GAY RESORT
MURDER SHOCK

GAY RESORT
MURDER SHOCK

PHILLIP SCOTT

alyson books
los angeles

MANUFACTURED IN THE UNITED STATES OF AMERICA.

THIS TRADE PAPERBACK IS PUBLISHED BY ALYSON PUBLICATIONS,
P.O. BOX 4371, LOS ANGELES, CALIFORNIA 90078-4371.

FIRST PUBLISHED BY PENGUIN BOOKS AUSTRALIA LTD.: 1998
FIRST ALYSON BOOKS EDITION: JULY 2003

03 04 05 06 07 🅰 10 9 8 7 6 5 4 3 2 1

ISBN 1-55583-757-3
(PREVIOUSLY PUBLISHED WITH ISBN 0-14-026950-9 BY PENGUIN BOOKS AUSTRALIA LTD.)

LIBRARY OF CONGRESS CATALOGING-IN-PUBLICATION DATA
SCOTT, PHILLIP.
    GAY RESORT MURDER SHOCK / PHILIP SCOTT.—1ST ALYSON BOOKS ED.
    ISBN 1-55583-757-3 (PBK.)
        1. PRIVATE INVESTIGATORS—AUSTRALIA—FICTION. 2. AUSTRALIA—FICTION.
    3. GAY MEN—FICTION. I. TITLE.
    PR9619.4.S38G395 2003
    823'.92—DC21   2003041808

CREDITS
COVER PHOTOGRAPHY BY CHRIS KAPA.
COVER DESIGN BY PENGUIN DESIGN STUDIO.

PROLOGUE

I lay stiffly in my hammock as the warm sea air caressed my chest and tickled my nostrils. I fought off a sneeze. My piña colada (or penis collider, as we call them here) was sitting within reach, but my fingers couldn't break out of their clench long enough to grab it. Heaven knows, I was trying hard to relax. My ideal holiday involves keeping completely still unless sex is taking place—then I allow myself some leeway— but in this case the film of tropical sweat on my forehead was not the result of erotic exertion. Nor was my stillness suffused with postcoital joy. No, I was quite simply rigid with shock.

Sex was the furthest thing from my mind. The closest thing to it, geographically speaking, was a set of headphones attached to a portable CD player through which I could hear Madama Butterfly slowly and ravishingly dying. It was a comfort to know someone was worse off than I was—namely that hefty Italian geisha Cio-Cio-San.

The CD player was an optional extra in this gay holiday package. (The extras ranged from windsurfing to wigs.) Strictly speaking, I wasn't here on a holiday: a junket, yes—although my official responsibilities at this moment were far from clear. I closed my eyes and tried to think rationally, but the soggy tranquillity of the island overwhelmed me. Or perhaps it was the piña colada: They contain about 120 percent alcohol.

Steeling myself, I rolled over in the interest of cultivating an even tan. As I did so, I heard a crack and felt a sharp pain shoot across my left buttock. I held my breath.

Every so often, since my accident with the fishhook, I find myself suffering the odd twinge. At my age I suppose it's to be expected: After all, I have achieved a half a century. The pain usually goes away by the time I count to a thousand. Today, however, some soreness lingered in an unpleasantly localised area. The cracking sound was unusual, too: sharp and kind of permanent.

I cautiously prodded the sore spot and discovered blood on my finger. I peered into the hammock: Nestling in a crevice, alongside some of my most tender and personal appendices, was a crab—slightly the worse for wear and definitely crabby.

"Eeek!" I ventured.

I hopped off the hammock and shook it about hysterically. The crab plopped onto my foot. I leapt to one side, too far for the cord on my headphones to stretch, thereby wrenching the CD player from its position on the table and slamming it into the trunk of a palm tree. The music stopped.

I removed the headphones and dropped them on the crab. It zigzagged away, stunned. I picked up a small rock and took aim, but the critter had learned its lesson: It hastily flicked sand over itself and vanished from view.

Cautiously, I climbed back into the hammock. My sound system was no longer working. The batteries had fallen out, and I could only find one of them. I noticed my cocktail had disappeared. One of the houseboys must have removed it. They were attentive above and beyond the call of the hospitality industry, but I wished they wouldn't sneak around like that. It was extremely unnerving under the circumstances.

I shuddered, and then, of course, the images I had been trying to keep out of my mind came flooding back. Hideous images of the night before, of the sickening moment when I stumbled across the body.

I guess I should start at the top.

CHAPTER 1

Once, many years ago, when Sydney was a hick town with no gay ghetto to speak of, there was a swampy area of land somewhere southwest of the Central Business District. Farmers pronounced it useless: too boggy for cattle and too near the sea for grain. It was also unsuitable for football matches, hotted-up car races, private schools' outdoor choral concerts, and the thousand other mindless pleasures the city fathers enjoyed on their weekends.

Everyone ignored this vast acreage, assuming that some day it would be eliminated during the course of natural erosion. And the sooner, the better. After all, what could be done with an inaccessible swamp full of waist-high stunted scrub, asked the city fathers? These fathers were by definition heterosexual, yet a few of them knew very well the answer to that question: The swamp was, in fact, one of the largest and most active beats in the southern hemisphere. For fifty years, day and night, it was jumping with a lot more than ticks and mosquitoes. The fathers, had they ventured deep into this wasteland, would have been surprised to discover many well-worn tracks, nooks, and crannies, and several native rock paintings explicit enough to excite the most jaded anthropologist. But they never did. The place remained a hive of unmentionable activity, and everyone was happy.

It couldn't last, of course. Much to our eternal discomfort, along came the airplane. Generally regarded as a step forward for mankind, this flying people-mover nevertheless had significant drawbacks, the most pressing of which was that it required somewhere to land. "Eureka!" shouted the city fathers—with one or two notably quiet exceptions. "We'll build our airport on that useless old swamp." Thus closed a clandestine chapter of our city's lurid past.

Queens, however, have long memories. A few generations later, when the tiny workers' cottages surrounding the airport were old enough to be nouveau again, gays and lesbians moved there in droves, drawn by the area's historical resonance and "renovator's dream" real estate. Amongst the previous generation of barflies and displaced persons there soon appeared a glut of muscular young men in shiny shorts and pale brown-lipped girls with shaven heads and an abundance of ear jewelry.

The new generation of city fathers weren't too happy to see the international gateway to their city surrounded by trendy street trash, but rather than do the obvious thing and move the airport, they conceived a nastier and cheaper form of vengeance. They rerouted existing flight paths directly over the most heavily populated streets. Death by deafening was the plan.

So where do I fit into this picture? Right in the middle, unfortunately.

Not that I'm a muscular young man in shiny shorts. I never was. I'm simply a semiretired opera lover, hoping for some peace and quiet so I may slip my favourite soprano, Renata Tebaldi, into the CD player, larynx first, and bask. I have no expensive tastes in, for instance, men, which is just as well. My meagre income from investments and private pupils—to whom I teach beginning Italian—is barely enough to cover everyday inexpensive tastes. I'm off luxuries.

I'm also over shorts, my wrinkly, scar-crossed knees being the prohibiting factor. Distinguished grey temples, a sexy old-fashioned widow's peak, "artistic" hands—these are the physical attributes I'm prepared to present to public view. I've been told my bone structure is a photographer's dream, although it's getting harder to pinpoint as gravity goes to work on the surrounding flesh.

I suppose I'm one of that quiet breed of gay men: the silent minority. The thought of public protests, chanted slogans, or glittering parades chills me to the marrow. Which is why, on this particular Saturday in March, I was not attending the annual rally in my local park.

Drag Artists Against Aircraft Noise had begun as a one-time-only event and was so popular and ineffective it had blossomed into a much-publicized community bash. But I had restaurant plans that evening and was passing the time sprucing up the frame of my newly double-glazed front window.

Double glazing is regarded as the least inadequate way of blocking out the earsplitting sound of passing aircraft. It simply involves building new windows inside your existing old ones at considerable expense. To this end, I hired a very cute boy named Justin from GayGlaze. He made a rather slapdash job of painting the frame, but I didn't notice until he was no longer standing in front of it.

So there I was, that balmy afternoon, with one foot on my bookshelves and the other on a chair, a small brush in one hand and a tiny tin of white gloss enamel in the other. The glorious strains of Verdi's celebrated *Requiem* wafted up from my speakers.

I was leaning as far over as I could to reach the crucial but elusive spot in the top right-hand corner when there came a loud rapping outside the very window I was painting. The sound jolted me, and I dropped the pot of paint, which landed on its side on the shag pile and rolled the length of the floor, spilling its sticky contents as it went.

At the same time, seemingly in slow motion, the chair slipped out from under my foot and did an impressive complete somersault. I grabbed at the bookshelves. They rocked precariously, tipping several heavy volumes onto my face. I had no choice: I let go and threw myself to the mercy of the four winds. Actually, I threw myself onto an upturned chair. My last memory was of a solid coffee-table book, *Colourful Fish of the Barrier Reef,* finding its mark right between my eyes.

Next thing I heard was, "Caro! Caro mio! My God, speak to me! Are you breathing? Tell me! Can we talk?"

A face swam into focus, amongst the fish. I recognised the dark eyes, the short blond hair, and the mischievous but concerned expression.

"Paul?"

"Marc, don't move. Let me see if anything's broken."

The pain took this opportunity to register on my personal Richter scale of injury. It approached record levels.

"Am I bleeding?" I whined.

"No."

"I am! I can feel it! My arm is lying in a pool of blood!" I lifted my hand to my face, but had difficulty focusing. Tentatively, I licked my index finger.

"It's not blood," Paul snapped. "It's paint."

I coughed and spat.

"How did you get in?" I asked.

"Through the laundry window. Now, lie still and don't try to gossip."

"I slipped. Something startled me."

"That was me. Oh, dear. This looks like a broken leg. In fact, it's broken right off. Caro, I'm afraid your chair is fucked. Hope it wasn't a valuable antique. Mm, apart from that—"

"Ow!"

"Sorry. You're looking very pale. *Very* pale! Better tell me where you keep the poppers, just in case."

"What?"

"I take it back. The paleness is white paint."

Slowly and painfully, I sat up.

"I was touching up the window frame," I murmured.

"Nice job. I like the floor, too. Are they planning to bring the highway through here?"

He dragged me gently to my feet and we staggered to the kitchen. For once, I had no objection to Paul's opening a bottle of my champagne.

Actually, we first met over champagne, when Paul bowled up out of the blue, demanding Italian lessons. At the time he had a foolish yearning to sing opera, instead of the show tunes he was mangling nightly on stage. He'd brought along a bottle of Carrington Blush; the best way to learn, he insisted, was to drink in the knowledge along with cheap alcohol. He'd learnt no Italian except *caro*, a camp term of endearment. He never sang opera and never again provided a single drop of bubbly. Now, even though he's roughly twenty years younger than me and thinks about nothing but sex, Paul is my best friend. The thought makes me feel strangely pathetic.

"Now, caro, close your eyes while I rub a bit of the old metho on your nose."

"Ach! Thanks."

"Good as new. Drink up. No!—that's the metho. Try the champagne. Why are you always trying to kill yourself?"

"I'm not. It just happens."

"Well, on to important matters. How do you like my new T-shirt? It looks white, but it's really a very, very pale blue. Hugely expensive but worth every hard-earned lira."

He did a quick turn around the room. The T-shirt had a V neck and came to an untimely end an inch or so above his navel. It showed off his tan and hugged his small but overworked chest.

"The pale blue brings out my eyes, don't you think?"

"Your eyes are brown!"

The eyes in question looked confused. "Are they? I suppose you're right. Damn! I've been had!"

"Not the first time. It still looks sexy."

His face brightened. "It does, doesn't it! That's the important thing; the eyes are incidental. I need to impress some important people tonight."

7

"Oh? Where?"

"At dinner with you, of course."

I sighed. "Oh, that's right, I'd forgotten. I don't think—"

"Caro, you're not going to cancel—you mustn't! How will I ever cross the poverty line if I don't make it big in television? You promised!"

"What *are* you talking about?"

"Your friends, natch. Won't your television friend be there? You invited him 'specially for me!"

"Grant's only a writer. And he hates actors. He says they change his dialogue all the time and make it worse."

"I'm not an actor, I'm in musicals! He's bound to like me. So will the rich lawyer. Maybe I'll get somewhere with *him*!"

"Newton? Forget it. He has a boyfriend, and I don't want you coming between them."

Paul chuckled. "We'll see about that. What's he like, this so-called 'boyfriend'?"

"I've never met him. He's a photographer. I've got one of his books: *Heavy Fish of the Barrier Reef*. Remind me to give it to you as a present."

"He doesn't sound like too much of a threat. Photographers are *mucho* unattractive. They spend all their time in the dark, experimenting with chemicals. I needn't worry. Look at this!"

He lifted up his T-shirt.

"What is it? A birthmark?"

"Very funny, caro. It's a tan! Muscles and a tan, and they don't come cheap. I've been to the gym four times this week! Can you imagine it? Once I even worked out."

"It's only a casual dinner. You needn't have gone to so much trouble."

Paul languidly refilled our glasses. "Well, I've got to do something! Work's thin on the ground. Two years ago there were five or six big shows on; now it's a toss-up between playing a magic tree for school kids or bending over backward in a queer dance co-op. Either way, you're rooted. Why can't this

Grant write a part for me in his soapie? What's it called again?"

"*Surfside Motel.* You'd better learn the name if you want to impress him."

"There, you see? I know plenty about surfside motels. I've woken up in them often enough. I'm perfect for it—I'm even blond at the moment."

"So I see."

"And so are you! Come with me to the shower. We've got to get that white gunk out of your hair. You look like Pepe Le Pew."

As I quivered in the bath, feeling the hot water coursing from head to feet, I began to morph into something vaguely human. Paul gently scrubbed my scalp. Rather than get his T-shirt wet he stripped it off completely. I patted his thigh.

"Ah-ha, signs of life! Is that better, caro?"

"Yes, thanks. Now I feel like going to dinner."

"Good! Here. Wipies."

He dried my face gently.

"You've got a black eye, and your backside is purple! Have you been slingin' it round the Bunker lately?"

"Of course not."

"Didn't think I'd seen you. Well, let's get you dressed. Something loose and comfy would be best. A bustle is *out.* Got any caftans?"

"Hundreds."

"I hope they're not too revealing. You're a bit on the hairy side."

"I'm Italian."

"That's no excuse for sloppiness. A back wax and a chest clip and you wouldn't know yourself."

"Waxing hurts, doesn't it?"

"No pain, no gain! It's nothing, compared to the things you usually do to yourself. Oh, caro!" He stopped in his tracks. "I completely forgot in all the carrying on. I've got incredible goss. The most awful thing happened today. Have you heard?"

"No. What?"

"You haven't? Wait till you do! It was devastating!"

"*What*?"

"Well. Do you know a drag queen named Vasselina?"

"No."

"She used to be Rhoda Dendron in Melbourne, but she went down-market when she moved here."

"What about her?"

"Well, she was doing a routine at the Drags Against Aircraft Noise thing—'This Is It,' you know, that old Melba Moore number? Anyway, a plane flew over, one of those little ones that sound like a blender full of broken glass, and what do you think happened?"

"She couldn't hear the music and got out of time?"

"No! Better than that! A propeller fell off the plane and *whack*! Right in the beehive!"

"Is she dead?"

"Yup! That was it, as Melba Moore once said."

I suddenly felt peculiar and tingly above the ears. "My God, that rally was just around the corner! It could have happened to any of us!"

"I saw it all. We were having such fun till then. Big fat Victoria was running the show. You remember her?"

"I'm afraid so."

"She had the crowd in the palm of her chubby, bejeweled old mitt. You know how imposing she is. If she'd told those queens to pull out their dicks and set 'em on fire, they would've. Well, she got us all to make a Mexican wave—you know, where you jump up and act sort of like Mexicans? And she couldn't get it to stop! The wave kept going on and on, even when Vasselina got the chop. Blood, brains, and bouffant, and a crowd of big girls standing up and sitting down and screaming their tits off! It was a nightmare!"

"Paul, stop. I'm...I've been through...I just need to...I think I'm going to throw up."

CHAPTER 2

Newton Heath was a successful gay lawyer who did things in the right order: He became successful first and gay second, at least as far as the public eye was aware. He had built his reputation on controversial cases: defending developers, rapists, and suspected pedophiles. Whenever the supply of these occasionally dried up, he relished a good civil suit. He was especially fond of libel. I can't say he never lost a case but, as he admitted to me once, he never came out of the proceedings looking less than pristine.

I met Newton when, like Paul, he answered my ad for Italian lessons. He and some business acquaintances had purchased a villa in Tuscany, primarily as an investment. He had no thoughts of visiting the place until he discovered there was a vineyard attached. Suddenly, his enthusiasm knew no bounds. He decided to take a year's sabbatical and play the land-owning vigneron. (Like all barristers, Newton was a wine and food expert.) I helped him brush up his grass-roots Tuscan slang, and we kept in touch.

Predictably, he soon became a notorious Italophile, with exquisite taste in *ragazzi*. "I prefer 'em mature," he told me wickedly, "after they've been laid down for a minimum of two years."

He had gone so far as to cultivate a handsome Sicilian boy whom he had placed in charge of the vineyard. It lasted until the in-laws popped in unexpectedly. Then there were tears and recriminations all round, and the family assured Newton in their subtle way that his safety could no longer be guaranteed if he were to show up again in Sicily, Tuscany, or just about anywhere in the Mediterranean. Newton threatened to take them to court but, hotshot lawyer though he was, even he couldn't negotiate the maze of the Italian legal system, which in any case had its hands full with other matters.

Shrugging it off, Newton returned to Sydney and proceeded to style himself as Australia's leading Q.C., or "Queer Counsel," as he termed it. Whenever he had a new boyfriend or a swish new restaurant opened, I would hear from him. This time it was both.

"Marc, mate! Saturday night, me and the boys are christening a new Spanish joint not far from you. Don Cojones. You heard of it?"

"I think I've passed it."

"Mate, you're not past it—you're in your prime! Never say that!"

"I didn't."

"What was that? Bugger this. It's a bad line, I'm calling from some filthy take-away food bar up the coast; they don't have a bloody clue. *Turn the frigging radio down, love!* Sorry, Marc."

"Where are you?"

"I'll tell you all about it Saturday night. Nine. Don Cojones—right? We can't get a booking any earlier, so that's a good sign, I'd say. Hang on, Marc. *Turn down that crap country music, or I'll have you for breaching the peace!* Christ, I hate small towns."

"I don't think I can make it on Saturday, Newton."

"Why not? You must! I've got some exciting news—may even be a nice little freebie in it for you."

"I have a friend in town that night."

"A lover? About bloody time. Bring him!"

"No, no, nothing like that. Just a friend."

"It isn't a woman? I couldn't take another female. They've been driving me spare."

"No, no, it's a man."

"Well! No problem!"

"All right then. I'm sure you'll like Grant—everybody does. He writes for television."

"Good for him."

"My other friend Paul might be coming, too," I stammered, suddenly uneasy. Paul has killed more dinner parties than I've had hot take-aways, usually through a combination of tactlessness and recreational drugs. "It's probably too many people—"

"Bring 'em all! Christ, you're like an old granny at a christening."

So the arrangement was made, but I still felt wary. It was the usual dinner party quandary: Simply because people are friends of yours doesn't mean they'll instantly fall in love with each other. Paul can be wonderful company on his own, but he has a knack for pitting brother against brother and bringing out the belligerent side in total strangers. I don't know how he always manages it, but one way is by having sex with their boyfriends.

Because of the late restaurant booking, I arranged for us to meet Grant for a drink first at the local. After my brush with injury that afternoon I needed a few stiff ones to revive my capacity for small talk.

The local in question was an old pub called the Dominion. When I first moved into the area, it was a plain, ordinary, comfortable watering hole. Although not without the usual Saturday night fistfights or the odd derelict urinating lightheartedly in the beer garden, it was manageable and unthreatening most of the time.

However, times change. Recently, the space outside had been roped off and crammed with metallic tables and chairs, and now male models with attitude served focaccia and bottled boutique beer with a slice of lime stuck in the top. The derelicts sometimes returned, but not for long. The dismay on their stubbled faces told the story: They knew they were no match for your average gay waiter.

Inside, the decor remained virtually unchanged, the only upmarket addition being a state-of-the-eardrum sound system and eighteen extra speakers. Otherwise, the slimy, olive green walls and flaky-paint ceiling retained all the simple charm of yesteryear. Naturally, the simple charm of yesteryear's drink prices was well and truly a thing of the past.

It was eight o'clock by the time Paul and I respectively strode and limped our way there. It had taken Paul some time to style and restyle his hair into a state of petrified paralysis.

At that time of day, the front bar of the Dominion was usually quiet, populated by a few leftover tragedies from the night before and a clutch of lesbian pool players. Tonight, however, it was packed and buzzing. Everyone was talking about the incident at the rally.

"She was a mess! Nobody would even give her mouth-to-mouth..."

"They couldn't *find* her mouth, stupid..."

"It could have hit any one of us..."

"Yes, it's getting so a girl can't even lip-sync in public! This is a serious violation of our rights."

"I can't see Grant anywhere!" I shouted in Paul's ear.

"Let's have a drink while we wait," he called back. "The usual for you, caro? A pineapple screwdriver?"

"I'll have a Scotch."

"You got any change?"

"Change won't pay for a Scotch!"

"Sad but true. Better give me twenty bucks."

He turned away as my gaze was taken by a solitary figure in a distant corner. It was a man in drag casually cruising the room. He was dressed quietly, in a maroon outfit with matching jacket. A silver chain dangled across the front of his blouse. Attached to it was a small onyx crucifix.

I couldn't stop myself from staring. In spite of the outfit, he was downright luscious. He appeared to be young and his figure was tall and trim, if a tad masculine for the ensemble he'd chosen. His short, neat wig was ash-blond. He caught my eye and quickly looked away, a faint flush on his high cheekbones. Strange—did I know him from somewhere? Was it a fellow opera-goer slipping into drag in his spare time? Of course, that hardly narrowed it down.

In a flash, Paul was back with the drinks.

"You were quick!" I marveled.

"I'm a slippery little customer. Have you found Grant?"

"Not a glimpse. Why don't we try outside?"

As we edged our way through, Paul tossed his dance-trained hips in time with the music, a disco hit of the early '80s. There was no room for this kind of high-spirited gyrating, however. Just as we passed the pool table, Paul accidentally shoved me into a snooker player as she was about to sink the pink. The shot missed by light years.

"Shit!" she snorted and sent me a look of pure hatred such as I hope never to see again in our lifetime. I was taken aback by her appearance. She sported a bright-red Mohawk haircut and seemed to be wearing a roll of black masking tape.

"Sorry," I mumbled.

"I would've won that," she growled.

"Whoopsie," Paul quipped, flashing her a smile of the utmost insincerity as he dragged me away.

The beer garden was quiet. All the action was inside tonight. There was still no sign of Grant.

"Can we sit anyway?" I whined. "I'm aching all over."

"I'm shakin' and achin' all o-o-ver!" sang Paul in a girlie voice.

"Who is that supposed to be?"

"Elvis!"

"Elvis Streisand, I presume."

"She colours all my work."

We found a metallic table and chairs. The stainless steel chilled me to the bone.

"So how do you know this Grant? Does he, in fact, exist? Or is he your imaginary friend?"

"I've known him forever. When Andrew and I were together,

we saw a lot of Grant and his lover, Nick. Then Andrew and I split up, and not long after, Nick's visa ran out and he had to leave the country."

"Bummer."

"Grant was so upset, he took his laptop and moved to Queensland. He lives in a charming old guesthouse on the coast where he writes all his scripts. There's a gorgeous view. It looks out over the ocean and the islands: It's idyllic. Once every now and then he flies down to Sydney for a script conference. Not a bad existence."

"It sounds fine as long as *Surfside Hotel*—"

"*Motel.*"

"—*Motel* keeps running. But what happens if it gets the flick? Teenagers don't live forever."

"Grant will retire on his royalties, I presume. The show is seen in eighty-something countries around the world."

"Really?" Paul preened. "So is Granty-poo looking for a sexy young protégé whose career he can promote to his heart's content?"

"Forget it."

Paul looked deflated. "He's got one already. Bugger."

"I think so."

"You think? What's 'think'? We need to know!"

I pondered. I wasn't keen to dissect my friends' lives in the name of gossip, and certainly not with Paul, whose blab network would be the envy of Reuters. I knew very little about Grant's current attachments, anyway.

"Well, Grant says he's celibate."

"He *says*. But you don't believe him."

"Not really. He's always been too interested in sex. He must have some secret outlet."

"You make him sound like a sewer! Won't he tell you? You're his best friend!"

"No, I'm not."

Paul pouted. "I'd better ask the guy myself."

"Don't you dare."

"I'll be subtle, caro. I'll wait till we're in bed."

"Are you ready to order?" asked a bored voice. I looked up. A tall waiter hovered beside us, pen poised. He wore a starched white apron and had a negligible goatee.

"We're not eating, thanks," I answered.

"Then you'll have to go inside. This area's reserved for food." He folded his arms. Obviously, he'd had trouble with our type before.

"Isn't this the beer garden?" Paul asked sweetly.

"This area's reserved for eating, sir."

"But there's a quaint old sign that says BEER GARDEN and look! What's this I'm holding? Could it be a beer?" Paul slapped his forehead. He can be sarcastic at times. The wrong times, usually.

The waiter's lips thinned to breaking point. "Would you like me to get the manager?"

"Darling, I'd like you to get the clap."

"Right!" the waiter snarled. He turned to call in the big guns.

"What sort of focaccias do you serve?" Paul suddenly asked, all innocence.

The waiter swung back, fuming. "Vegetarian," he intoned. "Salami and cheese, mushroom—"

I looked at my watch. "Excuse me," I smiled. "Paul, it's getting late. One more round of the bar, and we should go."

"We'll have two vegetarian focaccias, please," beamed Paul. "One with lots of artichokes and the other with zillions of sun-dried tomatoes and a sprig of thyme. You *do* have plenty of thyme, don't you?"

The waiter gritted his teeth. "I'll inquire."

"You do that, petal."

The waiter swished away.

"This place is a dump," Paul remarked.

I glared at him. "Why did you order food? Just so we could sit here? We're about to go to dinner!"

Paul looked abashed. "You're right, caro, I got carried away. I don't want their overgarnished rabbit food after all. Let's hop it." Before I could say another word, he grabbed my arm and dragged me out of my chair, over the rope, and into the street.

CHAPTER 3

We can never go back to that pub after the way you behaved," I grumbled as we sped along the pavement.

"Who'd want to?" Paul sneered.

"You," I answered, "to ask for a job!"

He stopped in his tracks. "That was cruel and uncalled-for. I'm looking for work as we speak."

"Where? Here on the street?"

"It'd be better than waiting tables." We moved on. "Speaking of prostituting yourself, what's happened to your television friend?"

"I don't know. He must've smelt an actor."

"Rubbish, he just didn't understand your complicated arrangements. I'll bet he's at the restaurant already."

I slowed down as a herd of sharp pains began a stampede across my ribs. All this rope jumping and power walking was bad news for my recently battered body. "Ow!"

Paul slowed instantly. "How are you feeling, caro mio?" he asked.

"Like I spent the evening in a tumble drier," I said.

The restaurant called Don Cojones had changed its name, menu, and ethnic background five times in three years. It had opened with French-influenced Thai, switched to Greek, browsed through Malaysian, and of course done the obligatory gourmet pizza. Now as we approached I thought for a moment it had closed again, but no, it was simply dark. We blundered inside to be greeted by a familiar face peeping over an unfamiliar bow tie. It was Rodney: chorus boy and one of Paul's many ex-lovers.

"Hey! Hi, babe," Rodney drawled, giving Paul a big strong hug.

"We-hell! Waitressing! How the flighty have fallen. You remember Marc?"

Rodney's eyes swiveled languidly in my direction. "Oh yeah," he said. "How's it hangin'?" It was a rhetorical question; he turned his attention back to Paul. "This job's just temporary. I've got a show."

"Understudy on the Chippendales tour?" (Rodney was extremely well built.)

"No way. I don't strip anymore. It gave me tinea. No, this one's a rock 'n' roll tribute show. The Fabulous Fuckin' '50s or something. I'm the choreographer."

Paul's mouth fell open several inches. "The what?"

"Too much, isn't it? But I thought: Shit, anyone who can dance, can choreograph."

"That lets *you* out!"

Rodney grinned. "And it's worth a packet! I just sit back and watch hunky boys doing all the work."

While they talked shop, I peered into the shadows, trying to spot the rest of our party. Apparently, they hadn't arrived. Bored rigid, I studied the new decor. (I hadn't been here since the pizza incarnation.)

The dining area was very large, by inner-city standards, but the tables were few and far apart. "Rough" was the overriding theme: The poorest Basque mountain dweller would have felt right at home. The chairs were uneven slabs of wood and the walls were the colour of good solid earth, give or take the odd swipe of whitewash. Bang in the middle of the room, filling up valuable customer space, was a cracked terra-cotta pot containing a gnarled, bent shrub. Its thick, leafless branches suggested it had recently survived a nuclear blast. The most primitive aspect of the place was the lighting. Every meter or so, the wall sprouted a cast iron candleholder with fake electric candles glowing red and orange, each lighting a tiny area of the ceiling. The rest of the room was bathed in authentic Spanish-Inquisition gloom.

In a corner a thin, wispy haired youth sat on a stool and plucked on a drab guitar. A music stand stood nearby. Every few seconds he played a twangy discord, or stopped altogether, whispered "Shit!" and leaned forward to squint at his sheet music.

Paul and Rodney were now halfway through a critical appraisal of every "tribute" show they'd seen in the last five years.

"Excuse me," I butted in. "Can we please have a table?"

"Huh? Oh, yeah," Rodney mumbled. "Anywhere you like."

"We have a booking. A table for five."

"Right. Sit near the window, it's lighter. I'll bring you a jug of san-i-gra on the house." He winked.

"Sangria!" snapped Paul. "It's called 'sang-gree-ah,' you bimbo."

"Oh."

Rodney sashayed off and left us at a large, bare, uncomfortable table. Paul fumed, "Choreographer! He couldn't choreograph Siamese twins to shit side by side."

We sat in silence waiting for the promised sangria, which never came. In fact, everyone in the place was waiting—except Rodney. Just as I was beginning to wonder whether it was a "do-it-yourself" restaurant, the door swung open and Newton and his boyfriend were upon us.

"Marc, mate! Sorry we're late—I had a meeting! You haven't started, I see. Always the gent!"

"Not from want of trying. Newton, Paul Silverton."

"Hi, Paul. Mmm, cute. This is Hadrian."

Big kisses were exchanged all round. Although Newton could be domineering, his energy was infectious. Indeed, he had the stamina of a man half his age—which Hadrian undoubtedly was. They made a study in contrasts: Newton with his neat, smooth features, and grey crew cut, and this strange boy, who looked like a sedated basset. Hadrian had very long, very straight black hair. It swagged across his face like curtains drawn back to reveal beady eyes and a large nose. The effect suggested nothing so much as a peeping Tom. His frame was tiny, with skinny arms and legs, but enormous hands and feet—and, if I knew Newton's taste, that's not where it stopped.

Newton hardly paused for breath.

"What a day, eh? Were you there? Did you see it?"

"You mean Vasselina?" gushed Paul. "Wasn't it sensational!"

The basset shot him a look of disgust.

Newton continued. "I've been in meetings all afternoon. It's about time something was done about these bloody aircraft, and I'm just the man to do it. I've been talking to the Gay and Lesbian Rights Lobby. We've come up with an intriguing plan."

"What can they do?" I said.

"Only this! We're going to target the airlines, the government, the Federal Airways Corporation, the Pilots Guild—in fact, anyone who's got anything to do with these flight paths— and we're gonna challenge them under the Sexual Discrimination Act! I mean, they're sending their planes over the gay and lesbian areas. That's minority discrimination in my book! They can fuckin' pay for it!" He beamed.

"Is it possible?" I queried. "I thought that act was about individuals' rights. Sexual harassment in the workplace and so on."

He shrugged. "I intend to find out. Lovely, pristine legislation. The water's hardly been tested. Getting 'em into court's the way to do it! You'd actually be surprised how many judges live—or at least spend their free time—under the flight path. We may get a very sympathetic ear."

"It's a great idea," Paul enthused.

"I'd love to see something done," I argued, "but it's not only gays and lesbians who are affected by planes. There are other people, too."

Newton gestured dismissively. "Yes, yes, yes, I realise that.
But who are they? Vietnamese...Cypriots...ethnic minorities,
right? So I'm setting about organising a cooperative coalition
of minorities' representatives to mount this case. There's
only one thing bothering me, and I brought this up today: If
we get too many minorities together, we may end up with a
majority. If that happens, we're up shit creek."

"Why?"

"Because the majority haven't got a leg to stand on. By
definition, they're the discriminators."

"Can't a minority discriminate against another minority?"
I asked.

Newton shook his head. "That's not the point at issue. In
my opinion, what we've got here is officially sanctioned discrimination on a topographical level." He rubbed his hands
together in gleeful anticipation of these legal proceedings
which, I sensed, would be long, drawn out, and lucrative.

He turned the laser of his attention onto Paul. "So, you work
in the realm of dreams and bullshit!" He grinned broadly.

"Who, me?" said Paul.

"In television! That's what Marc told me. Or is that a front?
Are you a charming and rather good-looking rent boy?"

I could swear I heard Hadrian growl.

"My friend Grant is the TV writer," I interjected. "He's not
here yet."

"Ah!" Newton looked around. "Neither is that fucking
waiter." He resumed his cross-examination. "So what do you
do, Paul? Tell us in your own words."

"I'm in show business."

"No business like it, I believe. An actor?"

Paul took a deep breath and raised his chin defiantly.
"Actually, I'm a choreographer," he announced.

"Well! I'm fascinated."

"Me too," I added in amazement.

"Been in the business long?"

"All of twenty seconds," I suggested.

But Newton's attention had wandered. "I wonder if Pepe is running the kitchen tonight," he queried. "I should have a look—they'll be wheeling us out of here on a stretcher if we wait any longer. Pepe's the chef. A great friend of mine. That's why I want to support the joint. I defended his brother a couple of years ago on a rape charge. You know these hot-blooded Spaniards! I got the bastard a reduced sentence, so I'd say they owe us a discount!"

He sprang up and bolted off toward the kitchen.

"Newton's as energetic as ever," I observed to Hadrian. "I don't know how you keep up with him!"

"What do you mean?" he said suspiciously.

This rather took me by surprise. "I just mean... keep up with him."

"You think he's seeing someone behind my back?"

"No! No, of course not."

He glowered. "You don't have to pretend."

"I'm not. Honestly." It seemed like a good time to change the subject. "So, um, how's the photography going?"

"OK."

"Well, that's good. I love your collection *Colourful Fish of the Barrier Reef*. It made a deep impression on me. Literally."

"Thanks," Hadrian murmured and almost smiled. "I got pretty wet doing that one."

"Yes." I paused. "You would."

"Fish being underwater most of the time," Paul added.

The conversation lapsed awkwardly. I glanced at my wrist-watch. It was after 9:30. Clearly, Grant wouldn't be joining us. Perhaps I'd given him the wrong address. Whenever things go awry, I always assume it's my fault. No doubt there would be a message for me at home from some other restaurant: "I waited until 2 A.M. Where were you? Have you been murdered or something? If so, please call ASAP."

With a sudden flourish, Newton returned, dragging after

him a short, swarthy man wearing an apron and a greasy, deflated chef's cap.

"Here he is!" Newton crowed. "This is Pepe, boys and girls, and a damn good chef he is too!"

Pepe smiled sheepishly.

"I'll order, if you're all OK about that? Fine. Pepe's family are Catalan, so we'll have the specialties of the region. The pollo con gambas de Palamós—a nice big serving of that all round. And pork! Anything unusual you do with pork! And I fancy esquiexada de bacalao—that's a bunch of leeks, olives, tomatoes, fish, and stuff with lashings of oil—patata con butifarra del perol on the side, that's potato with butter and sausage—aaah...and crema Catalana? None of this is specifically on the menu but Pepe doesn't mind, do you, mate?"

Newton swung around and kissed Pepe fulsomely on the cheek. The embarrassed chef waited a millisecond for the second kiss, European style, but it was not forthcoming. He shuffled back to the kitchen. At the same moment, Rodney appeared with a jug of sangria and two glasses.

"Here's your snagri...here's your drinks."

Newton took the jug and sipped from it. Rodney turned to leave, but Newton reached out and grabbed his sleeve.

"Who mixed this?" he thundered.

"Um, me," said Rodney.

"Pah! I thought so. It's crap—we don't want it. You can open this perfectly fine Australian red." Newton shoved two bottles of wine into Rodney's surprised hands. "And I don't mean next Christmas!"

He turned back to us.

"Sexy, but a complete idiot. Probably a dancer slumming it."

"He is!" Paul enthused. "He *is* a dancer. Not a choreographer."

Everyone stared at Paul for a moment, then we plunged back into conversation, or at least Newton did. He was ebullient this evening. Over a sensational dinner, he took us through the most interesting cases he had been involved in during the year. One of them, which particularly intrigued Paul, involved a well-known television actor who had been the victim of a campaign of media innuendo concerning his sexual practices. This nationwide heartthrob—Lachlan (a.k.a. Lachie) Turner—had been mentioned in a magazine article about male prostitutes called "Boyz on the Make," when one of the boyz casually dropped his name. Turner decided to sue.

"So he should!" Paul cried. "A person's sex life is their own business!"

My jaw dropped. "You don't believe that!" I scoffed.

"I do too. Except in the case of Lachie Turner. How fabulous! I always knew he was gay."

"I didn't say he was!" Newton roared. "That was the whole point of the suit, for Christ's sake!"

"Who is this Lachlan Turner?" I asked. "I've never heard of him."

"You cultural philistine!" laughed Newton. "Lachie's the star of *Good Cop, Bad Cop.*"

"You must know him!" added Paul. "He's that gorgeous blond one. The good cop, natch. Bad cops are always bald."

I merely shrugged.

"Honestly, caro! He's only the biggest pinup boy in the country. All my friends worship him, and now we know their adoration is not misplaced!"

Newton continued. "I argued, perfectly legitimately, that these unsubstantiated personal revelations were not in the public interest, in spite of the fact that the public was busting a gut to get the dirt. Ergo, the paper was in the wrong. Of course, it helped that their star witness was a no-show."

"Where was he?" I asked.

"Dunno. I'll tell you where he *wasn't*: in court! They couldn't produce any such piece of garrulous trade. Just quietly, I heard they couldn't locate the kid anywhere. Disappeared! Poof!" He clicked his fingers.

"That's very suspicious, isn't it?"

"Not really. He probably didn't want his flimsy accusations torn to shreds under my cross-examination. Or maybe some P.R. guru paid him to get lost—that's assuming he ever existed in the first place! I wouldn't be surprised if the whole thing was a media beat-up."

"If a big star like Lachie Turner is gay," ventured Paul, "he should stand up and say so."

"And kill his career stone-dead?" I countered.

"Possibly," said Newton, "but not if it's handled right. I'm inclined to agree with Paul. It's important for celebrities to come out, but for the right reasons, not simply in order to make news for a bunch of homophobic vultures. I guess *Bimbeau* magazine'll have second thoughts next time, after coughing up eight-hundred fifty thousand bucks!"

At this point, further discussion was interrupted by the arrival of crema Catalana—an utterly delectable Spanish version of crème caramel. I made a mental note to abduct Pepe some time and keep him prisoner in my kitchenette where he could churn out these miracles to my heart's content.

Pepe eventually served coffee, by which time we were virtually alone in the restaurant. Rodney seemed to have pirouetted off home, and the bad guitarist had long since given up on his instrument. For the first time since I'd swan-dived into a bucket of paint, I felt relaxed.

Newton lit up a cigarette and grinned at me with a twinkle in his eye. "Time for my big news!" he announced. "I was saving it till now. I'm involved in the most fabulous project, and it's going to make me a hell of a lot of filthy old moolah. Do the words 'New Heaven' mean anything to you?"

"No," I answered wittily. "I'm not all that *au fait* with the old heaven."

"It's a gay resort," muttered Hadrian.

Newton glared at him.

"It's not *a* gay resort. It's *the* gay and lesbian holiday destination of the 21st century! An entire island paradise 100 percent gay–owned, run, operated, funded, and decorated! Ex-National Park, or as good as. It used to be called Crab Island, but we couldn't keep that moniker, could we? Considering what crabs mean to most of us."

"What do you have to do with this resort?" I asked.

"I have a financial interest, naturally, and I put the Australian consortium together. We're in partnership with Gaytour International, an American-based gay holiday group who already operate a couple of island resorts. One's in the Caribbean and the other's off the coast of Scotland, of all places! But this is the biggie. We're building the accommodations et cetera to five-star specifications. The rooms are sensational, the food's gonna be swish, it's all as environmentally friendly as it can be without compromising our high standards of luxury, and it was designed by a queen, so there are bars everywhere!"

"New Heaven," I mused.

"Don't you love the name? I thought of it myself. The Yanks are over the moon. They wanted something Greek and sleazy, along the lines of Mykonos or Lesbos. They suggested Queeros—"

"Queeros!" Paul exclaimed. "That's so P.C.!"

"Not much fun, is it? And 'Homos' would sound like a Lebanese dip. Whereas 'Heaven' resonates: It conjures up this clear image of—well, heaven!"

"Why not just call it 'Heaven'?" I asked.

Newton frowned. "We prefer 'New Heaven.' It's unique, it's vibrant, it's now. Also, it's available."

"Some other company owns the name 'Heaven,'" explained Hadrian, "and they won't budge."

"It sounds divine!" Paul raved. He looked longingly at me. "Take me there, daddy!" he drooled.

"We haven't launched the Australian campaign yet. Most

of our clients will be from the States, and we're publicising our tits off over there. They love how it's off the coast of *Queens-*land. They think the whole bloody country's gay!"

"They'll soon come down to earth," I observed.

"No, they'll be too busy having fun. We can take 300 guests at a time, and I don't need to tell you boys, it ain't cheap. Of course, there'll be merchandising galore. This is a very big operation. Hadrian's been taking shots for a major coffee-table book and a calendar, though he'll be doing most of the shoot later on."

"Portraits of men in the wild," he whispered.

"Beefcake!" Newton practically shouted. "And lesbian shots. Whatever lesbian beefcake is called."

"Fishca—" Paul began.

"Don't be tacky," I interrupted.

"There's only a few staff up there at the moment," Newton continued, "but we're coming in on time and under budget— well, more or less. Anyway, the hard part's over. Naturally I'm coordinating the whole thing personally. When we get the right team together, all well-oiled and turning over smoothly, I'll ease myself out, so to speak." He laughed coarsely.

"Newton hates to delegate," said Hadrian.

"When does it open?" Paul asked.

"That depends what you mean. The grand opening, with selected celebrities and gay icons—the usual bludgers—that's some months away. But we actually open for business in a few weeks. We're giving it a dry run to iron out any bugs. There's always problems with a project this size. We're taking a bunch of die-hard Americans and leading lights of the gay and lesbian milieu up there for a week on the house. And Marc, old mate, you're invited!"

"But I'm nothing to do with the gay milieu."

" 'Course you do. You're our average fag on the street. Your opinion counts." His face took on a slightly predatory look. "Once you've seen it you'll be dying to invest."

"Invest?"

"Settle down, I'm not pushing you, but it *is* a fantastic opportunity. We can talk about that later."

Paul was practically falling out of his T-shirt with enthusiasm.

"Caro, you must go! God knows, you could do with a holiday after your injuries."

"What injuries?"

"Oh, I fell off a chair. It's nothing."

Newton was adamant. "Then I insist! You can relax, lie in a hammock the whole time. You don't have to do the programme."

"There's a programme?" I asked.

"Oh. there are activities—bush-walks, water aerobics, and stuff like that. Don't worry about it! I wouldn't do 'em myself. Stick to the disco and bar areas. Let the staff take care of you. I can assure you, each and every one of them is drop-dead gorgeous and a trained masseur. One or two are untrained masseurs." He winked. "They're the best kind."

"Handpicked by Newton personally," Hadrian muttered darkly. I had forgotten he was there.

"Naturally!" Newton chortled. "Except the girls, but I have complete faith in Claire, our lesbian coordinator. Of course, there may be activities you'll be only too delighted to join in! There's a sauna in the gym."

I shuddered. Saunas aren't really my cup of vapour.

"Dances, shows—the staff will be performing nightly as part of their duties, and I predict they'll be talented, energetic and *very* sexy." He suddenly looked deep-and-meaningfully at Paul. "We're looking for someone to run that side of things. A director who's good with dancers. Do you direct too?"

Paul smiled modestly. "A little," he lied.

"Why don't we give you a go, then? We'll need to put on a show for the special guests! If we like you and you like us, we can come to some arrangement."

Paul's face glistened with scarcely suppressed joy. "I'll have to check my availability," he said, "but I'm 99.9 percent sure I can do it."

"I'll take that as a yes," said Newton, ruffling Paul's hair. "Welcome aboard. You too, Marc!"

It looked like I'd be heading for the subtropics. It seemed as good a way as any to recuperate. Besides, it was impossible to say no to Newton, especially when he uttered the magic words every diner wants to hear at the end of a long, satisfying meal.

"This is on me."

CHAPTER 4

A week or so later I was sitting in a shadowy auditorium in the Sydney Opera House, trying not to listen to the loud conversation taking place next to me.

"When is this thing gonna start?"

"Any second. Relax, Tony—uh, Terry."

"I'm bored, but."

"Shhhh!" This sound emanated from the lungs of a distinguished opera critic who happened to be seated in front of the conversationalists. It struck terror into the hearts of anyone remotely connected with the arts, but had no effect at all on his intended victims They continued to chat.

"Let's go up to Oxford Street if we don't like the show. Can we?"

"Maybe."

"Go on, there's a new place opening tonight. E-Male."

"Really."

"It's all like, computerised. Virtual Dance Party."

"Shhhh!"

With a scurry, the orchestral strings broke into their busy little fugue. It was Act 1 of *Butterfly*, one of my subscription evenings at the Sydney City Opera. I must admit, I had missed the last three in the series—on purpose, in two cases, and accidentally in the third. I had absented myself from *The Magic Flute*, an opera so preposterous that even I find it hard to swallow, and it was also my happy privilege to miss something by the ghastly and unmusical Benjamin Britten. The other occasion was an opera I desperately wanted to see, a new production of Puccini's *Girl of the Golden West*, but unaccountably I misread a 5 for a 6 on my ticket and turned up twenty-four hours too late. If it had been Wagner, I might still have caught the finale.

Madama Butterfly was ample compensation. It's a favourite

wallow, associated as it is with my all-time idol, Renata Tebaldi. We wouldn't be hearing Signora Tebaldi tonight, of course. She would never have toured as far afield as Australia—unless Maria Callas had first.

Our current Butterfly was a rising star on loan from the San Francisco Opera, a Slovakian soprano whose name I'd never had enough nerve to pronounce. San Francisco critics raved about her purity of tone and vocal stamina. Rumors that reached me privately tended to concentrate on her shortness and considerable girth. A prominent West Coast opera queen christened her Madam Butterball.

My date for the opera was supposed to be Grant. When he'd failed to turn up at the Spanish restaurant, and I'd returned home to a blank answer-phone, I rang him the next morning. He was full of apologies and forehead slapping. There'd been a particularly difficult script meeting, he explained, which had gone on and on.

"I'm trying to get a gay character up in the series, love. Local schoolteacher, you know—private tutorials after hours, gets into hot water, suspicion all round, suspended by the panicky headmaster—then the whole class tops the state and he's suddenly a saint."

"Sounds good," I remarked.

"It is, but it's taken a year for the producers to even consider it. I thought we'd be pinning the story line down yesterday, but no! The meeting was about ruddy Stonewall instead!"

"Stonewall? I don't follow you."

"Lovey, you and I know Stonewall's a pivotal date on the old pink calendar, but the producers didn't. They've just found out, and they're livid."

"But what's Stonewall got to do with *Surfside Motel*?"

"Marc! My dear, I'm shattered. Don't you watch the show? Don't you unplug the phone, draw the blinds, and whip off your undies religiously every weekday at 6:30?"

"Not every day."

"Not ever! For your info, Stonewall is the name of the seaside town where these motel malingerers live. I named it that as a private joke, just to amuse myself and a few friends—but some idiot complained."

"Hell."

"The network's a bunch of nervous nellies, shitting themselves over the ratings. You can't explain to them that a crank's a crank. They extrapolate one loony into a percentage of the viewers and think a million people are cringing in horror. Then they panic. Rory, our E.P., is frightened of his own shadow! Mind you, his shadow *is* pretty frightening. Anyway, with all this on my plate, I forgot about our date. Mea culpa! How can I make it up to you?"

"Set me up for life."

"What about a cautiously extravagant night on the town?"

So we'd arranged to meet at the opera, and now here I was, stood up again! Eau de rodent lingered in my nostrils. Grant has been snowed under with work ever since I first met him, thriving on several projects at once, and it never affected his punctuality. Something else was going on, and I suspected homo hormones might be involved. But there was no time to speculate, as the sweeping melodies of Puccini hauled me out of my seat and La Butterball made her entrance.

Madama was the textbook definition of rotund. Unhappily, the requisite Nipponesque eye makeup served to flatten out her nose, so her face appeared less Asiatic than broad Eskimo. Also, Butterfly is meant to be in her teens, not a pudgy aging spinster. However, there was no doubt our diva had vocal chords from heaven. Her tone floated through the theatre like warm, orange fog and enveloped everything. Right from her first appearance it gave me tingles, and when we got to the great Act 1 duet, I simply closed my eyes and sank into the sound as into a vat of golden syrup. Without the visual element, everything made sense: She was young, vulnerable, and ardent. *That's what opera's all about,* I thought as I kept my eyes glued firmly shut.

When at last we poured out after the final curtain call, exhausted from applauding and basking in a moist emotional afterglow, I felt restless. Grant's nonappearance had left me vaguely wanting more. The foyer bar was closed, and I headed impulsively toward Oxford Street.

The traffic was thick, even though it was getting close to midnight, and I drove around listlessly searching for somewhere to park. Eventually, I found myself in a narrow, dark alley, the kind to be avoided at all costs. I heard a car door slam somewhere up ahead. Assuming the car would be leaving, I drove up and waited. And waited! Why do people fart around for so long before they drive off? It never happens in films.

I wound down my window. The car, a black sedan, was definitely populated. I could see the lone occupant sitting vacantly behind the wheel, staring into the distance. I beeped politely and waved a frantic pantomime of "Are you going?" But the driver continued to look straight ahead.

Feeling impatient, I backed up, hopped out, and walked over casually. The windows were quite foggy. Peering in the passenger side, it took me a few seconds to recognise the driver as the older half of the couple who'd been chattering all through the opera. "Will you be leaving?" I called, tapping on the hood. With a sudden jerk, up sprang the boyfriend from some place below sight-level.

"Piss off!" he yelled.

"Oh! Sorry," I fumbled.

The driver turned and glared at me through glazed eyes.

"Um, did you enjoy the show?" I asked, grinning foolishly as I backed away.

All at once the motor started. They lurched into the street and sped away, nearly running over my foot.

I parked—very poorly—and strode briskly toward Taylor

Square. The quickest route to the bars was via the notorious Wall, an avenue bounded by a high stone wall on one side and a hospice on the other where young boys on the game traditionally hang out. The thing to do, if you go this way, is to appear bored and casual and act like you walk along this street several times a day as an unavoidable necessity. If your body language manages to convey all that, the boys leave you alone. Needless to say, I failed.

"Lookin' for someone, mate?" a tired young kid asked loudly. "Hey? Lookin' for somebody?"

"Aren't we all," I replied stupidly. (Why couldn't I just say "No"?) As I increased my walking speed to the outer limits of casual, he caught me up.

"Come on, mate. I need some money. I'm gonna be chucked outta my place tonight. Come on. I'm good."

"Please leave me alone."

"I'm here till late. Are you lookin' for someone?"

"No."

His tone shifted from pleading to aggressive. "Just havin' a perve, are ya?"

He turned on his heel and sauntered away. I had to pass three or four others before I reached the main drag. By the time I reached the nearest hotel, I was a nervous wreck. I longed for a drink, but one glance told me it would be impossible. The bar was so crammed with patrons that they spilled out onto the pavement and into the gutter.

Clusters of buffed men stood around clutching their beers, cruising, or chatting. One boy was dancing in the street. I watched him distractedly. Clad in silk shorts and a football singlet, he cut a trim figure as he pirouetted his way deftly out of the path of an oncoming bus. Springing off the road in the nick of time, he landed in a camp curtsy beside me. With a jolt, I realised it was Paul.

"Buy a flower from a poor girl, mister?"

"Hello, Paul."

He frowned. "What's wrong, caro? You're not getting into the spirit of things. Come and celebrate my farewell."

"What farewell?"

"I'll be in heaven tomorrow—New Heaven, that is. We're starting rehearsals!"

"Already?"

"Darling, zero hour is only a week away. I have to stage two entire numbers, plus have sex with the busboys. My work's cut out for me."

"I didn't know it was happening so soon. I should ring Newton and get my flight organised."

"You must, caro. You could use a week's veg-out on a poofy island. You're looking rattled."

"I am. This area intimidates me. The boys at the Wall gave me a hard time."

"Just say you're Drug Squad and tell them to move along. Works for me."

"Take me for a coffee somewhere quiet."

We ambled around the corner to a late-night coffee shop, Yankee Doodle's. No trendy new establishment, it had been quietly plodding along since the '60s. A garish blue and pink neon sign anchored it in that bygone yet newly fashionable era. Fluorescent windows on either side of the door displayed row upon row of blanched cheesecakes and limp pastries which, under a more flattering light, might have looked edible (though probably not at one o'clock in the morning). Inside were booths, milk bar–style, with lacquered seats in faded red. Lounge music from the café's heyday bled from tiny speakers above the counter: Herb Alpert and the Tijuana Brass.

Paul squealed a request for two cappuccinos, and we flung ourselves roughly against the warped, tough vinyl. A sleepy-eyed Mediterranean woman slammed two weak coffees on the table, slopping most of the liquid into the saucer. She sighed, as if to suggest this was inevitable, then wandered away. Paul soaked up the spilt coffee with the pages of one of the free gay newspapers that lay just inside the door.

"Funny about that aircraft accident," he commented as a brown stain spread over the headline POLICE USELESS SAYS DRAG QUEEN.

"What about it?"

"Haven't you been following? It's quite spooky. I mean, you'd think a plane minus one propeller would have landing difficulties, but none of the aircraft that day reported any such thing. And then the police brought in some old fuddy-duddy to look at the propeller. After they scrubbed it and got all the makeup off, he identified it as an antique: a relic from the 18th century or something."

"They didn't have airplanes then!"

"Well, whenever. Before my time. So that kind of linked it to an air show which was on that day out at Halstrom Park. None of those little planes are supposed to go near a major flight path. Could cause a nasty accident."

"It did!" A thought came to me. "Surely somebody must have seen the plane as it flew over?"

"I suppose so, but by the time we knew what had happened, it was bound for the wild blue yonder. Anyway, it's not our problem, is it? Finish that cold revolting muck and get a good night's sleep. I'll call you from the resort. You should be fully informed on any goss before you arrive. If you're good, I'll save you a dancer."

I gulped the remaining coffee while Paul paid. "I'll get it. I'm a working girl now," he leered.

We kissed each other a fond *arrivederci*. I trudged back to the car, taking a long circuitous route to avoid the street of a thousand arseholes—an old joke, but apt. There were no further incidents. By the time I reached home I was virtually asleep. I flung my clothes onto a chair and was heading unswervingly for bed when I noticed the answer machine flashing away. It was so late. Could the message wait? The machine won, as it always does. The caller was Grant.

"Marc. Are you there? Marc? Damn, bloody damn. Don't tell me I've missed you. Shit, shit, shit. Well, by the time you hear this you'll know I can't come to the opera. Don't be annoyed with me. I didn't get down to Sydney today. There's too much happening up here.

"I can't talk to your machine. I'll call again tomorrow. I mean, really, Marc, it's extraordinary. It's always been so peaceful, but some idiot's been building a resort out on one of the islands and the ads have just appeared. The new place is exclusively for gays and lesbians! The locals are foaming at the mouth! Darling, I can't tell you—they'll be organising lynch mobs any minute. I suppose this is the end of my casual trips to the beach for research into shallow teenage angst. Anyway, there's no point anymore, I know *Surfside Motel*'s about to country, and we're about to cop it head-on. I—"

The beep sounded, cutting Grant off midstream. A second message quickly followed.

"It's me again. I didn't mean to rant on, Marc, but things are awfully hectic." He stopped. I thought the message was over. Then he resumed in a thick voice. "I've got personal problems too—I'm at my wit's end, actually. So, anyway... um...I'm really sorry about tonight. We'll talk soon. Ciao, sweetheart. Hope you enjoyed Mrs. Butterball."

I'd never heard Grant so agitated.

CHAPTER 5

I hadn't gotten around to asking Newton exactly where his playground of the rich and bent was, but Grant's message put it firmly on the map. By a strange coincidence, I knew the place well.

Grant lived just outside of a town called Murphy's Inlet. It was cozy, small, and tacky in an indistinct coastal way. There was a long beach bisected by the inlet, a few battered RV parks, then farther inland the town itself, which consisted of one main road, a post office, several pubs, the Seabreeze Guesthouse, an historical museum, a sports oval, and a few more RV parks. Recent additions included a shopping mall and cinema centre.

Adjacent to these were the municipal council chambers and employment office, which occupied an elegant, heritage building. The stately old pile had been decorated to death with a dozen different shades of mauve and magenta, then strangled by feral fairy lights. The effect was akin to finding your grandmother drunk in the gutter post–Mardi Gras.

The most unusual and striking landmark was a church, which sat in hilly country at the back of the town. Simple folk had worshiped on this spot since the 1850s, and the mossy foundations of their old church were still visible. More recently, a nondenominational sect had bought the land—they'd decided to make Murphy's Inlet their regional headquarters—and swiftly erected an enormous structure. The Church of Divine Intervention was a combination chapel and drive-in: You parked in one of the 200 available spaces and tuned into God's word. The central edifice was colourfully painted in red and white stripes. Except for the towering crucifix, it could have been a vast KFC outlet.

Grant had moved to Murphy's Inlet just as the new church opened for business. Local residents were skeptical to begin with, he told me, but soon accepted the sect, especially when it brought more tourists into town. Grant personally regarded the whole thing as a hoot, and even attempted to drag me along one Sunday evening.

"Give it a try, dear," he'd said. "You may be saved!"

"I hope not."

"The pastor's dead-sexy."

"Grant, it's a principle of mine to avoid religious ceremonies. Even if they are gay-friendly."

"Darling, who said they were? Anything but."

"Well, you said the pastor was sexy."

"Oh, yes, but she hates us! Poofs are in for the great chastisement on Judgment Day, apparently. It sounds like S/M Heaven! Personally, I can't wait."

In spite of the exciting presence of the Church of Divine Intervention and its greatly chastising pastor, the town continued to go about its business of barely surviving. Its decline was hastened a year later by the Department of Roads. They downgraded the old highway and replaced it with a multi-lane freeway that bypassed Murphy's Inlet altogether. The town was quietly and happily disintegrating when it came into the orbit of Gaytour International.

I left a message with Newton's answering service, but he didn't call back until late in the week. He sounded snowed under.

"Jesus, what a shitfight! The Americans are here already, a week early, to take advantage of some cheapo airline deal, and we're not ready. I've only got a skeleton staff in the kitchen and a handful of cleaners. I mean, shit! There's all these jobs and we can't seem to find local kids to fill 'em! Can you believe it?"

"You know what people are like, Newton. They're skeptical of new ventures."

"Skeptical? Murphy's Arsehole or whatever it's called is chocker with unemployed youth. What the fuck's wrong with them? You'd think they'd want to earn some easy money making beds. We had one girl—you wouldn't read about it— she didn't like the cleaners' uniform! Sorry, but she only wears purple! She'll be wearing purple if I get hold of her. Christ, I'll end up washing the frigging sheets myself! I've had to cancel meetings in Sydney all week."

"If things are too busy, don't worry about me—"

"Don't be bloody stupid. Can you come Monday? The weekend flights are full up with the official party, press, and that lot."

"Monday's fine."

"Good, 'cause I've organised it. Qantas Flight 502 to Mackay via Brisbane, 6:30 Monday morning. Someone'll meet you at the airport there and drive you to our boat. Hang on— Watch it! Just put it down there. No—Jesus, Hadrian! Why do you have to clean your lenses in here? You're a bloody menace."

"Pardon?"

"Sorry, Marc. I've got Hadrian underfoot. Gotta go. Cheers, mate."

I hung up, wishing I could have flown out a day or so earlier and organised a visit with Grant before racing off to the island. Now I'd have to try to catch up with him on the way back.

As it was, I had very little time to get myself ready. I needed to postpone my Italian students' lessons till further notice, see about my mail, and most important, buy a new swimming costume to replace the faded, shapeless tragedy I found at the bottom of my underwear drawer. This I accomplished after a lot of soul-searching and turning away at the last moment from the doors of fashionable boutiques. Finally, I hauled myself off to a large and impersonal department store, where I bought a pair of tastefully baggy swimming shorts in an unremarkable bottle green.

I packed a few tropical things, like my only two T-shirts—

one a sleeveless pink tie-dye, the other emblazoned with SHOP TILL YOU DROP '91—and threw in a paperback I'd been meaning to catch up on, *The Bedside Book of Coming-Out Short Stories, Vol. 6.* I added a handful of condoms and lube packets in case of an emergency—all a good decade past their use-by dates—and a pair of binoculars to set the ball rolling. Now I was equipped and ready for everything.

On Monday morning I set my alarm for 5:30 and woke up on the dot of four. Not wanting to risk going back to sleep, I dithered around as best I could and got to the airport an hour early. This was just as well. When I turned up at the prepaid ticket counter, they had never heard of me.

"Nooo," said a tall, balding man with a pale mustachioed smirk, who was standing behind the counter. "No Petrucci here. Are you sure that's the name?"

"I know my own name!" I replied, flustered.

He rolled his eyes. "Could it possibly be reserved under a company name?"

"Oh—um, yes. Try Gaytour International."

His eyebrows shot skyward. "Gaytour...gay...gayyy... Nope."

"This is ridiculous. I'm going to the New Heaven Resort. Newton Heath booked the flight. I'm a VIP guest! Sort of."

"I'll look under Heath, shall I? No, nothing. Sorry. Do you have a reference number for the booking?"

"Um, no."

"You wouldn't have mistaken the day?"

"Of course not!" I snapped.

He flounced just a little. "Perhaps you need to make a phone call."

"To whom?"

"I don't know, sir, but you're holding up the line. People are waiting."

I whirled around. There was one person behind me, a beady-eyed schoolboy.

"Look," I said, "when the flight fills up and there's one seat left over, that'll be mine!"

"It certainly will, sir—if you *buy* it."

"Pardon me," chirped a high voice, "but did you say you were going to New Heaven?"

I turned again, stunned. The kid had spoken.

"Ah, yes," I answered.

"Then we're travelling together." He pushed past me to the counter. "There should be two tickets under Journey's End Travel." He turned to me in explanation: "Journey's End has an exclusive deal with Gaytour."

The balding man smiled pleasantly. "Here you are. Enjoy your flight." He glared fleetingly at me as he handed the tickets across.

We dragged our bags over to the check in. "Thanks," I murmured to the (rather attractive) schoolboy.

"No probs. You must be Marc Petrucci."

"Yes."

"Pleased to meet you. I'm Delia Scott-Merman. Journalist."

I peered at her as I limply shook her hand. My schoolboy was a woman! How could I have mistaken such a thing? Mind you, she was slight of build—a boyish figure, one might say—and sported a short haircut. She didn't use makeup: The youthful reddish splotches in her cheeks were completely natural. She wore grey slacks and a maroon blazer. She was young but she smiled with a slyness that betokened a certain maturity.

We boarded in companionable silence and settled into the inhumanly shaped seats. I scanned the music channels for something escapist but—alas—there was no Tebaldi. The only opera available was the three tenors singing "Nessun Dorma." I put my headset away, deciding that *dormire* would be preferable. No sooner had I closed my eyes than Ms. Scott-Merman clicked into chat mode.

"I've heard all about you," she confided. "You and I are the last two stragglers. The Yanks have been up there for almost a week."

"I can't believe Newton forgot to mention Journey's End Travel," I sulked.

"Oh, Claire organised these tickets. She's much more efficient than Newton. He rants and raves all over the place while she simply gets things done. But that's the difference between queens and dykes, wouldn't you say?" She smiled sweetly.

"You know Claire well?" I asked.

"We're friends."

"Ah," I said. "I'm a friend of Newton."

She didn't bat an eyelid. "I know. I'm amazed you're going up so late. I'd have thought they'd need you sooner. You'll be run off your feet!"

"No, no," I answered. "I'm there to take it easy. Treat it like a holiday."

"Oh?" She arched an eyebrow. "Fair enough. It's a bludge for all of us."

I resented her tone. Somehow she'd managed to make me feel guilty for accepting Newton's offer. But why shouldn't I have a free holiday once in a while?

"What paper do you write for?" I asked.

She smiled. "I'm freelance. Profiles, mostly. In-depth pieces. You know—we could pool our resources here. With your connections you could give me some background about the place."

"I don't know anything."

She grinned craftily. "Course you do. I've been wondering how the mainland people feel about all these queers turning up on their turf. What's it called: Murphy's Inlet?"

I recalled Grant's phone message. "They're suspicious, I'd say."

She laughed. "I'd say so too! Isn't this area a centre of some fundamentalist cult?"

"The Church of Divine Intervention. Apparently, they're pretty quiet. I don't take all that preachy stuff too seriously."

"Well. You're Mr. Cool, aren't you!"

What on earth did she mean by that? "Don't go quoting me or anything," I stammered. "I'm no expert. I've got a friend living in the town."

"Mmm. Handy. What else can I ask you?"

I was beginning to feel trapped. "I'm sure I couldn't tell you anything you don't already know."

"No? Nothing about a certain mystery man, for instance?" She smiled enigmatically.

"I'm sorry—who are you talking about?"

"That's the question, isn't it! I've heard Gaytour is lining up a major celebrity to head their campaign. He'll do all the ads, talk shows—the lot. You know who it might be?"

"No."

Ms. Scott-Merman looked skeptical. "Honestly!" I added.

A grim, determined expression came over her face. "I'm going to find out. And so should you! Isn't it part of the job?"

"What job?"

Delia seemed to think I was another journalist. I was about to correct that impression when she leaned over and gripped my arm savagely. "Will there be celebrities in our group?" she asked.

"There might. I don't know. Ow. My arm—"

She let go. "I'm leveling with you here. I know we're all brothers and sisters, a united community, et cetera, but I'm a newcomer and the competition's fierce. Just between us, I haven't been a dyke for long."

"Oh." (It seemed like the polite thing to say.)

She shrugged dismissively. "I need the real story, not just the P.R. spin! It's my living, you know? If I don't get published, I starve. Simple as that."

I felt sympathetic. "I understand," I said, stroking my throbbing forearm. "If I hear anything about any celebrity I'll tell you."

"Anything about anything!" she cooed, her intensity

vanishing. "You never know what might be important. Thank you, Marc. I guess you haven't seen this!"

She opened her bag and took out a folded photocopied sheet.

"What is it?" I asked.

"Ah-ha!" she gloated. "It's a prototype of the New Heaven brochure. Hot off the press! Look here." She indicated with her finger. "This part interests me no end."

I peered. There was nothing but a blank space and a very faint circle scribbled on the original page.

"There's nothing there."

"That's right. It's obviously where the celebrity head shot is going. But whose head? That is the question."

"Do you mostly write about celebrities?"

"Quite frankly, I prefer investigative journalism. So much of what happens in our society is fundamentally unfair, don't you agree?" She shrugged. "But celebrity pieces sell. Some people are always news."

With that, we drifted off into our own little daydreams— at least, I did. In fact, I slept through the second leg of our journey. Delia shook me awake to say that we were landing in Mackay.

Once safely on the ground, we waited for our bags. Mine, as usual, might have been tagged with a sticker saying SEND OUT LAST, IF AT ALL. By the time they came, we were virtually alone in the terminus, with the exception of a tall, grey-haired woman. She walked briskly over.

"Delia! Welcome!" she said, embracing my travelling companion rather formally, then turned to me with one of her hands outstretched. "And you must be Marc. I'm Claire Bornkamp." She paused and added with a wry expression, "It's Dutch. Sorry to rush you both, but we must get back ASAP. The Jeep's right outside."

Within moments we were speeding off down the old highway toward Murphy's Inlet, where the ferry was waiting. I scarcely had time to take in the green hillsides and paddocks as they flashed by. As soon as the road reached the sea, the tang of salt air hit my nostrils like a wave of amyl at a dance party.

"Marc," said Claire, "Newton would like to see you the second we arrive."

"Fine," I said.

"What's the hurry?" asked Delia.

Claire turned to me. Her capable expression had slipped into a look of grim resignation.

"It's a pain, but we've got a contingent of Murphy's Inlet people over this afternoon. Local big shots. God knows the Americans are enough to cope with! Now we have to turn around and pat these self-appointed moral guardians on the head. We tried to stall them—give you time to get properly briefed—but they wouldn't hear of it."

I was somewhat confused. Why should I need to be briefed?

Delia spoke up. "Give 'em a quick tour and get rid of them."

"We'll try," answered Claire. "They want to see the whole place. They're just plain curious, really. Newton's doing his best to send the Americans off on a bush-walk so they won't be around to bother our new 'guests.'" A smile flitted across her lips. "The Americans don't wear very much."

"So what?" remarked Delia. "Isn't this the new millennium?"

"You'll see what I mean. A lot of them are pierced and tattooed, and there's the odd transsexual. We just don't look like a Christian fellowship camp! Of course, I'm not complaining about that! Anyway, we'll give this Inlet mob a drink, a swim if they want one, and a mini-seminar in the conference room. You'll be in charge of that, Marc. I know it's short notice, so just wing it."

I was stunned. "Me?" I croaked.

"I'll help you as much as I can, but I think you should run the show. Talk to 'em about acceptance with a capital *A*. I'm sure you know what to do. I'm looking forward to seeing our community liaison officer in action!"

"Community liaison officer?" I mumbled.

Delia leered at me. She must have known about my executive status all along. I felt strangely weak.

During the half-hour ferry trip to the island, the water was utterly calm, and our little ferry glided along on a sea of blue velvet. I threw up four times.

CHAPTER 6

The island was twenty to thirty kilometers long and shaped like a half-moon, with the main beach and new resort complex nestling inside the crescent. The terrain behind the resort was hilly and covered in a dense subtropical forest. At one end of the island, a mountainous plateau jutted unexpectedly out of the trees, its towering cliffs providing a natural shelter to the beach. There was, apparently, another beach hiding around the back somewhere, but generally the island's coast met the ocean in sheer walls of rock. It was a two-hour trek to the second beach, up through a thickly wooded ridge and down again.

The resort itself was virtually vertical. Built up the side of the hill in strata fashion were three levels of luxury motel–style apartments linked by a steep road and two sets of stairs, one for guests and one for staff. There were no lifts or buggies. To get anywhere you had to walk.

The main reception area nestled at sea level and ran parallel to the wharf and past the communal swimming pool. Here, too, were the main bar, the dining room, and a large activities area that could be used for everything from morning aerobics to a late-night disco and dance spectacular. Tucked away behind it was the conference room. On the second level were the administrative offices and at the very top, where the land flattened out somewhat, were the male and female swimming pools, a nine-hole golf course, a covered luncheon area, and a fully equipped gymnasium. Each building was crowned with a tropical style thatched roof made from woven palm leaves and padding.

By the time we docked, I was feeling very hot under the collar—and not just because of the humidity. For once, it was a relief to see Paul. Clad in minuscule Aussie Boys swimmers, he stood on the wharf waving frantically, a ridiculous grin on his face. With him were two simply gorgeous boys wearing identical T-shirts, blue shorts, and silvered sunglasses—the angelic uniform of New Heaven.

"Hello, caro mio!" he cried as he hugged me, even though he was dripping wet. "You must have a swim, it's bliss-in-a-pool."

"Let me get organised first," I panted.

"I'll take you up to Newton's office," said Claire, and glanced at her printout once more. "Boys, take Ms. Scott-Merman to her room, 212, and Mr. Petrucci's bags to 213."

"We'll be next to each other," I remarked convivially to Delia, though she didn't seem to hear. She stood, mesmerised, staring up at the tiered levels of the resort. I had to admit it was an imposing construction.

"Please, let's get moving, can we?" Claire snapped. Without a word, the two boys picked up our bags and trotted off toward the stairs with a silent Delia in tow.

"That's Darren and André," Paul explained breathlessly. "Ain't they cute? André's French-Polynesian or something. He's the one with the eyes. Darren's the one with the dick. Who's your mute girlfriend?"

"Just a journalist."

"A pack of them got in yesterday. There's one or two who can do an 'in-depth' with me anytime they like."

"Shouldn't you be rehearsing your routines?" snapped Claire, evidently not the world's number one Paul fan.

"We're on a break," he chirped. "We're way ahead of schedule. Besides, I'm thinking water. A swimming motif. I'm on the verge of a major inspiration!"

"I can't wait to see it," she muttered. "This way, Marc."

"See you in your room, caro!" Paul called as he sprinted back to the pool.

Claire shook her head. "Newton and his protégés," she growled to herself.

As we strode along, passing reception and the bar area,

I took stock of Claire. She was, as I said, probably in her mid 40s. Deep-set lines had settled around the corners of her mouth, giving her a general air of determination. She wore little makeup, though I noticed two small, expensive-looking earrings. Her cotton suit was staff-blue but well-tailored. Her fingernails were long and painted a deep crimson, a blazing contrast to the rest of her businesslike demeanour.

Our conversation was stilted, to say the least. I got the distinct feeling Claire was in some kind of emotional turmoil and was working hard to keep a lid on it.

"Do you know Delia well?" I asked breezily. Claire looked straight ahead. For a moment I thought she hadn't heard me.

"Who?"

"Delia. The girl I flew in with."

"Oh," Claire shrugged. "She's doing a story on the place."

"I thought you two were quite good friends."

"No." Claire came to a halt and turned to me. "Gaytour has a strict 'no freebies' policy. You should be aware of that." She exhaled ferociously. "Please excuse me, I'm not myself today. When we get rid of these locals, I'll be able to relax again. Up this way."

We climbed a flight of stairs, popped through a STAFF ONLY entrance, dashed along a corridor, and stopped outside a door at the end marked NEWTON HEATH. The door was slightly ajar, but Claire still knocked.

"Yeah?" came Newton's booming voice from inside.

"Marc Petrucci's here," called Claire.

"Marc! Come in!"

Claire slapped me on the back in an "all yours" gesture and strode away. I entered one of the most luxurious offices ever seen this side of the Equator. An enormous desk faced the floor-to-ceiling window, from which you could see right across to the ocean and all of the south end of the island.

Immediately below spread the branches of a tree thick with chattering parrots.

On the back wall hung a big black-and-white photo of a man wearing nothing but an elaborate Venetian carnival mask. The anonymous gentleman's penis was half in shadow but was still clearly gigantic.

An air-conditioner hummed in the corner. Newton was seated casually at the desk, which was covered in faxes and folders. Opposite were two comfy-looking office chairs, one of which was occupied by a muscular man in a mauve golf-shirt and urban camouflage slacks.

"Newton," I began, "Can you please explain—"

"Marc, am I glad to see you!" he interrupted. "Have a seat. Allow me to introduce Hiram. Marc Petrucci, Hiram Hudson."

The man shot out a hand, which I shook. He wore several chunky gold rings and a bracelet.

"Like the British explorer," I commented lamely.

He gave me a frosty smile. "That's Henry Hudson. There ain't no similarity."

Hiram's hair was reddish with streaks of grey still discernible in spite of his military clip. He flicked his head to one side, and I was reminded suddenly of the American eagle.

"What's in a name?" said Newton cordially. "Hiram here is practically Mr. Gaytour International in person, Marc," he continued, shooting me a conspiratorial glance. "We're very honoured to have him here this week. Most unexpected, too."

"It's a hands-on company," crowed Hiram. "Nobody's too big—or too small—to take an interest in the big picture. We are the big picture of the future, Mr. Petrucci: gays and lesbians. Lesbians and gays. It's about Pride, and it's about big bucks. You read me?"

I fought the impulse to say "loud and clear." I lost. "Um, loud and clear."

Mr. Gaytour International smiled. "Marc's our boy," he said to Newton.

"I knew you'd think so," Newton grinned. "Now if you don't mind, Hiram, I've got to brief Marc fully for this afternoon's session, and we don't have a lot of time."

"Go ahead," said Hiram. He rose and crushed my hand again. He stood at least a foot shorter than me. "I'll be there!" he barked encouragingly and marched out of the room.

I sank back into a chair. Newton immediately opened a drawer in his desk and took out a half-empty bottle of whisky and two shot glasses. He filled them to overflowing.

"Here," he said. "This might help."

"Newton, what the hell is going on? What have you put me in for?"

"I know, I know, mate. I'm sorry, all right?"

It was serious. I'd never heard Newton apologise before.

"It's all because that short-arse prick arrived out of the blue." Newton's voice had dropped to a whisper. "I mean, he honestly does represent the entire American investment, and he could pull out at the drop of a hat. It's not likely, so far down the track, but if he did, I'd be saddled with a whopping big debt. The place cost a packet to build, as you can imagine. Without Gaytour's international connections, we'd be up Shit Inlet. Trouble is, Hiram's so fucking hands-on. I had to think of a title for you to make it look good."

"Community liaison officer!"

"Yeah, well, we all make mistakes. See, I wasn't expecting the Murphy's Inlet crowd over here until the grand opening. You'd have been long gone by then, and I'd have gotten a real liaison officer. It's just a big pain in the bum they're coming today." He suddenly laughed heartily. "I'll be interested to hear what you say to 'em. Apparently, some of them are pretty fucking shitty about the whole idea."

"I'm no public speaker at the best of times," I quavered.

"Well. That's good news."

"What will I say, for God's sake?"

"Tell 'em it'll be good for the area: tourism, money, youth

employment. You know: bullshit. We've been careful with the environment and we paid handsomely for the place, so the previous owners have no complaints—"

"What previous owners? I thought it was national park."

He stroked his chin. "I don't think I said that. We could never have got it if had been commonwealth land. No, it was privately owned, the whole island. The Murphy family bought it from the governor in 1899. Pre-federation sell-off."

"Murphy, as in the inlet."

"Yeah. Like I told you, it was called Crab Island. That's another bloody problem: These fucking crabs are all over the bloody place. Anyhow, there was only old Mrs. Murphy left here. When she died, it came on the market and I swooped! If you see an opportunity, grab it with both hands—crabs and all! The old girl left no will, so the executors tracked down her closest living relative, who turned out to be a phony art dealer I defended ten years ago. He lives in London now, but we keep in touch. He put me onto it. We're naming part of the golf course after the old lady: The Iris Murphy Memorial Ninth Hole."

"How sweet."

"Silly old bag. Well, let's work this out. It's one o'clock now. The Yanks are having lunch, and they're pissing off to Murphy's Beach at two, all except Hiram, of course. Our chef has packed hampers, and I'm hoping they won't be back before six. The Inlet gang gets here around two; we'll give 'em drinks and mouthwatering delicacies, the grand tour at three, more drinks, and then your little Q&A at, say, five-ish? Shouldn't take more than half an hour. Get 'em on the ferry, then we can have a bloody good dinner and a bit of fun, like in the brochure. Incidentally, I'll give you one of our brochures so you know what you're talking about." He winked. "I'm sure you won't let us down."

He shuffled around the papers on his desk and eventually handed me a black-and-white pamphlet. It was identical to the one Delia had shown me on the plane. The space for the photo was still blank. "Tell me," I asked, "are you getting some famous name to endorse the place?"

"How do you mean?" He looked up.

"A celebrity."

"It's an idea. Why do you ask?"

"Someone told me you were. A journalist."

He slapped his hand down hard on the desk. "Jesus! Already? Which fucking journalist?"

I felt uncomfortable. "Does it matter?"

"Of course! Who was it?"

"A lesbian writer I met at the airport. She was only guessing."

Newton got up, walked around behind my chair and put his hand on my shoulder.

"Marc, mate, this is between us. Christ, I thought I was the only one who knew about it! Claire doesn't know. Nobody does. Yes, there's a celebrity I've been wooing, if you like, to front the campaign. It's at a delicate stage of negotiation, by no means definite, so we have to keep very quiet! If this person hears a hint of a rumour, it's all off. Kaput. OK? Now you better get to your room and suit up. Where have we put you?"

I stood up. "213, I think."

"Good. That's on this level. Ask one of those spunks I've hired to show you the way. I recommend Darren." He started to usher me out, but before he opened the door I laid my hand on his arm.

"Newton, please—who's the celebrity?"

He gave me his best courtroom scowl. "You'll keep this to yourself?"

"You know I will!"

He leaned close. "The Dalai Lama," he whispered.

I could still hear him laughing in his office as I closed the door.

Room 213 was pleasant and spacious, with a queen-size bed and a balcony looking down over the main pool, but I was too fussed to enjoy the view. I flung my bag onto the bed, unpacked a few things, and sat miserably at the corner desk staring at a blank piece of paper.

This activity produced no results, so I browsed through the brochure Newton had given me. It listed a formidable range of entertainment to tempt the holidaying queer person: swimming, golf, tennis, picnics, dance parties, karaoke, and so on. Most of these delights were marked with an asterisk, the words "Not available yet" scrawled up the margin. There was a safe-sex message, with a reminder that lubricated condoms were supplied in all rooms and other sex aids might be purchased at the New Heaven Boutique behind reception. Admirable, I thought, but probably not the way to mollify the locals. There was a map detailing the layout of the resort and the track to Murphy's Beach. What there *wasn't* was a community liaison column entitled Handy Hints for Beginners.

I needed a drink. I searched for the minibar, but alcohol was evidently "not available yet." On top of the fridge sat a porcelain water-jug and two tall glasses. I quickly poured myself a stiff one and gulped it down. It tasted revolting—stale and strangely fishy. I peered into the jug. Two tiny dead crabs were floating on the sludgy surface of the water.

I began to wonder if more of these creatures were lurking around. I was in the process of stripping my bed when there was a knock at the door.

"Caro! Is anybody home?"

It was Paul, now fully dressed in lime Lycra pants and a chest-hugging tank top that stopped short just below the nipple line.

"Coming for a swim and a tan-up?" he asked. "I've got sun-screen stuff. Three-Plus."

"I can't, Paul."

"Why not? Look, caro, they haven't even made your bed. How slack! Let's call Darren and André to do it. They can tuck themselves right in!"

"I'll do it myself, then I have to prepare something to say. Didn't you know I've got to pacify a lot of local small-businessmen this afternoon?"

"Sure. All available staff are required to attend. Should be a hoot!"

"What will I say?"

"I don't know. Tell them to mind their own small business."

"I'm supposed to liaise with them."

"So, liaise. Come swimming with me and forget all about it."

I sank onto the unmade bed, and Paul started to massage my shoulders.

"Caro, you're always so tense! You mustn't let these things get on top of you. There are plenty of cute men around to do that!"

"It's worrying me, Paul."

"Let's think: There must be a way. Didn't you once teach languages to a bunch of yuppie teenage girls? Darling, if you can handle that, you can handle anything."

"I didn't handle it too well, I recall."

"Doesn't matter. Approach this the same way. How did you prepare for your girlie lessons? Hmm? Tell Paul."

"I used to write the day's vocab on the blackboard, take them through it—you know, put each word in context, then give them exercises."

He clapped his hands with glee. "Too camp! Well, do something like tha—answer a few curly questions and Bob's your aunty!"

"If you think that will work—"

"Can't fail. Now, come swimming."

I shook my head. "I can't."

"Suit yourself. But there's no need to worry. You'll be a smash! It'll run for decades! See you backstage afterward. We'll scan the reviews over supper."

Paul kissed me solicitously and flitted off.

He was right: It was all in the preparation. I recalled that during my teaching days I would reproduce regional maps of Italy on the blackboard in intricate detail, using coloured chalks. Perhaps that was the way to go: Dazzle them with penmanship. In the next hour I made several draft copies of the island map, adding little dragons in the clouds and sea monsters for that dash of cartographical panache. I even took it upon myself to name a couple of natural landmarks. "Lake Renata" was a favourite.

I was completely immersed when there was another knock at the door. Now what? I checked the time: 2:45.

"It's open," I called.

To my surprise, Grant strode in. "Mr. Community Liaison, I presume? May one come in?" he beamed.

"Of course," I said, giving him a long hug. "I'd offer you a drink, but there's only crustacean cocktail."

He threw himself on the bed. "Not for me, dear."

"What are you doing here?"

"Darling, I might ask you the same question. You could have knocked me over with a sequin when I heard you were working for this Gaytour outfit!"

I wiped my brow. "I didn't know myself till I got here. I thought it was going to be a holiday. Suddenly I'm in charge of the complaints department! Newton dropped me in it."

"Newton's your chum, is he?" Grant looked contemptuous. "Terrific."

"Do you know him?"

"By reputation only."

"I must introduce you. If you'd bothered to come to dinner that night, you'd have met him."

59

"My loss, no doubt."

"It was: He paid for the meal. So are you with this local group?"

"Yes, lucky for you. You remember June, who runs the guesthouse?"

"Of course. How is she?"

"Not too well. I'm here in her place."

"I see. So, " I pleaded, "fill me in, for God's sake. What's the story?"

He took a deep breath. "I feel like a double agent or something. Where to begin? A lot of the townspeople are hot under the collar about this whole thing. Frankly, my love, it's a no-win situation for you. On one hand, they're aghast at the thought of a bunch of deviants slumming it in their very midst; and on the other, they're angry because the pink tourist dollar won't be spent in their tacky little shops."

"Are you against New Heaven, too?"

"Oh, I suppose not, though it won't do me any good for a number of reasons. Poor June's business will be the most affected. She used to do a roaring trade in jaded old tarts looking for a bit of peace and quiet. People like you, for example."

"Mmm."

"But I wouldn't worry about that, Marc. There's something else going on. I mean, these people get excited for a minute, but they're basically lethargic. That's why I like it here, as you know. It's tranquil, conducive to creativity. By the way, I still have a job on *Surfside,* though Lord knows for how long! The point is, these nice ordinary people are being whipped into a frenzy by someone."

"Who?"

"I don't know, but I wouldn't look much farther than the Church of Divine Intervention. Our Woman of the Cloth is a sneaky brute."

This sounded tricky. "What should I do?" I moaned for the umpteenth time that day.

"Compromise, darling. I mean, look at the size of this place. They'll never keep it going. There's just not enough of us. Oh, I can see Mardi Gras and Midsummer Festival packages et cetera, but what about the rest of the year? We do have a winter here, you know. We have a monsoon season with cyclones and the whole shebang. The weather can be ghastly! No good for a bunch of fussy old queens. So why not open the place up to, you know, *them*?"

"'Them?'"

"Heterosexuals, love. Families of 4.2. School-holiday nature-study groups. Japanese honeymooners. *That* them!"

He seemed perfectly serious. I thought instantly of Hiram Hudson. "I don't think the management would consider it for a second."

Grant snorted. "Well, it makes sense to me," he said. "Financially, they're mad if they don't. And the good Murphy-siders wouldn't feel quite so threatened."

"You could suggest that plan to Newton," I offered.

He grinned. "Have no fear, I shall."

CHAPTER 7

I found my way to New Heaven's conference room half an hour before my community liaison debut was scheduled to start. Its interior was reminiscent of those tropical back rooms common to 1940s melodramas: mouldy rendered-cement walls, rattan blinds, plain old chairs, a lazy fan circling above. What I'd assumed would be a brand-new corporate facility was in reality the oldest building in the resort.

A whiteboard had been tacked up on the central wall and I attacked it with gusto and coloured pens. Within twenty minutes it was adorned with a detailed many-hued map of our island paradise. I stepped back to appraise my work. Modestly, I had to admit it was superb! My mapmaking abilities had not deserted me in those happy years since I had parted company forever with multilingual schoolgirls.

Claire was the first to arrive. Seeing that I was ready, she swiftly rounded up the guests, who gradually took their places. I tried to avoid direct eye contact with my audience, but even peripherally it was not difficult to distinguish the locals from the journalists.

The Murphy's Inlet team, sitting close together in the centre of the room, was a vision of floral-print cotton (ladies) and long white socks (gents). The men, though of varying ages, all specialised in lightweight shorts with very thin belts, and durable shirts with wet underarms. Only one of them transcended the drawbacks of this unattractive ensemble by virtue of his pale green eyes and dark lashes—not to mention a tanned, taut body obviously used to working out. Unmistakably a wolf in cheap clothing. I decided to look to him if I needed to calm my nerves.

The journalists, many of them sweltering in inappropriate

black denim, moved languidly up the back. Some were sculpted young men sporting message T-shirts like COME OUT, COME OUT, WHATEVER YOU ARE. There were a couple of solid, formidable lesbians of a hard-won middle age and a few younger dykes who might have stepped from the covers of a glossy magazine.

Accompanying the journalists were a pair of overly neat young men sporting silk ties and expensive haircuts: These were the "special package" travel agents. They kept apart and appraised the decor with a jaundiced eye.

Last of all, in the front seats were the New Heaven staff, including Paul and Hiram Hudson. Neither afforded me much relief in my stage fright. One of the gorgeous boys, Darren, was among the last to arrive. He sat down directly in front of me, panting slightly, and stretched out languorous legs, which ended in a pair of tight floral shorts. He glistened healthily with good, honest, masculine sweat, and was far too distracting for comfort. I searched for a friendly face. Where was Grant?

Claire looked tired and exasperated. "The tour was hell," she confided quietly. "As soon as Newton gets here, start for God's sake." I glanced at my watch. It was just after five. Paul bounced over.

"Love the map, caro," he said, nodding encouragement. "But you look like shit warmed up. Relax! Take a deep breath, close your eyes, and hold it till I tell you to stop."

"I don't want to."

"It'll relax you. Trust me, I'm a performer. I know these techniques. Now, eyes closed. Good. De-e-ep breath in. And hold it."

I did. The hubbub in the room slowly receded, replaced by a shrill high-pitched tone. Little darting amoebas swam before my eyelids till my head span. Finally, I had to exhale.

"Is that long enough?" I panted, opening my eyes. Paul was over near the door, engrossed in conversation with André, the other gorgeous boy. Claire and Hiram were peering at me with concern.

"You OK?" barked Hiram.

"Yes, yes, fine," I replied dizzily. "Just a simple relaxation technique."

"Well, get going."

"But Newton's not here yet."

"Too bad for Newton," Hiram remarked.

Claire stood up. "Oh, I'll find him. He's probably arguing on his mobile somewhere. You'd better start. It's ten past." She strode grimly from the room.

"Ah, Hiram," I said, "since you are Mr. Gaytour International, I wonder if you would care to open this, um, session."

"Sure," he grinned, and without pause, shouted in a voice louder than God, "Hey!"

The babble ceased immediately. Paul and a few others rushed guiltily to their seats.

"My name is Hiram Hudson," Hiram began, "and I represent the American investors in this island paradise we call New Heaven. As you know, Gaytour International offers very popular gay and lesbian vacation packages in the Caribbean—also in Scotland—and now we're bringing this unique opportunity all the way to Queensland, Australia. We pride ourselves on being at the cutting edge of the hospitality industry. First, there was ecotourism—that's to say, your environment-based holiday package—then there was agri-tourism, your agricultural-based package, and now there's us: aggro-homo-tourism! Speaks for itself. I got a lot more to say, but instead I'm gonna hand you over to our expert here. Let's hear it for our community liaison officer, Marc Petrucci."

Paul clapped enthusiastically. "Bravo!" he screamed.

"Thank you, Hiram," I began confidently. There was an expectant hush.

"Ladies and gentlemen, distinguished guests. As you can see, behind me is a detailed map of the island and the resort, which I've gone to the trouble of reproducing here. Feel free to make your own copies."

"Why?" asked somebody.

"Sorry, what?"

"Why?"

"I thought it might be helpful in, um, acclimatising you."

"But we've got the brochure."

I frowned as I realised my elaborate map was redundant. I'd never quite decided what to do next. "So," I faltered, "if there are no further questions—"

This tack took everyone by surprise. The room was stunned and silent, till a stocky, red-faced man from Murphy's Inlet spoke up.

"Why don't you go back where you come from?" he called.

"Um, is that a question?"

"Yair, it's a bloody *good* question!" Some of the locals tittered.

I had a sudden brain wave. "Would you mind identifying yourself, sir?"

He leaned back in his chair, folding his brawny arms defiantly over his gut. "I've got nothing to hide. Merv Jackson's the name. Alderman Merv Jackson, chairman of the land and development subcommittee."

"And you have some objection to a gay and lesbian resort?"

"We all do, more or less."

"I see. Is your objection personal or official?"

"Council's yet to find a way to close this place down, but don't you worry, we will! Listen, I grew up in Murphy's Inlet. Now that I'm retired, I'm back here and I'm interested in the history of the place. It's got a lot of historical significance. You mightn't think so. But what are people gonna say if we get overrun with a whole bunch of poofters and, er—"

"Dykes!" called a female journalist from the back.

"What about our children? That's the important thing!" said a woman in a cotton-print frock.

"Very bloody sneaky when you put in the development

application," the alderman continued. "Not a word about gays and...so on back then."

"Lesbians!" called the journalist again. "We do exist."

"Yair. Well, I've got a fair idea what you lot need."

"We're here and we're queer!" chanted a couple of youthful voices.

"There's enough of that sort of thing on television," snorted Alderman Jackson, "without having it shoved down your throat in real life! Reasonable people find this whole business absolutely disgusting."

"Good!" I said. "This is all sounding very healthy. Get it out in the open."

"Don't try anything like that, pal!"

"What I mean is, to answer your question, Mr. Jackson, going back to where we came from is precisely what will happen. When the resort is fully operational, we'll be bringing in groups from all around the world and a week later they'll be flying out again. All their needs will be met here, on the island, as you saw from your tour. None of our tourists will be spending any time in the town, except to transfer from the bus to our boat, and I can assure *you*, madam," I addressed the lady in the cotton frock, "the changeover will take place only during school hours."

"Good one, caro!" cried Paul.

"That's rubbish!" yelled a female journalist. "Surely they'll be coming in on the weekend. And anyway, why the hell should we stay out of town? Are we lepers or something? I'll go into town if I want to. I'll walk straight into the pub!"

"Over my dead body," shouted the alderman. "You can head back where you come from!"

The journalist stood up. "Where do you think I come from, you stupid clown? From a town just like this!"

"Let's not descend to name-calling," I snapped at her irritably. "Do you have a question?"

"Yes! Is Gaytour International out and proud, or just a

bunch of money-hungry predators exploiting the queer market?"

This one stumped me for a second. "Well. I think the name says it all. 'New Heaven.' It's unique, it's vibrant, it's—um—available."

"They can call the joint Prickville if they like," she answered. "It's their attitude I'm interested in."

"May I remind you," I said, using my severest teacher's tone, "that this is not a press conference. It's a community liaison, uh, thing. Now, are there any more queries?" A ripple of laughter spread through the room, for some reason. This would have been a good point for Grant to help me out, I thought, but he, like Newton, was inexplicably absent.

"I have something to say." I looked up. The request came from the good-looking man with green eyes.

"Certainly," I beamed. "And you are?"

He stood slowly, and I might add, breathtakingly.

"I am Pastor Matthew Paramor of the Church of Divine Intervention." Calmly and expertly, he surveyed the room. The humble townsfolk and male journalists watched him in rapt adoration. I bit my lip. This could be tricky.

His face broke into a relaxed, winning smile.

"This is the 21st century, isn't it?" he asked offhandedly.

"Yes," I answered, pleased to be on top of the facts for once.

"It was a rhetorical question," he replied gently. "What I mean is, we are all modern people. We all live in the current climate. We recognise that there is a diversity of attitudes, a number of differing lifestyles, and it is the individual's pre-rogative to live exactly the way he or she wishes—within the law of the land. I'm sure we all agree with that."

There was a general murmur of consensus.

"It seems today that everyone has an agenda, doesn't it? And that's our right! You've got your agenda, these people have theirs, and I have mine. And who can truly say one per-son's agenda is more important than another's? God created us all, whatever our agendas may be, whether they agree with one another or not. We're all equal in His eyes, and we all have our basic human rights. I mean, that is your bottom line right there."

This was sounding all very reasonable and conciliatory. I uncrossed my fingers.

"Did I mention God?" he continued. "I believe I did. And it's no surprise, is it, to discover that God has an agenda too. Why should He miss out?" There was general laughter at this. "God's been around a hell of a lot longer—pardon the expression—than I have. Longer than the good people of Murphy's Inlet. Longer than the partners of Gaytour International. As far as we're concerned, God and His agenda have been around since that very first holiday resort, the Garden of Eden. Now that was some resort! I wish I could've had a guided tour of that one!"

I started feeling uncomfortable again. Where was this heading?

"I wonder if you could get to the point, Pastor Paramor," I said.

Several of the audience stared at me.

"That's no way to speak to a preacher!" clucked a fat woman in a pink shift.

"It's OK," smiled the pastor. "But let's get back to the Garden of Eden. God made his agenda clear right from the start. He created Adam, a man, and Eve, a woman, and said 'Go forth and multiply.' And to help that little process along, He gave them the urge to do it. The sexual urge."

"Yahoo!" remarked someone. (I suspected Paul.)

"To cut a long story short, we all know what happened: Adam and Eve disobeyed God, ate from the Tree of Knowledge, and got themselves a brand-new agenda! They started this whole complicated chain that leads to our modern world full of contradictory options, which are all equal and all viable"—suddenly he was at full voice—"and all overshadowed by the long-standing, cosmic agenda of God!"

"Yes, well, thank you very much—" I began.

"You may say," the Pastor persisted, in this less relaxed tone, " 'All this Garden of Eden stuff: What's it to do with me? I wasn't there!' But, my friends, God continues to reveal His agenda to us. We in the church believe in divine intervention, as our name implies. And God Himself will surely intervene in the matter of this resort. He will give us a sign, as He invariably does. It may be a bolt from the blue, it may be fire or flood or"—he paused for emphasis—"it may be plague. I cannot say. It isn't my place to divulge the details. But if I know God, there'll be no mistaking the intent of His holy will."

He smiled once more. The Murphy's Inlet crowd applauded as the journalists scribbled away avidly. It was at this moment I noticed Grant, looking flushed and disheveled, tiptoeing in the door.

"Thank you for your contribution, Pastor," I mumbled hurriedly. "Anyone else?"

I looked beseechingly in Grant's direction. He avoided my gaze.

"Aaahh," came a voice, theatrically imitating a yawn. "Well, that was boring."

It was Paul.

"Paul, I don't think—" I started, but he was on his feet.

"Listen here, Rector Rectum, or whatever you call yourself. Can you answer a question for me?"

Alderman Jackson sprang to his feet, but the Pastor gently motioned him to sit. "I'll try," he answered evenly.

"That tacky monstrosity of a drive-in your friends have put on the hill over there—is that one of God's signs? Because honey, if it is, God better get a new sign-writer!"

"Shame on you," cried a voice in the crowd.

"Shame on me?" Paul shouted back. "The shame's on your poor old town. Or were you all thrilled to have the place turned into a tasteless heap of trash?"

"That's enough," commanded the alderman. "At least their development application was clear!"

"God will punish you," another man shouted.

Paul leapt onto his chair. "Whoa! Is God going to interfere with naughty little me? He sounds like a dirty old man. Luckily, I'm divine too!" He roared with maniacal laughter. "Here I come, out of the blue!" He back-flipped off the seat and landed in an elaborate curtsy. "Ta-daaah!"

The Alderman was on his feet. "I've seen enough," he snapped. "Council permission for this resort is withdrawn!"

"You can't make that decision," snapped the dyke journalist.

"See if I bloody well don't!"

"Redneck idiot!"

"Close the place down!" yelled someone else.

"You're ripping us off! Nobody's been paid!"

"Go to hell!"

"You *will*!"

Everybody was shouting.

BANG! A huge explosion went off, almost in my face. The clamour ceased. As I reeled back, I saw Hiram, one arm extending upward where his hand gripped the butt of a smoking revolver. Miraculously, the bullet had missed the fan and gone through the ceiling.

"Siddown and shut up," he ordered. Predictably everyone did, myself included.

"Now listen to me," he said. "I'm Hiram Hudson, from Gaytour International. You got that? OK. We gave you folks a tour, we gave you a drink, and we gave you a chance to air your opinions. I don't want you to forget that. Our Mr. Petrucci here"—I ducked as he gestured toward me with the gun—"he's done his best to be friendly and conciliatory. That's fine. He's in P.R., and he's a pro. Me, I don't feel so friendly. New Heaven's been built, it's goin' ahead, and I don't give a faggot's fuck if you people like it or not. Now get off my land!"

Everybody sat stock still. Hiram turned to me. "Get rid of 'em," he hissed.

I stood. "Thank you very much, ladies and gentlemen, for this, um, frank exchange of views. All very encouraging. It's now—let me see—five minutes to six. The ferry will be leaving directly. This meeting is adjourned."

CHAPTER 8

A tempting glass of Italian red and a plate of field-mushroom risotto lay before me. I reached for the wine, my third in as many minutes, with an unsteady hand. I instinctively felt my community liaisability left something to be desired. On their way back to the ferry, the Murphy's Inlet brigade shunned me as though I were the Antichrist. Even Grant, clearly in one of his moods, bade me a monosyllabic farewell. Nor were the gay and lesbian scribes happy with my performance. One had asked me about my credentials, and another had pointedly remarked that he didn't recall seeing me at the Mardi Gras AGM. The only person who gave me any support was Paul.

"Excellent show, caro," he mumbled as, mouth full, he plonked his lasagna-laden plate down beside mine. "You had them in the palm of your hand."

"I'm not so sure. The meeting didn't achieve a glimmer of reconciliation."

"Leave them wanting more, darling. Speaking of which, can I top you up?"

"Thanks."

We were in the spacious dining salon on the ground level. The rest of the staff had finished eating and were now flirting in the bar area with a gaggle of journalists. Another group had congregated there too. They looked like a gymnastics team with no age quota. Young, old, or indeterminate, they all wore tight-fitting stretch fabric over shapely, pumped-up bodies. Their chatter was loud, positive, and uplifting. These were the Americans.

I'd come to dinner at the last moment. My first port of call after the meeting was Room 213, where I had spent an hour in bed curled up in fetal position, gibbering mindlessly.

Eventually, however, hunger had triumphed over self-pity, and I reappeared in public.

"Is Newton around?" I asked Paul.

"Haven't seen him."

"He must have heard all about my fiasco. I bet he's in his office right now, organising me a one-way dogsled to the Gaytour resort, Siberia. "

"Whooo! Marc!" sang a tipsy voice, as Delia ricocheted her way toward us, clutching a cocktail. She collapsed into a seat opposite.

"Cheers!" She downed her drink in seconds flat and turned to Paul. "Delia Scott-Merman, hi."

"I'm Paul."

"And what do you do round here, Paul?"

"I'm in a creative role. Consultant choreographer."

"Ah, fun! When do we get to see your fancy footwork?"

"Tomorrow night," he announced, "if I'm satisfied it's ready! I'm très picky."

"Me too. Tell you what. If I like it, I'll do an interview." Delia turned her attention to me. "Marc! How are you bearing up? You look a bit shaken."

I was still recovering: Paul's shameless self-promotion never fails to stun me. "Oh, I'm fine," I said.

"I thought the seminar went pretty well," Delia said brightly.

I was staggered. "You did?"

She shrugged. "Considering. Who was that man who fired the shot?"

"Oh, Hiram. He's Mr. Big of Gaytour. Rather an extreme way to break up an argument."

"An argument? Oh yeah, of course." She seemed momentarily distracted. "So! Have you learnt any more about you-know-what?"

"No, I haven't."

She smiled. "Me neither, but keep trying."

"What are you two talking about?" Paul demanded.

"I'll tell you later," I said.

"Now don't sit in here gossiping," trilled Delia. "Come and join us in the bar! That's what I popped over to say." She lurched to her feet. "I'm on a roll tonight!"

"I haven't finished eating," I protested.

She staggered away, as Paul held my face in his hands. "If you have goss," he stated in serious tones, "you are duty-bound to pass it on."

"It's nothing," I said. "Delia's got it into her head that some megastar has been hired to play 'Goddess of New Heaven' and do all the promotions."

"Wow! I wonder who it is!" he enthused. Does caro know?"

"Get that sly look off your face. I asked Newton, and he said there was no such person, although he thought it was a damn good idea."

"It is! Coming to the bar, then?"

I demurred. "I don't feel like mixing. I'm going to bed."

He looked disgusted. "You can sleep alone in a nursing home when you're senile—in about six months' time. Here, we boogie! Now listen to me very carefully, 'cause I've got a surprise for you." He leaned close. "Meet me tonight, round eleven, at the lunch area on the top level."

"Can't we have lunch tomorrow?"

"It's another kind of lunch. Promise! You know where I mean? Next to the men's pool, up the stairs and to the right."

"What for?"

"For the view! You'll adore it. Money back if not completely satisfied!"

With that he skipped off. I bypassed the bar and headed for my room, where Tebaldi was lying in wait, wrapped in a plastic bag at the bottom of my suitcase. I had no intention of venturing out until morning, at which time I confidently anticipated breakfast would be served. My agenda, as Pastor

Paramor might call it, was henceforth reprioritised toward serious relaxation.

I listened to Act 1 of *Butterfly*, then chucked my head-phones to one side and tried to doze, but it was impossible. I was still too fired up by the events of the day. I was swelter-ing, too. The air-conditioner in my room was "not available yet." I lay in sticky stillness.

Outside, *la notte tropicale* called, ripe with the promise of insect bites and adventure. At 11:15 I reviewed Paul's invita-tion. Maybe there was a late-night bar operating at this luncheon area? Eventually, I threw on my clothes and ambled up the road.

At the luncheon area there wasn't a light on anywhere—and no sign of life either. The trellised pagoda lay still and silent. Murky, eerie shadows, cast by the misty moonlight, shone through the trellises creating faint surreal patterns on the polished floor; potted plants, succulent in the sunshine, took on a bending, breathing nightlife of their own, as they stirred imperceptibly in the hot evening breeze. Sounds of subtropical night creatures, with all their implicit menace, broke the silence.

I felt lost in this mysterious, threatening landscape. I peered into the gloom, straining to see or hear something familiar.

A gentle lapping of water against tile and a low murmur of conversation suggested a presence in the pool nearby. I wandered over and saw a couple of silhouettes, outlined weirdly by dim lights under the surface of the water. Two men were swimming. One of them might have been Paul, but I didn't like to interrupt. I was not dressed for a dip in any case, though as I looked harder, it became clear the swim-mers were naked.

I turned my attention back to my surroundings. My eyes grew accustomed to the darkness. I could make out the glass doors of the cafeteria. Tables and chairs were stacked neatly in a corner. An orange glow appeared for a second—the ember of a cigarette—and I realised with a jolt that there was a dark figure slouching beside the pile of stacked chairs. I couldn't see the face, but he raised his head slightly, and a glint of light flashed across the surface of his spectacles.

A rustling to my left made me turn, and I now perceived two more dark figures, one leaning next to the trellis pole and another a few feet away in the shrubbery. The second one nodded at me. I nodded back, out of automatic politeness.

This area was apparently your genuine, good old-fashioned beat. No wonder Paul had been so excited. Well, I thought to myself, why not?

I decided to move to a less obvious spot. I felt silly standing in the centre of all this clandestine activity. Casually, I made my way over to a potted palm and nestled into its sweaty foliage. It had been years since I'd last found myself in this situation, yet the old frisson was there and it all came back to me—rather like riding a bike, another favourite activity of my youth.

Suddenly, my radar clicked into full alert. I sensed footsteps. One of the figures was moving toward me. A second later I felt the pressure of his fingers in my hand as he turned me around to face him. Our bodies were inches away from each other in the blackness. He seemed a mere boy; I could make out a mop of hair in silhouette, a strong profile and a pair of broad shoulders. He opened his mouth and rocked me with a blast of peppermint.

"Whoa," I whispered.

Daintily, he reached up and removed his gum—where he put it I don't know. Then his lips were on mine and we kissed. Without a word, I put my arms around him. He wore no shirt, and I rubbed my hands gently up and down his warm back. His skin was smooth and dry, in spite of the tropical humidity. I let my fingertips trail over his shoulders and down his chest. There was the slightest friction between his pecs where he had shaved. (Was it too soon to talk about commitment? Probably.)

He stepped back slightly, took my hand, kissed it and placed it on the front of his pants.

"Mmm," he crooned.

I stroked him gently, luxuriating in the waves of peppermint that came with increasing frequency. Words like "bingo" and "jackpot" drifted into my mind. He leaned close to my ear.

"Hey," he whispered softly.

"Hey," I replied.

"Wade," he said.

"Right now? Well, if you like."

"Huh?"

"Hmm?"

"Wade is my name."

"Oh. Hi. Marc."

"I like to know names. I guess it's uncool."

"No, no. Shall we go to my room?"

"Uh-uh. I wanna do it out here."

He held me tight. I buried my face in his hair as I nuzzled his neck. His fingers were undoing my belt.

"Are you sure?" I asked.

"You want it. You know you do."

Goodness, I thought, *Americans really do talk like that!* Moreover, he was 100 percent correct.

"It's not too private here," I said.

"I got a rubber," he replied vaguely. Another second and I wouldn't be going anywhere, due to trousers-round-the-ankles syndrome.

"Not here," I whispered. "Let's go around the back."

"Cool."

Lickety-split, I fastened my pants and took his big, warm hand. I had no real idea where we were heading, but it didn't matter much. I was feeling quite rejuvenated.

"Behind that wall," I suggested, pointing to where the cafeteria backed into a patch of bush. We edged along the wall, our backs to the warm bricks, until we reached a natural clearing. It was dark, dry, and well-hidden.

"How's about here?" he asked, and before I could agree, he kissed me hard once again. Suddenly, he pulled away and held me at arm's length.

"What's that?" he asked in a tone of utter distaste.

"What?" I said, mentally running a personal hygiene check.

"That smell."

I sniffed. He was right. A strange, pungent odour caused me to catch my breath. Sharp and irritating, it smelt like barbecued rancid meat marinated in fabric softener.

"I don't know, I— aaachuu!" I sneezed violently. "Sorry."

"It's over here," he said, moving farther along the wall.

"Wait!"

"What?"

"Don't leave me." I stumbled toward him. "Where are you?"

"Right here, man."

I reached out to grab him and found myself toppling. I had tripped over a muddy log. I braced myself, and landed with a bump on the ground. The smell down there was unbearable. With a growing sense of disbelief, I realised that the log was, in fact, a human leg.

I yelled. A yellowish light flickered on—my companion held up a cigarette lighter. "Shit!" he said.

He came closer as I jumped to my feet. There before us, half concealed in the bush, lay the body of a man. He was on his back. In the dim light I could just see that he was partly clothed: the legs of his jeans were intact, as was the left sleeve of his shirt. But his upper body, from his nose down to his crotch, was half eaten away. The shadowy pool I saw around him must have been blood.

"Oh!" I exclaimed, clamping my hand over my mouth and nose.

The light flickered out.

"Acid," the boy muttered. "That's what we been smelling."

"Acid?"

"This guy's got it all over him. Don't touch him! I'm gonna light up again."

I screwed up my eyes, but I still had to look.

"How, how did he…" I began. "Oh shit, I know who it is! It can't be! Give me your lighter." I held out my hand. Everything went dark again.

"Here. You got it?" he whispered. "Be careful. It's a Zippo."

I flicked the lighter on. My hand shook as I leaned as far as I dared into the bush.

"God in heaven!"

"What?"

"I think I'm going to faint."

"Get back!"

He grabbed me by the collar and pulled. I stumbled, feeling the cigarette lighter slip out of my hand. Instantly, there was a crackle of heat and light. I watched in horror as the already seared remains of Newton Heath burst into flame.

CHAPTER 9

"Claire, wake up! It's Marc." After what seemed like hours of knocking, I was finally rewarded with the appearance of one suspicious, bleary eye.

"Who is it?" she drawled.

"Marc! The community liaison offi—for heaven's sake, it's me!"

"Whaddya want?"

"Newton's dead!"

"Whaa?"

"I just found him."

"Oh, yeah. G'night."

The door began to close again. In desperation, I kicked it savagely. A bleary, reproachful eye returned to its former position.

"You pay for any damage," she mumbled, but the eye was going through a gradual process of enlightenment. Without forewarning, she threw the door wide open.

"What did you say before?" she demanded.

Claire was completely naked, as anyone might be who was dragged from her beauty sleep in the steamy subtropics. I'm afraid I was mesmerised. One sees thousands of photographs of breasts, but right up close, in the flesh, the sight was a rarity for me, particularly when the breasts in question had gleaming metal rings through the nipples. After a moment I realised I was staring.

"They're nice." I stammered. "Have you had them long?"

"Since puberty."

"The rings, I mean."

"Bloody well come in!"

I followed her into the room and sat on the unmade bed. I was relieved to see we were alone. My hands were shaking.

"I don't suppose I could have a drink?" I pleaded.

"Whisky?"

"Thanks."

She poured out two shots of whisky, finishing off an already depleted bottle. She flung herself into a chair and crossed her legs, rather like Sharon Stone in that film, only all over. Her face recovered a suggestion of its official welcoming look from the afternoon, which merely served to emphasise the change in the rest of her. Her formerly neat hair was a mess, her eyes red and puffy, and of course, her blue suit was missing.

"I believe you said Newton's dead?" she asked politely.

I took a sharp breath. I'd momentarily forgotten about it. "I just found his body. He's been murdered I think."

"When? Where?"

"Up near the top pool. He was lying in the bushes round the back."

"Are you sure he's dead?"

"Yes!"

"Did you give him mouth-to-mouth? Bang on his chest?"

"No. He was covered in some sort of acid." I shuddered. "I'm afraid I set fire to him. Accidentally."

She looked dumbfounded. "Murdered, you think? God almighty! Have you told anyone else?"

I shook my head.

"But you—what did you say? You burnt him?"

Uncomfortably, I downed my drink in one swish. "Just a bit."

"Are you a complete idiot?" she asked—rather rudely, I thought. She began to throw on some clothes. "You'd better show me. You didn't actually touch his body, did you? Or move it?"

I gulped. "Yes, we, uh, rolled him into a sort of fishpond." I smiled weakly. "He was on fire."

Claire eyed me warily. "Who's 'we'?"

"One of the Americans was with me."

"Who was it? What's his name?" she asked.

I frowned. My mind was a complete blank. After all the excitement, my short-term memory was shot to bits.

"Um, it was a funny name. Started with an M, I think."

"Can't you remember?" She sounded slightly hysterical. I shook my head again.

"Well, what does he look like, then?"

I couldn't recall that either. "It was very dark. He's...young," I offered lamely.

"Jesus. Where is he now?"

"I don't know. He disappeared as soon as we put Newton out." I detected a note of regret in my voice, although the American boy and I could hardly have continued with our previous business under the circumstances.

Claire grabbed my hand. "Come on then," she snapped.

She dragged me after her as we bounded back toward the luncheon area, up warped wooden stairs marked STAFF ONLY. It proved a more direct route than the one I'd used and, almost immediately, we were back at the scene of the crime. It was darker now. The moon had snuck thoughtlessly behind a cloud.

"Where is he?" Claire whispered. She produced a nifty flashlight no bigger than a fountain pen.

"Behind the kiosk thing."

She flicked on the beam, and the trellised area was suffused with a soft glow. It was empty, as was the swimming pool.

"Over there." I pointed.

I was hoping the whole thing would prove to be a crazed tropical nightmare, but no such luck. There at the back of the kiosk was the charred track we'd created as we kicked the burning corpse around in a frenzied attempt to extinguish the fire. Avoiding the acid had made this particularly difficult and it wasn't until we'd shoved poor Newton into a fish-pond, previously unnoticed in the dark, that the bluish flames had flickered out. This pond was some twenty or so feet from where we'd found the body and, sure enough, he was still there—a black, soggy, blood-caked mass, half submerged in the water.

"Oh!" exclaimed Claire. "The Japanese carp!"

She shone the torch closer, and the light flashed back at us, reflecting off something shiny: Newton's eye. His wrecked, staring face was twisted round to the side, gazing directly at our feet. It was a face I'd known so well: grinning, glowering, animated—alive. No longer. I felt bitterly ill.

The water shuddered with the darting of the carp. One of them must have nudged Newton's head because it casually turned and his face slid back beneath the pool's surface. Claire and I both jumped. I grabbed her and, bending over, dry-retched in the direction of her midriff. She pushed me away.

"Stop it," she commanded. "Pull yourself together."

We stood glued to the spot, trying to take in the implications of the situation.

"This mystery boy," Claire mused. "Did he lead you to the body?"

I blinked. "You think he murdered Newton?"

"If it was murder, and it sure doesn't look like he died of old age, then somebody must be responsible."

"I think it was my idea to come here," I confessed. "You know, step out of the public gaze."

She stared at me.

"I didn't kill him!" I protested. "He's a friend."

She pursed her lips. I wasn't sure she entirely believed me. Then she snapped into action. "I'll go back and call the police," she announced. "Actually, I'll tell Hiram first. We've got to try and play this down. First of all, let's pull that thing out of there. The least we can do is save the carp. They cost a fortune. Grab his legs."

I did, and dragged Newton's body onto the track. Neither of us looked at it.

"What will I do now?" I asked pathetically.

"Go to your room," she answered, headmistress-like, as though I'd committed an embarrassing breach of etiquette. "I dare say Hiram will call a staff meeting in the morning."

I did as I was told. Exhausted, I lay my head on the pillow and closed my eyes, but sleep eluded me. I was haunted by macabre images of Newton. During his sojourn in the carp pool, the acid had continued it's implacable work: the burns on his body had turned deep, menacing shades of purple and indigo, and his disintegrating flesh had fallen away in tatters. I had to get the repulsive picture out of my mind, but not even a dose of grand opera could distract me. Too many people come to an unpleasant end in opera.

I tried, as a mental exercise, to conjure up the name of the American boy whose whirlwind romance with me had been peremptorily nipped in the bud. *His name started with an M, didn't it? Mack? Mike? Hmm... Was it B? Bud? Bryce? That sounded closer. Bart? I would have to go through the whole alphabet. Aaron? Adam? I'd known a boy named Adam once. Red hair, quite well-developed, years before it was the fashion...*

There was a sudden knock at the door. My eyes sprang open. It was broad daylight, and rays of harsh sunlight punched into the room. I looked down at myself in surprise and disgust. My legs were coated in charcoal, mud, and heaven knows what else. My shirt was soaked through with sweat.

The knock came again, louder.

"Caro!" called a voice.

"Paul?" I answered. I swung off the bed and hobbled to the door. He barged in and immediately shut the door behind him.

"Yech! Filthy old man, you," he grimaced.

"I know, I know. I need a shower," I replied.

"Me too," he beamed, tearing off his speedos. "It's so warm out, I'm stickier than a half-eaten toffee apple."

I discarded my clothes and gingerly nudged them into a corner with my foot. Paul wrinkled up his nose.

"I'll explain all this in a minute," I said.

"No need," he replied breezily. "I bet I know what happened! Let's see… you found our friend Newton's dead body at the beat and fried it to a crispy golden brown. Good guess, huh?"

My mouth fell open.

"Shower time!" sang Paul, pulling me after him.

"How did you know?" I floundered as the water pelted down on us.

"All will be revealed, but first Paulette will soap your back. You've obviously been through hell."

"I have indeed."

"Let me give you a massage."

The spray was cool and comforting, and so was Paul. He is very good under a shower, as he himself will admit. In this case, he concentrated on my neck and shoulders. They were, predictably, tense.

As we dried off, our chat resumed. "I stumbled across Newton," I explained. "I was being cruised by an American boy."

"As we had hoped!"

"We were looking for somewhere private to go and literally walked into the body. Then I dropped the American's cigarette lighter and *woof*!" I paused uncertainly. "Is that the story you heard?"

"More or less. Was it really murder?"

I thought hard. "It must have been. He had acid all over him. Well, all over his upper body—neck, chest, and stomach. There was even some on his face. I suppose it could have been an accident, but it looked like the stuff had been thrown. If he'd done it himself, he most likely wouldn't have got his nose in it."

"Eeew. Sounds messy."

"He's a hell of a mess now!" I felt strangely guilty. "Thanks to my setting fire to his body and chucking it in among the fish."

Paul patted my hand. "We all panic occasionally."

True. I was panicking at that very moment. "Paul! What am I going to do? I'll be in huge trouble when the police come. I've moved the body over and over again…"

"And washed away any fingerprints."

"Shit!"

"Don't worry, caro. Sit down."

I sensed a hint of self-satisfaction in his demeanour. "Paul," I said, "you haven't told me where on earth you heard about this. What were you up to last night?"

He smiled. "All shall be revealed, but first I must stress that I've done you an enormous favour."

I didn't like the sound of this at all. I pulled my complimentary toweling robe around me and waited apprehensively. Paul lay on the bed, still nude, with his knees in the air and his hands clasped behind his head.

"You know me, caro," he began. "I love all mankind equally and without prejudice."

"Can we do without the self-congratulatory ode?" I asked.

"I'm just trying to explain that although my taste runs to younger men, I have occasionally been known to entertain tender feelings for the mature gent. Under certain circumstances."

"Involving the mature gent's credit cards."

He ignored me. "Just such an occasion transpired last night, when I had it off with Hiram."

I choked.

"He's rather fun, actually," Paul continued. "I mean, it's a bit like a military campaign: attack, repulse, regroup, new strategy, attack, subdue, and at a given signal the troops go right over the top!"

"Who won?"

"It isn't whether you win or lose, et cetera. Now I'm one of his 'spoils of war.'"

"You were spoilt already."

"You and I know that. So I'm lying back, wondering

whether another skirmish is in the offing, when all of a sudden I felt a painful sensation in my left nipple. "Are you putting a nipple clip on me?" I asked Hiram and he said no. Anyway, to cut a long story short—"

"Too late."

"There was a filthy great crab biting me on the tit! Naturally, I ran screaming to the men's room. And who should come rapping at the door while I was dabbing away in there but our beloved lesbian coordinator, Claire. I overheard everything. She'd just returned from your private viewing of Newton, and she was pretty worked up." He looked me squarely in the eye. "It's Claire's opinion that you yourself, personally, are the guilty party."

"Me? Why?"

"Who knows? She thinks it's fishy that you fiddled around with the body the way you did. She figures you deliberately obscured the evidence. She got you to drag Newton out of the pond so your prints would be on him again."

"But the American boy can vouch for me. Sort of."

"She doesn't believe there's any such person. She said you pretended you couldn't remember his name."

"I couldn't! I still can't!" Despite my shower, I had broken out in a fresh sweat. "What's going to happen now?"

"Hiram's taken charge. He's already mobilised the boys in blue. Two local cops from Murphy's Inlet took Newton away early this morning, but they're not senior enough to do the investigation. Homicide men from Brisbane will arrive around lunchtime, wearing lightweight coats and funny old porkpie hats. The top pool's been roped off. Morning tea may be delayed. Otherwise everything's running smoothly."

"Bugger morning tea, I'm going to be arrested!"

"No, you're not, caro mio," he beamed. "Hiram will see to that."

Now I was completely confused. "I don't follow you."

He stretched out, smiling lazily.

"This is where yours truly comes in. Hiram and I had a long discussion about the whole thing right after Claire left us. He was desperate to see more action at the front, so I had him over a barrel. To tell the truth, I think he found the idea of a brutal murder quite exciting! He's never been mixed up in bloodshed before."

"You surprise me."

"No, Grandma Gaytour leads a quiet life. He's basically an accountant. Spent exactly zero time in the armed forces, needless to say. Anyway, where was I? Oh, yes. I was brilliant. I began by pointing out that there was no reason why you should find it necessary to murder anybody and that, if we were going to point the finger, we might start with Newton's enemies rather than his friends! Claire, for one, hated his nuts with a passion."

"Did she?"

"She never tried to hide it. She thought he was a bully and anti-women."

"She was right! What did Hiram say?"

"He ate it up. He was never comfortable with the idea that you did it. He respects you too much, thinks you're the cold-blooded corporate type, above that kind of rough stuff. He admires you immensely."

"I'm nothing of the kind."

Paul snorted. "Don't tell him that! I built you up even more afterward. Coffee?" He ambled over to the facilities and set out two cups.

"Well," he continued, "after hearing how much Hiram admires you, I let slip about your previous detective work. I told him you'd been a professional—what is it called—gumshoe, and that I'd had the great honour to work with you on some of your celebrated cases. He was intrigued."

So, I must say, was I. Paul has turned stretching a point into an art form, but this was the limit. We had indeed investigated a murder together, the one and only murder I'd ever been associated with. It was that of a young opera singer named Jennifer Burke who had been unceremoniously shoved over a cliff. I shuddered to recall the amateurish, haphazard way we'd gone about it. Admittedly, I did finally discover who the murderer was, but it all ended very unpleasantly. Never again, I'd vowed.

"Besides," Paul continued blithely as he handed me a cup of coffee, "Hiram has his own theories, even at this early stage. He's convinced it's an outside job. Murder is death to the hospitality industry. Hiram thinks it was done to knock New Heaven on the head."

"I'm sure it will."

"Hope not. This is a good gig."

Paul downed his coffee—not a tricky feat, since it was cold.

"Didn't you boil the water?" I asked, spitting out my first mouthful.

"I thought I did. Whoops, there's a teensy red button you're supposed to press." He smiled, and yanked his swimsuit on. "Never mind, Hiram will give us some real coffee. We're supposed to meet him at 0800 hours." He glanced at the bedside clock. "That's now."

I shut my eyes. "I've had three hours sleep!"

"Plenty. Now get dressed, caro. We have a lot of people to see before the cops get here."

I stopped in my tracks.

"He's not going to ask us to investigate this is he?"

Paul bounded to the door. "Not ask. Hire!"

"Oh, no."

Paul slapped me lightly on the cheek. "Would you rather be behind bars?"

Fortunately, he didn't wait for my reply.

CHAPTER 10

When we found him, Hiram was floating across the downstairs pool, spread-eagled atop a slim-line, inflatable cushion. He was decked out in gold-framed, blue-tinted sunglasses, a military cap, and swimmers that resembled a length of camouflage-coloured string and covered approximately 90-percent less than they should have. No one else was in sight. Evidently Hiram had cleared the pool for his private staff interviews. When he saw us, he waved vigorously, putting himself at grave risk of capsizing.

"Hit the water, boys!" he called out.

"Last one in's a breeder!" cried Paul, who was underwater in a split second. He surfaced right next to Hiram's float with such a cheesy look on his face that Esther Williams's sparklers would have been superfluous. I took a little longer, as I needed to disrobe and preferred to descend daintily into the shallow end. My bottle-green swimmers elicited a fit of barely suppressed giggling from Paul and a wolf-whistle from Hiram, both of which I chose to ignore.

"I admire a hairy back," Hiram remarked as I surfaced alongside. "Don't let nobody tell you different."

"Thank you," I spluttered. "I won't."

He reached over and fluffed my hair in a fatherly gesture—though he couldn't have been more than five years my senior.

"Buddy," he said grimly, "I wanna see how much of a man you are." He was about to find out. The legs of my swimming trunks were ballooning full of water and the waist felt dangerously loose.

"Um, what do you mean?"

He smiled, looking even grimmer. "I think you know what I mean. This Newton business. It's bad, boys. Real bad. God-damn it, I can't believe I underestimated them crazies from the mainland! I wanna know which of 'em did it, and I wanna know why, where and how! Marc, this is your jurisdiction, the area of community liaison."

"Is it?"

"I am fully aware that what I'm asking you to do is above and beyond the call of duty."

I swallowed. "You want me to investigate?"

He nodded. "Young Paul here tells me you guys work together. Well, as from now you'll work for me. Undercover. OK? I'll make it worth your while."

"We'll do it!" cried Paul.

"Great," Hiram nodded sagely. "I knew I could rely on you, Marc."

"But—"

"As soon as you've talked to Homicide this afternoon, I want you to get off this island and head back to Murphy's Inlet. Report to me at 0800 in forty-eight hours. Don't rest till you've got something."

"But—"

"Yep, you're absolutely right, I'm sending you deep into enemy territory. It won't be no goddamn picnic. I don't have to tell you: homophobia is an ugly thing. I can't abide it. It's tantamount to discrimination, and we know where that leads! Them homophobes oughta be horsewhipped!"

"Hiram," Paul fluttered, "what exactly *is* horsewhipping? I've always wondered."

Hiram seemed momentarily at a loss. "It's, well, it's a disciplinary measure involving horses."

"Ah."

I finally managed to butt in. "Hiram, there may be one or two problems."

"Such as?"

"Well, the police. After all, I moved the body."

Hiram snorted, making his opinion of the police perfectly clear. "'Course you did! Man, I know what you were thinking:

Get this corpse outta here! Get him back to his office, any place where we can maybe minimise the damage of this incident. You had Gaytour's interests at heart. I'm not saying it was the best thing to do, but it shows loyalty."

"I'm worried the police won't think it was the best thing to do, either."

"Well, they ain't gonna know shit. As far as they're concerned, you and Claire found that damn body exactly the way it was—in the carp pool. And don't you worry your head about Claire none. I had a word with her this morning." He pursed his lips. "I kinda hinted we may be forced to give this Queensland resort the ass. I sure hope not, but if it happens, I suggested she could be looking at a new position with Gaytour International. Something big." He winked. "Ambitious dykes are a pushover."

I wasn't so sure.

"There's another problem," I sighed. "One of the American boys was with me when I found Newton."

Hiram removed his cap, immersed it in the water, then draped it over his face. "That's better," he muttered. "I was getting warm here. Now what were you saying? I couldn't hear ya."

"An American boy. Last night."

Hiram tapped the side of his nose through the cap. "Our boys won't be no trouble. The guys we gotta worry about are them journalists. I mean, shit!—this is one helluva story. They get back into town, they're gonna blow this murder sky high. You know the press! Goddamn homophobes, every one of 'em. Same the world over. So we gotta see to it the story that gets out is the *right* story! You with me?"

"Um... "

"Sure y'are!"

"But..." I was confused. "We don't know the right story, do we?"

Hiram shook his head, more in amazement than in reply. "The story is, we play our cards right, and us gays and lesbians are gonna come outta this smelling like roses. So—we got a deal, boys? Let's shake on it. I don't wanna put you guys on the payroll as detectives—it looks kinda fishy—so how's about we file it under 'miscellaneous expenses'? Fifteen hundred a week sound fair?" Hiram punched me on the shoulder. "I guess this ain't nothing but petty cash for you, Marc, but it might be fun, hey? Sure it will! Now get going! I gotta talk to some of them journalists right now." He whipped off his cap and sunglasses. "But first, how about twenty quick laps? Yeah! Let's *move!*"

Without further warning, he rolled into the pool and was off like a two-stroke mower toward the other end. Paul kept pace alongside with effortless grace. I struggled away in the same direction but soon gave up. Stamina is not really my forte.

I was soon up the pool steps and surreptitiously slipping back into my robe. I seated myself at the nearby bar and tried to act like a man who had just completed twenty laps without even noticing. Here, too, the resort was deserted, apart from a couple of well-built bar staff. I swiftly ordered a piña colada.

For the first time that day, I managed to think about the situation. I was still in a state of disbelief, completely overwhelmed by all the implications of Newton's murder. I closed my eyes and tried to concentrate on specifics. Any specifics! I was sure of one thing: It couldn't be as cut and dried as Hiram suggested. I knew Newton pretty well, and I was quite aware of the dazzling number of enemies he'd made during his career. No doubt the local residents of Murphy's Inlet were among them. But was that the whole story?

My thoughts returned to our convivial dinner party of only a few weeks before. Newton had talked with an advocate's relish of taking on several private and public bodies. He was all set to ruffle feathers over the flight path issue, and, knowing him, he would not have been happy until he'd stirred up plenty of trouble. But were those official feathers ruffled enough to lead someone to commit murder? And if so, who?

PHILLIP SCOTT

Another memory surfaced from that dinner: the image of
one extremely disgruntled boyfriend. Hadrian had been har-
bouring murderous impulses all night; he could scarcely conceal it. If looks could kill, Newton would have been dead
before he ever left the vicinity of Don Cojones. Hadrian war-
ranted a thorough investigation, and so did Claire, if Paul
was to be believed, but how could I follow up any of this if
I was stuck in Murphy's Inlet?

"One piña colada, sir."

At my elbow stood Darren, the strapping houseboy.

"Call me Marc," I insisted.

Darren flashed his perfect pearly whites. "I was at your
meeting."

"Yes, you were, right there in front."

As he stretched languidly, I reflected—not for the first
time—that his legs were among the most lovely and evenly
tanned I'd ever had the pleasure to ogle.

"Where is everybody?" I asked.

"It's early. Those guys don't get up yet." He casually patted
his stomach. "Mind if I join you?"

"Please do," I choked invitingly.

He pulled up another chair and unfolded himself across it
like a priceless tapestry. I gulped my drink.

"I s'pose you handled those bozos the best you could, considering you don't know much about the place."

"I've only been here a day," I protested. "Less!" Criticism
from this unexpected quarter had rather ruffled me.

"I mean you don't know Murphy's Inlet."

"Yes, I do," I said huffily. "I often stay with a friend…"

"Nah," he remarked, offhandedly swatting a mosquito.
"You gotta live there. I did." He yawned and crossed his arms
in an arrogant pose. He wasn't as attractive as I'd thought,
after all.

"Well, how would you have run the meeting," I asked
pointedly. "if you were in my place?" There was a sarcastic
edge to my voice, but Darren failed to notice.

"One thing's for sure: I wouldn't have let the pastor give his little sermon. It gets the rest of them too excited. 'Course, those God-botherers don't scare me. I know 'em."

"I suppose, if you were born and raised in the area—" I began.

"I didn't say that," he interrupted. "I just worked over there." He ran his fingers through his hair. "You want another drink?" he asked abruptly.

"Yes, thank you," I answered with some formality and handed him my empty glass. "Another one of these."

He grinned smarmily. "Better have mineral water. You wouldn't want to be pissed when you talk to the cops."

"What do you mean?"

"Relax! I know you found Newton's body last night. You and Claire."

"Yes. We found it together—at the same time."

"I had to rope off the whole top area at six o'clock this morning. Was I crapped off!" He laughed.

"You don't seem very upset about Newton's murder," I ventured, automatically slipping into detective mode.

"Murder, was it?" He raised his eyebrows. "Yeah, well, I'm not surprised. He had it coming, I reckon."

"What do you mean?" I snapped.

He paused for a moment, carefully considering his reply. "That guy was no Mr. Popularity, you know? I mean the way he breezed in here, pushing people around, telling us what to do, like he owned the place."

"He *did* own the place!"

"Yeah, so what? He wasn't going to run it! Was he ever in the hospitality business? Nah! He just felt like throwing his weight around before he pissed off back to Sydney, back to the shady deals and big bucks. Well, some of us here are professionals, you know? Jeez, man, you're one yourself!"

I gave him a coy smile.

"How would you like to take orders from someone who

doesn't know what they're doing? I could run this resort the way it should be run. It's not so easy that any arsehole can do it."

A question occurred to me. "Who was going to manage New Heaven after Newton left? Claire?"

He tossed his head contemptuously. "Claire's only the Lesbian Coordinator, and the boys outnumber the girls ten to one. Rumour was Newton was going to bring in a manager." The boy glared. "We all thought it was you."

I felt vaguely uneasy. "God, no!" I replied hastily. "I'm only here on a break."

"Yeah, I know that now. A little bird told me." He shot a glance out to the poolside where Paul was toweling himself down. "Same again?" Darren leapt to his feet.

"You advised me to stick to mineral water."

"The customer's always right," he smirked, flicking the waistband of his shorts.

"What do I owe you so far?"

"Nothing." He waved a hand dismissively, then leant over and whispered, "This'd be a top resort if I was running it. I know how to show people a good time."

"Mmm."

"Just in case anybody asks!"

He strode back to the bar, where he instantly fell into conversation with the other bartender and showed not the slightest sign of mixing my drink.

I closed my eyes. I'd hardly slept, and the humidity was making my head ache. Gradually, I realised that my foot was itching uncontrollably as well. Examining it, I found four mosquito bites, one exquisitely located on the tip of my little toe. I scratched frantically, finally managing to draw blood and pave the way for serious infection. I was a zillion miles from a holiday mood. Finally, I decided to fetch my headphones, get a fresh drink, settle down in a hammock and enjoy myself for a while even if it killed me! Unhappily, it nearly did.

Paul was waiting beside the restaurant when I trudged back from my one-on-one with Crab Island's resident crab.

"Caro! You look hideous. Let's do breakfast."

Resplendent in a flimsy sarong with a gleaming GAYTOUR GUEST STAFF dog tag around his neck, Paul dragged me to the self-serve, where we confronted voluminous plates of tropical fruit, yogurt, and sundry dried goodies. I discovered I was ravenous. Giving the health food a wide berth, I piled my plate high with chipolata sausages, potato fritters, poached eggs on a bed of spinach, and big buttery muffins. I smothered the lot in hollandaise. Paul, who would normally have gorged himself, settled for a slice of pawpaw, a segment of passion fruit, and two plums.

"You shouldn't be eating that gunk," he mumbled, picking passion fruit seeds from his lower gums. "Think of the old ticker."

"What's the matter with you?" I asked. "Since when do you subsist on stoned fruit?"

"I've met some very nice stoned fruits," he quipped. "It's for my figure; there's too much competition around here. This diet is the exact same one Fergie uses."

"The resemblance is striking."

"A girl must be vigilant. Can I have a teensy bite of your sausage?"

"Are you asking me? Or practising lines for Hiram?"

He batted his eyelids. "He's going to take me back to the States and foster my career."

"What career?"

"I'm thinking of becoming a star. A gay icon, in fact! We're planning a one-man show that'll make me the belle of New York. I thought I'd kick off with a routine on a huge blowup globe—you know, like the Earth—and sing "I'm Sittin' on Top of the World"! What do you think? Hiram doesn't like it. He wants me to open with "Big Noise From Winnetka." His grandfather was born there or something. Whatever. I'll need to look my best. Flabby icons are a turnoff."

"I'd say we have more pressing things to worry about."

"Mmm? Oh yes, yes. We have to find this murderer for Hiram. My future Tony Award depends on it!"

"But God knows where we start. There are so many possibilities."

"Name one."

At that moment, Darren appeared beside me and slammed down another frothy pink cocktail. Leaning down, he kissed Paul lightly on the lips. "Morning, babe."

"Hi, Dazzle," smiled Paul.

"Drink?"

"Not for *moi*!"

"Suit yourself." And he was gone.

Paul gazed raptly after him. "'What a piece of hunk is man,' as Shakespeare once said."

"There you are," I replied. "He's a possible suspect."

"Him? Why?"

"Newton pushed him around and he resented it. He told me so just now."

Paul shrugged. "Newton pushed everyone around."

"Well, Darren's a professional, or so he claims."

"Ha! I wouldn't be surprised..." Paul blinked. "Of course! How could I have been so blind? That explains it."

"What? What explains what?"

"Our boy's a hooker. I knew I'd seen him before! I mean, you'd never forget that tush, would you? I bet he worked the Wall."

I shuddered. "The Wall? Are you sure?"

"That must be the reason..." Paul started to blush, something I'd never seen in all my born days.

"The reason for what, exactly?" I asked.

GAY RESORT MURDER SHOCK

"Oh, nothing."

"Paul?"

"Caro...oh, all right. It sort of explains why he more or less turned me down."

My eyes opened wide in astonishment. "You mean there goes a male human being, presumably in full command of his senses, who failed to succumb to your celebrated charms? Surely you don't expect me to swallow that?"

"I hope you're not rubbing it in," he pouted. "It happened last week at the top pool. I could have persevered, but I had other dish to fry." His expression brightened. "But if he only comes across for hard currency, obviously it wasn't personal."

"Obviously not."

"Now can we drop the subject?"

"Happily. Let's get back to something less tacky, like murder. If we're going to do this efficiently, we need a modus operandi."

"A computer?"

"A plan, you idiot."

"Don't speak to me like that! This is not *Ren and Stimpy*." He leapt to his feet. "I do have a plan, as it happens. We ought to check out a few places for clues. We won't have a hope in hell once the homicide girls get here."

"That's true," I admitted. "Let's have a poke around Newton's office."

Paul laughed smuttily. "We wouldn't be the first."

He grabbed my hand and we quickly headed up to Newton's office in the administration section. We reached the STAFF ONLY door to discover it wide-open. The corridor was empty.

"What are we looking for?" Paul whispered.

I had to admit I had no idea. Clues? Signs of a scuffle? "We're simply looking," I said, reverting to the Mount Everest quip, "because it's there."

We crept forward stealthily, although as community liaison

officer I had as much right to be in the staff area as anyone else. Newton's door was slightly ajar.

"Somebody's inside," Paul hissed. "Sprung!"

He kicked the door wide open, or rather, as wide as it would go without impediment.

"Shit!" cried a voice. Hadrian staggered from behind the door carrying a large cardboard box. Carefully, he put it down on the desk, then rubbed his lumpy red knuckles. He seemed even more morose than usual: grumpiness tempered by grief.

"Oh, it's you," he muttered. "You scared me to death."

"Sorry," said Paul unconvincingly.

Hadrian slumped into a chair. "You heard what happened, I suppose." He looked at me. "Of course, you found him. Was it very bad?"

I was solicitous. "You don't want to know."

"Yes, I do!" he shrieked. "Nobody will tell me a damn thing!"

I was completely taken aback.

"All right, calm down, I'll tell you! I was taking a midnight stroll. I am prone to insomnia, you know. Anyway, there he was in a pool full of Japanese carp. Quite expensive, I understand."

"What?"

"Japanese carp. They're colourful—"

"I know what they are!" he snapped. "I've photographed them!" He closed his eyes. "Oh, God, it's all too much," he whimpered. I glanced at Paul, who was leaning against Newton's desk with a blank look on his face. Hadrian opened his eyes again. "What are you doing here?" he asked suspiciously.

Brilliant improvisation was called for.

"Nothing," improvised Paul.

"I was looking for you," I added quickly. "I thought you might be here. I was a bit concerned about you." (Actually, I hadn't been sure he was even on the island. I'd seen no sign of him the day before.)

Hadrian looked up. "Concerned about me? Why?"

"I thought you might be upset."

"I am!" he blurted out and began to sob. I sat beside him and patted his hand.

"Don't cry, Hadrian," I said.

"I will too," he blubbered. "I'm an artist! I don't believe in suppressing my emotions." He threw his head back and bawled, hand his meagre body rocking back and forth. "I can *use* this!"

Paul began to lift Hadrian's box off the desk.

"Put that down," Hadrian sobbed. "Just leave it alone, will you?"

"What is it?" Paul asked.

Hadrian sniffed and dabbed at his eyes with his sleeve. "Some stuff I need in the darkroom." He smiled pathetically. "I took fantastic shots yesterday. I went on that bush-walk with the Americans, and I got some guy to strip off. That's the beauty of being a photographer—you can get people to do that." His smile faded. "Not that it matters now." He sniffed again. "Excuse me, I'm about to lock up."

My eyes darted about the room. I hoped a clue or two would make an appearance, but no, I needed more time. Hadrian took a deep breath and picked up the box.

"Hadrian," I said, adopting a serious tone. "Clearly, Newton was murdered. Do you have any idea who would do such a thing?"

He shook his head. "No," he replied blankly. "Everybody always seemed to like him."

His answer knocked me sideways. The boy must have gone through their relationship with his head in the sand! Or somewhere else equally dark.

"He was a lawyer," said Paul, stating the obvious. "Surely he would have made a few enemies?"

Hadrian screwed up his face. "They'd never kill him," he grunted. "They wouldn't dare!"

He started to lug his mysterious personal effects toward the door, then stopped short as Claire stepped in, blocking the way.

"Where are you going with that?" she demanded.

"They're my things! I need them in the darkroom."

"I don't think anything should be moved," she countered. "The police wouldn't like it."

"It's my stuff, Claire," he whined. "I haven't touched anything else."

She turned her gaze on me. "And what do you think you're doing? Haven't you caused enough trouble?"

"I'm helping Hadrian," I stammered.

"No, he's not," said Hadrian.

I grinned inanely.

"We could ask you the same thing, Claire," purred Paul. "Why are you barging into somebody else's office?"

"I popped in to see nothing had been tampered with."

A grin oozed across Paul's face. "And how would you know if it had?"

She sniffed dismissively. "You better get your precious little butt down to the auditorium and rehearse! Hiram is very keen for everything to continue normally—as though nothing had happened."

"I'm leaving," panted Hadrian. "Please let me past, this is heavy."

"Yes," I said, hauling myself to my feet. "We'd all better get out and leave the police to make their inquiries."

Claire regarded me skeptically.

"Come on, caro," said Paul chirpily. "Come and watch me choreograph. They can't get enough of my talent! There's one particular routine I'd really like you to see." He winked and patted his bottom, a gesture I found totally puzzling.

"No, thanks," I answered wearily, thinking of my upcoming police interview. "I've got some rehearsing of my own to do."

"But, caro..."

"Run along," ordered Claire. "I have business to discuss with Marc."

She closed the office door behind him. I was cornered.

"Hmmm," she said.

"Claire, last night when we found the body, some of the things I told you... well, um..." I fumbled to a halt.

Out of nowhere, she suddenly slapped me in the face.

"Ow!" My ears were ringing. Three or four Claires swam before my eyes. "What was that for?"

"Get yourself organised!" she snarled. "Our story's never going to convince them if you pussyfoot around like some doddering old fool."

"I gather you've spoken to Hiram," I mumbled, rubbing my cheek.

"The fate of this whole enterprise depends on your police interview, so play it cool and keep it short. You and I went for a stroll together and found the body in the fishpond. OK? I'll back you up. Forget about your grubby little adventure earlier on. You needn't tell anyone about the beat."

I nodded.

She sighed. "God knows, I'm not a conservative woman. I understand human sexuality—I celebrate it! I know all about letting yourself go wherever the feeling takes you. But one thing I can never fathom is what drives you silly old poofs to stand around for hours fiddling with yourselves in public places. It just doesn't seem like much fun."

She pushed me up against the door.

"Why did you do it?" she asked accusingly.

"I don't know. I...felt horny, I suppose. Silly old poof that I am."

"Not that," she said. "Why did you kill Newton?"

I gasped. "I didn't! I already told you!"

She eyed me warily, her arm still pressing into my chest. "Yeah, maybe you didn't," she conceded. "It's hard to imagine you planning a murder, let alone carrying it out. But you did mess around with the body, for whatever sick reason—and I warn you, if the necessity arises, I will have no hesitation in telling the authorities everything I know. Don't forget that!"

A burst of manic laughter nearby made us both jump.

"Jesus Christ!" Claire exclaimed.

Four kookaburras sat watching in the tree outside Newton's window. I relaxed, and Claire finally let me go. She seemed shaken.

"Get out," she said.

CHAPTER 11

It was at about this stage in the proceedings that my crab-infested holiday haven began to feel downright menacing. It was becoming less like New Heaven and more like plain Old Hell. Maybe it's me. I seem to be unnaturally sensitive to undercurrents of danger. I have a sixth sense in place to sniff out the threat of bodily harm. (When you've burnt yourself ironing as often as I have, you learn to be wary.)

On the surface, the place looked for all the world like a travel brochure come to life: the sun effectively bright, the sky appropriately blue, and the scrub deep and luxuriant. But beneath that glossy veneer, a touch of something was lurking. Would I be too film-noirish if I called it "evil"? Suddenly, the sun was a dangerous presence, the sky all too suspiciously clear. Suddenly, the thick vegetation concealed a world of spying, slithering life forms, semihuman and filled with malignant intent.

Now, where everything had been peaceful and still, there was constant, inexplicable movement. Leaves rustled, branches swayed, doors eased open or closed silently, and the dappled sunlight rendering it all uneasily indistinct. Which of those little movements was random—the innocent manifestations of Mother Nature going about her everyday business—and which were driven by a deeper, darker agency?

These unwelcome revelations occurred as I returned, sore and sorry, to my room. I leapt onto my bed, ripping and crushing one of the useless maps I had made of the island. Such elegant work! I smoothed it out while attempting to get my thoughts in order.

What I primarily needed to know was when the killing had taken place. Paul and I, in our ad hoc discussions so far, had started from the wrong end. We were already asking "why?"

when the first question we had to answer was "how," and "how" depended to some extent on "where" and a great deal on "when." If Newton had been dispatched some time after seven P.M., it ruled out any involvement by the Murphy's Inlet crowd, who had all sailed away at six. (I could just see Hiram leaping for joy over that!)

Alternatively, suppose Newton had been killed some time during the afternoon? Then the Americans—and Hadrian—were in the clear, happily occupied on their trek, but the Inlet people were implicated.

I wondered what Newton's relationship had been with his gay guests from the U.S. They'd been here almost a week. Plenty of time for bonding of one form or another and, if I knew Newton, he'd have explored every avenue of the Americas without fail. Of course, even if Newton had been bonking the lot of them senseless, it didn't prove anything. It only pointed the finger back at green-eyed Hadrian. To make matters more complex, any one of the journalists or staff could have done it at any time, day or night.

I stood, my mind boggling, and gazed out the window at the lost paradise. It really was a marvelous view.

At that moment a movement caught my eye. There was something in a tree—a tall tree with thick leafy foliage jutting out above the surrounding rain forest. I screwed up my eyes to focus; the tree was a fair distance away from the resort area, and yet there seemed to be a man in it! A strange blob-like man, squatting in the branches—unless it was a trick of the light? No! He moved again. I was certain he could see me.

I swung around to search for my binoculars but when I looked back, he'd disappeared. This was odd. There was an abundance of men in the vicinity, but why would any of them want to do something kinky like climb a tree? Especially a tree as remote as that one? It seemed the height of foolishness (and discomfort).

I was just deciding I'd imagined it when I noticed another

movement, this one far from imaginary. Claire, accompanied by two men who could only be detectives, was marching up toward my room. I cursed inwardly. I'd been planning to fit in a stiff brandy before the police interview, and now it was too late. I glanced around the room. It was a mess. I smoothed the bedclothes, kicked my shoes and some other rubbish under the bed, and rinsed the coffee cups. Should I offer them something to drink? I was checking whether I had enough sachets when the knock came.

Claire was all smiles as I opened the door. "Marc, these gentlemen are from Brisbane police headquarters. They'd like a chat about our little misfortune."

The closer of the two flashed a badge. "Detective Brian Williams, and this is Detective Lee. May we come in?"

"Of course. I'm expecting you. Coffee, anyone?"

"No, thank you," replied Detective Williams.

"Tea, if you've got it," said Detective Lee.

Claire backed out, grinning like a woman on the verge of a nervous breakdown. The police made themselves comfortable. As I switched on the kettle, I concentrated on readjusting my expectations. I had presumed the homicide police would be fat, middle-aged, hard-boiled, red-nosed, and intimidating. I'd also seen them, in my mind's eye, dressed in ill-fitting '60s gear: beige safari suits, to be exact. I couldn't have been more mistaken. These two policemen were young—neither could have been much over 30—and rather attractive in their taut, fit way. They wore plain shirts and navy blue shorts. Long white socks—which can be a very sexy look against tanned legs—were their one concession to officialdom. A surreptitious glance over the aforementioned shorts revealed several bulges, none of which suggested a revolver. I breathed a sigh of relief. At least they wouldn't shoot me.

I poured the tea, and we politely got down to business.

"We understand your desire to keep this incident as quiet as possible to avoid bad publicity," began Detective Williams.

"That's why we're speaking to people in their rooms."

"Very good of you," I said brightly.

Detective Lee piped up, in a high pitched voice. "This resort is exclusively for gay men and lesbians, yeah?"

"Yes. But what's that got to do with it?"

He merely shrugged.

"It's only important insofar as it may lead our inquiries in a certain direction," explained Detective Williams. "I understand you knew Newton Heath well?"

"Relatively well. I wouldn't say we were all that close."

"He arranged a job here for you."

"Community liaison officer, yes."

"I guess that means you're pretty familiar with Murphy's Inlet," broke in Detective Lee.

"Reasonably."

"Ever lived there?"

"No."

He raised his eyebrows, indicating that in his opinion I was spectacularly underqualified for the job. "Were you involved sexually with the deceased?"

I fought the desire to say "before or after?" "No, never," I answered. "We were just friends, that's all."

He nodded and stared out the window.

"When did you last see Newton Heath alive?" asked Detective Williams.

"Let me see, it was lunchtime yesterday. About one-ish. We had a meeting in his office. Hiram was there, from Gaytour International. Hiram Hudson."

"Like the British explorer." Detective Lee grinned.

"Yes." I was too nervous to contradict him. *Let Hiram fight his own battles,* I thought.

"We'd like a statement from you about how and when you discovered the body," said Detective Williams. "Take notes, Bing."

I started. "Bing Lee?" I asked.

"A nickname," he replied. "You were saying, Mr. Petrucci?"

"Well, I couldn't sleep—the humidity you know, I'm not really used to it yet. So it must have been about midnight I decided to go for a walk. We went to the top pool. It's cooler up there, you see—"

"I'm sorry," Detective Williams interrupted. "We?"

"Oh, er, me and Claire."

"Claire Bornkamp," he stated.

"That's right," I said.

"Why?" asked Detective Lee.

"What?"

"I asked why. Why did you go for a walk with Ms. Bornkamp?"

"Um... I don't know. She couldn't sleep either."

He smiled. "And how did you know that?"

"I don't quite follow you."

"It's perfectly clear," snapped Detective Williams. "Did you wake her up and suggest a walk in the moonlight, for instance?"

"In the moonlight?"

"Did you run into her by chance? Or did you arrange to meet her at a certain time?"

I was aghast. "Is that what she told you?"

"I'm asking you," he answered.

I was even more aghast as the penny dropped with an almighty clang. "Claire's a lesbian," I said.

"So I believe." He cleared his throat discreetly. "Tell me, are you in a relationship yourself at the moment? Any men friends or whatever on the scene?"

"N—no. Not at present."

"Hmm."

"For heaven's sake! I'm not seeing Claire! I mean, really! She's the last person..." I was speechless.

The Detectives glanced at each other. " 'Methinks the lady doth protest too much,' " smirked Detective Lee.

"Now, look here!" I huffed.

Detective Williams turned to me gravely. "We're trying to find a murderer, Mr. Petrucci. We're not here to blow anyone's cover, pardon the expression. If you're not romantically attached to Ms. Bornkamp, what other possible reason could you have to take her out walking in the middle of the night?"

It began to dawn on me just how smart Claire had been. I'd be getting into very deep water now, if I didn't go along with her convenient explanation. I put on my best sheepish expression.

"It'd mean the end of my job if the management found out. Claire's too," I admitted. "Not to mention our standing in the gay community." I risked going over the top. "But what am I supposed to do? When you find yourself falling in love..." I couldn't continue; the much-abused word stuck in my throat.

"I understand," Detective Williams said reassuringly. "Believe me, this won't go any further. I've cautioned the witness, too."

"Sorry?"

"Somebody saw Ms. Bornkamp answer the door to you," said Detective Lee. "She was ready and waiting. Yeah?"

A vision of Claire, clad only in body jewelry, came back to me with startling clarity.

"Who saw us?" I queried nervously. (*And what else had they seen,* I wondered.)

"I'm afraid we can't divulge that information. As I say, the person has been cautioned." Detective Williams folded his arms. "Now, please continue. It was hot. You went for a walk."

"Yes, well. I thought the little pool where the Japanese carp swim would be rather romantic so I took her there. The body was in the pond, or most of it was."

"Did you touch anything?"

"No, no. Of course not!"

Detective Lee looked me in the eye. "You didn't pull him out of the water to see if he was dead or alive?"

"Well, I may have done. But that's all. He was a dreadful mess."

"What did you do then?"

"We went back to our rooms. Claire told Hiram, I think, and Hiram rang the police."

"And what did you do?"

"I went to sleep."

"So now you could sleep perfectly well?"

"Yes. At first I didn't think I could, then the next thing I knew it was morning. Funny, isn't it? The shock must've tired me out."

"I see," said Detective Williams. "Now would you be good enough to give us a brief account of your movements between the time you last saw Mr. Heath alive—about one o'clock, you say—and the time you and your girlfriend found his body?"

I cringed. "Certainly. After the meeting I came back here to prepare my talk."

"Were you alone?"

"Most of the time. I had two visitors. Paul Silverton and Grant Breen."

"What time did they call in?"

"Paul was first, about 1:30, I suppose. Grant came about an hour later. They didn't stay long."

"What did you talk about with Mr. Breen?"

This surprised me. "Oh, well, I asked him how the people in Murphy's Inlet felt about the resort. He works over there. He seemed to think we shouldn't limit ourselves to gay and lesbian clients. I told him to speak to Newton about it."

"I see. And after he left?"

"I worked on my lecture, then I went to the conference room around 4:30. I copied my map onto the white board. I said my piece and answered a few questions. We finished just before six. Then I had dinner, came back here and hopped into bed."

"Thank you, that's very precise. You didn't sleep, though."

"No. I listened to opera on my headphones."

"Counting the hours before your assignation."

"Something like that."

"You chaired the meeting from five P.M. until six P.M.?"

"Yes."

"And who attended?"

"Oh, the Murphy's Inlet people, the journalists, and the staff. The Americans were off on a bush-walk."

"Did anyone fail to attend?"

"Yes, Newton. We held up the start, waiting for him." I thought it was high time I got some information out of the police for a change. "When was he killed? Do you know?"

"We can't tell you that!" Detective Lee glared accusingly.

"Please. He was my friend. You must have some idea."

Detective Williams was silent for a moment. "We've received a preliminary report," he said slowly. "It seems to indicate he'd been dead seven hours or so when you found him. Of course, it's less accurate than it might be, because of the time taken to transport the body to the mainland."

"Thank you. This is absolutely appalling. I hope you find the culprit."

"Oh, we will, Mr. Petrucci. Did Newton Heath have any enemies that you are aware of?"

I nodded. "I know he made enemies in his legal work. He used to boast about it!"

"We'll certainly look into that. Are any of his legal colleagues here on the island?"

"I don't think so."

"And who else?"

"Pardon?"

It was Detective Lee's turn. (I don't think he liked me.) "Who else didn't make it to your meeting?"

I suddenly remembered: *Grant! He'd only turned up at the very end.* I didn't know what to say.

"Er, nobody."

Detective Williams looked pained. "Now, come on. You've been most co-operative so far."

"He's protecting her," sneered Detective Lee.

"Oh, you mean Claire?" I blurted, trying not to appear relieved. "Yes, now that you mention it. She went off to look for Newton. Never returned. I had no support whatsoever!"

"OK then. Anyone else?"

"No." I went on the attack. "Why ask me these things if you already know the answers?" I demanded.

Detective Williams smiled. "We have to verify other people's testimony. Not everyone tells the truth, you understand."

"Of course. Sorry."

Detective Lee pounced up and walked to the window. "Nice view," he commented. "Quite a pretty place, this."

"You should book in," said Detective Williams.

His fellow officer shot him a dirty look. "Cut it out, Brian," he grunted.

"Tell me something," I said. "Do you think the locals would try to stop this resort from going ahead?"

Detective Williams gave me an appraising smile. "That's your theory, is it?"

"No, I'm just asking."

"Well," he said, "As far as I'm concerned, homosexuals and lesbians, unless they break the law, ought to be treated no differently than normal people. That's official. We've just attended a course about it." (Detective Lee rolled his eyes heavenward.) "But your locals don't change their tune so easily. Personally, I doubt they'd welcome all this."

"They'll see hell freeze over first," added Detective Lee. "'Specially here in the Bible Belt. Thanks for the tea."

"Oh! Have we finished?"

"Yes, and thank you for your time, Mr. Petrucci. Detective Lee will type this up."

As I escorted them out, I asked, "What if I want to leave the island?"

"After you've signed the statement, you can go or stay as you like. You're not under arrest, you know! Let me see, you're based in Sydney?"

"That's right."

"Well, we have your address and contact number if we need them."

I closed the door and rushed straight to the bathroom. I turned on the cold tap, full pelt, and stuck my head directly under it—partly to cool down and partly to wash away the stain of my newly acquired bisexuality.

CHAPTER 12

O nce Queensland's finest had trotted off it was definitely time for a dose of *morbidezza*. Nothing less
than the death of Mimi could soothe away the anx-
iety I'd accumulated during my unnerving police interview.
I felt so guilty, I may as well have flung the acid in Newton's
face myself and dumped him in a piranha pond for good
measure.

Everything about this murder was ridiculous and perplex-
ing. Who keeps acid on a tropical island, for God's sake?
Refusing to think about it any longer, I loaded spruce new
batteries into my sand-blasted CD player and clicked in
La Bohème, Act 3. (Not Act 4, my favourite: I didn't want
Mimi to die too soon!) The heat was oppressive. I peeled my
clothes away from my body and offered my naked self up to
the twin deities of Puccini and Tebaldi. The gentle opening
bars, depicting a sub-zero Parisian winter, brought the anticipated cooling effect. I drifted away, borne by the sublime
drama of high tessitura and hearts on sleeves.

I was deep in trance-like concentration when an abrupt
sforzando chord jolted my eyes open. I blinked several times.
There, standing at the end of my bed gawking was the gorgeous Darren. I lay a limp hand over my groin in a pose reminiscent of Botticelli's *Venus*.

"Yes?" I inquired.

"The door was open," he remarked. "Are you packed?"

"Pardon?" I took off my headphones.

"Packed. Ready to go."

"No. Where?"

"Hiram wants me to take you over to the mainland. He
said you should get started."

"Get started?"

"He said you'd know what he meant."

Without further ado, he dragged me to my feet and helped me fling my few meagre holiday togs into a bag. Really! I could appreciate Hiram's haste to pin the dastardly deed on someone, but I couldn't see how my giving lunch a miss would make a heap of difference. And where was Paul, the boy genius behind my new role as international gay and lesbian sleuth?

"Have you seen Paul?" I asked Darren as we rushed off toward the dock.

He stopped, reaching into his pocket. "Oh yeah, he gave me a note for you."

He handed me a crumpled New Heaven brochure. Paul had scrawled something illegible in the blank "celebrity" section. His writing is not easy to decipher under the best conditions and this had evidently been dashed off in a hurry: he hadn't even dotted the i's in his usual way with little stars. The note read: "Caro. Got to stay and see performance through. Show must go on. Will phone you at June's. I HAVE SOMETHING!"

I shuddered. The last time Paul said "I have something," every man within a ten-mile radius had rushed to change his bed linen.

Soon Darren and I were speeding across the water, putting New Heaven behind us. I hadn't even had time to fret about seasickness (to which I am prone). Fortunately, the channel was still smooth and calm and our trip rather exhilarating. With the wind blowing through my hair in time-honoured fashion and salt spray splooshing into my eyes, I gazed peacefully at the blurry marine-scape. My departure was the nearest thing I'd had to a holiday activity since I had arrived.

Still, the speed with which I'd been ousted continued to bother me. There had been no opportunity to speak to Paul, nor to anybody else. I began to wonder if there wasn't a more sinister motive behind Hiram's initiative. I didn't think

Hiram had done Newton in—why would he?—but what if he was protecting someone? If Hiram was in cahoots with a murderer, I'd have little chance now of finding out. The man had hired me to investigate the murder, then promptly removed me from the scene of the crime and all the possible suspects! It seemed increasingly suspicious. However, there was nothing I could do about it for the time being but sit back and gape at the gorgeous scenery.

Darren gazed back at me as he manfully steered our course, flashing a ready smile each time the boat jolted. I began to notice a strange expression on his face, which I'd have called "respect," if I didn't know better.

"Hiram got you out of there in a hurry!" he shouted above the roar of the motor.

"That's what I was just thinking."

"What'd ya say?"

Suddenly, everything was tranquil. All I heard was the lapping of the water's surface against the side of our boat. Darren had cut the engine.

"What are you doing?" I asked.

"Thought we might drift for a bit. Have a talk. Not in any great hurry, are you?" he replied.

"No, not particularly. But why?"

"Why not?"

He stretched out. I gave his body a good long look, but this time from a different perspective: It was clear that in a one-on-one confrontation I wouldn't have a prayer. The boat was miles out from land. Fearful thoughts flashed through my mind. I was completely in his power. If I vanished, who would be the wiser? Was this Hiram's real plan—to silence me? He must have thought I knew something already! But what did I know? *Niente.*

Darren yawned. "Nice out here."

"Mmm. I'm sort of over it now," I hinted.

He grinned.

"So why has Hiram got you out so quick, I wonder," he mused aloud. "Some of the Yanks are desperate to get away. They're important guys, billionaires. They don't wanna get mixed up in—what were they calling it?—a "murder scenario." But does old Hiram look after them first? Nope! He looks after you. You must be pretty fucking important." He fixed me with that look eagles give rodents in nature documentaries.

I felt a familiar sensation: the sharp fingernails of panic creeping down the back of my shorts.

"What do you want?"

He didn't answer directly, but mused to himself. "What do I want? Good question. I want to make an honest living like any other guy, but things are fairly tough just lately." He smiled. "Not that I'm asking for charity."

I smiled back, equally insincere. "Why should you? You're young, good-looking, talented..."

"I've got talent all right." He rubbed his chin. "I'm real sorry you're gonna leave us. I was thinking you and me might even get a bit friendly."

This sounded like a step in the right direction. "It would be nice to part friends," I stammered.

"We haven't gotta part at all," he said confidingly. "Not if you don't want to. You're staying on at the Inlet, right?"

"Well, yes, for a short while."

"Great! I might be back there soon."

What was he getting at? "Darren, is this a business proposition?"

He laughed. "You got the picture." He glanced at the island, now on the horizon. "New Heaven's had it, so I'm thinking of getting into a different line of work."

"Are you sure? Hiram seems to think as long as things continue normally—"

He shook his head. "You wait." Then he lifted his foot and rubbed it against my shuddering thigh. "Y'know, I'm feeling a bit horny right now. I'm quite into older guys."

"Thanks!"

"As clients." His foot reached my crotch. "You into anything special?"

"Not particularly."

"Some mature guys like to do a father-and-son thing. We could pretend we just got in from the footy or something. Take a shower together, fool around." He adopted a nasal adolescent voice. "Daddy, show me. Teach me what you know—I'm a fast learner. I'll make you proud of me, I promise. Oops, there goes the soap. I'll get it! Hey! What's that? Heck! Mum's home early. That's her key in the door! We better stop! Stop, Daddy! Mum's gonna walk in and—"

"Stop!" I cried. "Please! That's enough."

"Just giving you a sample."

"I'm sorry, that's not my style of thing at all. Anyway, my mother was Italian. She'd have gone straight to the kitchen to prepare dinner."

"No worries. We'll come up with something." His foot still nestled menacingly in my groin.

"Er, what if I'm not interested?"

Darren gave me a long drawn-out stare. Then, without warning, he shoved his foot hard against my waist. I lost my balance, flailed my arms, and immediately felt the cold water. The tiny boat pitched.

"Careful," he drawled. "Pretty deep out here."

I held on tightly and righted myself. "I'll be extremely careful!" I panted. "And, um, I'll be staying at the Seabreeze . Why don't you keep in touch?"

"Thanks. I'll do that." He patted my knee reassuringly. "We'll have fun, Marc. Guaranteed."

"Money back?"

"Ha! You're a real comedian."

"Can we please get moving now?"

"Sure thing!"

A second later the motor groaned and spluttered once more,

and we were headed for the mainland. As soon as we docked, I bade Darren a hasty farewell and trudged up the road to the guesthouse, well and truly shattered.

June wasn't expecting me, but she had plenty of room and welcomed my visit with ancient open arms and an apricot sponge. I felt I was more than merely an old and valued lodger: I was a living symbol of the time when business had flourished at the Seabreeze.

Grant, with whom I'd hoped to catch up, wasn't in town. Script crises on the soap opera had required him to fly out to Sydney early that morning. There was nothing left for me to do but relax. I whipped out the Discman, plugged in the power, and Tebaldi took up where she had left off. It was dark outside when June tapped at my door.

"Marc? You there, love?"

"Yes, June?"

"There's a man for you. On the phone. Says his name's Harpo."

"What?"

"Harpo. Like the Marx Brother."

I followed her downstairs to a dim alcove occupied by an antique telephone. "Not a very common name these days," she declared as she shuffled away. I picked up the receiver.

"Hello?" said a familiar voice.

"Harpo?"

"Caro, what did you say? My mobile must be dying."

"You called yourself—oh! Caro. Not Harpo."

"What are you babbling about? Pull yourself together, darling, we've got work to do. As soon as this shitty old show is over I'll join you and we'll throw ourselves into the investigation."

"Yes, well," I replied. "I don't think I can do much good over here. From what the police said, the murder happened seven hours before we found the body. In other words, around the very time I was doing my community liaising."

"That's why Newton didn't show!"

"Precisely. The thing is, it eliminates as suspects the people who were there. That includes the Murphy's Inlet people, the journalists, you, and most of the staff. Plus, the Americans who were away on their bush-walk."

"What are you saying? He did it all by himself?"

"No, of course not."

"Perhaps someone snuck away from the meeting."

"I think I'd have noticed."

"Hadrian wasn't there!"

"He was with the Americans, so he said."

"He's going back to Sydney in the morning."

"Damn and blast, this is impossible! I haven't got a clue."

"Well, I have! Did Dazzle pass you my note?"

I had forgotten, not surprisingly. "Yes," I said, "and I still suspect that one! I get the feeling he's capable of anything. By the way, you were dead right. Your friend Darren's a rent boy, and I get the feeling he's only slightly cheaper to rent than the Palace of Versailles."

"I knew it! The slut."

I pulled the soggy paper out of my pocket. "Your note says you've got something."

"Yessiree, babe! Nothing less than a genuine certified Clue with a capital C!"

"When you've finished congratulating yourself, will you let me know what it is?"

"Maybe."

"Don't be coy."

"OK. Remember when we were in Newton's office? Well! While you were keeping boyfy occupied, I spied a fax on Newton's desk and voilà! Move over, David Copperfield. In a flash and before your very eyes, said fax had vanished into my back pocket! I tried to tell you."

"Is that what all the bum-patting was about?"

"Natch! What did you think?"

"I thought it was your celebrated impression of an orang-utan. So what does this fax say, exactly?"

"It's from Newton to...somebody. It doesn't really spell it out."

"Can you read it to me?"

"I don't actually have it on me just now. I'm in the jacuzzi. HI, KIDS!"

I jerked my ear away from the receiver.

"Caro, you still there? My dancing boys are coming over. I'd better go. Why don't I fax it to you? You can ponder over it in bed. Is there a creaky old fax machine up there at Mandalay?"

"You're joking."

"I'll send it tomorrow then. Where to? The post office?"

"No. That'll be too public. I'll find a fax somewhere and let you know."

"Call my mobile. Not before ten. *Ciao bella*!"

I spent an unpleasant night dreaming I was the Tallulah Bankhead character in the film *Lifeboat,* and woke at dawn. It was ludicrous. I got less sleep in this panoramic paradise than I did at home under the planes!

I tiptoed down to the roomy kitchen, trying not to wake June, and made myself a coffee. This took longer than it should have, as I dropped an entire carton of milk and had to search for towels to soak it up. I was rummaging through a cupboard under the stairs when the phone exploded into the silence. I answered.

"Seabreeze Guesthouse."

"Marc! Is that you? It's Grant. What are you doing there?"

"I'm a guest."

"Well, you're just the woman I want to speak to! How extraordinary. I was about to ring that ghastly Crab Island as soon as I'd had a word with June."

"She's asleep."

"Whoops! She's usually an early riser. Anyway, will you tell her I won't be back for a couple of weeks? She likes to know. More importantly, your aunty's usual digs in the city have shut up shop. Can I park my carcass at your place for a while? I promise I'll redecorate."

"Of course. What's up?"

"Oh, one thing and another. By the way, have you seen the news? Newton Heath's ugly mug is everywhere. He was murdered!"

"I know, I was there. So were you!"

There was no response. For a moment I thought we'd been cut off.

"Grant?"

"Yes, yes, I'm still here. The paper says he was killed in the middle of the night."

"No, that's when the body was found. By me!"

"How ghastly for you! Was death swift and painless?"

"I don't think so."

"Good. The man was an arsehole."

He seemed recklessly flippant. "Grant, listen to me. You'd better stop saying things like that. Have the police spoken to you?"

"Lord, no!"

"Well, they probably will," I warned.

He groaned. "That doesn't sound like a load of laughs."

"What happened to you anyway? You were so late for the meeting."

"I'm sorry about that. I know you're a riveting speaker but I went for a walk. Nothing personal."

"That's when Newton was murdered."

"Fuck! Was it? Oh, God, I hate my life."

"Grant, think! What did you do after you left my room?"

"Yes, well, I trudged around looking at that tasteless resort with the others, everyone mightily unimpressed. Finally we were introduced to Newton. I told him I wanted a chat in private and—shit, this is sounding worse and worse—we had a real screaming match! An absolute ball-tearer. I was so wound up—you know how I get—I just needed to go off alone and cool down. I hate scenes, unless I've written them myself."

"What were you arguing about?"

"I can't tell you."

"You've got to tell me!" I roared. "Don't you see what kind of trouble you could be in?"

I sensed he was beginning to panic. "I had a bone to pick with Newton. I went over specifically to confront him. In fact, poor June wasn't sick at all. She was itching to see the place, and I talked her out of it!"

"You told me you'd never met Newton."

"I hadn't till then."

"What was it about?"

"Oh, boyfriends, what else! You know I've been having a bloody difficult relationship lately. He's a gorgeous kid, but a bit confused about a few things. I discovered he'd been 'associating' with Newton, and it worried me. Not a good influence, to put it mildly. I really don't want to tell you any more. I need to keep this very quiet."

"When you were out walking, did you see anyone?"

"No! Oh, wait—some woman spoke to me. Wanted to know if I'd seen Newton."

"It must have been Claire. Was she tallish, smartly dressed?"

He paused. "I can't remember, to be honest. I was in such a temper."

"Well, I bet *she* remembers! You'd better go to the police yourself."

"Should I? They haven't been my staunchest allies in the past."

"No, but it's the best thing to do. Be cooperative. You've got to clear yourself right away."

He sighed. "Yes, yes I will. I should have gone straight to your little function. At least I didn't miss the best part."

"That parson of yours was a nightmare. He went on and on and on…" I stopped in my tracks. The possible significance of Pastor Paramor's preaching abruptly dawned on me.

"Hello? Testing?"

"Grant, I have to go."

"Well, before you do, is there a key to your house flitting around, or do I climb through the laundry window?"

I told Grant where to find the spare key and slowly replaced the receiver as my brain began to grapple with a new idea. Perhaps I'd started off on the wrong foot. Was Hiram right after all about Murphy's Inlet?

Somewhat reluctantly, I cast my mind back to the meeting. Pastor Paramor was an experienced preacher, I reflected. At least half the crowd were hanging on his every metaphor. He must have known he could hold them for—what, twenty minutes, easily? Suppose he had been giving somebody time—creating an ecclesiastical window of opportunity—to perpetrate a hideous act that even an atheist like myself knew to be theologically frowned upon. The murderer could go about his business uninterrupted while the rest of the population sat happily enthralled by the padre's rhetoric. As for motive, it was perfectly clear from the tenor of his speech: Get the gays.

The Church of Divine Intervention. Ha! They had to be kidding. Only a fool would buy that "God shall do the dirty work" routine. The silver-tongued sermoniser was predicting Newton's murder at exactly the same time it was happening! There was even a touch of fire and brimstone in the use of acid as a murder weapon.

I was staggered by the clarity and certainty of my vision. Real "road to Damascus" stuff. What I should do about it was another matter. I could hardly swagger into church, hurling accusations around like some pregnant ex-girlfriend at a wedding. No, this would require subtlety. Luckily, Paul was still on the island.

That reminded me: First things first, I had to locate a fax machine. If Paul's clue was genuine, it could confirm my new theory. On a hall table by the phone was a local district paper. I swiftly scanned the ads for businesses with a fax number. I noted dozens of adult video exchanges, none of which operated out of fixed premises, and a tacky travel agency promising seven nights in Manila with certain "conditions." *Typical,* I thought! Murphy's Inlet, while throwing up its collective hands in horror at the thought of gays and lesbians, was happy enough to tolerate all sorts of heterosexual sleaze! None of these businesses owned a fax.

Finally, I found two possibilities: the Eagle Tavern, a pub that had live rock music every night of the week, and the Murphy's Inlet Historical Society Museum. Instinctively, I felt more inclined to try the pub. I tore out the appropriate page, squared my shoulders and prepared to step out into what Hiram had so correctly termed "enemy territory."

CHAPTER 13

It was one of those muggy midweek mornings up north when the air is clogged with moisture and frogs that sound like drag queens are having endless altercations with tropical birds that sound like Jewish mothers in sitcoms.

Although it was still early, the good folk of Murphy's Inlet seemed to have been up and about for hours—at least those of them with jobs to go to, that is, which was about one percent. The local milk bar crawled with activity. A lank-haired girl slopped wide-rimmed cups of water and froth on the counter for two harried housewives as they held a clandestine conversation on the subject of domestic violence. Farther along the main street, a bright young lad lugged racks of clothing out of a large shop onto the pavement. On the racks hung "crocodile season" singlets, complete with bloody rips.

I wandered, lonely as a pariah, past these local emporiums, wearing sunglasses and a terry-toweling hat, disguised as a man who was not the New Heaven community liaison officer. I think it worked. The stares I got were merely suspicious, not viscerally threatening.

I found the Eagle Tavern without much difficulty. I picked up the odour of stale beer a block away. When I tried the doors, however, they were all bolted. I squinted through the frosted glass window and was able to make out a few dim figures inside. From their slow yet regular arm movements I deduced they were drinking. I tapped on the main door, softly at first, then more briskly. After some time, a red-eyed bald man with grey stubble and a very large gut opened the door.

"Not trading yet, sir," he slurred.

"But people are drinking," I pointed out.

He looked back over his shoulder. I could clearly see four

or five locals seated at the bar with beer cans cradled lovingly in their hands.

He turned back. "I believe you are mistaken." He started to close up again. I blocked the door.

"I just want to use your fax," I protested.

He gave me a polite but dentally challenged smile. "Shove off, mate," he suggested tactfully, and forced the door shut. I heard the bolt fall back into place.

Humph, I thought. Wait until he needs something from me! Then we'll see who has the siege mentality.

Realising the pub had been a mistake, I settled on my second choice: the Murphy's Inlet Historical Society Museum. It sounded quaint and welcoming. Perhaps they'd even do a Devonshire tea.

Naturally, the venerable institution was situated at the opposite end of town, right on the outskirts. By the time I reached the place, I was hatless and perspiring. A gentleman of historical bent was perched on a stool, a tin of heritage-colour paint in hand, touching up an external doorjamb.

"Good morning," I said breezily. "Is the museum open?"

"Yair." He turned to greet me. His expression did a 180-degree about-face as he recognised me, and my heart sank quicker than the Titanic. It was unmistakably Alderman Merv Jackson himself.

"Whaddaya want?" he growled.

My face was concrete. Nothing would unfix my smile. "Oh, I was interested in researching some local history."

"Come to snoop, have ya?"

"Just healthy curiosity. Is the curator in?"

"That's me."

"Ah ha. Alderman Jackson, I believe. I'm Marc Petrucci." I held out my hand. A slight breeze caressed it softly. After a moment I pulled it back.

"Why aren't you over on the island with all them poofs?"

I waved dismissively, realising belatedly how campy the

gesture must have looked. "Oh, I've resigned," I said.

"Is that so?"

"It wasn't the opportunity I'd first thought."

Merv grinned malevolently. "And they had a murder, hey? That oughta close the joint down!"

"Possibly."

"Good! Bloody glad to hear it."

"Yes, well. I'm returning to Sydney very soon."

With unexpected dexterity, he climbed down from his stool.

"Come in, then. Your dough's as good as anyone else's, I daresay. It's five bucks."

I paid up and followed through the door, carelessly brushing my sleeve against the new paintwork. I had the impression he'd sooner throw his fax into a volcano than let me get my hands on it, but I felt I should persevere.

"Here," he grunted, thrusting a dusty, monochrome pamphlet into my hand. "Our catalogue."

The museum, like its big brother the council chamber, was a converted homestead. The kitchen and bedroom painstakingly recreated those of a bygone era—or rather eras. The kitchen furniture ranged from a cupboard that predated the British presence in Australia to an "Early Kooka" stove from the 1920s.

A fragile chair sported a set of patchwork covers and cushions that indicated an early manifestation of colour-blindness in the district. I gazed at this monstrosity in nauseated awe.

"My granny made that," announced Merv with pride. "Now come and have a butcher's at the real exhibits! You reckon you're interested in our history."

He led me to the large front room and switched on a pallid single-globe light. Crowded around the walls were dozens of faded sepia photographs of the town, the townsfolk, and their machinery. Below the pictures were glass cases, some quite large, jammed into every square inch of space. I stared into one. It was hard to make out what artifacts—if any—lurked behind the murky glass.

"Don't strain yourself," smirked the alderman. "That one's empty. Sent away for cleaning."

I gingerly stepped over to the adjacent case. Inside hung a rusty bucket with a rough rectangular hole cut into it. Underneath, a card read: BUSHRANGER PATRICK MURPHY 1854-1882.

"Murphy hid out here from the state troopers," explained my guide. "He's the Murphy the inlet's named after. Survived on nothing but fish and fruit for six months!"

It didn't sound like such a hardship to me.

"So that's his original, ah, fruit bucket?" I murmured.

"Headgear. Wore it at the infamous siege of Crook's Creek when he robbed the post office. Stole 300 head of sheep the same day, reached the inlet by nightfall, and decided to stay put."

Merv was obviously impressed with Murphy's exploits.

"Why didn't he eat the sheep?" I asked.

"Eh?"

"During the six months."

Merv shook his head. "They got away."

I reexamined the helmet. The designer hadn't considered comfort a priority.

"Like Ned Kelly," I suggested.

"Hmm," he grunted. "Murphy did it first."

I stepped back.

"Mind your head."

The warning came too late. With a crack my skull came into contact with something sharp and metallic. I reeled around to confront a peculiar mobile, suspended precariously (and dangerously) on wires in the middle of the room. It was a sheet of metal, twisted but gleaming.

"You'll be all right," drawled the alderman, without bothering to examine me.

"What on earth is this thing?"

"Part of a plane. The U-2, built by the Yanks as a spy plane."

I seized at the chance to ingratiate myself. "Ah, yes," I remarked, dropping into my teaching voice. "One of these got shot down by the Soviets in about 1960, I recall. And it was the U-2 that Kennedy sent over Cuba at the time of the missile crisis."

Merv stared at me, gobsmacked by this informed observation.

"A piece of the fuselage I'd say. Where did you get it?" I asked him.

"Picked it up cheap. Bloody things were always falling to bits."

I nodded sagely. "Fragile, you see. They had to be, to fly at 70,000 feet." I continued with the earnest momentum of a cable documentary. "Of course, the record altitude had been set in '59 in the Starfighter, the good old F-104!"

Merv glowed. "You keen on planes?"

I played it cool. "Used to be," I admitted. "One of my interests."

He nodded slowly. "I'm ex-RAAF," he said. "Flew a DC3."

"Ah. Fancy."

"You fly yourself?"

I pursed my lips. "Not really."

The truth was, I'd reached the limit of my expertise. I knew nothing more about this subject. It was simply that, for a very narrow period of two to three years in the early '60s as I was entering my fraught and frustrated teens, I'd conceived a deep and abiding interest in a school friend named Colin—who was himself mightily interested in planes. Together, on weekends, we lay on his bedroom floor constructing Airfix models in all their intricacy. While Colin prattled on about altitudes and the sound barrier, I hung around in a miserable cocoon of sexual distraction, nearly out of my mind, thanks to the lethal combination of desire and airplane glue. I can't say romance ever blossomed. He exposed himself to me at the movies once, but that didn't count—it was *Twelve O'clock High,* so he wasn't himself.

I snapped out of my nostalgic reverie. It seemed Alderman Merv Jackson had mellowed toward me a fraction. I was all set to wax lyrical about faxes when he fixed me with a challenging stare. "You wanna go up?"

I gulped. I knew he didn't mean upstairs.

"Up?" I glanced at my watch. "Is there time?"

"All the time in the world. Council owns a Cessna, a little beauty. She's just over at the airstrip, and I've got carte blanche. Lemme show you the countryside, hey? Make up for doin' me block the other day. It wasn't you I was cranky with. It was all them filthy poofs."

I raised my eyebrows. Apparently, my smattering of aircraft knowledge had rendered me heterosexual (or possibly neuter).

"Can I use your fax?" I demanded.

"Ar yair," he answered offhandedly. "When we get back. Come on!" He clicked off the light and whisked me out into the sultry morning. At the door he turned and grinned wickedly. "I'll only charge you half-price for the flight. Fair enough?" He didn't pause for a reply, but hauled me after him into a battered old truck.

As we bounced along a dirt road toward the airstrip, the atmosphere between us changed tangibly. The alderman lost all interest in chitchat and concentrated intently on his driving. He appeared preoccupied.

The day was warmer and stickier than ever. I gazed dreamily at the passing countryside. In this humidity, a storm couldn't be far away. Out to sea, the sky was almost black. The road, apparently a secondary route, began to climb snakily into the high country at the back of the town. In the valley below crouched the gaudy headquarters of the Church of Divine Intervention, its bright red panoply shrieking at the cool greens of the surrounding landscape. We made a wide circle up behind it.

Seeing the holy eyesore reminded me of my brilliant murder theory. Now would be a good time to question Alderman Jackson, since I seemed to have gained his confidence. Specifically, I wanted to find out if the pastor had a right hand man, preferably a convicted murderer, who may have been lurking about while the community and I had liaised. But before launching into detective work, I decided to charm the councillor a bit further.

"Any other aircraft are around here, Merv?" I asked in a tone of total fascination.

He grunted, without looking at me. "A few." His manner discouraged further conversation. I relaxed down into my half of the lumpy seat.

Suddenly, without warning, my companion hauled the wheel around and our truck made a sharp turn off the road and into the scrub. Tires screeched on the loose rubble, and I was thrown off balance, banging hard up against the door, which burst open. I threw out an arm, fumbling to hang on to something, and inadvertently grabbed Merv's thigh.

"Oops! Sorry, mate," I said, slipping into a ripe *basso profundo*.

The alderman said nothing, but immediately stopped the truck. I froze. Not for the first time in my life, I regretted having watched the movie *Deliverance*. We had come to a halt in a small clearing amongst dense bushland high up behind the town. There was nothing remotely resembling an airstrip to be seen.

I wondered what to do next; neither of us had moved. My door was open, but if I made a run for it, he could easily catch me up. He probably kept an arsenal of rifles in the back— I wouldn't have a hope in hell of getting away. I cursed myself inwardly for my stupidity. Here was I in prime redneck territory, and I had blithely flitted off on a joyride with the king of the homophobes.

Merv turned his head slowly to stare at me. I tried to

make a move for the door but he grabbed my forearm and held me firm.

"Where you goin'?" he whispered. His voice was hoarse.

"To stretch my legs?" I suggested. "It's been a long drive."

He didn't reply, but tightened his grip. My fingers were beginning to go numb.

"You're hurting me," I mumbled.

He just stared. "A real man can take a bit of hurt," he answered quietly.

I swallowed. I could feel him sweating profusely.

"Y'know," he confessed, "it gets lonely round these parts."

I winced. Which parts? I didn't like this turn of the conversation one tiny bit! "Yes, well, Merv. When you're on your own a lot, um, a person can lose a sense of perspective. So they say. You ever been married?" I queried cautiously.

"Yair," he said. "Bitch walked out on me."

"Oh, I'm terribly sorry."

"Nah. Good riddance."

Once again, there was an uneasy silence. The alderman was breathing with some irregularity. Even through my pins and needles, I could feel the excitement mounting.

"Is the airstrip nearby?" I inquired with the feigned nonchalance of a tourist in a war zone.

He ignored my question. "I don't like women," he continued. "Never had much time for them."

"Indeed."

"Them women over on the island—lesbians!" He forced the word out. "They make me want to vomit! Them poofters too. Poncing around like stupid bloody girls. I tell you, that little bastard who was taking the piss out of our padre: If I'd had a rifle there, he woulda been dead meat!"

Now I was sweating, too. Agreement seemed like the best way to go.

"Yes, Paul can overdo it sometimes. He means well."

"Paul, is it?" Merv sneered. "He'd better not show his pansy face in Murphy's Inlet. Men are men, fuck it!" He suddenly exploded. "It's natural! Men are strong, not weak. We like men's stuff. Sports! Planes! The company of real bloody men!" He softened. "Like you," he added. "What's wrong with that, hey?" He gritted his teeth. "That make you some kinda fairy?"

I could see what was coming, of course. Heaven knows I've had a multitude of sexual experiences over the years—most of them delightful—but I've always found that the least successful couplings occur when both parties are in it against their better judgment. Such a situation had arisen occasionally toward the end of my now defunct relationship, the result of boredom and long-running unresolved tiffs.

I'd also experienced it in entirely different circumstances, when dealing with a person or persons not entirely comfortable with their sexuality. Technical expertise was not their strong suit. I was inclined to place Merv Jackson squarely in this category. After a few such encounters, I'd developed a simple, reliable rule of thumb: When in doubt, don't bother. I was certainly in doubt at the moment, but to put the rest of my rule into action would be tricky.

"Merv—" I began.

"Shut the bloody door," he interrupted as he began to ease himself out of his pants. At precisely the same moment, the dark clouds made a unanimous decision and tropical rain pelted down. Within seconds, it was impossible to see out the windows. Clearly, we wouldn't be going anywhere even if we wanted to.

I returned to the task literally at hand. The alderman's shorts were no longer an encumbrance but hung on the central gearshift, a piece of equipment which paled into insignificance by the side of the equipment now revealed.

"Get your pants off," he shouted, above the roar of the downpour.

I stalled. "Have you got a condom?"

"What?"

"A condom! Have you got one?"

"No." (I wasn't surprised. I doubted they came in an XXL.) "So what?"

I was firm and emphatic. "No sex without a condom! Preferably two. It's far too risky."

"There's nothin' wrong with me!" he snorted. "Or you either! That's for fairies, not blokes like us! It's God's way of wipin' out perverts!"

It wasn't hard to guess where he'd picked up this offbeat sample of religious dogma. Now the ignorant cretin had me riled.

"It's you I'm thinking of!" I yelled. "I don't want you to catch anything. I've been over on that island with the fairies! I've used all their toilet seats! One after another."

He grabbed me hard by the shoulders. "Shut up now," he commanded. "Time to take it like a man."

With that ominous cliche, I knew we'd reached the point of no return. There was only one thing left to do. I grasped his supposed indicator of "real manhood" with both hands and pumped vigorously. Overhead the sky rumbled and the rain increased in its intensity.

"Looks like we're in for a long wet," I said conversationally.

"What are ya doin'?" he cried. "Not that! Don't do that! I... uuhhhh..."

"Do you want me to stop?"

"Yair... no...uuhhhh! Can't we do somethin' else?"

"No!"

I redoubled my efforts, working like a milkmaid possessed. I had a plan, but it was going to require all my considerable skill.

"Oh, those lesbians," I bellowed. "Just think what they get up to, Merv!"

"Aaaahhh!"

"Can you imagine? With their soft hands and their pierced tongues... Sometimes they shave each other..."

"Stop! Uuhhh..."

Now Merv was writhing, slamming his palms into the faded upholstery.

"I'd like to be a fly on the wall when those lesbians get together! Wouldn't you? When they think nobody's watching..."

"Nooooooo!" He was screaming.

"And the fairy boys, Merv! Some of them are even bigger than you! They'll do anything and everything. Anywhere, with anybody! Whenever they feel like it!" (That at least was true.)

"Uh...uh...uh... "

"Are you close??"

"YEAH!"

I let go, braced myself and punched him as hard as I could in the face with both fists. Blood trickled from his nose, but I didn't wait to see which end he would deal with first. I kicked open the door and threw myself out into the pouring rain. Then I ran.

CHAPTER 14

I ran as though my life depended on it (which I suppose it did). I stumbled over logs and slipped in the wet, but kept running back to the road and down the hill, the way we'd come. My hands were throbbing, my legs aching, and my shoes completely saturated. With every second step I sank into a puddle but I didn't stop to look back. I just kept on frantically running, stumbling, and sticking to the hilly side of the road.

After about fifteen minutes, seeing no sign of Merv, I paused to catch my breath. The shower continued at full pelt. I wiped the streaming face of my watch: It was well past noon. It would probably take me hours to walk back. I trudged on, occasionally glancing over my shoulder in case the truck should come bearing down on me. It was during one such glance that I stepped into a ditch by the side of the road and plunged headlong into a prickly native shrub.

I squealed in agony, rolled back into the ditch, and lay face-down in a pool of soft, wet clay. Then my ears pricked up—there was a distant rumble behind me. I lifted my head to see the headlights of Merv's truck piercing the sheets of rain. The truck came rattling down toward me, picking up speed. In panic I cringed back into the ditch, closed my eyes and fervently reembraced the Catholic faith I had so casually discarded some years before.

A second later—it seemed like an eternity—I looked up again. The coast was clear. He had driven past! I dragged myself, muddy and soaking, out of the ditch. Farther down the hill I saw the truck careering wildly from one side of the narrow road to the other, dangerously out of control. I watched in amazement as it approached a sharp curve, lurched sideways over the edge, smashed through the bush, and ricocheted down into the valley.

I limped along till I reached the spot, then stood still for some moments staring at the deep clay furrows where the truck's wheels had left the road. I wondered what I could do, but quickly realised the situation was hopeless. I could see where Merv's truck had come to a halt. It sat in a tiny gully—upright, but leaning to one side, like a child's forgotten toy. If I tried to climb down there it would take hours, presuming I didn't get lost en route. There seemed to be no sign of smoke or flame. The alderman would have been shaken up considerably, but after our recent unappetising tête-à-tête, Merv's well-being was way down my list of priorities. I decided to get back to town without further ado.

As I hobbled on down the road, the rain finally ceased and the sun's rays returned with a vengeance. In an instant the clay dried on me, making it so difficult and painful to walk that I was forced to remove my shirt and trousers. In this sorry, semi-clad state I stumbled into Murphy's Inlet. Not once during the two-hour hike did a vehicle pass by.

Eventually I was right back where I'd started, at the end of town where Merv's museum was situated. Desperate as I was to get to June's and soak in a cleansing tub, I was also of a mind to achieve something—anything—to make the ghastly day worthwhile.

I staggered up to the museum and tried the door. It opened. Merv hadn't locked up. *Why would he,* I thought? There was nothing for anyone to steal except Murphy's old bucket.

I soon located the alderman's office. The phone and fax machine snuggled temptingly on a desk in the corner. Masses of old faxes, council meeting agendas, and bills lay haphazardly about. Merv was evidently no bookkeeper. I fished deep in my mind for Paul's mobile number. *Miracoloso!* It came to me at once. I picked up the receiver and dialed.

A very proper lady's voice answered. "This call is to be diverted to another number," she intoned. Beeps followed, then Paul's familiar message twittered down the phone. Just hearing his chirpy voice made me feel better. "I'm not here right now, I'm prancing around up north with a lot of mouth-watering dancers! Aren't you jealous? Now leave a message after the beeps 'cause I'm dying to dish the dirt. We must catch up. Oh, if you're offering me work, I'll take it!"

"Paul, it's Marc. I've had the most putrid time. I'm in Murphy's Inlet at the history museum. There's a fax machine, but if you're not there, forget it. I can't stay here. Call me at June's, will you? I've got a theory—and plenty to tell you."

As I replaced the phone, a green manila folder jutting out from beneath a pile of museum catalogues caught my eye. In the same childish script I'd seen under the bushranger's bucket, it read: "Crab Island Development Application." I opened it. Inside were several letters and memos. The top one boasted a Murphy's Inlet Shire Council letterhead. It was a photocopy of a letter from Alderman Jackson to Pastor Matthew Paramor of the Church of Divine Intervention. It was dated some months before and marked "Personal and Confidential." My eyes scanned it avidly.

Dear Matthew,

As per our phone conversation, I'm afraid there is nothing in the ordinances to reverse the decision on Crab Island Development Application #QGT 83c. It's the last thing we all want, but planning and environmental guidelines have been adhered to, and I wouldn't be surprised if one or two state government palms weren't greased. I regret to inform you that building work is, as you suspect, nearing completion. There is nothing I can do through official channels at this stage.

On the other hand, as you suggest, getting a resort up and running is not easy, and council will certainly look closely at operational issues once the building's there. We would also be amenable to any further development on Crab Island, should your organisation acquire the land or come to some future arrangement with the present owners.

Personally, I'm inclined to believe the current resort may find the situation discouraging, one way or another. I know we are in basic agreement on this.

On the matter of our forthcoming trip, I have faxed our requirements to H.P. and will forward you the timetable. I emphasised our proposed take-off could be no later because of the time it will take us to reach our target and commence our return journey.

Sincere regards,
Merv

I scrutinised the letter uneasily. It struck me as immensely fishy, especially the part about the church coming to an arrangement with Gaytour International. From what I knew of the players on both teams I couldn't see it happening in a month of Sundays, even if God divinely intervened and drew up the contract Himself.

I shoved the folder down the front of my ruined clothes, slipped in an extra museum catalogue for good measure, and sneaked out of the building, stopping only for a second at the till to retrieve my five dollars. I noticed I'd left muddy footprints all over the place. Alderman Jackson would have a fair idea of who had been snooping around his office. Still, our relationship could hardly get any worse.

I returned to the guesthouse via the beach. It was a longer walk, but another sodden old beachcomber was unlikely to cause comment. All I could think of was a brimming hot bath, followed by an equal amount of June's chunky minestrone.

It was getting dark as I dragged my wretched body up the front stairs. A welcoming light shone in the kitchen. I entered timidly, not wishing to alarm June with my dilapidated demeanour. I found her sitting at the table, staring into space.

"Hello?" I said.

She looked up at me vacantly. She appeared upset. Her hand clasped a damp tissue.

"Where have you been, love?" she asked. "You look like shit." (So much for alarm.)

"It's a long story. I ought to have a bath right away."

"Someone's in there," she replied tartly.

I rubbed my hands together. "Well, what say we tuck into that fabulous minestrone of yours?"

She shook her head.

"June, what's up?"

Her voice quavered. "Grant's been arrested! For murder!"

"When!?"

"This morning. He called me from the cop shop at Sydney Central. They think he killed that feller on Crab Island." She choked back a sob.

"Oh, God!" I gave her a big hug. "Don't be upset, June. It's obvious Grant didn't do it. The idea's just too ridiculous!"

She glared at me. "He said you told him to go to the police. The minute he walked in, they arrested him. Now he's in prison!"

"I did suggest he cooperate, but I never thought..."

She smiled sadly. "You never do, love."

Above us, I heard a door open and close.

"Bathroom's free," she said. "He's been in there for ages. The water won't be too hot. Well, I'll put on some soup." I'd been grudgingly forgiven.

I trudged up the stairs, reeling under the impact of her shocking news. Grant! How on earth could the police even think such a thing? But even as the thought whizzed through my mind, I realised how bad it looked for him. He'd arrived late to the meeting, he'd been alone with Newton, and they'd had a screaming match over a boyfriend.

As I rounded the corner to my room, I walked smack into a young man wearing nothing but a towel, which promptly dropped to the floor.

"Oh, I'm sorry," I stammered.

"Home at last! Now behave yourself."

"Paul!"

"Caro! Ugh, where have you been? The brick pits? You look worse than a piece of performance art."

I fell into his arms. "Let's just say I have a strong desire to return to the comparative safety of the inner-city slums. You can keep your tropical paradise. Too many traps for young players."

"True, oh, queen."

"What are you doing here, anyway?"

He looked me squarely in the face. "You know your friend Grant's been fingered, as they say in criminal parlance?"

"June just told me."

"You're not her favourite little fairy at the moment!"

I shuddered. "Don't use that term, please."

He looked quizzical, then shrugged it off. "Come in while I dress, and I'll tell you what I know."

Like mine, Paul's room was spacious and warm. I sat on his bed as he wrenched on a T-shirt and went to work strenuously on his hair.

"What do you want, caro? The good news or the bad news?"

I gave him a wan smile. "Bad news first."

He nodded. "We're off the case. As of this afternoon."

"Oh. Why?"

"Well, for one thing, Hiram's satisfied. He's delighted Grant got arrested. Just the type of murderer he had in mind: a complete outsider. When he heard it was all your doing, he sang your praises high and low! You should've been there. Then he sacked us."

"How did you know about the arrest?"

"When I didn't receive your phone call, after waiting and waiting, I called here and got June. She'd just heard."

"Were you sacked as choreographer as well?"

"Kind of. Basically, Hiram's decided to close the whole place down until all this unpleasantness blows over—after the trial and so on."

"Oh, my God—Grant might be put on trial!"

"Everybody's clearing out. All the journalists raced back to cover Grant's arrest, and most of the Americans are off tonight on a special chartered flight nonstop to the States. And," Paul looked solemn, "the really baddest bad news is: Hiram's not taking me to that Great White Way."

"Where?"

"New York, New York." He sniffed. "Start spreading the news, caro. I'm not leaving today or any other time."

"Oh, dear. Is it all over between you?"

He looked pained and sat next to me. "Comfort me," he whined. I held his hand and patted it gently.

"What's the good news?" I'd almost forgotten there was any.

"Oh, yeah. Hiram paid us off. Fifteen hundred for me, twenty-five hundred for you! You get a bonus for convincing Grant to give himself up."

"But I didn't!"

I lay back on the bed. I was aching, fatigued, and famished.

"Too bad, caro. We were almost real, true detectives."

I pulled him down next to me.

"We still are, Paul. More than ever. We've got to find this murderer and save Grant. It's the least I can do! I must see him. Let's fly back to Sydney first thing tomorrow morning."

"Might as well. There's no use hanging around here any longer."

He was probably right. Even though I still had grave suspicions about Pastor Paramor, I certainly didn't wish to run the risk of bumping into Merv in the street. He was probably out searching for me right now, swathed in bandages with arms outstretched like Boris Karloff in *The Mummy*.

"Caro?" Paul had assumed his serious face.

"Yes?"

"What if Grant *is* the murderer?"

I thought for a minute. "Then I want to be absolutely certain of it! And, when I get some strength back, I'll tell you all about my very amusing day."

We headed downstairs, drawn onward by pungent soup smells wafting up from the kitchen. As we reached the bottom step, Paul stopped me. "There's something else! Remember the gorgeous Dazzle?"

"Gorgeous like a python."

"Hmm," Paul mused. "There *is* something snaky about him, but I can't put my finger on it!" He giggled.

"What about Darren?"

"He wants to move to Sydney, and I said I'd put him up."

My mouth fell open. "Is that wise?" I ventured.

"Why not?"

"Well! I mean, are you sure you want a prostitute living in your flat?"

He grinned. "It pays the rent!"

CHAPTER 15

G rant and I went to bed once, in 1973. (Most people went to bed with each other in 1973.) It was an era of experimentation, and honey was the favoured additive of the time: in soybean coffee, in carob-studded muffins, and, not least of all, in lovemaking. Because we chose the sex option on impulse, as you do, no prior shopping was involved, and our lack of preparation was our downfall. We knew it was de rigueur to lick honey off each other's firm young torsos, but amazingly, Grant's communal household had run out of the stuff. We ad-libbed with marmalade. Ill-advised, I'm sorry to say. The result was a disaster, sticky in all the wrong ways. All we could work up in the end was a giggle. A firm and lasting friendship bloomed.

Although he comes across as a traditional middle-aged queen these days, Grant was quite the activist back then, demonstrating for gay equality, or at least visibility. Sexual liberation was his personal project. Self-effacing as I am, I was his precise political opposite. In fact, he once had a T-shirt made up for me that read: WE'RE QUEER, WE'RE HERE, CAN WE GO HOME NOW? Even so, Grant would drag me along to help swell the numbers at various seminal events, one of which was the first Mardi Gras march in June 1978. Nothing like the corporate-sponsored parades of today, it was a stroppy, sequineless affair complete with mandatory bashings and arrests. Grant was one of the fifty or so who cooled their heels as guests of Her Majesty. Not me, though. When the parade turned ugly, I snuck into the nearest cinema and stayed there for two consecutive sessions of *Heaven Can Wait*. I've avoided Warren Beatty ever since.

At that time Grant was having an affair with Andrew, a young chemistry student. They sat side by side in their cell singing revolutionary songs like "Get Happy," but after this exciting start, the relationship had nowhere to go but under. Andrew transferred his youthful chemistry to me and became my partner for eleven years of officially unrecognised bliss. Grant didn't seem to mind. In any case, our domestic life was so low-key I think he soon concluded he was well out of it. Andrew and I were homebodies. We socialised very little after the initial stage of showing off, preferring to stay in. I had my opera, and Andrew had whatever it was that amused him.

After Andrew dumped me, Grant offered me a consolation prize. We spent a pleasant week together in Tasmania. (Grant was sentimentally attached to the southern isle, having been born there).

Another memory stirred. Around the age of 40, I'd gone through a brief fatherhood fantasy and begun to feel I was missing out by not having children. I confessed as much to Grant. "Come on," he replied and took me out to a suburban Pizza Hut. We spent an entire Sunday afternoon there, and I quickly realised that child rearing was not an activity to which I was remotely inclined.

All this shared history came back to me in a rush on my return to Sydney. Indeed, it weighed down on my conscience. I felt responsible for Grant's predicament, and I intended to set things right.

As soon as I'd unpacked, I rang the police station where he'd been nabbed. But Grant was no longer in the state! Since the murder was a Queensland matter, the authorities had whisked him off to Brisbane where he was being held prior to his appearance before a magistrate. This was an unforeseen set-back. I simply couldn't afford a return trip. Greatly discouraged, I spent an hour trying to get Grant on the phone. When they finally did put me through, he was less than expansive.

"Thanks for your wishes at this time," he said. "Your sympathy is appreciated."

"It's all a misunderstanding."

"You're telling me. I can't believe it's gone this far." He lowered his voice. "Between you and me, the police are totally incompetent. All they've got are a few tidbits of circumstantial evidence."

"Are you sure? They might have a witness!"

"To what?"

"The murder!"

"I hope so."

"Why?"

"'Cause I didn't do it, you stupid girl!"

"Sorry. I forgot. I'm a bit stressed."

"Well, you take to the baths and relax. We'll never even go to committal. I'm seeing the magistrate this morning. She's bound to throw it out."

"Grant, a word of advice. Don't call the magistrate 'she'."

"What if it's a woman?"

"Play it by ear. But above all, don't worry. Paul and I are going to track down the real murderer."

Grant went strangely quiet. "Marc, lovey, you've done enough. Really. Please leave it alone. I've got a lawyer, why don't we let him handle all that? I have to go. Room service just arrived."

He hung up and I replaced the receiver, slightly miffed. A simple word of encouragement would not have gone amiss— a "my life is in your hands" kind of thing. Still, I wasn't about to let Grant's lack of faith get in my way.

I was making coffee when Paul rang.

"Caro, can we meet? We've got to talk, and I have to stay out of the flat. Darren's bringing home a client."

"I told you so. Come over here then."

"Yeesss, I could do that. Or we could go to a stunning new café that opened while we were away!"

"Oh, no," I said. "I'm fed up with your stunning cafés and their attitude. I don't like being insulted and ignored."

"This one isn't like that. Apparently, it's a sheer delight:

plain, simple fare, and they fall over themselves to be nice. I'm dying to try it."

"Oh, all right."

"Good. It's Café du Bois in Queen Street. Where the Greek jeweler's was."

"What? That jeweler's fixing my hall clock!"

"Not anymore. See you at three! Ciao!"

Much to my annoyance, Paul was right. The jeweler, an old gentleman with bad eyesight and brown teeth, had shut up shop. His store had been replaced by a cavern of polished wood. The floor, walls, ceiling, and stairs at the back all consisted of gleaming new timber, the various grains crisscrossing attractively. The bare tables and uncomfortably straight-backed chairs were likewise made of wood. The place smelled like a lumberyard.

When I arrived on the dot of three, Paul was already seated at a table close to the street. He likes to observe and grade passing trade during the odd lull in conversation. He was wearing an old favourite T-shirt that featured a traditional portrait of Our Lady placed over a pumped-up male torso and the caption MUSCLE MARY in rubric script.

"Caro!" he called, and beckoned me inside.

"Paul, you're early," I said as I joined him, my chair legs screeching against the polished floor.

"I had to get out quick smart," he answered. "Dazzle runs a strictly confidential service."

"That boy is trouble."

"Don't lecture me, please, Marc. If I want to shack up with the most perfectly proportioned male ever sighted since the Jurassic Era, I will shack."

He gave me a goofy look. I'm afraid I knew all too well what it meant.

"You're obsessing!"

"I'm taking him under my wing," he countered. "Besides, nobody refuses *me*! I'll wear him down, and when

I do, it'll be Christmas!" He grinned. "White Christmas."

"Just like the ones you used to know. Well, be careful. He behaved very suspiciously with me on the high seas."

"Caro..." Paul paused. "I don't mean to be rude, but what are you staring at?"

I shrugged. "I can't help noticing," I remarked, "that your hair is blue."

"Ah, so it is. I forgot. Do you like it?"

"It's...bright."

"You're not wrong. Darren helped me. I adore it. It's such a streetwise look. It seems to say, 'I don't give a shit.' "

"Don't you?"

"Of course I do! I'm desperately hair conscious!" He sighed. "You'll never understand fashion, Caro. This colour is *mucho* underground."

"I'm sure all those sweet old women in bowling clubs would be pleased to hear that."

"Don't laugh at lawn bowls. It's poised to become the next retro sensation. Are we lunching?"

He shoved a menu at me, a printed sheet tacked onto a slab of wood. I was studying it when I unexpectedly lurched backward. Someone had grabbed the back of my chair, almost wrenching it out from under me. The culprit was a chubby dark-haired boy on roller skates—our waiter.

" 'Scuse me," he said. His voice was rather strident. "I thought I was going to slip over. It's this floor. Have you boys decided?"

"I'll have the scrambled eggs with baba ghanoush on toasted olive bread," gushed Paul, "herb salsa on the side, and a long black."

"OK," the waiter answered, jotting it down. "And for sir?"

"I'm toying with the gooseberry cheesecake."

He leaned close and whispered. "Go for it! It's *to*-tally unbe-*lieva*-ble."

"That sounds like a recommendation. All right, I will."

"To drink?"

"A strong flat white."

"Marvey. Here we go!" He held on to my chair for a
moment, then veered off toward the bar.

"Now," said Paul, "down to business." He reached into his
pocket and pulled out a crumpled page.

"What's that?" I asked.

"The fax I never sent you. The one I nicked from Newton's
desk. It's fascinating. You just can't put it down!"

"I've got something to show you, too." I handed him the
folder marked "Crab Island Development Application." "I
stole this from the museum in Murphy's Inlet."

Paul beamed. "We're so businesslike, aren't we!"

"That's one word for it. Read the top letter, it's the interesting one. Alderman Jackson writing to Pastor Paramor."

"Eyes down." Paul held up a booklet. "Is this part of it?"

"No. That's the museum's catalogue."

I scrutinised Paul's fax. It had been written by Newton,
and a faint red circle in the corner indicated it had been
transmitted. It was dated the day before the murder. The
recipient was tantalisingly identified only by the initials B.F.
It read:

> For Christ's sake, what are you on about? I thought we had
> an agreement didn't we? Let me reiterate: You do a couple of
> photo sessions with Hadrian, sign a bit of harmless blurb to
> the effect that New Heaven is where you go to chill out, then
> we quietly place the ad in a few gay papers where it'll do us the
> most good. Only your gay fans will see it! Maybe a TV ad,
> later on, but late night, definitely. Does that sound so difficult?
> You have a big gay following, you know, like it or not. You are
> a very attractive man. For God's sake, let's meet and iron the
> whole thing out. I'll be back in Sydney next week. I'll take you
> to dinner, and don't get in a tizz about anybody seeing us. I'm
> always out with celebrities.

All I want from you is a simple endorsement. You don't even have to "come out"—not literally. It's a resort, not a hard-core porn video! (Although if you ever do one of those, put me on the mailing list! Joke.) You needn't worry about the trashy magazines—they're terrified of us! As for the loonies and obsessive fans: Yes, I agree it's a worry, but every star has them. I've got one or two myself! I don't think our proposal would make a scrap of difference to those people. Might even get them off your back!

Look—if I can help with anything, I'd be glad to. I've got a billion connections, as you know.

You see? I AM YOUR FRIEND! Call me! We must get together soon.

Yours,

Newton

I looked up. Paul was studying me intently.

"Well?" he asked.

"You haven't read that file already!"

"I flicked through it. I'm more interested in what you make of Newton's little note"

I sighed. "Well, B.F. is obviously the nameless celebrity."

Paul slapped his palms on the table. "Read between the lines, caro! B.F.! It must be boy friend! Newton was having a raging affair behind Hadrian's back—which we know Hadrian suspected—and this fax confirms it!"

"So you think Hadrian killed him?"

"Naturally! Hadrian was in Newton's room before we got there. Remember? And that fax was sitting on the table right under his little red basset-like eyes. He must have seen it."

"Wasn't that after the murder?"

"Well, he got wind of it the day before, OK? And get this: I believe I know what was in the box he was moving out of Newton's office. Remember all that weird hedging and carrying on? I'll bet you that box contained the murder weapon."

"Photographic equipment?"

"Precisely."

"But Newton didn't choke to death on a tripod!"

"Caro, don't be obtuse. What do photographers fiddle around with in their darkrooms? Chemicals, developers, stuff like that. Acids!"

It hadn't occurred to me, but I could see Paul's point. "You're pretty sold on Hadrian," I remarked. "Suppose B.F. doesn't mean boyfriend?"

"What does it mean, then? Bigfoot? Betty Ford?"

"And what's all that stuff about obsessive loonies?"

"Well, Hadrian strikes me as loony. Don't you think so?"

"Yes, but did Newton?"

My train of thought was interrupted by another lunge behind my chair. The waiter was upon us again, unfortunately not bearing our long-awaited food.

"I'm so, so sorry, guys," he crooned, "but we only opened last week. It's not running smoothly just yet. The bad news is, we're out of the cheesecake, and the baba ghanoush went mouldy overnight, though most of it looks OK. Anyway, sorry, sorry. We've got everything else. Would you like to see the menu again?"

He urged menus onto us.

"Just a coffee for me," I said, handing mine back.

Paul mused. "Second choice! I'll have the omelette Du Bois with chili bread, but no pulped cucumber relish."

"Right away!" our waiter beamed. "I'll bring your coffees now."

He swirled around stylishly, skidded wildly, and fell sideways into an empty table, which he pulled over on top of himself.

"It's cool, I'm fine," he called weakly.

"I told you they fall over themselves," said Paul.

I returned to the matter in hand. "Hadrian is definitely a suspect," I said, "but so, perhaps, is Claire."

"What makes you think that?"

I frowned. "Didn't you tell me she hated Newton?"

"So did three quarters of the world's population. Have you got any other reason?"

"Well, she went off searching for Newton and never returned. Why didn't she come back to my seminar?"

"Because she resented you being there. On her turf."

I was stunned. "You think so?"

"Obviously! You were clearly a case of jobs for the boys! Newton brought you in from nowhere, an unknown with no experience. Then he gave you this special appointment which turned out to be pretty damn important, and Claire was shitty! She went off in a huff."

"And ran into Grant, also in a huff. A very huffy atmosphere altogether. Perhaps she found Newton in his office and huffily let him have it."

Paul looked skeptical. "Then what? Retired to repair her nail polish? If she *had* killed him, she would have raced back to the meeting quick smart to establish an alibi."

I was lost in admiration. "Paul," I said, "when did you get this logical?"

He smiled coyly. "I've started reading thrillers."

At this moment we became aware of a sick gurgling sound emanating from the restaurant kitchen, accompanied by raised voices. Suddenly, a gaunt man in an off-white apron came striding across the room toward us. I don't recall whether he was wringing his hands, but he certainly looked as though he wanted to.

"I'm terribly sorry," he began in a familiar strain. "Your food's on its way, but our espresso machine's packed up. They assured me this wouldn't happen again, but what can you do? We only opened last week." He smiled miserably.

"I'll just have a glass of water then," I sighed.

His smile was replaced by an expression of utter disbelief. "We have fruit whips," he said. "Or chinotto—"

"I don't want fruit whips or chinotto."

He pursed his lips. "Water's on the side table. Help yourself."

"I don't think I like this place," I muttered as he strode away. With an effort, I refocused my mind onto the subject of our suspects. "Well, if you don't think Claire did it, what about the Church of Divine Intervention? They wanted the gays and lesbians out and voilà! As soon as news of murder leaked, Hiram put everything on hold."

"Including me!" Paul perused the filched file. "Who's H.P.?"

"Where?"

"Quote: 'I have faxed our requirements to H.P.'"

"I don't know."

"Phooey! H.P.! B.F.! All these pissy initials. Someone's trying to hide something from us."

"There's a barbecue sauce called H.P."

"People don't fax their requirements to a barbecue sauce." He wrinkled his brow. "And all this taking off and reaching our target. What's that about?"

"It sounds more like a military operation than a holiday," I said sourly.

Paul's eyes lit up. "Caro, I do believe you've hit it! A military operation! A bombing raid, in fact! H.P.—Halstrom Park! Where the planes were, the day Vasselina got propelled to glory." He briskly flicked through the catalogue. "And this seemingly innocent museum is chocker with old airplane parts!"

"I nearly decapitated myself on one of them."

"There's even a propeller, look! Messerschmitt, 1938." He held up the dim photograph.

"It's huge. I didn't see anything like that."

"Of course not! They chucked it at Vasselina."

I looked up. "Jackson and Paramor nicked the council's Cessna, bombed the drag acts with their ghastly artifact, and buzzed off back to Murphy's Inlet."

Paul clicked his tongue. "Looks like these religious types don't regard cross-dressing as an art form."

I reread Alderman Jackson's letter. "There's more to this than knee-jerk homophobia," I said. "It's all about property. Look. The church wants to move in and acquire the island cheap and then get a ready-built luxury resort as a bonus. They've got the shire council on side. They probably aim to turn the place into a Christian retreat."

"Oh, my Lord. Can you imagine it? Sandals and acoustic guitars and big old pots of very strong tea? How revolting!"

"I don't know about sandals. This feels like a very ambitious project. Jackson says, "We would also be amenable to further development." I paused. "Who owns the controlling interest in the resort?"

"According to Hiram, he does. Very smug about it, too!"

I frowned. "That's a pity. I was hoping it was Newton. That might have given these bastards more reason for killing him."

"Language, caro, puh-lease! You're starting to sound heterosexual."

"Sorry, but I feel strongly."

"Anyway, those 'bastards' couldn't have done it. Jackson and Paramor were both present and accounted for at the meeting. They did most of the talking!"

"I know, I know. We must find out more. We'll never get anywhere sitting around starving in coffee shops. It's time to act!"

So we started to draw up some plans, just like true professionals. Paul was to search out the location of Hadrian's studio. It was high time we paid him a visit. My own work would involve a few hours on the phone, checking the details of Vasselina's demise. For example, was the fatal propeller part of a 1938 Messerschmitt? It shouldn't be too hard to confirm, as there had been a volley of newspaper coverage. I would also need to ring someone at Halstrom Park. If we could place Alderman Jackson and Pastor Paramor at the scene of that crime, we might eventually link them to Newton. I was convinced that one or other of these roads would lead us to the killer.

I had a spring in my step as we strode back to the car. At last our investigations were getting somewhere! I dropped Paul off at his flat and dithered around at home, but I was a caged beast. The tension and excitement were too much. My blood was up and not even the most elevating passages of Puccini could calm me. I was in the mood for *Götter-dämmerung*. When you get like that, there's nothing to do but prowl. I washed my hair and selected my sexiest T-shirt, black and not too tight. I'd been through a long dry spell and was determined to go mildly berserk.

CHAPTER 16

I t was early evening by the time I got to Oxford Street, not the most exciting time of the day or night, but Legends was open. I popped up to the comfy first-floor lounge, where the DJ specialised in screaming disco stars of the '70s. It was one of the quieter rooms on the strip.

The bar was almost deserted, so I snuggled into a cozy spot near the window where I could see the clientele arrive and stare into the street below if I felt like it. It was a perfect position, and although I'm not especially skilled at cruising, I nonetheless felt confidently cuddly and refreshingly mature.

I sipped a Black Russian and let my mind wander. I thought about Newton's fax to the uncooperative celebrity. I really couldn't see any indication that they were having it off. Paul was mistaken. It was simply a business letter in Newton's regular over-the-top mode. Even so, I had the feeling I'd missed something. Was it to do with those enigmatic initials: B.F.? I wracked my rapidly relaxing brain and remembered that Grant had gone to confront Newton over the matter of a boyfriend. What if they were one and the same: Grant's boyfriend and Newton's celebrity? Grant hadn't mentioned whether his friend was famous, but it stood to reason. He was always meeting celebrities in his line of work.

I would have to discover this elusive B.F. character's identity. Maybe Delia Scott-Merman had managed to root him out. She had struck me as persistent. Whether she was prepared to pass on such information, under the Freedom of Gossip Act, was another matter.

I got a refill and shut my brain down for the night. By now, the lounge had begun to fill with quite a cross section of lizards. All the cutest men were in couples, naturally; it must have been Monogamy Night.

Eventually, a man about my age plonked himself down in the adjacent window seat. He was very tanned, balding, and had a heavy five o'clock shadow. He stretched out his legs, glanced around briefly, then stared out of the window. I appraised his neatly packed blue jeans and red T-shirt, over which he wore a cheeky leather vest. He seemed approachable. This might be just the thing, I thought to myself. I got a dazzling smile all ready to spring into action the moment he looked across again, but he just kept gazing into the street below. After a while, I did the same.

The boulevard was bustling, a passing parade of scene queens amongst the regular misfits and drunks who made their home there. Every so often, an absolute god would lope into view. One, a big, tousle-haired blond in a tight sleeveless top, impressed me particularly. I ogled him as he sauntered up the street. When he was directly opposite he looked up, smiled, and waved. I was taken aback. If I knew someone that gorgeous, surely I'd remember! I waved back tentatively. He suddenly skipped into the traffic and ran across the road toward me. "Hey!" he cried as he landed on the pavement beneath my window.

"How are you doing?" called the man in the adjacent window seat. I slunk back down into my chair and sipped my drink uncomfortably. "You off to the club tonight?" the man shouted.

"Yeah! Right now!" the boy called back.

"I thought you were flying home to the States?"

"Tomorrow!"

"You have a good trip."

"Guess I will! See ya!"

"See you, Wade!"

Wade! As the boy darted back into the traffic, the name hit me over the head like a book about tropical fish. It was him! I jumped to my feet, bumping the table and upsetting my drink. The tanned man looked up.

"Where's that boy going?" I demanded.

"Sorry? Who?"

"That boy. Wade! Where's he going?"

The man's lips assumed an expression of enigmatic amusement. "Minnesota, I believe."

"I mean now! Oh, never mind," I fumed. I shoved a twenty-dollar note into his hand. "Here," I said. "Pay for my drinks, and have one yourself." His eyes opened in astonishment as I left him and bounded down the stairs.

Out on Oxford Street I peered about frantically. Every person of every possible sex suddenly had blond hair and a white T-shirt. "Wade!" I screamed to no avail. It was hopeless. Then I spotted him on the opposite side of the street, looking in the window of a leather goods shop. "Wade!" I cried again, but he didn't hear me and began to amble away. I sprinted, desperately trying not to lose sight of him behind the multitude of buses and cars cluttering up the concourse.

An opportunity to cross finally presented itself, as soon as a bus had passed. The boy was still in sight. I braced myself and waited on tenterhooks. The bus pulled up and the doors banged open. Nobody got off. As the seconds ticked by, I gritted my teeth in impatience. The driver stared at me, as though I were an imbecile.

"Are you getting on?" he shouted.

Belatedly I realised I was standing at a bus stop. "No!" I snapped.

The driver raised his eyes heavenward, slammed the doors shut, and drove away, just in time to reveal Wade disappearing into a dark doorway farther up the road. I ran toward the spot, but when I got there, the door was shut tight and locked. It was a metallic door painted black, sandwiched between a newsagent and the Salvation Army thrift shop. There was no sign around to suggest what was housed there, though I had a vague idea—the windows on the floor above were completely blacked out. I knocked several times, tentatively at first, then more loudly, but got no response. I stepped back, despairing.

As I did, a man sauntered toward me. He was short and built like an old-fashioned wood-burning stove. He appeared to be sweating, even though he wore very little. His entire outfit was black leather, comprising boots, shorts, vest, and cap. He sported a white moustache, pointed at the ends, and on close examination appeared to be in his early 70s. He looked me up and down for a split second, then reached to the top of the doorframe and pressed a tiny black button that I hadn't noticed. With a buzz the door unlocked and the old man shoved it open, revealing a stairwell on the other side.

"Excuse me," I said quickly, "but is this the, er, club?"

"Too right it is, petal," he replied in a wheezy voice. "It's known as the Bunker."

"The Bunker!"

He smiled, propping the heavy door open with some difficulty. "A charming gentlemen's health-and-leisure facility. Come down with me. You'll love it."

I hesitated. The name was not unfamiliar to me, thanks to Paul. I haven't led an entirely sheltered life, but compared to that boy I'm a total novice. He's seen and done everything—and will describe it energetically. Yet even Paul admits you have to draw the line somewhere. The Bunker is where he draws it. I found myself unnerved to discover that a place I'd always presumed to be an urban myth did, in fact, exist. A muscle deep inside me contracted involuntarily.

"Make up your mind, dear," the man gasped. "This door's heavy."

"Oh, all right," I said, thinking of Wade, and we both headed inside. The door slammed shut behind us with a clang.

The stairwell was very dark, lit only by a single violet globe. At the bottom was an alcove, which opened out to reveal a dingy second door adjacent to a barred window. The old man walked straight through the door, closing it in my face. I tried to push it open, but the studded iron panel wouldn't budge.

Not again! The metalworkers' union had done very well out of this establishment, I thought sourly.

"Are you a member?"

I turned to be confronted by two beady red eyes lurking behind the window grill. They belonged to a pale, sandy-haired man who seemed not to have had a wink of sleep for some years.

"No, I'm not a member."

He yawned offhandedly. "Thirty-five dollars, please."

"What?"

"Thirty-five. That's a month's membership."

"I don't want a month, I want to go in now! Just for a minute."

He smiled, revealing an ill-sorted set of discoloured teeth. "We don't do memberships by the minute."

"One night, then."

"It's a week minimum. Twenty bucks."

"Why is it twenty for one week if it's thirty-five for a month?" I huffed.

"Special offer."

I snuck a peek in my wallet. Twenty would completely clean me out. If only I could grab Wade, I could take him somewhere else. Like my place!

"I'd like to speak to the manager!" I said.

"He's inside."

"Oh, damn it." I produced my wallet and bade a heart-rending farewell to my last twenty dollars.

The door swung open, and I stumbled into pitch darkness. I reached out to my right and touched a slimy stone wall. I appeared to be in a corridor. A purple glow dimly illuminated the far end, where hazy figures wafted in and out of the shadows.

I edged along the passage. As my eyes grew accustomed to the dimness I saw doorways on my left. I was passing a series of rooms. Some of the doors were open, others were ominously ajar. Way off somewhere I could hear suggestive groaning. I quickened my pace till I was opposite an open door. "Wade?" I whispered. I heard a sort of rustling noise in response. I peeked in. The dimly lit room seemed empty. I took a step forward.

Inside was a bench and a leather hammock, the latter suspended from the ceiling by thick metal chains and swinging slightly to and fro. I reached over and stilled it. The leather was thick and tough. I sniffed. The air was permeated by a chemical odour, like some cleansing agent years past its use-by date.

"Kiss the floor!"

I almost leapt out of my skin. I spun around, my heart thumping. There, standing against the wall, legs and arms akimbo, was a naked man. When I say naked, I don't mean he was completely unadorned: he wore boots and an executioner's mask, and several metal things wedged into various hard-to-get-at parts of the body. He flexed his pumped-up pectorals.

"Did you hear me, slave?" he barked, in the same commanding though high-pitched tone. "Get down on that floor. Lick it."

I gaped. "I will do no such thing," I replied.

"Kiss that floor, worm!"

"Kiss it yourself," I snapped. This was getting beyond a joke. Why did I keep finding myself in these unbelievably sleazy situations? Things like this never happened to me when I taught languages to upper-class schoolgirls.

The masked man gulped. I glared at him. "Aw, poop," he said. "I knew I couldn't do this. I'll never be the master." I toyed with the idea of making a quick getaway. "Give me a hug?" he asked piteously, and tore off the mask. "Please?" He had quite a pretty face: big, clear eyes and Cupid's bow lips.

"Come here," I said, and he slumped into my arms, a dead weight.

"I'm no good at this at all," he sobbed.

"Shh, yes, you are," I whispered, patting him encouragingly on the bum. "Cheer up. I'm sure somebody will lick the floor for you." (Although frankly I doubted it.)

"I'm a failure. My voice is all wrong."

"No, it's very authoritative. You must be in the army or something."

He looked up, his cow eyes wet with tears. "I am. I'm in the SAS."

"Ah, well, there you are. You see? Now I'm looking for a friend of mine, Wade, so I have to go. Otherwise I'd stay and slurp all over the place."

He smiled. "You're sweet. You remind me of my dad."

Not *this* again, I thought! I maneuvered him onto the bench.

"This Wade guy," he said. "Is he American?"

"Yes! Have you seen him?"

"He's got a tattoo on his shoulder? A mutant ninja turtle with big balls?"

"Er, possibly."

He frowned. "I thought you said he was your friend."

"He chews gum. Peppermint, I think."

"Yeah, that's him. He's probably playing pool. There's a recreation room around the corner."

I bade my wannabe master a quick goodbye, and found myself back in the dank corridor. I couldn't see any sign of a recreation room—in fact, I couldn't see anything much at all. I inched along the cool brick wall. I'd just about had enough of this when the wall gave way, and I lurched wildly into another pitch-black alcove. I had no idea where I was, but I instinctively knew I wasn't alone. And then I smelled the pungent odour of peppermint.

"Wade?" I whispered.

"Huh?" came a voice.

"Wade! Is that you? Come here!"

There was a pause. "'Scuse me, guys," said Wade. The aroma became stronger. "Where are you?"

"Here!" I said.

"Where?"

A warm finger poked me in the eye.

"Ow!"

"Sorry, man."

And then I felt his arms encircling me. He drew me into a massive clinch and kissed me violently. Pleasant memories instantly surfaced—memories of a simpler, more innocent time—before our gruesome discovery. After a passionate few minutes, feeling myself drifting into a peppermint coma, I lay my head on Wade's hard warm chest. He was wearing a sweaty singlet. I ran my hands down his back and discovered he was nude from the waist down. We languidly kissed once more.

"Mmm," he moaned. "Say, who is this anyways?"

"It's Marc," I panted.

"Ah, yeah..." he replied vaguely.

"We once ignited a corpse together."

Wade stopped what he was doing and held me at arm's length. "Oh, shit!" he exclaimed. He grabbed me tightly and shoved me out the door. We bumped up against the wall in the corridor.

"Ow! Hey—" I said.

"I been thinkin' about that," Wade grunted, continuing to push me along. "Yeah, like, a whole lot! Let's get outta here."

"Yes, we must talk. Look, whatever you may be thinking—"

"In here!"

I twisted my head around. "No, not there!" It was the sling room. "Somebody's using it."

"So?"

"Er, well, it's not good manners to barge in, uninvited."

"You're cute." He peered cautiously into the room. "Whoever it was, he's gone. C'mon!"

He forced me through the door and slammed it shut behind us. In the dim purple light I could see him at last. He was staring at me, slowly nodding his head.

"Wade—" I began.

"How'd you find me?"

"Sheer luck," I said.

"I'm leavin' tomorrow."

"Yes, I know. Um, have you spoken to anyone about what happened?"

"Nah."

There was an awkward gap in the conversation.

"Is that a mutant ninja turtle?" I asked.

He glanced at the tattoo on his shoulder. "I was a kid," he sighed. "Everybody makes mistakes."

"Yes, well."

"Marc, listen, man, I didn't tell nobody what you done. OK?"

"What did I do?"

"Don't worry 'bout me. I know nothin' about nothin'— it's between you and him. Whatever. It's cool." He smiled conspiratorially.

"Now look here," I blustered, "I know I led you to Newton's body, but you must understand, I never had the faintest idea…"

His eyes shone in the half-light. "You didn't murder the guy?"

"No! Of course not. Surely you remember how surprised I was when we found him! You must believe me."

He nodded. "Yeah, I guess I do."

"Good. Well, at least that's settled." I relaxed slightly. "I'm so pleased to see you again. What have you been doing with yourself? Enjoying Sydney? You certainly know your way around…"

He looked at me strangely. "Say you killed him."

"What? I didn't!"

"Say you did."

"But I didn't!"

"I know, but say you did! Just say it! Say you, like,

slaughtered him, and then dragged me over to have sex right there. Right over the body."

"What?"

"It's such a turn on, man! I can't stop thinkin' about it." I noticed he was growing very animated.

"Wade? " I hesitated. "Are you feeling all right?"

"I feel great! But just *say* it! Like, talk me through it. Let's do it over again!"

"I don't know…"

Gently, he nibbled my ear. "Can't we have a little fun?" he whispered. "I really like you, yeah?"

"Me too. You, I mean."

"So what are you scared of? We got all night. Don't ya get off on a bit of weird sex?"

My heart sank. "I don't know, Wade. Is it really necessary to…?"

But by that time he'd given up on me and had decided to play all the parts. Grabbing my arms, he steered me around the room.

"Let's go this way…" he murmured stagily. "Over here. Say, what is that? Oh my Gaaaad! It's a dead body, man. Fuck, it's like a corpse. And there's acid all over. Oh, man! Hey, you wanna set the guy alight? You bet! OK, here. Use my Zippo. Yeah! Take that, you asshole! Burn, baby! Burn! Oh, fu-u-u-u-uck!"

Suddenly he was tearing my clothes off me. The sling was swinging and, not to beat around the bush, I succumbed to the moment. As one usually does.

It was the beginning of an unusual but romantic and memorable evening. Terribly disrespectful to Newton, of course—yet, somehow, I think he would have wanted it that way.

CHAPTER 17

T he next day, Wade soared off to Minnesota for good, or at least until the Mardi Gras after next, but first we indulged in a costly Oxford Street breakfast together. He seemed disinclined to return to the subject of Newton's death, but I insisted, explaining that I was investigating the murder on a private commission from Hiram Hudson himself. This whitish lie impressed Wade deeply, and he told me everything.

After he'd helped me dispose of the body in the carp pool, the poor boy had suffered a troubled, sleepless night. At the first light of dawn he'd headed straight for Hiram, begging to be kept out of any official inquiries. Apparently, Wade had a "record" back home concerning unpaid parking fines in five different states (which I must say struck me as frivolous). Hiram had advised him to make himself scarce but privately assured him that no "gay or lesbian" would be implicated in the murder, let alone held responsible for it. This assurance lifted a great weight off Wade's impulsively tattooed shoulders. He continued to enjoy what was left of his holiday in Sydney and gave no more thought to dead bodies, except when prompted by a surge of hormonal activity.

So far our conversation had shed no light whatsoever on Newton's murder, but when I asked him about the bush-walk to Murphy's Beach, however, he was much more informative.

In spite of being nominally attached to a travel agency, Wade had no interest in views, scenery, or the myriad wonders of nature. He had come to New Heaven for one reason alone: to get his rocks off. So when Newton suddenly insisted the American contingent wander off on a four-hour trek, Wade was disinclined to go, reasoning that four hours spent gawking at unique native foliage was four hours wasted out of his jam-packed sex life. Still, he tagged along, encouraged by the promise of a foaming nude frolic in the surf at Murphy's Beach.

Forty-five minutes into the walk, Wade had fallen behind the others and found himself in the company of the only Australian in the group, Hadrian. The two of them chatted for a while until Hadrian, not one to miss an opportunity, asked Wade to pose au naturel. Just about every man Wade ever met suggested this—but Hadrian had the added inducement of a camera.

Wade agreed, stripped, briskly pumped up, and fell into three or four tasteful poses, making much imaginative use of Tolkienesque ferns and dappled sunlight. Hadrian's shutter clicked away, and a good time was had by all until Hadrian's attention wandered. He suddenly became agitated, saying that he needed to get back to the resort and develop the film immediately. When Wade tried to accompany him, Hadrian insisted that he had to go alone and that Wade should catch up to the other Americans. Then he scuttled away and Wade never saw him again.

It was this strange change in Hadrian's behaviour that had been worrying Wade ever since. "I saw the picture of some dude they charged," he said, "and I was thinking, like, did they get the right guy?"

"I don't think so." I patted his knee.

Soon it was time to go. Even though I was hardly at my most alert, I generously drove Wade to his hotel and on to the airport, where we exchanged addresses. As he kissed me goodbye, Wade promised to look me up next time he was in Sydney. I had the distinct feeling that, given time, our relationship could have turned into something deeper and slightly less kinky.

On my groggy drive home I mulled over Wade's story. If Hadrian had turned back after forty-five minutes, he would have arrived at the resort some time around 3:30 P.M., an hour and a half before my meeting. In other words, he not only had motive; he now had opportunity. And why had he been in such a hurry? I desperately needed to find him.

Not this morning, however. I'd been up all night with Wade and looked forward to a hard-earned nap. Unusually, I was able to park within a block of the house. My front gate was wide open—I generally leave it latched when I'm out—but I was too tired to care. I staggered inside, showered, donned my turquoise silk dressing gown with the Chinese dragon (for private indoor use only) and splashed boiling water over a sachet of chamomile tea. I slid a quiet CD into the machine— Tebaldi's exquisite song recital with piano accompaniment— and started upstairs. Out of the corner of my eye, I spied the insidious flickering light of my answer phone on the hall table.

Sighing with impatience, I played it back. It was crammed with messages, mostly from people I'd never heard of.

"Mr. Petrucci, this is Antonia Chang of Ashburn and Bell, solicitors. We are executors of the estate of the late Mr. Newton Heath. Would you be kind enough to return my call as soon as you can? I'm contactable on…"

"Message for Marc Petrucci. Please call Ted Fuller at *News Limited*. The number's…"

"Yes, Mr. Petrucci. How are you? I'm from 2ZAP FM, Current Affairs Radio. We'd like to do a phoner about the Heath murder. Could you buzz Wendy Hollier on…"

"Hello. This is Celeste Ireland. I'm a reporter for *Queer Scene,* Australia's leading gay and lesbian newspaper. I'd like to talk to you urgently about Newton Heath. Please call me at home on…"

"Aren't you home yet, you dirty, dirty thing? Yes, caro, don't deny it! You were spied out on the prowl last night by hundreds of my henchmen. And you were spotted this morning, gorging bagels and bean sprouts with some hunk. Well, spill the beans! Ring my mobile and do it now! Incidentally, Hadrian uses a studio in Alexandria. I think he lives there too. I called by last night—see, at least one of us was being good!

He wasn't receiving. I didn't leave my card. We should try again today. Phone me!"

"Marc? I hope this is the right number. It's Delia Scott-Merman. I think we should talk. Call me any time on my mobile…"

"Martin Leak from *Leak on Sunday*. I'll call back."

"Wendy Hollier here, 2ZAP FM. I'll call again later."

In a tizz I whacked the "off" button. I'd seen a couple of newspaper headlines about Newton's murder, but why did everyone suddenly want to grill me about it? I detest being put on the spot. I wiped all the messages except for Delia's and the solicitors'. Perhaps Newton had left me a legacy? It was the least he could do considering all the trouble he'd caused.

I climbed the stairs to my bedroom. Disrobing, I glanced out the window as I usually do to check whether I should have closed the curtains, and I was alarmed to see a police car double-parked outside.

As I stared, the doorbell rang. I grabbed my robe and rushed to answer the door. Now what? Had they changed their minds about Grant and set their sights on me? Or had I done something else? Police always bring out a deep feeling of guilt—a throwback to the days when my "tendencies" automatically made me an outlaw.

A policewoman stood at the doorstep.

"Marc Petrucci?" she asked brightly, frisking me with a professional eye.

"That's me."

"Nice robe. I'm Constable Smith. Do you have any I.D.?"

"Er, not on me."

"I can see that."

I found my driver's license. In the photograph I bear a striking resemblance to a groper. She frowned at it, and I flushed. "The photographer asked me the time, and just as I looked at my watch, he snapped the shutter. That's why my mouth's open and I'm sort of looking down."

She grinned, then handed it back apologetically. "I have a summons for you. We tried last night, but you were out."

"A summons?"

" 'Fraid so." She shrugged, holding a nasty looking document out to me. "The court requires you to appear at the committal hearing of Grant Breen. In the matter of the Heath murder."

It was so official, I lost my cool. "I don't understand! Why me? I..."

"Relax, Mr. Petrucci. It's just routine." She smiled. "Here, you'd better take this. It'll explain everything."

She handed me a brochure. The cover featured a glossy photo of a policeman grinning at a housewife whose expression was one of delighted surprise, as though she'd won a Christmas hamper. Above this was printed the title: YOU AND YOUR SUMMONS.

Inside there were brief, uplifting messages from the sheriff and a high court judge, among others. There was even an entry form for a "court competition," a regular monthly raffle open to witnesses and interested parties such as friends or family of the accused. I was intrigued. Entrants were required to answer a series of simple questions on procedure, such as: "Are you permitted to bring the following items into court: (a) video camera, (b) lunch, (c) concealed weapons?" I couldn't find any reference to a prize. Perhaps the winner got his or her friend's sentence reduced.

"Is there a prize?" I asked, looking up, but the constable had gone. I checked the summons. The hearing was only ten days away! I had to contact the court officer immediately and make arrangements to be in Brisbane on that day. The court would pay for my travel and accommodation.

I reheated my tea in the microwave and flipped Tebaldi back to track one. As my head hit the pillow, the phone rang. Exhausted, I dragged my weary body downstairs once more.

"Marc Petrucci?"

GAY RESORT MURDER SHOCK

"Speaking."

"Where've you been? I left a message."

"I'm sorry, who is this?"

"Celeste Ireland from *Queer Scene,* Australia's number-one gay and lesbian—"

"I don't have anything to say to the press. I'm sorry."

"I get it," she replied. "Pathetic."

"I beg your pardon?"

"How much are they paying you for your story?"

"Who?"

"You tell *me*! Channel Nine, whoever."

"Nobody's paying me anything. Now if you'll excuse me, I'm going back to bed."

"It's eleven o'clock in the morning."

"Is it? Well, I've had a full night."

"And while you sleep the day away," she continued forcefully, "what's happening around you?"

"A jumbo jets lands every two minutes."

"I'll tell you what's happening. The country's edging its way into a state of right-wing homophobic frenzy! They already think we're sick. They already think we do nothing but fondle their kids. They reckon we've got more money than they do, enjoy ourselves too much, and now they think we're psychopathic killers as well! Just like in the movies. You're happy with that scenario, are you?"

"No! Of course not."

"Then tell your story, man! Have you seen the dailies? 'Camp Killing at Gay Resort'! 'Screaming Queen Drops Acid'! I mean, it's stereotyping of the worst kind. The one and only place you'll get unbiased coverage of this murder is in the gay papers. We must speak out! Proud and loud! You sat on the fence in your community meeting, but the time for that is past. You owe it to Newton to speak out now."

I gave in. "Yes, all right. I'll—I'll just get my tea."

I was tired and shaky. What was I going to say? Anything I

told her about the murder might be in contempt of court, and I certainly didn't want to make things any worse for Grant. Shakily, I retrieved the receiver.

"I'm back."

"Good. OK. Tell me all about this Church of Divine Intervention."

"I don't really know anything about them."

"Well, you ought to! You were Gaytour's community liaison officer! What about the rumour that one or more high office holders in this so-called church are heavily closeted homosexuals? What do you think about that? Would you like to see them outed?"

I couldn't believe what I was hearing.

"Who told you that?" I stammered.

"I have my sources. And frankly, mate, I have a gut feeling you know a heck of a lot more than I do, but I'm writing this piece up with or without your cooperation."

"I am cooperating! But nobody's linked this murder to the Church of Divine Intervention."

"Not yet. So what do you know about the murder?"

"Wouldn't that be, er, sub judice?"

"In my professional opinion, no, it wouldn't."

"Ah. Well, I did discover the body. With Claire Bornkamp. She's the New Heaven Lesbian Coordinator."

She paused. "Right. And?"

"Um, he was covered with acid."

"We all know that! So what else can you tell me?"

"Er, nothing."

The journalist sighed. "Worse than useless. So is the resort opening as planned, or not?"

"Well, er, that remains to be seen."

"Sounds like a 'no' to me. Right, thanks very much."

I waited for the next question, but there was silence at the other end. She'd hung up! I had an uneasy feeling the interview hadn't gone well. I determined to do no more of them.

By now I no longer felt sleepy. I sat at the kitchen table and pondered. Who could have been hinting to the press about some churchgoer's penchant for "real men"? I nodded. Paul, of course, who else! I rang him at once and got Darren.

"Paul's not here. I sent him out for some beer."

"Well, could he call me when he gets back?"

I rang off and walked restlessly around the house, looking for some useful pursuit to fill in the time. Beside my bed lay a pile of unwashed clothes from the resort, still salty, sandy, and probably crab-infested. I gathered them up, blundered out to the laundry, and shoved them into the washing machine.

Outside the laundry window a gentle breeze stirred the yellowing leaves of the old Liquidambar, my favourite of the two trees in my yard. I gazed at it, admiring its early autumnal hue. As I stared, a significant fact gradually came to me: The window was wide open. But I hadn't set foot inside the laundry since my return! I suddenly recalled the open gate that greeted me when I'd arrived home.

I wandered nervously from room to room, checking for signs of tampering. Nothing, it seemed, had been touched. Very odd, I thought. I'd been burgled before, like everyone else in the street, and the results had been instantly obvious: alien smudges on the wall, an unusual scent in the air, increased living space produced by the absence of TV and video. The notion that some felon had broken in simply to stand still and look around made my flesh creep.

It occurred to me, not for the first time but more forcefully than ever, that a cold-blooded killer was still on the loose, someone who could throw deadly acid into a lawyer's face without so much as a second thought. Furtively, I slipped back inside and locked the window shut, just as the silence was shattered by the screaming jangle of the phone. If I was a cat, I now would have had around six and a half lives left.

I picked up the receiver with a trembling hand.

"Caro?" whispered a distant voice.

"Paul, is that you? Why are you whispering?"

"I'm on my mobile."

"Where are you?"

There was complete silence. "Hello?" I called.

"Not so loud!"

"Where are you?" I whispered.

"I can't stay chatting," he replied. "Don't go ballistic, caro, just help."

"Help?"

"I'm in Hadrian's studio. I thought I'd be a stickybeak, so I kind of snuck in—there was no one here—but now somebody's come back and…" He stopped mid-sentence.

"And what? Hello? *Hello?*"

"Shhh!"

"Is Hadrian there?"

"No, other people. They don't know I'm here. I'm in a cupboard."

CHAPTER 18

I drove to the address Paul had babbled hastily over the phone, found Hadrian's building, and parked in a half-hour zone nearby.

I was in a light-industrial part of the city, consisting almost entirely of old warehouses. Some were home to businesses that sold hotel kitchen fittings or specialised in automotive rust-proofing. Others were used for storage. Many of the buildings I passed had been converted into residences. These ranged all the way from newspaper-strewn squats to glassed-in solar-powered edifices, the latter lovingly made over and daubed in pastel versions of the same browns and greys they'd been before. The block where Hadrian's studio was situated fell somewhere in the middle of these extremes. On the outside it appeared derelict, but inside, I suspected, lurked all the comforts of home and hearth—not to mention several video-art installations.

Paul had been unable to see who was in the studio or what they were doing. He had heard giggling and water running from time to time, and once somebody said quite clearly, "Now close your eyes." Then he'd heard a high-pitched squeal. Paul had guessed his unknown, unknowing captors were women and that Hadrian was not among them—unless he was being deliberately mute. Paul was about to tell me what floor he was on and how to get there when the call was abruptly terminated. I hoped that didn't signify discovery.

I scoured my mind for a plausible excuse to get into the studio and sniff around, and decided to keep it simple. I would be an anonymous customer of Hadrian's, come to pick up some prints. What I would do when I found Paul was another matter. I literally had no idea. Creative spur-of-the-moment ad-libbing would have to suffice.

First, however, I needed to find the entrance. There were

two doors on street level, both shut. One was a rusty, metallic roller-door, with NO PARKING DAY OR NIGHT printed on it in faded red paint. Adjacent was a smaller door, smeared with street graffiti and equipped with an ancient buzzer panel. It serviced fourteen flats, but there were no legible name tags left, and half the buzzers had been removed, leaving little holes with orange wires sticking out. Nowhere was there any mention of Hadrian's name or photographic studio. His business must have relied exclusively on word of mouth.

Slowly and deliberately I pressed all the existing buzzers. The speaker on the panel made no response, save the odd crackling sound. I was about to go when a raspy voice said: "Yeah?"

I leaned in close. "Hello?" I shouted. "I'm looking for Hadrian—" I stopped short. I didn't know his second name. "Er, Hadrian, the photographer. I have to pick something up." There was no reply. "Hello? Are you still there?"

I waited but nothing more happened. I couldn't even tell which flat had responded. I was wandering away for the second time when I heard a low-pitched electronic hum. I gazed about. It took me a moment to ascertain that the hum came from the speaker: the raspy-voiced person must be unlocking the door for me! I lunged just as the noise ceased. The door didn't budge. I pressed all the buzzers again and waited. This time no one answered.

Whistling cheerily, so as not to look like some felon lingering with intent, I strolled around the side of the building and down a dead-end alley. Here I found an ancient fire escape clinging rustily to the bricks. It ended abruptly in midair. The bottom step loomed three or four feet above my head. On each level of the fire escape was a narrow platform and a steel door. The door on the second floor was warped and slightly ajar.

Lining the curb stood a row of green plastic garbage bins, the large type with wheels. I had no alternative. Selecting the strongest and least smelly bin, I wheeled it to a spot beneath the stairs. Carefully, I climbed on top. Knees wobbling, I reached for the fire escape and awkwardly managed to raise my left leg onto the bottom step. In this unattractive position my body seized up. A searing pain shot across my lower back, a legacy from my recent ballet with the tin of paint. Gritting my teeth, I kicked my other leg off the bin and against the brick wall. The momentum set the bin rolling away down the alley, where it careered headlong into another one, knocking them both over and spilling rotting garbage into the street. I clambered onto the stairs and sat rigidly, holding my breath. No one came to investigate the clatter. When all was quiet once more, I snuck up to the fire door and, with remarkably little effort, forced it open. I slipped inside.

I found myself in a large uninhabited room divided by partitions. Evidently, it had once been a makeshift suite of offices. The walls and bare wooden floor were thick with dust. Dismal sunlight struggled in through two grimy semicircular windows. The smell of mould was everywhere; my breathing instantly turned asthmatic. In a corner I spied some cardboard boxes, broken wooden chairs, and .a pile of rubbish covered with a filthy tarpaulin. At the far end was a door with chipped paintwork and a frosted glass panel: my way out.

This was not Hadrian's floor. Clearly, nobody had set foot in here for years. Yet, as I wended my wheezy way through, I realised my initial impression was wrong. A trail of stark foot-prints adorned the dusty floor. They led to the pile of trash, where they became confused and blurred. Following them, I bent down and pulled back the stiff old sheet of canvas. A dozen cockroaches scuttled in all directions, one of them up my trouser leg. I stifled a cry and hopped back, dislodging the misguided creature.

I stared at the mess I'd uncovered: crates, yellowed papers, and stained curtains, all inexpertly arranged to cover up two white plastic containers. These, in contrast, were clean and new. The labels grimly announced the word POISON. I peered closer and read the following warning: DANGER! HYDROFLUORIC ACID. AVOID CONTACT WITH SKIN OR EYES. DO NOT INGEST. NEUTRALISING AGENT: CALCIUM GLUCONATE.

I caught my breath. Acidic fumes wafted into my nose and eyes—the same fumes I had last inhaled behind the lunch area at the top of the resort. I straightened up and sneezed. Immediately, there came a sound—a scuff or bump—possibly from one of the disused offices. I froze. When nothing further happened, I snuck cautiously toward the door. The old offices all seemed to be empty. I must have startled a rat, I told myself, or someone decided to practise Irish dancing in the flat above. In either case, it was time to move on.

The door, which fortunately had no lock, opened into a dusty foyer. There I found an old goods lift, a cage of thick mesh wire. I pressed the cracked button on its tarnished brass plate and waited. In its own good time, the elevator arrived, preceded by ancient swinging ropes.

I got out on the next floor. The landing was markedly cleaner than the one below, though it smelled faintly of vomit. There were two flats on this level, numbers 3 and 4. Number 3 looked derelict, but the door to number four was painted a dazzling bright green. Across the top in purple script were the letters H & F. Crossing my fingers and hoping the H referred to Hadrian, I knocked briskly.

After a moment the door creaked open a fraction, and I was face-to-face with a skinny young woman. She had pale eyes and fuzzy pink hair; a single silver stud nuzzled her lower lip. Gentle music wafted in the background—a bamboo flute or some such primitive instrument.

Before I could speak, the girl screwed up her face and sniffed the air. "Have you been sick?" she said accusingly.

"No," I answered.

"Oh. Must be the junkies in number three. Did they open the front door for you?"

"I suppose so."

She nodded. "Nobody else will. I won't 'cause I don't wanna get ripped off?"

She had that irritating and peculiarly Australian habit of finishing phrases with an upward inflection.

"What do you want?" she added, glaring suspiciously.

"I'm looking for Hadrian. The photographer."

She shrugged. "He's out. Try again tomorrow, but ring first?"

She began to close the door.

"Wait—" I said. "May I come in?"

"I'm in the middle of a shoot," she answered. "Hadrian's not in."

"I know, but I'm meant to pick up some prints. He said they'd be ready."

She peered at me. "I don't know you, do I? What's your name?"

"Marc, P—um, Petrie."

"Nah. Hadrian never mentioned it. He hasn't been around much lately."

I smiled sweetly. "Please, can I just see if my prints are here? I need them urgently. In fact, I must have them today!"

"OK." Reluctantly, she opened the door. "But I'm busy, like I say. I can't be looking for stuff."

"That's fine, I'll do it myself. I know exactly what I'm after."

I stepped into a room the same size as the one directly below. Here, too, were a couple of old office partitions, but in every other respect the place couldn't have been more different. There was colourful junk everywhere: mattresses, weirdly shaped chairs that stuck out at odd angles, bean bags, desks covered in magazines and photographs, daunting sound equipment, and gigantic dyed cloths hanging from the ceiling. There were enough kitsch ornaments to document the 1950s in scrupulous chronological detail.

Each wall was painted a different colour. Beside the window, a vivid blue cloth had been attached to the wall and rolled out onto the wooden floor. Big hunks of polystyrene were arranged on stands nearby, and a camera balancing on a tripod stood several feet away. The girl strolled over to it, flicked on a blinding spotlight, and peered through the lens.

The camera was pointed at a queen-size bed bedecked with black satin sheets. Lazily draped across the bed was a woman, absolutely naked, her skin painted a deep violet. I stared. On various parts of her body were arranged a number of large garden snails, each one pink with a crimson circle daubed on its shell. They looked like tiny, brittle breasts.

"Hi," said the naked girl, though she didn't sit up.

"Hello there," I replied.

"This is Lou." remarked the photographer. "I'm Fog. Lou's posing for me. It's a series called *Jardin du Désir*. That means 'garden of desire'?"

"Ah. Well, don't mind me, I'll just find my photos."

"Have they moved?"

"Pardon?" I asked.

"I was talking to Lou."

"Some of them," Lou answered. "The one on my arm's moved right up. These other guys haven't moved at all."

"Right, we'll wait awhile," said Fog, angling the light. "We wanna get some, like, snail trails in the shot."

They both giggled. "Bugger, one's fallen off," said Lou.

"You think it's dead?"

"Dunno."

I left them to their erotic gardening and pretended to search for photos. This was easy. There were millions of prints lying around. I worked my way along toward the partitions, examining various pictures and occasionally muttering, "No, no..."

The partitioned area, I reasoned, was the only place Paul could hide. I reached it and casually slipped around the corner. There I discovered a mattress on the floor, a dressing table, a chest of drawers, and a reading lamp in the shape of a Victorian streetlight. On the walls were framed prints, mostly of nude young men, though there was one nude older man: Newton. His outfit consisted entirely of a broad smile and a barrister's wig. He was holding a briefcase, but it covered none of the essentials. The most extraordinary thing about this au naturel portrait was that it appeared to have been taken on the steps of the Supreme Court! How that was done, I could not imagine. I gazed into Newton's face—he had a devilish look in his eye—and I felt a pang of sorrow. He'd been fun in his bullying way. He was also the only one of my Italian students who'd ever paid up promptly.

Snapping out of my reverie, I spied Hadrian's wardrobe against the far wall. It was one of those big old mahogany affairs, but had been reupholstered using full-length mirrors. One of the mirrored doors was open a fraction.

"Paul?" I whispered.

I crept across and grabbed the door handle, then stopped. Standing behind me and reflected in the mirror, was Fog. She had a tense expression on her face and held a long, dull kitchen knife.

"What are you doing in here?" she choked.

"Looking for the prints. Could you put that down?"

She didn't move. "This is private! I don't even come in here? And you just walk in off the street? You're a friend of the junkies in number three, looking for something to nick, I bet!"

"Nonsense!"

"Clear out, or I'll call the police!"

The situation required some decisive fast-talking. I adopted my most genial tone. "Please, just put the knife away. Honestly, you're completely mistaken. I hate to be intrusive, but I must have those prints. I couldn't find them in the other room."

"Why do you need them right now?" she asked accusingly.

"Well, I, er, I run a gallery. We have an exhibition opening tonight. Tonight, for heaven's sake! Hadrian's work is absolutely crucial to the success of the thing. I really don't know why he hasn't been in touch. He should have brought the pictures over to us a week ago!"

Fog slowly lowered the knife. "Yeah, well, he's had a lot on his plate recently."

"That's too bad, but I'm frantic! I had no choice but to come here myself."

She cleaned her fingernails with the point of the knife. "I know all the galleries. Which one's yours?"

"It's a new one."

"Called?"

"Queeros. The Queeros Gallery. In Darlinghurst."

"The name doesn't, like, ring a bell."

"It's very new."

She grinned. "All right, then. But the shots won't be in here. This is his bedroom. Come on, I'll help you. I'm taking a break till the snails do their stuff. Lou's gotta get a bit more, you know, slimy."

She marched out of the bedroom. In a flash I hauled open the wardrobe door. "Paul!" I hissed urgently. There was no answer. I prodded the shirts and jackets inside, but none of them seemed to conceal a young homosexual. I was baffled. Where could the stupid boy be hiding out?

I wandered back to the main area. Lou still lay on the bed, chuckling quietly to herself. Fog was sifting through piles of pictures on an ironing board.

"This is all pretty old," she muttered. "What's in your shots?"

"Hmm? Oh, you know. Men."

"Thought so. It was that or tropical fish." She looked up. "Queeros, huh? You showing queer art?"

"Yes. Gay, lesbian, queer. Whatever you call it."

She sniffed. "They're not all the same thing, man!"

"No, no, of course. I know that."

"So, you gonna have a look at *my* stuff?"

"Certainly!" I beamed. "Um, do you have a bathroom?"

She pointed. "Behind the orange curtain."

A section of the room I hadn't noticed before was cordoned off by two hanging drapes. Gingerly, I peeped behind them. The area was bare, except for a toilet. Up against the wall perched a small washbasin, and farther over, a shower recess. Between these was an open window. I stuck my head out. It was a sheer drop of three stories. Not even Paul was that swashbuckling!

"Here!" Fog called as I ambled back in. "Is this them? I haven't seen these before." She handed me a manila envelope. I pulled out half a dozen black and white ten-by-eights. The top four were the beefcake pictures of Wade. I sighed. He was truly photogenic! *Well,* I thought, *I may as well hang on to them as keepsakes.* The two shots on the bottom were your basic island scenery: a figure on a distant cliff top and a lot of bushy foliage.

Fog peered at them. "Not Hadrian's best work," she commented. "There's heaps better stuff."

"No, no," I replied hastily, as inspiration struck. "Look, could I use your phone? I absolutely *must* ring my partner at the gallery to let him know we've finally got them."

Fog agreed, and I picked up the phone and dialed Paul's mobile. As the digits clicked into place, the air was filled with a loud ringing. Lou's bed rocked. She screamed and sprang up, sending the pink snails flying. At the same time, Paul scrambled out from underneath. "Ah-ha!" Lou cried and attempted to kick him in the head. Missing him entirely, she tumbled onto the blue cloth, which came ripping off the ceiling with a jerk and fell over her.

"Junkie!" yelled Fog, raising the kitchen knife. Advancing toward Paul she squashed several snails underfoot. "Damn," she cried, looking down. "They took me ages to collect!"

"Caro!" shouted Paul as he grabbed my hand. We raced out the door and hurtled down the stairs.

"Pervs! Scum!" Fog bellowed after us. We kept running.

I didn't recover my usual Zen-like calm until safely inside the car, which, incidentally, had acquired a parking ticket. Paul was giggling like a drain, while I made a concerted attempt to control my breathing.

"Caro," he chortled. "You were just brilliant! The Queeros Gallery. Fantastic!" He paused. "Are you OK? You probably shouldn't run like that at your age."

"What were you doing under the bed? You said you were in the closet."

"I couldn't stay *there,* now could I! When they slipped off to the bathroom to glam up I tried to sneak out. I didn't make it!" He smiled broadly. "At least we got a souvenir. Let's see."

I realised I was still clutching the envelope. I handed it over.

"Yummovision!" he drooled. "Who is this person I'm falling in love with?"

"That's the boy who found Newton with me. I bumped into him again last night. His name's Wade."

"Wade? I'd sooner plunge!"

"Will you stop!"

"Sorry, caro." He gave me his puppy dog look. "So, are you going to introduce me?"

"Wade's gone back to the States." The puppy dog sniffled. "But," I continued, "I'll share some interesting information he gave me."

I repeated Wade's tale of the bush-walk and capped it off by explaining how, in my attempt to rescue Paul, I had stumbled across the concealed acid. I scrabbled around in the glove box for a pen, and wrote down "hydrofluoric": I wasn't about to forget any other important names.

"Hadrian's our man," Paul remarked.

"So it seems," I mused. "And he's lying low. But still—"

"Still what? Let's get him! I always thought he was a creepy little shit."

I shook my head. "There's more to it, surely. The police

could easily have found out everything we've uncovered. Yet they've decided the evidence points to Grant. They must know something we don't."

He stared at me, looking puzzled. "You don't think Grant did it after all?"

"No, I don't, but there are so many unanswered questions. Why did Hadrian leave the bush-walking Americans in such a hurry?"

"To run back and fry Newton. Right?"

"Mmm. But if that was his intention, why go off hiking in the first place?"

"To establish an alibi."

"Not a very good one. Americans can be self-obsessed, as we know, but surely they'd have eventually noticed he wasn't around."

"I give up, caro. I still say we need to find Hadrian."

I sighed. "We can never set foot in that studio again."

"Tricky. Well, Plan B: We go to Oxford Street for a coffee and drool over Wade's glossies." He shuffled through the pictures, sifting out the bush shots. "These two are duds!"

"You mean because Wade's body is not all over them?"

"Yes, that, of course, but they're also blurry and naff. Looks like he took them in a huge rush."

I peered across at them. The silhouette figure on the cliff reminded me of something: the cover shot on a record I'd owned as a teenager. It was the Wagner opera *Siegfried*. (I'd gone through a brief Teutonic flirtation.) The cover had shown a fat German tenor dressed up and posed as the young god-warrior. "That man is no chicken," I said. "Not Hadrian's usual choice of model."

Paul nudged me in the ribs. "Caro, look at this! There's a face!" He pointed at the bush in the other picture and, sure enough, I saw the blurry suggestion of a round face, a fair way off, and half hidden by leaves. "It's not very clear."

I squinted. "I've seen him somewhere before...up a tree, in fact!"

"What?"

"Yes! I was in my room on the island, waiting for the police interview and staring out into space, and I saw this man sitting in a tree."

"What was he doing?"

"Just watching."

"Who is he?"

"I haven't the faintest idea, but it was definitely him. How weird."

"Caro! What if Hadrian was going back to develop these pictures? Pictures of a dirty old perv lurking in the bush?"

"But why?"

"Strange unfathomable reasons of his own!"

I mused. "Wade said Hadrian was in a hurry. He wasn't sneaking off in a devious murdering kind of way; he was rushing like mad."

We sat for a moment trying to get our thoughts in order. Who was this ubiquitous voyeur? What was he doing on the island? Had we found yet another contender for the coveted role of Newton's assassin? I glanced up and caught sight of a parking inspector striding toward the car as if he were a piranha heading for an upturned canoe. I quickly started the engine. I did not intend to get my ticket upgraded.

As I sped away, Paul turned to me.

"Caro," he said, "we're very confused, aren't we."

"Yes," I answered.

CHAPTER 19

Ashburn and Bell's reception area was like every reception area the world over, a carpeted no-man's-land. It contained the usual Pro Hart reproductions and dog-eared *Who* magazines. Indeed, the place reminded me so much of a dentist's, my molars began to throb involuntarily. I had to remind them sternly that it was not my dentist I was about to confront but Newton Heath's solicitor, one Ms. Antonia Chang. My molars took some convincing.

In the week that had elapsed since our farcical visit to Hadrian's studio, Paul and I had achieved precisely zilch. Hadrian was definitely not answering the phone, so I was quite unable to discover any more about his photos or the blob-like man they depicted.

I had combed the newspapers for pieces on the Vasselina incident, but there was not a hint dropped about the make of the propeller. Halstrom Park clammed up on me as well. When they realised I was not inquiring officially, they told me the police weren't releasing any details and actually slammed the phone down in my ear.

Most disappointing of all, our acid lead seemed to have run out of steam. Paul had thoughtfully arranged to get some new head shots taken by a taciturn photographer friend of his who lived in Bondi. During the shoot, Paul bombarded the poor man with queries about photographic chemicals. Hydrofluoric acid was not one of them. Furthermore, although they could be nasty, none of the chemicals a photographer might use was strong enough to kill a person on the spot. We were back to square one.

Frustrated at every turn, I looked forward to a sizeable bequest from Newton to ease the pain. Oh, I knew I was probably kidding myself, but what had started out as a fanciful idea had taken hold over the week. After all, I had aided Newton in his Italian "episode." He'd always said he owed me a debt of gratitude. What better way to repay the debt than bequeath his Tuscan vineyard to the house of Petrucci? It was certainly the kind of full-hearted gesture Newton would have reveled in: generous, but at no inconvenience to himself.

I was sampling a late-picked chianti in my mind when a tall young man came striding down the corridor. I stared compulsively at his distinctive features: blond hair and dark-brown eyes. He looked disconcertingly familiar, very reminiscent of the young Tab Hunter (a leading light of my early fantasy life). He averted his eyes as he passed.

I'd turned my head about 180 degrees to watch him—old habits die hard—when a voice behind me coughed gently.

"Would you come in please, Mr. Petrucci?"

The speaker was a slight, well-groomed young woman wearing a light grey suit and green scarf. Her smooth Asian features were framed by a large pair of circular tortoiseshell spectacles. She wore her long hair tied back and secured with a mother-of-pearl comb. Under her arm she held a spiral-bound folder. I followed her down a cluttered corridor and into a cramped ancient office full of files and bookshelves. There was a small window that offered a view of a similar office across the street.

Ms. Chang sat at her desk and began to sort through a pile of papers. She indicated a chair opposite.

"Please sit down," she said with a warm but automatic smile. "Excuse the clutter, won't you? We're moving to new premises next month. About time, too."

As if on cue, I heard a deep rumble and was startled to see a series of faces glide slowly past the window. Children, little old ladies, young couples wearing backpacks—all gazed curiously into the room. Ms. Chang paid them no heed. "The monorail's right outside," she commented dryly. "Can't say

I'll miss all the attention." She clasped her hands together on the desk. In contrast to her neat appearance, I noticed her fingernails were bitten down to the quick.

"Thanks for your time," she began. "As I mentioned on the phone, I'm presently trying to put Newton's estate in order." Her eyebrows registered a slight tremor.

"Is it about the will?" I asked, unable to contain myself any longer.

"Have you found one?" She flashed me a look of mild surprise.

"Er, no."

"Thank God. We've quite enough already. They're turning up everywhere."

It was time to bite the bullet. "So has he left me a small bequest?"

"Did Newton say he was leaving you something?"

I cleared my throat. "Not in so many words."

"Well, I'm afraid I can't reveal the contents of the will—wills—but, just between ourselves, don't hold your breath."

"Oh. What about the villa in Tuscany?"

"That was sold six months ago." She smiled sympathetically. "Now, I wanted to talk to you about New Heaven. I understand you are one of the investors brought together by Newton—"

"What?"

"Please, let me finish. You are part of a consortium he put together to purchase a controlling share in the New Heaven Resort, in partnership with the American parent company Gaytour International. Correct so far?"

"No!" I gasped, jolted out of my Tuscan reveries once and for all.

Ms. Chang removed her glasses and began to clean them absentmindedly with a small cloth. "No? Your name appears on several lists amongst Newton's papers as a substantial contributor. Gaytour have confirmed this. Your name's on the list Newton submitted to them on...let me see...the fourth of September last year."

"I'd never heard of New Heaven in September! Not even in October! How much did I contribute?"

"Seven-hundred thousand dollars," she answered.

I reeled.

"But," she continued, "I'm having difficulty tracing any evidence that the money was, in fact, paid. Did Newton provide you with a receipt, or would you possibly have a copy of the contract? He was inclined to make handshake deals, as I'm sure you're aware."

"Water! Could I have some water?" I begged huskily.

"Of course, help yourself. It's there by the window."

I stood up shakily, hobbled over, and poured myself a glass of water. I downed it in one and poured another. Seven-hundred thousand! Did this mean debt collectors would camp on my doorstep for the rest of my days? I envisaged rough, hairy repo men in dungarees, carting off my Tebaldi collection in their uncaring arms.

"There's been some mistake," I croaked.

Ms. Chang flourished a paper at me. "I've unearthed this letter of agreement," she said. "It's basically an IOU, but it would be legally binding."

I scanned it incredulously while a rumbling carriage full of gawking tourists read the fine print over my shoulder. Sure enough, it stated that I, Marc Petrucci, do hereby et cetera, et cetera, forthwith to the tune of seven-hundred thousand bucks.

"I never signed this!" I protested, flourishing the form with more than a hint of hysteria.

"I know," she replied blankly. "Neither did Newton."

I stared again at the paper. She was right.

"All I want to know," she said in a tone she might have used to address a recalcitrant child, "is whether you hold a signed copy of this document in your possession."

"I've never seen it before in my life!"

She nodded. "Did you contribute any money at all to the purchase?"

I shook my head vehemently. "The first I heard of the damn place was a few weeks ago when I had dinner with Newton and he said come up for a holiday. Only it wasn't a holiday! I had to chair a meeting with a lot of vile Christians and journalists and I had no idea what I was talking about and he was killed! That's all I know!"

"Just as I feared." Ms. Chang sighed. "Well, thank you again for your time." She stood to show me out.

"Hang on," I said, "Is that it?"

"Yes, thank you."

"But what's this about? Am I involved in some kind of fraud?"

She shrugged and returned to the desk. "I suppose I owe you an explanation. Regrettably, it's the same story I've been hearing all week. None of the so-called contributors seems to know anything about the deal. It's looking as though Newton simply made up a list of names out of his head."

"What for?"

"He was taking what appears to be a typical Newton Heath risk. He wanted a half-share in the resort. He seems to have been reluctant, shall we say, to allow Gaytour the controlling interest. Understandable, I suppose, since he'd spent most of his personal savings in acquiring the island itself."

"Is that why he sold his place in Italy?"

"Yes, and several other assets. Rather reckless of him."

I nodded. "That was Newton."

"Indeed. It appears he bluffed. He fobbed the Americans off with promissory notes and updates of the A-list until he could get extra capital together."

"But—" I could hardly take this in! "What happens now?"

"That's up to Gaytour, I'd say. They've inherited the debt. The initial capitalisation was expected to cover building costs. A lot of those people still haven't been paid. Staff as well. So Gaytour may decide to make up the shortfall, gain the controlling interest, and then they're free to do whatever they like with the place. They could run it at a loss if they need to, or sell up. I suspect they'll sell. A murder is bad publicity, don't you think?"

"Yes, indeed." The significance of what she was saying started to sink in. "So Hiram will own the whole place?"

"Hiram? Oh, the director of Gaytour. No, no, Newton's heirs will still hold a stake in it, unless Gaytour International buys them out too, as will the members of Newton's consortium who did contribute."

"Oh? Some of them did?"

"Only one, so far. The actor, Lachie Turner. He was here just now. You passed him in the corridor." She laughed lightly. "I got his autograph—I felt like a kid asking for it."

We shook hands. "I won't hold you up any longer," I said.

She smiled, this time with a genuine twinkle. "I almost gave you heart failure, didn't I. Sorry."

Once outside the solicitor's offices, I paused to lean against the building, nonplussed. Nothing ever seemed to be what it seemed! Now I'd discovered a whole new level of chicanery, raising even more questions. Why wasn't Newton prepared to let Gaytour have the majority share? The answer to that, at least, was easy: The man had been a control freak. If he involved himself in any project, from a dinner party to an international resort, Newton had to be the boss. On the other hand, Hiram was a control freak too. Perhaps Newton hadn't trusted him.

Wandering the city streets, I concocted a new theory. Suppose, I argued, after months of stalling, Newton had actually been about to acquire the capital he needed for his controlling share in the resort. What was it he'd said, that night at Don Cojones—"The hard part's over"? Suppose he'd told Hiram, but Hiram wanted control for himself? Hiram couldn't have killed him, but one of his acolytes may have. There was no way of confirming that all the Americans went on the bush-walk. One or two might easily have stayed behind. I suddenly thought of Wade, and his gleeful reenactment of our grim discovery. Wade was lovely to look at, heaven to touch, and all those things, but you couldn't call him sane. Cutely unhinged would be closer to the mark. Could he have followed Hadrian back to the resort after all? It was doubtful, but not impossible.

The subject of gorgeous young men led my thoughts in the direction of Lachie Turner, the only genuine investor on Newton's list. That was no surprise. He'd owed Newton a favour after the exorbitant *Bimbeau* magazine payout. Was Lachie the mystery man in Newton's fax? Was he B.F.? I recalled very clearly how Newton had hedged around the subject of Turner's sexuality, as well he might if he was having trouble convincing the fellow to become the face on the New Heaven billboards. And was Lachie also the young man Grant had been fighting with Newton about? It seemed to make sense. *Damn it,* I thought. *Everything keeps coming back to Grant!*

Focussing briefly on my surroundings, I noticed I was passing a pub, and abruptly decided to slip inside. It was ideal: a quiet bar in the late afternoon, plain, sterile, and virtually empty, just the place to veg out, as Paul would say. I hiked myself up onto a barstool, and glanced longingly at the rows of spirits. I could treat myself. How about a piña colada for old times' sake?

Out of nowhere, an unpleasant truth dawned on me: Hiram had thought I'd sunk seven-hundred grand into the New Heaven project! Was it any wonder he showered me with praise after my feeble performance as community liaison officer! I felt a flush of retrospective embarrassment. Word of my supposed wealth and influence had even spread to the staff, I realised, recalling my peculiar conversation with Darren in the speedboat. Everyone had been treating me with kid gloves while I acted like a buffoon. Damn it, I wanted a drink!

"Hello?" I called.

From the other end of the room, a broad black T-shirt came

swaggering along, with granite arms and a small head attached. As he got closer, the barman's surly expression turned to one of delighted recognition.

"Hey! How's it going, Marc!" he purred. "It's Rodney! Remember me? Friend of Paul's?"

He leant over the bar, kissed me full on the lips and ruffled my hair.

"The choreographer," I said as his face fell into place.

"Ah, that didn't work out. Rehearsals ate right into my gym time. What'll you have? It's on me, babe, anything you like."

"OK, Rodney, thanks. A piña colada."

"What'd you say?"

"How about a vodka and tonic?"

"Can do!" He turned to make the drink, but clearly had no idea where anything was. "Um—yeah...I might have one myself, to keep you company."

"Do. Are you still working at the Spanish restaurant?"

"Don Cojones ? Nah. They closed it down. Hygiene regulations."

"Really?"

"You shoulda seen the kitchen, it was gross—I knew somebody'd catch salmonella before long."

"Mind you, the chef was excellent."

"Pepe? Oh yeah, the best. He's up on charges. Criminal negligence."

My drink started to taste faintly greasy.

"Hey," he went on, "is Pauly back in town?"

"Yes."

"Working?"

"No." Rodney tried not to look pleased. "I'm surprised you haven't run into him," I added.

Rodney filled his impressive chest with air. "I spend all my time working out," he exhaled. He sipped his drink, and his expression grew thoughtful.

"Marc—remember when you and Paul came into Don Cojones that time?"

"Yes."

"The other queen with you—the rude cunt—was that the guy who got murdered?"

"Newton. Yes, it was."

"Wooo! So who did it?"

"I don't know."

He winked outrageously. "I reckon you do! You're the man who knew too much! Just been readin' about you. Don't tell me you haven't seen it!"

He sashayed away and returned with a stained copy of *Queer Scene*. I grabbed it out of his hand. I could scarcely believe my bulging eyes! There on the front page was a mug shot of a seedy-looking character; indisputably, it was me. Where on earth did they get hold of such a shocking photo? Beside it huddled the main story, enigmatically titled "The Man Who Knew Too Much."

"You better have a top-up," Rodney whispered.

Grimly, I began to read.

THE MAN WHO KNEW TOO MUCH

The mystery of the New Heaven Resort deepens. Police have charged Grant Breen, 49, of Murphy's Inlet, with the murder of leading gay lawyer Newton Heath. Breen is head writer on the long-running soapie *Surfside Motel*.

Gaytour International has refused to comment on rumours that the much-hyped gay and lesbian resort will not go ahead. Claire Bornkamp, recently appointed Australasian Community Liaison Officer for Gaytour, told me: "We're still very excited about New Heaven. The opening has been post-poned because of unusual weather conditions." She would not comment on the Heath murder.

Suspicions remain that the so-called Church of Divine Intervention, a dubious local religious sect, led by charis-matic preacher Matthew Paramor, 32, may have stood to gain from Heath's demise. Although links between Breen and the pastor have not been established, sources say the closure of the New Heaven resort was one of Paramor's key concerns. "They run the place," according to a former resident and ex–New Heaven employee. "There's no way they'd let that resort open." Locals in Murphy's Inlet are known to be openly hostile to dykes.

At the centre of the storm is former Gaytour employee Mark Petrucci, 50, of Sydney. Petrucci was a regular visitor to Murphy's Inlet, according to June Boggs, 68. Ms. Boggs runs a guesthouse in the homophobic town. "Mark's been coming here for ages," said Boggs. She could not confirm whether Petrucci is linked to Paramor's sect, but Petrucci has been sighted in the company of local alderman and sect member Merv Jackson, 55. Jackson has since left Murphy's Inlet, and his whereabouts are unknown.

Petrucci, a known associate of Breen, was uncooperative when I spoke to him, denying all knowledge of the cult. However, *Queer Scene* can reveal that Petrucci was a substantial investor in the resort.

It was also Petrucci who 'discovered" Newton Heath's body in remote scrub some time after the murder took place.

Clearly, Petrucci is more deeply involved in this affair than he is prepared to admit. When I asked Ms. Bornkamp why Gaytour International had fired Petrucci, she didn't know. "The US management make these decisions," she said, "I can't comment on their reasons." A disgruntled employee told me, "The guy couldn't get out of there quick enough."

Petrucci was emphatic on one point only. When asked whether the gay and lesbian resort would go ahead, he simply said, "No!"

I clung to the bar, petrified to leave, and rapidly polished off a succession of vodkas. I was in shock. Every rereading made the snide story appear more damning. I'd virtually been identified as the criminal mastermind behind Newton's murder! What's more, *Queer Scene* was the rag everybody read.

The hide of this journalist amazed me. She'd done all the talking herself, and how the hell had she found out everyone's age?

Eventually pangs of hunger clamoured for my attention. I bade farewell to Rodney. He refused to take any payment for the vodkas. "You're a celebrity now," he winked. I somehow sensed his days of tending bar in this establishment were numbered.

It was dark when I hit the street. I checked my watch: 7:10 P.M. I decided to treat myself to gnocchi at my favourite little diner, La Stupenda, a pleasant, homey hideaway, unchanged after 20 years—a most unusual phenomenon in Sydney. The restaurant wasn't far away, and though it was in the general area I wished to avoid, it was off the main drag. By a circuitous route, I could miss Oxford Street altogether.

As I took a shortcut through the park, a nasty thought bubbled up in my mind like overcooked risotto. The murderer, whoever he was, was somewhere out there, and had no doubt devoured the *Queer Scene* article with considerable interest. Having apparently gotten away with murder, he now found himself confronted by the mysterious Signor Petrucci, who apparently knew more than anybody else about the case, police included. If I were that murderer, I'd feel inclined to send Signor Petrucci packing. *A permanenza!*

I glanced over my shoulder to see if I was being followed. I wasn't, of course, and told myself firmly to calm down. There was no need to get melodramatic: That was the easy option. I forced myself to stay cool.

By now I was only one or two streets away from La Stupenda. I stared up at the dark terraces, some of them derelict, and had a sudden realisation: I'd approached from the wrong side! To get to where I wanted to go, I would either have to stroll past the notorious Wall, or else spend an hour retracing my steps. No, damn it, I was far too hungry for that. I clenched my fists and prepared to run the gamut of street boys once again.

As I approached the first couple of loiterers, I gazed into the distance, glancing neither left nor right. To my relief, they ignored me. Then, out of nowhere, it started.

"Ay, mate? How you goin'?"

"Got a light?"

"I know ya, don't I? Hey! You! Don't I know ya?"

"I don't think so," I mumbled, quickening my step. (I'll never learn.)

"Yeah!" he crowed back. "I seen ya in the paper. You're the man who knew too much."

"You know too much, do ya, mate? Whaddaya know, then?"

"You know where I can score?"

They both laughed heartily at this.

"It's not me," I protested.

"I seen your picture. Looks just like ya!"

"Hey! Man who knew too much! Ya got any plans?"

"Got any money?"

"What do you like? Ay?"

"Whaddaya know?"

"Piss off, you lot, and leave him alone! He's my client."

The last voice had a familiar ring to it. I cautiously peeked around. There, leaning against a parking meter, was a pair of long, shapely legs in teeny-weeny, fun-packed shorts, and a casual, superior smile.

"Darren!" I exclaimed.

"Look who's here. Come for some take-away?"

"Certainly not," I huffed. "I'm on my way to dinner!"

"You could thank me for getting rid of that street trash."

"Sorry. Thanks." I raised my eyebrows. "So what brings you out onto the street tonight? I thought you were a professional operator."

He sniffed. "I'm the only one round here! I like to keep my options open, that's all. I got my mobile, in case anybody answers the ad. Meanwhile, I hang out where the action is. It's plain business sense."

"I see." I began to move on. The street now seemed strangely deserted.

"Wait a sec," he said. "So you're the man who knew too much, are you?"

"Don't believe everything you read."

"I don't. You know fuck all. I know more than you ever did"

"I'm sure."

"That frigging story was meant to be about me! That's what she said."

I stopped as a sudden wave of anger swept through me. "It was *you*!" I exploded. "And here was I thinking Paul had shot his mouth off as usual. *You* told that journalist all that stuff, including how I couldn't get off the island quick enough! Well, thank you so *much*!"

Darren blinked. My unexpected outburst had stunned him. "It was s'posed to be about me," he repeated. "She didn't even use my name."

"I bloody well wish she had!" I shouted. "Then you'd be in the kind of trouble I'm in! I presume you're the 'disgruntled ex-employee'—and what else? Were you a member of that blasted church?"

"Not a member, exactly. I had business dealings with them."

"With that screwed up sleaze-bag Jackson, no doubt. Business dealings! How could you stoop so low?"

Darren grabbed me around the neck. I felt his strong fingers tighten.

"Darren…stop…I ca-an't breathe…"

His grip loosened, and I gulped for air. I would have to warn Paul about this maniac.

"All right, Darren," I panted. "I'm sorry I lost my temper.

You're right: You know a lot of things I don't. So why don't you tell me some of them?"

He looked wary. "Tell you what?"

"Whatever you know."

A slow grin spread over his face. "Information costs money," he crooned.

"How much?"

"Five-hundred bucks."

I gaped. "You're mad!"

"That's what I got last time."

"Really. From whom?"

"Can't tell you." He yawned ostentatiously.

"How do I know it's worth it?"

"You don't."

I made a decision. "I'll pay you for an hour of your time. That's what you're here for, isn't it?"

"Guess so. All right. A hundred and twenty."

I nodded, and Darren wrenched the mobile phone out of his back pocket and switched it off. "Right," he said. "Let's go. I've got the use of a room."

"No," I exclaimed, pulling him back. "We can talk right here."

Darren shrugged and hauled me across the street to a dark stone building, the annex of a rarely used church. We sat on the cold steps.

"Talk," I said.

"OK. I knew your mate Newton very well."

"He was a client?"

"Sort of. I helped him out a while back, and he's been helping me out ever since. Well, up until recently."

He glanced up and down the street.

"Is that all?" I asked.

"Yeah."

"But I don't even know what you're talking about! How did you help Newton?"

He shrugged. Then in a flash, it came to me.

"Lachie Turner!" I cried. "You're the sex worker in the Lachie Turner case. Newton paid you off to disappear so they could win the suit against the magazine!"

He said nothing.

"And he kept 'helping you out' so you'd keep quiet! You blackmailed him."

Darren remained tight-lipped and slowly gazed at his bulky, metallic watch. His eyes met mine.

"Well?" I demanded.

"Touch me," he whispered.

"Pardon?"

"Go ahead. I've got a great body, and you're paying for it." He stretched out his legs and languidly passed his tongue over his lips.

I stood up, found the cash, and roughly slapped it into his hand. "True," I snapped, "but if you were the last rent boy on earth, I wouldn't have sex with you at gunpoint."

CHAPTER 20

I needed to warn Paul as soon as possible. Darren was not only dishonest and unscrupulous. He was downright lethal. At the very least, I could imagine Paul traipsing up the stairs one afternoon to find his apartment stripped bare of every item worth more than five dollars. He could lose, in one fell swoop, his expensive runners, his grand-mother's tasteless costume jewelry, his Lana Turner mohair sweater, and his autographed picture of Barbra Streisand.

I finally got him on his mobile at 10:30 the next morning. It was ludicrously early by Paul Standard Time, but he was already up and about. In the background I could hear sounds of boisterous girlish activity and dance music.

"Caro mio. How nice of you to call." He sounded breath-less and crestfallen.

"What's all that racket? Why are you running?"

"I'm on the walking machine thingy at gym."

"You're at the gym? At this time of the day?"

He panted several times.

"Paul? Are you still there?"

"Sorry, caro. It just went up a hill."

"You don't need to do that! You're a dancer."

"Choreographer!"

"Whatever. You're fit enough."

"Darren doesn't think so," he replied. "He thinks I should spend more time bulking up. When I reach a certain level, he's going to spot me."

I had to put a stop to this. "Paul, that boy is dangerous. Do you understand? I hate to be blunt, but he's using you! He only wants you out of your flat so he can take dirty old married men back there and fleece them. You've got to get rid of him!"

"I'm glad we're on this subject," he gasped. "I've been meaning to talk to you about it." He took a deep breath. "Caro, I think this is it. This is the biggie."

"The big what?"

"Love! Lovely old love! I'm in it. I always wondered what it would be like. Oh, yes, regrets: I've had a few. Too many to mention, really. But all that's behind me. Those others never touched my soul. Dazzle is so much more! Shall I compare him to a summer's day? He's hot!"

"Stop it!" I snapped. "For God's sake! Darren's amoral, self-serving, violent…"

There was a pause. "Caro, you sweet old thing. You're jealous. Don't worry, this doesn't mean the end of our friendship."

I was losing my cool. "He's bad news! Believe me, I know!"

"It's true, you know everything. It's in the paper."

"Don't talk to me about that."

"I'm sorry, caro. I'd love to stay chatting but my abs need a workout."

"Your brain needs a workout!"

I slammed down the receiver. This was the limit! I'd seen Paul in this mood two or three times before, and experience had taught me that logic was wasted. I could do nothing but sit tight and wait while he put the rest of his life on hold and worked through the paralysis. Well, if I had to investigate alone, so be it.

My next move was clear. Grant's hearing was tomorrow, and I was flying up to Brisbane this afternoon. I'd been trying not to think about these legal proceedings. After all, I knew a few facts that, from a certain angle, could look bad for Grant and I'm not the world's most convincing liar. I prayed the questions wouldn't be too thorny.

As directed, I had been in touch with an officer of the Magistrate's Court, and they had promised to reimburse me for the airfare and pay a per diem of sixty dollars a day. That had seemed an extravagant amount, until I'd checked with a few inner-city hotels and come to understand that it wouldn't buy me enough water to take an aspirin. Finally, in desperation and against my better judgement, I rang my "ex."

Andrew and I had split nine years before, the best part of a decade. It was not your volatile break-up. There wasn't any china flung around or lines drawn down the middle of the carpet, no raised voices or neurotic dogs cowering under the chaise longue. No, our relationship was more like a spinning top: It had hurtled around to begin with, but eventually it fell sideways, slowed to a halt and lay there, getting in everybody's way.

We'd stayed in touch as "friends" for a while, in those first heady weeks of freedom after he moved out. Then Neil came slinking into the picture. Neil was a chemist, Andrew a sales rep for a drug company; they met at a convention. Cupid was evidently present, too, because a week later Andrew upped and winged his way north to the love nest where the two of them have nestled smugly ever since. At Christmas we exchange cards, and maybe once a year we chat.

I retain a very tender place in my heart for Andrew. It's Neil I can't abide. If ever I thought Andrew was a bit too anal, next to Neil he's a whirling dervish in a mud bath. Their house—sorry, home—is knee-deep in mats, coasters, and doilies, and each room exudes a different scented germicide. It's secreted through the walls, I think. But the real problem is Neil himself. He is far and away the most boring man who ever rinsed a plate so it would be clean for the dishwasher. Well, I reminded myself, I'd only be staying for two days.

I'd booked my tickets over the phone and was at the airport by two. I never thought I would be facing the same rude clerk at the prepaid pickup, but unhappily there he was: The balding pate and wispy moustache were unmistakable.

"Name please?"

"Petrucci."

I prayed he wouldn't remember our last fracas.

"Mmm. Petrucci..." He looked up. "Oh!" he exclaimed. "You!"

"Er, yes. Me. Marc Petrucci."

Unexpectedly, he beamed. "Darling, we've read all about you! You're the man who knew too much."

"I'm afraid so."

"And you're smack bang in the middle of that dreadful business. Didn't you discover the body or something? My Lord, it must have been ghastly!"

"It was. If I could take my ticket—"

"You know, I've got a friend who knew that man Newman—what was his name?"

"Newton Heath."

"Yes, *her*. And my friend said she had it coming in spades. People always say that sort of thing afterward, don't they!"

I was going to miss my flight at this rate. "Give me the ticket," I pleaded.

"'Course I will! Where are we off to today? Brizzie?" A look of disgust appeared on his face. "*Economy*? Tch! We can't have that, honey." He tapped away at the keyboard and tore up the existing ticket.

"Wha—"

"Here we go," he smiled, handing me a new ticket. "I've popped you into First. Have a pleasant flight."

"Thank you," I said. "Thanks very much."

"Don't mention it. And next time you want an upgrade, just ask for Stewart. OK? You'll never go hungry again, missy!"

"Thank you."

I was so stunned I left my beaten-up old suitcase behind at the counter and had to race back to retrieve it.

Brisbane isn't a town I know well. I had visited relatives there as a child, but when I returned briefly some years later, I discovered the entire city had been rebuilt from scratch. This was done not in the aftermath of any catastrophic natural disaster; it was merely the result of decades of entrepreneurial excess.

My first-class flight was smooth and delightful. Upgrading clearly agreed with me. I must have been a celebrity in a former life, like Shirley Maclaine. I felt completely refreshed when Andrew picked me up.

He looked well—he always had. He's only five years younger, but we seemed to have reached an age where five years makes a difference. His hair was still brown, though a little bit thinner. His waist didn't seem to have spread one centimeter. He wore a dark-blue suit, pale-blue shirt, and tie, presumably his work clothes. We met at the baggage carousel.

"Hi, Marc," he smiled. He put down his briefcase and hugged me. Every sensory receptor in my body remembered how well we had fitted together.

"Andrew, thanks so much for this. Thank Neil, too. I won't be a nuisance, I promise you."

"That's OK. In fact, Neil thought he'd be away this week, but it didn't work out."

"Oh."

"He'll be delighted to see you," he added hastily. "I booked a table at Brisket's tonight so we can all have a slap-up meal and a good old yack. It's five-star."

"Marvelous," I lied. Five-star meant the kind of restaurant in which I couldn't afford two toothpicks. So much for the sixty-dollar allowance.

"Now why don't I run you home?" Andrew continued

blithely. "We'll get you settled and cleaned up, and you can relax before dinner. What time's your thingo in the morning?"

"Terribly early, I'm afraid—9:30."

"Right. I'll be at work by then, but we'd better not make it a late night. We can go out to the bars another time, eh?"

"Of course."

"Neil and I usually retire early anyhow. Oh! Now tell me about poor old Grant! I couldn't believe it! Is he all right?"

On the way, I filled Andrew in on the whole messy saga, though I left out a few unnecessary details—such as what I'd been doing when I found the body. In spite of that, Andrew still managed to shake his head and mutter "How can you get yourself mixed up in things like this?" The idea that tragedy—or, for that matter, excitement—can happen to anybody would never occur to him.

I left Paul out of my narrative too. The last time I'd mentioned Paul, Andrew had concocted a whole scenario out of it and refused to believe he was simply a friend. "There's more to this, or I'm no judge of character!" he had simpered. In fact, he was dead right: He was no judge of character. "Men your age don't have platonic friends twenty-something years younger! I may be an old married woman, but I'm not naive!" Nine years down the track, he was still hoping to see me hitched again, probably to placate his guilty conscience. Well, I refused to oblige.

Andrew and Neil's house was a good deal grander than I recalled from my previous rushed visit. Initially, it had been a wooden cottage in the northern style, raised up on pillars with a wide verandah on three sides. When they'd first bought, they'd installed enormous picture windows, extended the verandahs and reinforced the outside walls with brick veneer. Now, however, the walls seemed to be made of sandstone, and there was a second storey. They'd also originally planted six umbrella trees on the perimeter of their property: "For privacy," as Neil put it. These were now monsters, dwarfing every dwelling for miles around and crowding each other awkwardly. The one thing that remained constant was the lawn, literally shaved to within an inch of its life.

Inside was equally unrecognisable. On the polished wooden floor, as reflective as the surface of an alpine lake, sat piss-elegant chairs, tables, and shelves that looked as though they'd just left the factory that morning. I'd never seen such pristine furnishings in my life. They'd have made Harrod's showroom look tawdry. Andrew obligingly carried my smelly old case upstairs. "You wash up. I'll feed Patty," he said.

"Who's Patty?" I asked.

"Patty the catty! She's a Burmese. You'll meet her later. Ah ha, I think I hear hubby's car in the driveway!"

"I'll be in the shower," I replied.

"Sure. There's an en suite by the way."

I stood under the steaming spray and tried to recall exactly what Andrew had been like when we were an item. He couldn't have been like this! When he'd said "Patty the catty," it was all I could do to stop myself regurgitating a kilo of first-class airline tucker. I strained my memory bank. He'd been quiet, admittedly, and very clean—but mostly we'd simply lolled around in our comfy old chairs. His was green, and mine was a deep maroon. We'd read the papers in bed or on the floor and only thrown them out when they'd threatened to take over.

We used to sit on the steps in summer and sip cask wine, admiring the liquidambar. When friends dropped by, we'd throw makeshift parties where everyone would camp it up and get lovingly drunk. Paul would have adored it all, but, I reflected, he must have been a precocious toddler back then. It all seemed as distant now as the Great War. And as futile.

After sprucing myself up for as long as I plausibly could, I had no alternative but to skip downstairs and greet Neil. He was reading a newspaper. When he saw me, he raised a hand while he finished some paragraph or other, then carefully folded up his glasses and placed them on a small table. Finally, he stood.

"Hello, Marc," he said, offering me his hand. "Good to see you."

"You too. Thanks for having me."

"Make yourself at home." (As if I could!) "Andrew will be ready shortly. We're eating out—did he mention that?"

"Yes, yes."

"It's his idea. Still, we haven't been out in ages. I suppose we've got to do something with our money!"

I laughed dutifully. "Well, then. How's the chemist's shop?"

"I have three stores now."

"Really! You must be run off your feet. I hope they're close by."

He looked puzzled. "I don't work in all three of them."

"Ah."

He paused, then shook his head. "Nasty business."

"I suppose so," I replied. "I always thought it sounded a bit dreary."

He frowned. "I mean this business you've got yourself involved in."

"Oh, that. Yes."

He leaned forward. "Hardly surprising, though, is it? This murder."

"What do you mean?"

"Well, I don't wish to be uncharitable, but the way some people make a song and dance about their sexuality in public! It attracts all kinds of undesirables."

I immediately thought of Wade. "Some are quite desirable, I've discovered."

Neil ignored me. "Now take Andrew and myself. We have a loving, committed relationship. That's not in dispute."

"I know."

"We have our own small circle of *simpatico* friends with whom we spend our leisure time. We don't go shoving it down everyone else's throat. How would you feel, Marc, if strangers kept waltzing up to you and screaming 'I'm straight! I'm a lesbian! I'm bisexual!' or whatever?"

"I'd feel like a therapist."

At this juncture, a sleek, lean cat sidled over and rubbed herself up against Neil's leg.

"Have you met Patty?" he asked.

"No," I said, and clicked my fingers. "Puss, puss, puss!"

She looked disinterestedly in my direction, then without warning, sprang into my lap. I reached out a finger to tickle her behind the ear. She hissed and lashed out wildly.

"Ow!"

Patty plopped triumphantly to the floor as I leapt up.

"She scratched me!"

"She's just being playful."

I stared at my tattered forearm. "I'm bleeding!" I snapped.

Neil jumped to attention. "Are you sure? Stay there! No, better idea, come into the kitchen." *He's more concerned about his furniture than the welfare of his guest,* I thought nastily. I deliberately rested my bleeding arm on the white material of his lounge chair.

Things went from bad to worse over dinner. Another friend of the loving couple had been invited to join us. This person was a local identity who apparently threw delightful Sunday lunches and liked opera. We said our hellos while waiting to be seated in the gaudiest eatery I'd ever encountered: a white starched, over-chandeliered, gold-festooned dinosaur which in Sydney would have been hooted out of existence, even in the Italian quarter.

"Lovely room, isn't it?" wheezed the opera lover, whose name was Janssen.

We ordered pseudo-Gallic concoctions from the extravagantly priced à la carte menu (mine was a coq au vin) and got stuck into the wine. I lapsed into a semicoma. My mind was so preoccupied with the oncoming ordeal of the committal hearing I had no energy to waste on the current ordeal of dinner.

"Janssen's an opera buff," Andrew piped up after a long stretch of peace and quiet.

"Yes, indeed," he admitted. "Do you enjoy the opera, Marc?"

"Sorry?" I said. "Oh, well—I'm Italian, of course. Tebaldi is my pin-up girl," I added.

Janssen mused. "Tebaldi, yessss. A gorgeous voice. Not much of an actress, though. I rather incline toward Callas in that respect."

"Maria Callas," Neil muttered in agreement.

"I wouldn't know," I answered, "I never saw her." I was a bit tart, but I hate to hear Tebaldi put down. Callas was never in the race as far as I'm concerned. From the corner of my eye, I saw a look pass between Andrew and Neil. *Now what?* I thought. Wasn't I allowed to hold an opinion on the matter?

"Marc," asked Janssen, "what have you done to your arm?"

"Hmm? Their cat scratched me."

"I'm so sorry," said Andrew.

"Don't worry."

"Surprising," Janssen mused. "Patty's normally so gentle."

"Yes, she is," agreed Neil.

"I beg to differ," I quipped.

We lapsed into silence once more. Our meal was apparently being prepared somewhere north of Siberia.

"Tell us about the murder," Andrew said.

"Oh, there's nothing to tell," I smiled. "I didn't have much to do with it."

"Why are you being called to give evidence, then?" Neil asked.

"I really don't know," I said a trifle defensively.

"Oh, Marc," exclaimed Andrew, "I forgot to tell you. Grant's lawyer left a message. He wants a quick word tomorrow before the hearing. I've written his number down. Now, don't glare at me like that!" This last remark was directed to Neil, who was scowling at his partner.

"You forget everything," Neil grunted. "You must be getting senile."

"Andrew's younger than me," I pointed out. Neil shot me a "that proves nothing" look.

"About this murder...?" Janssen prompted.

Andrew piped up. "Marc knew the victim, and the man the police have charged is an old friend of ours."

"And an old lover of yours," I added mischievously.

"Is he?" asked Neil.

Andrew's cheek displayed a cute maidenly blush. "Twenty years ago," he said.

"Newton, the one who was murdered, was a lawyer," I continued. "He was starting up a gay and lesbian resort called New Heaven, and I was up there on a sort of preview holiday. That's where it happened. Someone threw acid all over him."

Neil's face registered a look of severe distaste. "Why on earth would a lawyer waste his time with a project like that?"

I gritted my teeth. "I don't think it's such a bad idea! According to Gaytour International—that's the controlling company—heterosexuals can go anywhere they like for a vacation without getting hassled. New Heaven would simply offer gay men and women the same opportunity."

"Gaytour International," murmured Janssen. "Are they American?"

"Yes. They own resorts all around the world."

"Ah! Well, then. Americans." He chuckled.

"What about them?" I asked pointedly.

"Oh," he scoffed, "you know what Americans are like."

"Yes, I do," I said. "As it happens, I recently fucked one."

Silence reigned. Andrew looked as though he'd swallowed the cutlery.

"Ah, here's our food," observed Neil.

The meals arrived on a gold-leaf monstrosity of a trolley and, as I anticipated, the waitress had no idea who'd ordered what. She wasn't fazed, however. She simply plonked them down anywhere. We passed the plates around till we'd identified our own. As we opened our third bottle of wine, I took a tentative bite of my chicken.

"Mmm," I sighed. "The coq au vin is sensational!"

Andrew beamed. "Yes, the chef's very good here."

"Just as well," I remarked, glancing up at the chandelier that teetered precariously above our heads, "considering what the place looks like. I can't decide if it's a restaurant or a brothel!" I grinned.

"You're not a very tactful person, are you," murmured Janssen.

"Pardon?"

"Andrew here is responsible for the decor."

I was stunned. "Oh, um, sorry, I had no idea. Responsible? How?"

"It's my job now," he answered. "I do interiors. I don't work for the drug company anymore."

"They tried to send him interstate," Neil explained. "We couldn't have that, so he got out and we set him up in business. Doing very well, too, after only twelve months." He smiled coyly at Andrew—a sight so repulsive, Newton's corpse came in at a distant second.

I gazed at my ex. He was blushing again, a tiny red spot pulsating in each cheek and a damp glaze over the eyes reminiscent of a recently beached dolphin. I recalled this particular look from two or three pivotal moments in our relationship. It meant trouble; the waterworks were raring to go, without a doubt.

I floundered. "I didn't know you were interested in that kind of thing."

Andrew shrugged. "I am."

"You never said anything about it."

"Yes I did. You just don't remember."

"But you never did any interior decorating at our place!"

"I wanted to do plenty, but you were so damn attached to everything."

"Like what?"

Janssen raised a wizened finger. "Now, you two!"

Andrew ignored him. "Like those filthy old lounge chairs, for instance. I was dying to get rid of them. They didn't even match!"

"I've still got them," I protested.

"Don't tell me! After nine years? They must be decrepit!"

Neil stepped in. "Don't get upset, sweetheart. It hardly matters, does it?"

Andrew simply gulped. The other two looked expectantly at me. An apology was apparently required.

"Andrew," I said, "I'm glad you're doing something you enjoy and that it's so successful. Did you design your own house—home—as well?"

"Don't pretend, Marc. I know you hate it."

"No, I don't. How can you say that?"

"You *do*."

The table was now enveloped with a silence deeper and more chilling than the mist around Dracula's castle. We chewed our way resolutely through our meal.

"What were we talking about before?" said Janssen, rallying at last.

"Throwing acid in a man's face," replied Neil in a bored tone, as though it was something he did every day.

"Maybe I can pick your brain," I said to him. "You're a chemist. Do you know anything about hydrofluoric acid?"

He rolled his eyes. "I'm not an industrial chemist. I'm in retail."

"I could find out about it," murmured Andrew hastily, with a martyred look.

"Could you?"

"No trouble at all. I'll call up some suppliers. What do you want to know?"

"Oh, well, what it's used for, I suppose. Is it hard to get? That sort of thing."

"Most volatile substances are restricted," said Neil. He peered around the table. "Is anyone interested in dessert?"

"Not for me," Janssen mumbled.

"Right, then perhaps we should think about going. We'll split the bill four ways. It saves the trouble of working it out."

After his endless comments about how well they were doing, I'd half expected him to pay, but the magnanimous gesture simply wasn't in Neil's repertoire.

"Allow me," I said, producing my Visa card with a flourish. The anticipated objections never came. The others merely nodded in unison like judges in a French courtroom. Sometimes my generous nature goes too far.

Later that night, as I was about to drag my old body off to dreamland, there was a tap on my door.

"May I come in?" Andrew whispered.

"Sure," I said. He crept in and sat on the bed next to me.

"Neil's out like a light," he said. "You'll probably hear him snoring later. It'd wake the dead!" He smiled.

"I'm sorry I criticised your interior," I said.

"Oh, never mind that. Look, about your acid: I've just been talking to one of the chaps I used to work with, and he gave me a few details. It's very nasty stuff, apparently. Quite poisonous, too. You're supposed to handle it with gloves and visors. If it gets on your skin, even in a low concentration, the fluoride component eats into your vital organs and replaces the body salts so the organs break down."

"Lucky I didn't touch it," I gulped.

"Yes, you'd be dead by now. There was a horrific incident at a laboratory in Perth a few years ago…"

I held up my hand. "I've seen the effects already. What's

the stuff used for? Would a photographer keep it?"

"I couldn't say. It's a cleaning agent. It's used on iron casings, rocks, old glass—things like that."

"Camera lenses?" I asked urgently.

"I guess so. It eats away anything on the surface, though strangely enough it doesn't affect plastic. Is that any help?"

"Yes, thank you." I wiped my brow. Poor Newton, I reflected; he was doomed, whatever happened.

Andrew coughed awkwardly. "I was wondering about something."

"What?"

"Did Grant...well, did he do it?"

"I don't think so, though at the moment things aren't looking too good."

"Oh, hell."

"I'm trying to find the killer."

Andrew sighed. "You know, Marc, I do worry about you. I really think that at your age you should be in a relationship."

This was hardly a subject I felt eager to discuss. "I tried it once. Remember?"

"That was a decade ago. Being with someone back then—well, it was fun, but it wasn't essential. You know what I mean? What are you going to do when you get older?"

"Same as I do now, but less often! Look, I've got my opera and my interests. My life is excitement personified. So don't worry. You're a doll, but don't go matchmaking, all right?"

He squirmed. "Yes, oops! I should have known better."

It took a second to sink in. "What? Not that awful Janssen person? Surely you didn't imagine—"

"OK, OK. I knew it was dead in the water when he trashed Tebaldi."

He leaned over, took my head in his hands, and gave me a sweet, lingering kiss. In an instant the years fell away.

"I love you, you know," he whispered.

"I love you, too," I mumbled back. "But I must get some sleep."

"Ditto. See you at breakfast."

He crept out, gently closing the door behind him. From somewhere below, my ears detected a buzz not unlike a quartet of circular saws running at full throttle. For a very brief moment, and for a variety of reasons, I wished I had just a smidgin of hydrofluoric acid in my possession.

CHAPTER 21

I t was drizzling next morning: a cold, grey, judicial day. The waiting room in the new court complex was minus three on an ambience scale of one to ten. A few hard chairs constituted the entire decor. (Still, at least they hadn't let Andrew get hold of it!) My arrival had been duly noted, and a pleasant but anxious girl had brought me a cup of tea, reinforcing the sensation that I was awaiting major surgery in a large hospital.

Earlier on, I'd spoken to Grant's lawyer and we'd agreed to meet at nine. However, it was ten past already and there was no sign of him. Grant's hearing was first up before the magistrate, scheduled for 9:30. Just as I was beginning to think I'd have to go on "cold," the lawyer arrived in a flurry: a pudgy young man with slicked-down hair and heavy black-rimmed glasses. His stubby fingers clutched an overstuffed briefcase, which he dropped to the floor as he stretched out a plump pink hand.

"Marc Petrucci?"

"Yes?"

"How are you? Ross Costello, counsel for Mr. Breen."

He shook my hand limply, opened his bag, and produced a sheaf of papers. "I have a copy of your statement here," he muttered. "Yes, here it is. You'll want to check it through, I think."

I skimmed the document as Costello kept chatting.

"Mr. Breen tells me you're an old friend of his."

I looked up. "Sorry? Oh, yes. I am. I'd like to visit him."

He smiled. "You won't have to. I'm hoping the magistrate finds the prosecution has no case and tells 'em to nick off and start again."

"And discover the real killer."

"Exactly. But we'll have to verify your evidence. Another witness changed their tune completely in a second statement, and the case against Mr. Breen depends largely on that person's testimony."

"Who?"

"I'm afraid it's mum!" he whispered.

"Whose mum?"

"No, you know: 'Mum's the word.' It's imperative to undermine this witness's credibility—and the sooner the better—so I'll be cross-examining you."

"Why don't you just cross-examine the witness?"

"I can't call people in at this stage. That's the police's prerogative."

I was getting nervous. "Why did they call me?"

"The poor old coroner had a hard time with the body, it was so burnt and battered around. The court may require more detail from you on the state it was in when you found it."

I didn't care for this particular tack. "Why? We know the acid killed him. Didn't it?"

"No. Nasty as it was, the acid wouldn't have finished him off, not then and there. The coroner's finding was death by drowning."

My whole body went cold and limp. I felt dizzy.

"Are you all right, Mr. Petrucci?"

I put my hand to my forehead. Drowning? He couldn't possibly have been alive when Wade and I doused him in the pool. I'd swear he was dead! Wade thought so, too. But if he wasn't...did that mean I was the real murderer?

"I think I'm going to be sick," I mumbled, scrabbling in my pocket for a handkerchief.

Costello clapped me on the back. "It's often scary the first time. Don't you worry." He grabbed the statement and shoved it back into his bag. "I'm off," he said. "See you in court, eh? I don't know when you'll be called—not too long, hopefully. Have you got something to read?"

"What? Er, no."

"Should've brought along a murder mystery. Cheers!"

I sat, stunned, running through the horrific scene one more time in my head. We'd wandered along, Wade and I, in the dark. I'd bumped into Newton's body, lying face up in the parched scrub next to the track. When I saw his face, before I dropped the lighter, had there been any sign of life? It was a split second, but I was positive there had not been.

Suddenly, with a surge of relief, I realised I was forgetting what the police detectives had told me. Death had occurred between five and six P.M. But that was odd! If Newton had drowned, why did we find his body in the bushes? The body must have been moved!

In any event, I was not the murderer, and neither was Grant. The more I thought about this, the more I was convinced. Despite Grant's occasional tendency to rage and bluster, I knew how deeply he cared about people, and it was up to me to prove his innocence. The committal hearing would be my opportunity to alert the police to other possibilities—namely Pastor Paramor and Hadrian—which they had, so far, lazily ignored. There had to be some way I could work into my testimony the suspicious facts I'd uncovered: the acid hidden at Hadrian's studio, for instance, or the Church of Divine Intervention's violent homophobia.

After a long wait I was called. I have little experience of courts. Everything I know is based on the odd television drama. I was therefore quite surprised to be ushered into a very plain room indeed. It had none of the expected oak paneling or implacable, slow-moving ceiling fans: It merely looked like a classroom for very mature students. For some reason, this rather unnerved me.

The magistrate, a well-fed jovial character, sat behind the bench at the far end of the room. Before him was a long table with the police prosecutor at one end and a clutch of legal counsel, including Costello, at the other. The public gallery contained a handful of people who, from their slouching, I understood to be reporters. Grant didn't seem to be present.

I was sworn in and took the stand, which was, in fact, an uncomfortable seat. The prosecutor asked me to state my name and occupation, as another fellow handed me some papers.

"Mr. Petrucci, can you identify this statement?"

"It's the one I gave to the police."

"To Detectives Williams and Lee, on April 4 this year?" the prosecutor asked.

"Yes."

"Thank you. I tender this statement as evidence, Your Worship."

"Proceed," the magistrate mumbled.

"Mr. Petrucci, in your statement you describe your discovery of the body of Newton Heath. Just run through it in a little more detail, would you please?"

"Certainly. Well, it really started with that incident a while back with the aircraft—you remember, when a propeller fell off a plane and killed a drag queen? Vasselina, her name was—"

The magistrate interrupted. "Is this relevant?" he asked.

"Mr. Petrucci," said the prosecutor, "just tell us how you found the body. Newton Heath's body."

"Er, yes. Sorry, Your Honour."

The magistrate sniffed. "I am addressed as Your Worship," he said, "for the time being, anyhow." There was a polite rustle in the court. "Please continue."

"I found Newton's body just after midnight, in a pool of carp. They're fish. That is, I wasn't in the pool, the body was."

"At the New Heaven holiday resort," the prosecutor added. "Is that correct?"

"Yes."

"And you were one of the subscribers to the initial investment fund that financed this resort?"

"No, I wasn't. It's a long story."

"We have time, Mr. Petrucci," said the magistrate.

"Newton—that is, the deceased—put me down for seven-hundred thousand dollars without telling me. I haven't got that kind of money, of course."

"Excuse me, Your Worship," said Mr. Costello. "But this has nothing to do with Mr. Petrucci's statement."

"I'm merely establishing how well the witness knew the deceased, Your Worship."

"Why don't you ask him?" suggested the magistrate.

"Mr. Petrucci," said the prosecutor, "you were a friend of Mr. Heath's. Correct?"

"That is correct."

"So you recognised the body. Would you describe the scene for us? Take your time."

"It was dark. There were a few crabs here and there, scuttling around the place. Newton was lying in the pool, except for his feet, they were sticking out. He was sort of on his side, with his face turned around. He'd been burnt somehow. I thought it looked like acid burns."

"Are you familiar with acid burns?"

"N-no. Not really."

"Go on."

"Well, I pulled him out. He was dead."

"Were you alone when you made this discovery?"

I answered steadily. "No. I was not."

I gazed slowly around the court. There was silence. Eventually, the magistrate spoke. "I think we can do without the dramatic pause, Mr. Petrucci. Who were you with?"

"Er, Claire Bornkamp. She worked on the island too."

The police prosecutor continued. "In your statement, you say you were taking a moonlight stroll with Ms. Bornkamp."

"That's correct."

"So we may assume you are romantically involved with her."

"Yes. That is, I was."

The prosecutor shrugged and scratched the back of his neck. "For the record, Ms. Bornkamp's statement has already been tended as evidence." He smiled. "We have a slight problem, Mr. Petrucci." (I smelled a rat.) "There are conflicting versions of your story. According to Ms. Bornkamp's statement, she was *not* with you when you found the body. Would you care to *clarify* your testimony?"

My hands began to sweat slightly.

The magistrate cleared his throat. "Let me remind you, Mr. Petrucci, you are under oath. This is a serious matter, and it is imperative we are given a clear picture of the circumstances surrounding Mr. Heath's death. A man has been accused of murder, and it is up to this court to establish whether there is enough prima face evidence to prosecute. Do you understand?"

I nodded briskly. "Yes, I do, and, er, I plead the Fifth Amendment."

He glared at me. "The Fifth Amendment to what, precisely?"

"You know, that thing that says you don't have to incriminate yourself."

"You may be referring to a quirk of the American legal system, Mr. Petrucci. It doesn't apply here. You may incriminate yourself freely."

I was flustered. "All right. Well, um, Claire's right. I was out walking alone, because I couldn't sleep, and I found Newton, exactly the way I said. I ran straight to Claire's room and dragged her back to show her the body."

"Thank you," said the prosecutor. "So you lied to Detectives Williams and Lee?"

"Only about that part."

"Do you realise you committed an offense?"

The magistrate butted in again. "Why did you lie to the police, Mr. Petrucci?"

I blanched. Claire had put me in an extremely awkward position. Obviously, she'd stuck to our "official" story just long enough to secure her Gaytour promotion, then dumped me squarely in the excrement. *Well,* I thought crossly, *let her take the rap!*

"Lying was Claire's idea," I admitted. "To...protect my good name."

The magistrate blinked. "Pardon?"

"To protect my good name, Your Honour—Your Lordship."

He looked confused, but let it slide. "I see. Well, don't lie to the police in future, or your good name won't be worth protecting. Any further questions?"

The prosecutor resumed. "As regards the state the body was in, do you wish to change your testimony?"

"No, thanks."

"No further questions, Your Worship."

I started to get up.

"Wait a moment, Mr. Petrucci, if you would," the magistrate said. "We'll see if Mr. Costello has any questions for you."

"Oh, yes. Whoops."

Grant's lawyer stood and nodded pleasantly at me. "Mr. Petrucci, you say you were involved sexually with Claire Bornkamp."

I could no longer see a need to keep up this pretence. On the other hand, I'd already been warned once. I didn't wish to be exposed as a liar yet again.

"Yes," I replied half-heartedly.

"And Ms. Bornkamp was your superior in the resort hierarchy. Is that right?"

"Yes. She was the lesbian coordinator."

"Ah. So if she suggested a course of action, it would be diplomatic of you to go along with it?"

"Oh, yes."

"And you say she suggested you tell the police that you discovered the body together?"

"That's right."

He looked me straight in the eye. "Then why did she change her mind later?"

"I don't know. You'd have to ask her," I answered. Costello frowned.

"Mr. Petrucci has a point," said the magistrate. "Is Ms. Born-kamp appearing?"

"She's indisposed, Your Worship," advised the prosecutor.

"Indisposed! That's a damned nuisance," the magistrate replied. "In that case you may continue, Mr. Costello, but stop asking the witness for his opinion. He can't be expected to account for the lady's behaviour simply because he's involved with her."

"I'm not anymore."

"Be quiet, Mr. Petrucci."

"Sorry."

Costello ran his hands through his hair, then fixed me again with an encouraging but desperate smile.

"You say you went for a stroll that night because you couldn't sleep."

"Yes."

"Were you aware, Mr. Petrucci, that the top luncheon area of the resort operated during the night as a 'beat'—that is, an informal cruising area for homosexual activity?"

I blinked. This was unexpected. "I'd heard about it."

"When did Ms. Bornkamp discover what you were getting up to behind her back?"

The prosecutor leapt to his feet. "Your Worship, really! Objection! Who is on trial here?"

"Nobody is," the magistrate answered flatly, then glared at the lawyer. "What are you getting at, Mr. Costello? It's racy but is it relevant? Your client hasn't been mentioned once, to my knowledge."

"Your Worship," he answered. "The police's case against my client rests solely on Ms. Bornkamp's statement. I'm mere-ly questioning the reliability of that testimony. If her story swings back and forth on a whim, prompted solely by feel-ings of female jealousy, how much credence can we give to her statement?"

The magistrate looked unimpressed. "I thought we'd dealt

with this. Ms. Bornkamp is not on the stand. We know nothing of her motives. I'm afraid I am inclined to accept her statement at face value."

Costello turned to me. "No further questions," he grunted.

"You may stand down, Mr. Petrucci," said the magistrate.

I hesitated. "Oh, but I can't! There's new evidence."

The magistrate banged his gavel. I jumped. "This is not an episode of *Perry Mason*," he snapped. "We've got your statement. If you have more to say, you'll be given every opportunity at a later date, regardless of the outcome of this hearing."

"But Your Lordship, there's Hadrian's acid—"

"Mr. Petrucci! We have finished with you!"

The magistrate sat back and drummed the bench with his fingers. "I am concluding these proceedings at this point. I find Mr. Petrucci's evidence corroborates Ms. Bornkamp's statement. I am hereby committing Grant Aloysius Breen to stand trial for the murder of Newton Heath."

"What!?" I said.

Grant's lawyer gave me a withering look.

"Stand down!" the magistrate barked. "The hearing is closed."

"How did it go?" Andrew asked anxiously when he picked me up outside the court in his Saab.

"Could have been better," I admitted. "Grant's going to be tried."

"Oh, my God! It can't be happening, Marc."

"I know, but I'm determined to get to the bottom of this. It's just that there's so much devious activity below the surface, I can't begin to sort it all out."

He took my hand. "Don't get yourself killed!"

"That would certainly defeat the purpose." I smiled weakly.

CHAPTER 22

The cab bore me along past the grimy factories and grubby backyards that huddled between the airport and home. I gazed at the panorama of boarded-up windows, dingy shopfronts, and graffiti-covered walls. By no criteria could it be considered beautiful, certainly not compared to the lushness of the New Heaven resort or even the pastel pomp of Andrew's little suburban outpost. Yet there was nowhere else I wanted to be. My humble terrace was the centre of my universe, and after all this unaccustomed travel I longed to hear that familiar soprano, drink that strong coffee, and hide snugly away from the world. Of course I had urgent things to attend to, but first I planned a refresher course in day-to-day trivia. Staying with friends, even my "ex," always reminds me why I prefer living alone.

Imagine my alarm, therefore, when I discovered that the *thud-thud-thud* of dance music I heard as the taxi rounded the corner came from the wide-open windows of Villa Petrucci. I paid the driver and braced myself.

At my front door I tried pushing my key into the lock, only to find the door was already open with my spare key still in it—something no genuine resident of the area would do unless he harboured a death wish.

Inside, my worst fears were realised. I clicked off the pulsating CD and looked forlornly around my lounge room. Towels, shirts, and (of course!) Aussie Boys briefs were draped over every spare chair. The table was cluttered with champagne glasses, videos, and half-finished tubs of take-away Thai. Although it was five o'clock in the afternoon, all the lights were on and, I suspected, had been on for some time. In the distance I heard the shower running and Paul's light baritone belting out a ballad from a Sondheim musical. I eased open the bathroom door.

"Paul!" I screeched.

"Aaargh! Mother!" He flung aside the shower curtain and revealed himself, naked and dripping, his fists raised in a boxing stance. "Caro! It's you! Back so soon!" He stepped daintily out of the shower and embraced me. "I thought you were the late Tony Perkins in *Psycho*."

"What are you doing here?"

"Having a shower, what else! See? No more blue hair!"

I glanced behind him at my white tiled wall. It was spattered with blue. I moaned. "Paul, get dried then come and explain yourself. I'll be putting on the coffee."

"We're out of coffee, caro. But there's a used tea bag in the sink."

Within five minutes I'd managed to gather the stray clothes together in one pile and clear a mess off the couch so, if absolutely necessary, Paul could sleep there. I got the feeling he aimed to stay a while, and my premonition was amply confirmed by his sheepish expression when he finally emerged with an orange towel around his waist and a white one piled high on his head.

"You don't mind, do you, caro mio?" he squeaked.

"What's wrong with your own place?" I asked pointedly. "Don't you want to live with the love of your life?"

He breathed a heartfelt sigh. "Darren needs his own space."

"But it's your flat!"

"I know. It's a tricky question." He flung his wet towel on the carpet and tugged on a pair of jeans. "Although I always liked your house better."

"So do I. That's not the point."

"Can't I live here with you? Pleeease?" His bottom lip trembled.

"Don't get all emotional and girlie. You can stay for the time being."

He clapped his hands abruptly. "Good! Sorry about the mess, but I wasn't expecting you yet. Give us a kiss. I've been good, really!"

I kissed him. "There."

"You know," he smarmed, "old Renata's quite special! I played one of your opera CDs last night to lull me to sleep."

"Oh, which one?"

"Let me see, here it is: *Gianni Schicchi*. I picked it because it's the shortest."

"Lauretta's aria is divine." I started to hum the famous tune and Paul joined in, harmonising whenever he felt confident. As we reached a soaring climax, he grabbed my hand, gazed into my eyes, and beamed. Maybe it wouldn't be too inconvenient having him around.

Finally, after he'd taken several curtain calls, I managed to divulge the bad news that Grant was, after all, going to be tried. I could tell Paul was disappointed.

"Fuck 'em!" he scoffed. "If the police are so incredibly dumb, we'll just redouble our efforts! Which reminds me, to that end I have procured two of the most sought-after tickets this side of the Jesus, Son of God Tour!"

"Tickets to what?"

He mimed a drumroll. "Marc, you and your date—me!— will be attending the prestigious *Bimbeau*'s Choice Awards, to be held in the Robin Askin Room at the casino this Saturday coming. You don't have two dinner suits, do you?"

"*Bimbeau*'s Choice, as in *Bimbeau* magazine?"

"Clever, caro. You haven't totally forsaken popular culture."

"What are the awards for?" I asked dryly. "Academic achievement?"

"They're television awards. Best Actor in a Chicken Suit, Most Popular Personality of All Time, et cetera. *Bimbeau* readers pick 'em."

"I don't want to go to that!"

"Oh, yes, you do. There's always a hell of a party afterward. This year it's a gambling theme. Should be a blast!"

"No, thank you. Take Darren."

"I'd love to do that, upside down against a wall. However, we are going to the *Bimbeaus* with a purpose: We're going to nail Newton's celebrity, once and for all! He's certain to be there, so I've drawn up a shortlist with the help of your mate Delia."

My heart sank. "Paul! You haven't been speaking to a journalist?"

"I couldn't help it! She's been ringing and ringing. She's very cross with you, caro."

"Why?"

"For giving an exclusive interview to *Queer Scene*. She feels betrayed."

"Not as much as *I* do!" I rolled my eyes. "Paul, if there's one thing that damn article taught me, it's not to trust the media. More publicity is the last thing we need."

"I suppose you're right. But Delia did tell us about there being a celebrity in the first place."

"Then let *her* go to this shindig."

"She wasn't invited!" he crowed. He looked like the cat who got into the cream.

"I don't want to discuss it now. I'm hungry—and I've got plenty more to tell you."

"Goody! Let's eat out! There's no more food in the house anyway."

"All right. Get dressed, while I make up your bed on the couch."

His eyelashes fluttered longingly toward the stairs.

"No, Paul!" I stated. "You are not bunking in with me."

"But it's such a *bi-i-ig* comfy bed," he purred in a fruity French accent. "And I'm *vairrry* good at making love!"

"I thought you were in love with someone else."

"*Merde.* That's right. OK, I'll sleep with you, but no sex."

I burst out laughing. When Andrew urged me to find a soulmate, I doubt Paul was the prototype he had in mind.

We enjoyed a cheap dinner at the local Mexican, where I

made an expansive story out of the matchmaking meal I'd endured with Andrew and Neil, then steered the subject away to something more palatable: hydrofluoric acid. Paul agreed that our new information whisked Hadrian squarely back to the top of our list of suspects.

When Paul eventually started mooning over Darren, as I knew he would, I decided it was high time this romance was nipped painfully in the bud. I described our meeting in detail, then went on to reveal the sleazy part the boy had played in the Lachie Turner case and his subsequent blackmailing of Newton. Nor did I neglect to add my personal opinion vis-à-vis Darren's morals, motives, and general attitude. I didn't want to hurt Paul, but the truth had to be told.

Paul nodded earnestly.

"Caro, I'm shocked but not all that surprised," he said. "The boy has a lurid past, even a criminal one. It seems what Dazzle needs is the love of a good woman to show him the error of his ways and lift him up to a higher plane." He fluttered his eyelashes.

"You've lost your mind!" I exploded, but there was no point. I was wasting my breath. Instead, I turned my attention to the matter of Claire's duplicitous about-face.

Paul became very indignant. "Hiram was right! Claire would auction off her grandmother's next meal to get ahead. What other revelations did she come up with in her new, revised statement?"

"I don't know. But I wouldn't be surprised if she mentioned running into Grant at the time of the murder."

"Well, we'd better get onto her at once, caro! Before she goes and compromises our investigation any further."

"I suppose so. But how will we find her? There's no one on the island anymore."

He beamed. "That's easy! We'll ask Delia." He pulled out his phone and began punching in the numbers.

"Paul, she's a journalist..." I warned.

But it was too late: She'd answered. "Hello, Delia? Paul Silverton...I can hardly hear you. Where are you now? Really? Yes, yes, I know it...I'm out with Marc tonight, could we..."

A truck rumbled past the window and I missed the rest of their brief conversation. When Paul replaced his mobile, he was jubilant.

"How's that for efficiency? We're going meet up with Delia in half an hour's time. At the Wedge."

"The what?"

"The Wedge Hotel in Paddington."

He wrinkled his nose. "It's straight!"

"Paul—"

"Caro, isn't it about time we got something out of the media, instead of the other way round?"

I conceded. Paul had a point.

Twenty minutes later we walked into the Wedge. Whether this was the bar's official title or a fond sobriquet I couldn't say, but it was certainly accurate. The old building's three walls were wedged into a teeny space where two busy roads met in a fork.

On the ground floor, the inside walls had been painted a sultry dark purple in an ineffectual attempt to spruce up the ancient plaster. At the large central bar, everybody seemed to be enjoying themselves as if their lives depended on it. The roar of the crowd rivaled that of traffic outside.

We squeezed in amongst the clientele. Young men with bare midriffs and greasy hair, spiky black or bottle blond, flung their wrists this way and that in overtly camp gestures. Pale, short-haired girls with heavy makeup and lip rings smoked moodily and swigged bottled beer.

I tugged Paul's belt. "I thought you said this was a straight bar," I shouted.

"It is," he replied.

"Are you sure?"

He turned to me, a look of disgust adorning his normally beatific features. "What you see, caro, is the inner-city queer crowd. Most of them come from the film school a block away. They're gay and lesbian wannabes! They've taken up our look and our attitudes, but when it comes to the basics, they can't get it up."

We shoved our way to a gap at the bar. A single barman was serving down the other end.

"Can a real queen get a real drink!?" Paul screamed at the top of his trained voice.

The barman, who looked exactly like one of the patrons, only better, glided over to us. Languidly, he pursed his sculpted lips. "We don't want any trouble," he said.

"Trouble is my maiden name," brayed Paul, ordering a Long Island iced tea. "Look around, caro. Is there any sign of your friend?"

"She's not my friend!" I complained. "I hardly know her." I searched among the faces.

Paul waved to the barman. "'Scuse me," he pouted. "Is Delia Scott-Merman here?"

The barman nodded toward a stairwell in the far corner. "Try upstairs."

"Come on, caro. Bring your drink."

We plodded up a steep, narrow stairway to the next floor. A thwack of billiard balls greeted us on our entrance. Several pool tables were faintly visible through the swirling smoke. At each table, a group of bystanders lounged about casually. Some played pool, but their companions exhibited little interest. They were all ostentatiously cool.

There in the centre of it all stood Delia. She was about to play a shot when she saw us. She lifted her cue off the table, smiled grimly, then lowered it again and slammed a ball into a pocket.

"Game," she announced to her companions. They shrugged indifferently and wandered away. Delia put down her cue and staggered over to us. It was quite obvious she'd had a few drinks.

"Hello there, Paul," she said. "Who's your friend?"

"Delia, it's me!" I protested.

She continued to address Paul. "What does your friend want?"

"Now, now! To forgive is divine," Paul chirped brightly. "We need to get in touch with Claire Bornkamp."

"You might know where she is," I suggested.

She nodded vaguely. "Yeah, I know where she is."

"Oh. Good."

"Can't see any reason to tell *you*, though."

The other desultory matches had come to a halt during this brief exchange, as the room fell silent. Evidently, any degree of animation was something of a rarity.

"Why are you so angry with me?" I blurted out. Delia's unfriendly attitude was making me increasingly uncomfortable.

She fixed me with a pained expression, something like the look you'd give a cockroach that refused to die.

"I had nothing to do with that story in *Queer Scene*," I implored. "It's caused me no end of trouble! Honestly, Delia, I'm hardly the man who knew too much! If anything, I'm the man who doesn't know enough."

"So what *do* you know?"

"Plenty," I cried, "but none of it adds up. Claire may be able to clarify things. I've got to talk to her!"

Delia twisted the cue in her hands as a leer crept across her face. "All right, Marc," she replied. "You let me down by giving *Queer Scene* an exclusive. That was a low act. I don't know whether we're such good friends anymore. If you want something from me, you're gonna have to work for it."

"What do you mean?"

"Let's play pool! If I lose the game, I'll tell you where Claire is."

"That's a fabulous idea!" squealed Paul, who has an over-developed competitive spirit.

"And for every ball I sink, you've gotta tell me something I don't know."

"Doesn't seem very fair."

"Take it or leave it."

I was inclined to leave it. "How about an opera quiz instead?"

"I don't think so." She smiled spitefully. "You got two bucks?"

We grabbed an available table. Delia set up while Paul raced downstairs for more drinks.

With trembling hands I managed to break, having won the toss, and immediately sank one of the striped balls. It was mere beginner's luck. Delia lined up her shot carefully and sent two coloured balls spinning into opposite pockets at once. I was amazed.

"Two pieces of info, thank you, Marc," she said. "And they'd better be good."

I thought for a moment. I couldn't tell her anything I wasn't prepared to see distorted in print a week later.

"OK," I said carefully. "I've ascertained that there was a strange man hanging around the island, perving at everybody."

She looked less than interested. "Who was it? You?"

"Nobody knows who he was. He watched people from the trees."

"Like Tarzan," said Paul, as he returned and shoved a drink into her hand. It was a Long Island iced tea. He handed me a lemonade.

"Does this guy have something to do with the murder?" asked Delia.

I hesitated. "If I answer that, is it the second thing?"

"I guess so."

"Well, I don't know. He may have seen what happened."

She grunted. "That's not good enough."

Paul butted in. "We've got a candid photo of him."

"Can I have it?"

I considered her request. "Yes, all right. Why not?"

"Your shot."

I had an easy task: a striped ball quivered at the rim of one of the middle pockets. I took careful aim, but the white spun off the cushion at a tangent and missed it altogether. Delia casually potted another one of hers.

"Tell me about that religious crowd," she said, sipping her drink. "What's the story there?"

"OK," I said emphatically. "Neither Grant Breen nor myself are now, or have ever been, members of the Church of Divine Intervention."

"What kind of information is that?" drawled Delia. "You're also not pygmies! That tells me precisely nothing."

"The *Queer Scene* article inferred we had some connection to the cult," I answered huffily. "Now you know we don't."

She sniffed. In a burst of panache, I sank two balls. The second one was hers.

"You're in trouble now," she said gleefully. "So, who is the mystery celebrity?"

Paul piped up. "I already told you on the phone: we don't know."

"I'm asking *him*," Delia snapped.

I hedged. "There's a slight chance it's someone whose initials are B.F.."

"B.F.?" She shot a sideways glance at Paul. "You kept that little secret, didn't you! How do you know about these initials?"

"I'm afraid I have to protect my sources," I mumbled.

"Don't give me that crap," said Delia.

"It might just mean 'boyfriend,'" Paul added. "We'll find out at the *Bimbeau*s."

"You'd better! Call me as soon as you do."

We played on. Delia lost all semblance of good manners. I also knew that sooner or later I'd run out of these gossipy tidbits, which made me nervous and put me even further off my game. *Whack!* She did it again.

"Well?"

I bit my lip. "I could tell you something about New Heaven."

"Please do."

"It's up in the air." She glared in reply. "What I mean is, the initial investment was, you know, dodgy. Newton didn't manage to raise all his capital. The Americans now have control, but there's still a lot of money owed."

"Hmm. That's actually worth knowing."

With all the remaining concentration at my disposal, I potted a red and a yellow. This time, both were mine. I heaved a sigh of relief; we were nearly even. I was in with a chance. On my next shot I sank the white.

"Let's get to the murder," she suggested. "Paul mentioned that you were called to the committal hearing. Did anything interesting come up?"

"Well—the official cause of death was drowning."

She gestured dismissively. "I know the official outcome," she said. "Can't you give me something more? Any little thing that seemed odd or unusual? A fact, however trivial, that the media reports might have ignored? Anything will do!"

I shrugged. Delia was even more tenacious than the *Queer Scene* woman! My only option was to put her off the track somehow. Then it occurred to me: I could set her to work in the very area where Paul and I had been, so far, unsuccessful.

"Now that you ask," I mused, "They kept coming back to Pastor Paramor, the leader of the sect. They wanted to know what he said at the meeting, how he felt about gays and lesbians, and whether the church owned or had access to a light aircraft. It struck me as odd at the time."

Paul's eyes opened wide in amazement. Delia herself looked like a bulldog that had sensed the presence of a cat.

She stared straight at me. "Why would they want to know a thing like that?"

"One answer at a time!" I said brazenly, though I had no intention whatsoever of elaborating. I played my shot, failing to sink another ball. However, by some welcome fluke, I managed to snooker Delia.

"Making it hard for me, are you?" she grumbled.

She leaned low over the pool table, drew back her cue and sent the white ball flying. It ricocheted round the table, then with a shattering *thock* it rammed the black ball, which rolled lazily into a side pocket.

"Caro," Paul exulted, "you've won! Delia sank the black!" He clapped his hands, then lifted me off the floor in a bear hug. Delia seemed shaken.

"I lost," she muttered. "Shit!"

"These things happen," I chuckled magnanimously. "Claire's number, if you don't mind."

Delia ran her fingers through her hair. "I could give you the number," she said, "but she's not there."

"Where is she then?"

"Our Lady of Sappho."

"What?"

"It's a hospital," said Paul. "You know, the big one near the cemetery."

Delia smiled. "And you can forget all about visiting. She's in intensive care. I tried to see her as soon as I heard, and the sisters told me to come back in a week."

"What's wrong?"

In one broad movement, Delia drained her glass and slammed it down hard on the table. "She had a fall, apparently. She was drunk."

A wild-eyed schoolboy lunged at me, brandishing a snooker cue. In a strangely detached way, I saw that the cue was not wooden at all, but alive. I tried to scream, but my voice was paralysed. I balanced precariously on the edge of a precipice as he pressed the horrific object across my windpipe. "Bring the hydrofluoric!" he wheezed to his satanic minions who were drooling and capering in a corner. "We'll get a story out of him, or else!" I couldn't breathe. I saw stars and heard bells ringing as I tried to wrest the tremendous weight from my throat. The bells grew louder, and I was falling...

Struggling into consciousness, I recognised the comforting shapes and patterns of my bedroom. I lay on the far edge of my queen-size bed. Paul sprawled facedown in the centre, humming in his sleep. One heavy arm was stretched out and lay across my neck. Somewhere downstairs the phone rang.

"Move over," I gasped and pushed his arm away. Without waking up, he rolled over and nuzzled his pillow contentedly. I glanced at my watch: It was almost five.

I staggered to my feet and hobbled downstairs. My head throbbed in protest. The phone stopped abruptly, just as I lunged at it, knocking over a vase of dead chrysanthemums and spilling putrid flower-water all over myself. *Damn Paul,* I thought. Was it too much trouble to flick on the answering machine? I cleaned up the mess and was starting back upstairs when the phone rang once more. This time I made it.

"Who is it?" I asked crossly. There was silence at the other end. "Hello? Is anyone there?" Still no answer. I slammed down the receiver. It rang again immediately.

"Now, look here," I began.

"Is that Marc?" asked a shaky voice.

"Who is this? What do you want? It's five in the morning!" There was a pause. "It's Hadrian."

"Hadrian! Where are you?"

"I can't take this much longer," he whimpered. "What am I going to do? I think it's happening again."

"What? What's happening?"

His voice faded away.

"Hadrian! Are you still there? What did you say?"

"I think I'm losing my grip, you know? I get scared! I had a bad episode when I was a kid. I get scared and frustrated and then…I don't know. I've got to talk to someone."

"Talk to me!"

"I wanted to. I went to your place. I climbed in a window. But you never came."

I gasped. "That was you?"

"You were Newton's friend. You must hate me!" He sounded on the verge of hysterics.

"No, no. Calm down, Hadrian. Tell me where you are."

"I'm hiding where no one can find me and nothing terrible can happen."

I had to tread carefully. This could be our big breakthrough. I assumed my friendliest tone. "Why don't I meet you for a quiet, sensible chat. You can tell me what you think is going to happen—or what's happened already. How does that sound? We could relax and have a drink. Or a game of pool! Will we do that? Hadrian? Hello?"

He was sniffling. "It's too late now."

"It is, rather. Tomorrow then?"

There was a click. He'd hung up.

CHAPTER 23

aturday came, the day of the *Bimbeau*'s Choice Awards. I had done my best to talk Paul out of it. I loathe crowds, and besides, we had so much else to do. The investigation was hotting up, as they say, after Hadrian's revealing telephone call. Unfortunately, what he hadn't revealed were his whereabouts.

"Didn't he give you a teensy clue?" Paul asked for the umpteenth time as we squeezed into our One-Night-Hire dinner suits.

"No! Do I have to wear the vest? It's so tight!"

"Of course, caro. They may ask you to do an impromptu Noël Coward selection."

I groaned. "We ought to be searching for Hadrian, not swanning off to the casino. We should be combing his studio building from top to bottom. It's full of empty spaces and hiding places."

"Hmm," Paul mused. "Empty spaces and hiding places. Isn't that from *Les Mis*?"

"What?"

"Caro, if you hanker for a return engagement of *Attack of the Snail People,* go right ahead! I'm over dykes for a while. I'm putting all coalition activities on hold."

"But Grant's in jail and we're not doing anything!"

He patted me on the head. "Yes we are. Tonight we're bumping into Lachie Turner accidentally on purpose. Now, let me fix your tie. There! Elegantissimo!"

I looked like a dangerous escaped penguin in a straitjacket. Paul, on the other hand, could have given Fred Astaire a twirl for his money.

"It suits you," I remarked.

"I'm a dancer," he said simply. "Let's face the music, caro!"

Just as the final decade of the 19th century was marked by the arrival of the motorcar, so the final decade of the 20th witnessed the advent of the casino, at least as far as Australia was concerned. Glass and glitter domes were springing up like malignant mushrooms in every city, and Sydney was determined not to be left behind.

A vast gambling palace named Planet Playground had recently opened with a great amount of unavoidable hoo-hah. Situated on prime real estate at the edge of the harbour, it encompassed restaurants, conference centres, theatres, night clubs, a day nursery, and a retirement village, but was still a casino in all but name. While it was being built, the owners had wisely converted a nearby pier into a temporary casino, to put their expensively acquired license to work and get the public accustomed to gambling as a way of life.

Once Planet Playground threw open its massive doors, the pier casino became a superfluous adjunct to the main show. After a clandestine discussion, the owners decided to remodel the pier as a private landing strip and helicopter maintenance point for their own personal use. The remodeling was due to begin in a few months, once the inevitable clamour of public protest had died down. Meanwhile the place was being rented out for corporate functions like the *Bimbeau*'s Choice Awards. That was where Paul and I were headed in our specially provided shuttle bus.

We were part of a very elegant crowd. Because the "theme" of the night was gambling, all the men wore dinner suits and the women leaned toward low-cut satin gowns and long white gloves.

"Have you ever been to a casino before?" Paul asked me.

"I once saw one in Monte Carlo. It was shut."

"Well, in Australia gamblers don't dress up like this at all. They just shuffle along in whatever they wear around the house: cardigans, Ugg boots, and trackies." He glanced at our fellow bus-ees. "It won't be martinis for this lot. Mark my words, caro. They don't fool me with their hired tat! Beer drinkers to a man."

"Have you got the tickets?"

"It's by exclusive invitation. Don't fret, I RSVP'd!"

The pier was a long, narrow structure with the entrance at one end and water at the other. A canopy and potted palms graced the makeshift foyer, where guests lined up to produce their bona fides and receive a rubber stamp on the back of the hand. I'd wondered how Paul had managed to wangle an invitation to such a star-studded event. The answer became clear the moment we reached the baby-faced security man on the door.

"Breen," Paul announced, handing him the invitation. "And partner."

The boy checked his list. 'Mr. Breen—OK! Enjoy the night."

"You're not Breen," growled the person behind us in the queue. He was a thickset, jowly man with Beatle-length grey hair tied back in a ponytail. "Grant Breen's in prison! I should know. I'm the executive producer of *Surfside Motel*."

The boy on the door was confused. "Mr. Breen confirmed…" he said.

"Grant sent us along in his place," Paul explained lightly. "Nothing wrong with that is there, cute-face?"

The boy inhaled abruptly. He probably hadn't been addressed as "cute-face" very often. "The invitations aren't transferable," he said.

"Let's forget it," I said.

"Look," Paul ranted. "Don't you know who my friend here is? The Man Who Knew Too Much! Does that ring a bell?"

"Oh, yeah?" the producer butted in. "Read about it in the trade papers. Old Hitchcock classic. Remake for Pay TV."

I was momentarily at a loss.

"That's right," Paul announced.

The man patted the security boy on the shoulder. "It's OK, son," he whispered and then hauled Paul and me inside without further ado.

"Rory Van Dijk," he smiled, stretching out his hand. I shook it tentatively, crushing the business card he was handing to me. "Sorry about that little hiccup. These kids don't know anything. Had no idea you were in town. Been snowed under. You understand."

"Oh, yes."

He murmured in a gritty undertone. "Keeping my fingers crossed for Grant. Didn't know he was a friend of yours. Terrible business. We can't afford to lose him, can we? *Surfside* airs in eighty-seven countries, you know. Must grab a drink. Catch up soon."

As he lumbered away, I turned to Paul. He looked hugely amused.

"Who does he think we are?"

"Not a clue, caro!"

"Whatever the case, we're here under false pretences! How the hell did you get Grant's invitation?"

"It came in the mail."

"To my address?"

"Yup! Wasn't Grant going to stay with you?" he reminded me.

"That's right. Before he became a guest of Her Majesty."

"Ha! From one queen to another!"

In the area where we now stood were dozens of gambling tables—roulette, blackjack, wheels of fortune, and row upon row of poker machines. Members of the public crowded around them. At several blackjack tables, white-haired old ladies clutching their handbags appeared to be gradually betting away their life's savings one coin at a time, while more women could be found playing the pokies. These tough old girls had stiff hairstyles and knitted suits. They puffed on cigarettes and squabbled incessantly while playing two or three machines at once.

Suddenly, an unshaven man in a nylon shirt banged his fist on the roulette table. "That's it!" he bellowed. "I can't get another mortgage!" He produced a revolver and aimed it at his temple. In a split second, two burly security men overpowered him and punched him to the floor. They dragged him, swearing and screaming, right by us. As the desperate loser passed, he winked straight at Paul.

Watching this, I grew increasingly horrified, but I was alone in my reaction. Other guests either ignored the scene or gazed briefly and tittered as they passed by.

"Paul!" I clutched his arm. "Did you see what just happened?"

He laughed. "It's part of the 'theme night,' caro. These people aren't for real; they're actors. That little performance was put on for our amusement." He waved at the desperate man, who, having been thrown out, ambled over to join us.

"Hi, Jase," Paul said. "This is Marc."

"Hi," the man said. "How was that, baby? Break your fucking heart or what?"

"Marc was taken in."

Jase regarded me with amazement. "Were you? Not a bad gig if you ask me. I based the character on my old man!" He and Paul laughed uproariously. "You giving us something yourself?"

Paul lifted his chin. "Not tonight, Jasephine! We got invited!"

"Braggart! How is the bottom of the barrel these days? Well, off to the cleaners, I can't stay chatting!"

He ran back, preparing to go through the grisly scenario again, and we moved on. The room was bisected in the centre by a glamorous glittering curtain. It reminded me of a shower curtain my late friend Anton owned in 1976. He often wore it in the Mardi Gras parade.

Paul and I passed through the curtain and entered a huge room laid out for dining. There was seating for about two hundred, six to a table, and each table groaned under the weight of china, cutlery, and wineglasses. At one end of the room a red velvet curtain had been erected and a stage built in front of it. At centre stage stood a lectern. At either side loomed gigantic speakers. Glass panels around the room revealed a panoramic view of the harbour and environs—in particular the pier adjacent to ours, which was derelict and strewn with litter.

Paul and I found our table, which naturally turned out to be in the *Surfside Motel* section. We were the first there. A waiter instantly filled our champagne glasses.

"This is going to be disastrous," I whispered. "I don't even watch the damn show."

"Just say it's better than ever. That's all they want to hear." Paul peered at the rapidly assembling throng. "See anyone you know?"

"No," I answered sarcastically. "Alfred Hitchcock hasn't arrived yet."

Paul nudged me. "There's our boy!

He pointed toward the far side of the room. Sitting at a table, looking gorgeous and bored, was Lachie Turner. He was accompanied by two middle-aged men and three young women, who took turns fussing over him. The women were slight and remarkably plain in their features and outfits, hard to tell apart except for the colour of their hair: three very distinct shades of red. The men were more distinctive. They were wearing tuxedos that were a few sizes too small—it was clear a generation or two had passed since button and buttonhole last met their opposite number. From the polite way Lachie ignored these people, I presumed them to be television P.R. minions and bodyguards.

Paul nudged me. "Go and talk to him."

"Me talk? Why don't you?"

"I'm not very subtle, caro. Haven't you noticed?"

"But what would I say?"

"Mention New Heaven and wait for the bells to ring. Look!"

Lachie hauled himself to his feet and began to stride away from his table.

"He's going to the mens' room. Perfect! See? Doing the beat already!"

I clicked my tongue. "No! I won't."

"It might be the only chance you'll have all night. Once they start doling out those vile awards, we're stuck." He pushed me up. "Go!"

I fumbled my way through the crowd. By the time I reached the other side of the room, Lachie had disappeared. I found the gents' and snuck in. Fortunately, it was empty, apart from a single occupied cubicle. I stood at the urinal nearby.

"New Heaven," I whispered. There was no response. I tried another way. "Heavennn..." I sang softly. "I'm in *New Heaven*..."

This time there was a shuffling from within the cubicle. Encouraged, I started to speak.

"Excuse me," I said. "I wanted to see you..."

At that exact moment, the door to the men's room swung open, and another man lumbered across the room and stood adjacent to me. He unzipped and waited, rocking his ape-like body back and forth. After a moment he belched. I peered at his face: It was a complete blank. Inadvertently looking down, I noticed with a jolt that he was holding what seemed to be a salami.

"What you staring at?" he snarled.

"Nothing!"

It was high time my own bladder was pressed into service, to give my presence some validity. However, the stupid thing got stroppy and refused to cooperate. My companion glanced at me suspiciously. I smiled.

"Haven't I seen you on television?" I gushed insincerely.

"Probably," he grunted. "Brady O'Brien, *Footy at Five.*"

"Of course! Brady. I'm very pleased to meet you." I held out my hand.

"What do you think you're doing, pal?"

"Sorry. I was just going to shake hands. I'm a friend of—"
I raised my voice. "Grant Breen."

This brain wave elicited more shuffling from inside the
cubicle.

"Don't think I know him," mumbled Brady. "Is he Aussie
Rules or Rugby League?"

"Um, it depends on his mood on the day."

He stared at me as though I was talking gibberish. By now
I was getting impatient. When would this character leave and
let me talk to Lachie directly?

"I've got it now," Brady exclaimed. "You do one of them
lifestyle shows. Travel or something, right?"

"Travel, yes! Holiday destinations. Like New Heaven. It's
a gay and lesbian resort in Queensland..."

Brady suddenly lurched over and grabbed me by the lapel
of my coat.

"Oof!" I said.

Propelling me before him, he pushed me across the room
and slammed me into one of the cubicles.

"All right, mate!" he snorted. "I know what you're up to!
I dunno what you've heard, but I'm no faggot, get it? Them
nude calendar shots I did mean nothing!"

He jabbed me back into the room. Celebrity hunting
could wait, I decided. I headed for the door like the wind.
Once outside, I scurried behind a large potted plant and hid
there until Brady O'Brien had made his exit and vanished
into the crowd. Turning to go, I literally bumped into Lachie
Turner.

"Oh!" I said apologetically. "Wasn't that you in the toilet
just now?"

"What?"

"Nothing. Look, I'm Marc Petrucci, a friend of Grant's..."

He looked stricken. "Please leave me alone," he moaned,
and walked away.

I returned to our table. Rory, the executive producer, was there with his very young wife, a former star of *Surfside Motel*.

"Caro! We were wondering where you'd got to." Paul turned to me, flashing his cheesiest grin. "Rory and I have been discussing an upcoming role in *Surfside*. A young, idealistic teacher. He thinks I'd be perfect."

"No pressure," Rory mumbled. "Think it over. Talk later."

The waiters began to serve the meal which, in spite of the excess of cutlery and large plates, was absolutely minute. We were well into the entrée—a single, elaborately garnished shrimp—when the lights dimmed and the red curtains parted to reveal a large screen. "Here we go," said Rory's wife, already bored.

A well-known comedienne and radio personality entered to scattered applause and told a string of industry "in" jokes that meant nothing to me, though Paul was practically on the floor. She then introduced a series of fellow celebrities who presented the *Bimbeau*'s Choice Awards to their smug recipients, each award preceded by a film clip of utter incomprehensibility. We all clapped politely at the winners and drank heavily. Dessert eventually rolled around. It seemed to be a tiny cake of soap surrounded by chocolate shavings. By this time only one award remained. The hubbub diminished as our hostess returned to the microphone. There was no applause, though. Everybody was clapped out.

"Wake up, wake up," she chortled half-jokingly. "Nearly finished! Before the big one, I want to tell you about the party! Yes? Testing? One! Two!" There was a general stirring. "That's better. Now! When we finish here, that charming shower curtain will be pulled back and we're all going gambling! Isn't that fantastic? I'll be on the two-up. I might win a million-dollar contract!"

"That how you got your first one?" some wit called out.

"Yeah, it's called two-upmanship, now let me finish. In a moment, the staff will be handing out money for us to play with. Fake money..." The crowd jeered. "Don't be difficult! That fake money cost a packet! And here's the best part. Whoever has the biggest win of the night, the casino's gonna match it in hard cash!" Cheers broke out at every table. The comedienne smiled. "And it better not be Rory Van Dijk!"

"What she say?" Rory mumbled, pouring himself another dessert wine.

"But before that, there's one more award, the major award of the night. Yep, it's *Bimbeau*'s Choice for Most Popular Television Personality." The audience whistled and shouted; there were cries of "Me! Me!" The comedienne held up her hands. "To present the award, I'd like to bring on last year's winner, presenter of *Footy at Five,* Brady O'Brien!"

Brady stumbled up onto the stage, hurriedly tucking in his shirt with one hand and smoothing his hair down with the other. He gave the comedienne a kiss. She pulled a face and pretended to brush away the alcoholic fumes of his breath. As he stood, puzzled by the audience's laughter, she handed him an envelope.

"Thanks, love," he slurred, tearing it open. He read the name carefully in silence, then with a supreme effort, conquered his inebriation and stepped to the mike.

"I'm real pleased about this," he said. "He's a good bloke. Ladies and gentlemen, the award goes to Detective Blair Foster of *Good Cop, Bad Cop,* better known as actor Lachie Turner!"

His announcement was greeted by a thunderous ovation. Lachie stood shakily. He appeared anything but elated. Brady stepped back, almost toppling over, to allow Lachie to get to the microphone. The applause died down.

"Thank you." Lachie smiled a winning but strangely haunted smile. "I can't believe this. A couple of things I want to say. First of all, it's a pity the statuettes weren't ready in time. I'd sort of like to see what I won!" This got the biggest laugh of the evening.

"Seriously, I'm honoured to accept the award. *Bimbeau* magazine and I have had our disagreements in the past, but that's all over. There's no hard feelings at *Bimbeau,* and let me say, there are no hard feelings here either." He patted his chest.

There was more applause. "Smart kid. Diplomatic," mumbled Rory.

Lachie continued. "There's someone I'd like to dedicate this award to." The room went completely quiet. "He can't be here tonight, for reasons I think you all know. He's one of the great talents behind the scenes in our business, scriptwriter Grant Breen. We hope he'll be back with us real soon."

There was scattered applause. Lachie started to walk off, then changed his mind and lurched back to the mike, red-eyed.

"Grant," he said, "if you're watching—if they'll let you watch—I just want to say: you're the best! We're gonna beat this trumped up charge, don't worry. We..."

He choked. Nobody stirred.

"Grant, I'm sick and tired of this. I know you don't want me to say it, to keep it under wraps—well, I can't anymore! I love you."

Rory froze, his mouth agape. Brady looked helplessly offstage. The comedienne advanced on Lachie, but he shoved her roughly aside.

"I haven't finished," he snarled. "Did you hear that, you people? I'm gay, after all! So what? If that's the end of my career, too bad. I'd rather get a life."

He blew his nose, nodded, and, leaping to the floor, sprinted past the amazed guests and disappeared.

The buzz began almost immediately. Lachie's announcement had made the night for everybody, in one way or another. The comedienne stepped forward. "Well!" she exclaimed. "Now we're in the mood to take risks—let's gamble!"

There was a stampede toward the gaming tables. The curtain was ripped from its moorings and it seemed everyone was on the move, calling, whispering, shouting, desperate to repeat "I told you so" over and over again. Only Rory remained seated. (As we were later to learn, he had suffered a major coronary.)

Paul grabbed my arm as we were swept away.

"Caro!" he said. "Blair Foster! That's the name of Lachie's character! B.F.! I should have known!"

"Where did he go?" I asked.

"Outside, I think. Let's find him before he grabs a cab!"

"Don't you want to gamble?"

"We'll do that later. We've got our stamp to get us back in!"

We fought our way to the VIP exit and found ourselves out on the wharf. There was no one in sight. Off in the distance two security men lolled against a limousine, enjoying a smoke.

"Let's try around the back," Paul whispered. "If he hasn't left yet, he might be there."

We rushed along the walkway to the wharf's end; I heard the lapping of waves against the wooden foundations. A figure sat at the farthest corner, dangling his legs over the side, his distressed features barely visible in the dim light. We approached quietly.

"Lachie?" I called softly.

He looked up. "Oh, it's you. I've been sick." He blew his nose again.

Paul gently sat down next to him. "That was the most wonderful thing I've ever seen," he said. "You are a beautiful, beautiful man, and I hope he deserves you."

Lachie gave a bilious smile. "Thank you."

"Lachie," I said, "Paul and I are trying to help Grant—"

"He told me to keep away from you. He said you mean well but you mess everything up."

I was dumbstruck, but there was no time to argue. "I'm involved whether he likes it or not. I discovered Newton's body."

He groaned. "I know. Poor Newton. They were fighting over me, you know."

Paul took his hand. "Please help us."

"What has Grant told you?" I pleaded. "What happened?"

"I'll tell you," he said. "Only not here. Let's get away from all this shit."

Paul glanced at the stamp on his hand and shrugged. "Come on then," he said, helping Lachie to his feet. "Upsy."

"There aren't any cabs," I mused.

"My limo's there somewhere," Lachie answered and swayed. "Oops! Sick again."

We held his shoulders while he leaned out over the waves and donated one shrimp and a good deal of liquor to the fish below. Dragging him back, I brushed my hand against his collar and felt a sharp prick.

"Ouch. Something scratched me."

"Oh, sorry," he said. "My little crucifix has come undone. I wear it everywhere. Grant gave it to me."

I looked closely at the ornament, then at Lachie. A memory flashed through my mind.

"Good God, that was you!" I exclaimed. "In the Dominion Hotel! You were in drag. A little maroon number."

"I confess. It's the only way I can get out and hang in the gay bars without being Blair Foster. Though after tonight..." He gave a radiant smile. "I'm so glad I did that!"

Paul gave him a peck on the cheek. "Isn't he gorgeous?" he said.

We clambered into the waiting limo, and Lachie ordered the driver to take us to Gilda's, a late-night coffee bar in the city's newest, most swishy hotel.

The ambience there was ideal: low lighting, soft guitar music, and only a pair of interstate businessmen in a sombre wine-soaked stupor to share it with. Hot coffee was served straight away and we welcomed it, lounging in plush armchairs in a secluded alcove.

"That Claire woman," Lachie ranted, "for some reason she's trying to frame Grant. He doesn't even know her!"

"Start at the beginning," I suggested.

"Yeah, sorry. First of all, I should tell you that Newton wanted me to head the campaign, to be the face of New Heaven."

"I know."

"You do?" He blinked. "It was a big secret."

"I worked it out."

"Mmm. Well, Grant didn't want me to do it. A bad career move, he thought. I was unsure about it myself, 'specially after I'd sued *Bimbeau* over that piece they published. Of course, Newton hassled me to death. He said the lawsuit was history, I wouldn't have to give the money back. He was very persistent. Grant got the idea in his head there was something going on between us. I told him not to be stupid, but he's insecure sometimes—at his age and everything."

"Understandable," I agreed.

"And Newton was always calling, leaving messages. By the time Grant went to that stupid island, he'd blown things out of all proportion. He accused Newton of rape, theft, everything under the sun. They were all alone in the office—everybody was at some boring meeting—Newton was being typically horrible, of course, saying that if I came out of the closet, an old crock like Grant wouldn't have a hope of hanging onto me. That kind of thing. Then Grant punched him! Can you believe it? They actually had a fistfight! I mean, the whole thing was way immature."

He shook his head silently for a moment, then heaved a sigh. "Grant pushed Newton into the swimming pool, then he stomped off to calm down. He saw a woman who asked him where Newton was and he said, 'Drowning, I trust.'"

I frowned. "The 'drowning' line is unfortunate, but if that's the extent of their case—"

He flounced visibly. "It's not. They've got Claire Bornkamp's statement. She made up this bullshit story! She says she was looking for Newton and met Grant near the top pool and that

Grant was carrying a container of acid. She'd seen it earlier in Newton's office. Hadrian used it to clean things and kept it in the office 'cause it was safer there than anywhere else. She says, when she met Grant the container was empty, and he told her Newton was in the pool.

"But when she checked, Newton wasn't there. She tried the other pools—apparently, there's one down the bottom and another one—and he wasn't in those either, so she went back to her room. It wasn't till you found her later and showed her the body that she realised he'd drowned in the fishpond."

"We know that's a lie!" cried Paul. "Marc put the body in the fishpond himself."

Lachie turned. "You did?"

"Er, well, yes. Because he was covered in acid. I thought it might help. Then when I fetched Claire, we pulled him out again. I told her all about it."

Lachie brightened up. "Well, there you are! That proves Claire's lying, doesn't it?"

"We were right," said Paul. "Gaytour's determined to blame it on an outsider."

"At least she doesn't say she saw Grant hurl the acid," I said.

"He didn't!"

"We know, but somebody did right after that argument. Someone who must have overheard Grant and Newton fighting. Over you."

"So?" He looked so innocent.

"Well, it puts you in a vulnerable position, doesn't it. You ought to keep out of the public eye for a while. For you own good."

Lachie grimaced. "It won't be easy after tonight!"

"Don't worry," Paul added with a flourish. "Marc and Paul are on the case. We won't sleep until the puzzle is solved!"

CHAPTER 24

The next morning, however, we slept in: the only thing to do on a Sunday. With opera blaring downstairs and Paul cuddled up beside me snoring lightly, I felt less stressed than I had for months.

Since Paul had moved in, he'd made a genuine effort to conform to the Petrucci regime. He learned to confine his mess-making to one room at a time, promised to replace coffee on a regular basis, and even offered to make a contribution to the phone bill at some time in the future. During the preceding week he'd broken two champagne flutes and a plate, but I could hardly complain, considering my own breakage rate. And he'd been quite sweet, really; one evening he whipped up an old recipe of his granny for pineapple and prune cake. I was touched and quite sorry when I was forced to throw the soggy disintegrating mess into the trash. My next trick was to convince him not to do his vocal warm-up in the shower. This, I calculated, would reduce his shower time by roughly twenty minutes.

Around eleven the phone rang. It was Delia. She was more than a little terse.

"Thanks for nothing!" she snapped. "I thought we were helping each other."

"I found out who the celebrity was."

"You and the whole world. The story's dead in the water now! I'm taking a different line, namely, what's going to happen to Crab Island?"

"Don't ask me."

"I *am* asking you! You were quick enough to blab everything to that slag from *Queer Scene*! You told her the resort was kaput. Are you sure that's true? What are the Americans planning to do with it?"

"I don't know. I was misquoted."

"Serves you right. Well, I hear the whole joint is boarded up. Abandoned. What does it mean?"

"I'm sorry, Delia. Claire's the only one who might know, and she's under sedation in intensive care."

"Yes, yes, but didn't Gaytour fill you in before you left? Were they were getting cold feet because of the murder? Tell me!"

I was growing tired of this interrogation. "Stop shouting at me! I don't have to help you. It's not my patriotic duty, you know."

"I'm sorry," she said. A spiteful tone crept into her voice. "We have a saying in this business: If they're not with you, they're against you. In other words, there's no middle ground!"

She slammed the phone down with such force it made my ears ring.

"Who was that?" asked Paul, gliding down the stairs in my silk dressing gown.

"Delia," I grunted.

"Don't let her put you in one of your moods."

"What do you mean, one of my moods?" I demanded moodily.

"Snap out of it, caro mio. Think about nice things—like Lachie! Isn't he a living doll?"

I regarded Paul's rapt expression with skepticism. "Don't tell me Lachie Turner has replaced Darren in your affections!"

He collapsed, crushed, onto the nearest step. "Darren!" Paul spat the name out. "I don't know what one ever saw in the common little tramp. So far beneath one."

At last! "One had better kick him out of one's flat," I remarked.

"I don't think one would be able to handle it," he observed. "Maybe two or three. What am I going to do, caro?"

"I don't know."

He sprang to his feet. "I'll tell you what I'm going to do!

I'm going to watch television!" He pulled up an armchair and began fiddling with the remote. "I hate my life, and I need violent cartoons to cheer me up."

"I'll make coffee."

I was grinding some unusual coffee beans Paul had bought—they were spiked with Benedictine—when I heard a piercing scream from the next room.

I ran in, giving my arm a nasty bump on the doorframe in passing.

"Caaaaaaaro! I'm on the telly!" Paul was bug-eyed, scrutinising the TV screen. It displayed a series of still photographs of naked or seminaked men in the wild: swimming, splashing, hugging, sitting on each other's shoulders. The pictures had been taken from a distance and were poorly focussed, but this served to make them even more suggestive. The blurry contours in the distance were recognisable enough for me to identify the location as New Heaven.

"What program is this?" I inquired.

"Some current affairs thing."

I was startled to see an image flash past of a young man arching his back, a faraway, ecstatic look in his eyes: Wade.

"Turn up the sound!" I cried.

Paul did. A familiar voice was speaking. It was moderate, reasonable, persuasive, and smooth.

"Nothing more than a perverted parody of the Garden of Eden, a mockery of that paradise our Lord created for Adam and Eve—who were, fortunately for us, heterosexual."

"Paramor!" Paul exclaimed.

The scene returned to a studio set. It was indeed Pastor Matthew Paramor, seated opposite a glowering current affairs reporter, whom I'm sure had won a *Bimbeau* award the night before. (He certainly looked a little the worse for wear this morning.) The carefree nudes continued to disport themselves on a screen in the background.

"These pictures are...explicit," said the reporter.

"I make no apology for that, Martin," answered Paramor, pouring himself a glass of water from a jug. "These are the mild ones. Most of them could not be shown on television. It's horrifying. I feel it's my Christian duty to let the public know the perversions these people perpetrated. In that atmosphere, is it any surprise the mortal sin of murder followed?"

The camera switched to a close-up of the reporter.

"Where did you get these photographs?"

It clicked back to Paramor.

"One of our brethren took them, incognito."

"Isn't that trespassing?"

"A minor sin, I believe, compared to the orgy of evil they reveal."

"Reverend Paramor. This cult of your—"

"Excuse me, Martin, we're not a cult. We don't ask our members to commit suicide or ride in imaginary spaceships!" He laughed. "We are an unaffiliated church, the Church of Divine Intervention."

"Which is a breakaway sect from the Church of Earthly Intercession in the U.S."

Paramor smiled. "There are many churches, Martin; there is only one God. And He is angry. I'm sure I needn't remind you how God's retribution rained down upon those sinners at Halstrom Park not so long ago."

"Why have you gone public with these shocking pictures?"

"I thought good Christian people should see what Satan is up to. I must say, it is against the precepts of our Church to interfere. If we want something, we pray for it. And our prayers are always answered. We prayed for the blasphemously titled New Heaven resort to come tumbling down, and what happened? That wicked place has closed, albeit temporarily. In fact, one of our brethren, Samuel Pratt, has been installed on the island as a caretaker."

Up on the screen flashed a grainy picture of an odd round face. Across it ran the subtitle SAMUEL PRATT, CARETAKER.

"Caro! It's the blob!" Paul whispered.

"What are you praying for next, Reverend Paramor?"

This close-up was the closest of all, honing in on the pastor's perfect teeth. If Rory had been watching, he'd have had the clerical signature on the dotted line in a second.

"I'm in the business of saving souls, Martin. I want to save the soul of this beautiful natural paradise. We're praying for a 100-percent conversion!"

The camera swung back to the now cheerful face of the reporter. "And they might just do it! I'm Martin Leak. Back after this."

Paul switched off the set.

"That man was the blob in Hadrian's photo!"

"Yes, sneaking around the island taking, snaps of his own, and I doubt whether they were destined for the coffee table."

"What a low, filthy act. It's a pity you missed the picture of me—it came up very well! I was kissing André on the bum."

"How sweet." I paced up and down, recklessly spilling coffee over the carpet and furniture. "We're so close, Paul," I muttered in my sharpest Sherlock mode. "It all ties up with the ownership of the resort. Newton was keeping the place afloat—in a financial sense, I mean, not literally. Gaytour wanted control, which they got with Newton dead. Claire lied, probably to keep Gaytour out of trouble. Paramor, as we know, also wanted to take control of the resort, so he put Blob Man on the island to get compromising pictures, planning to use them to inflame the public's homophobia. That, combined with Newton's murder, would be enough to discourage gay tourists forever. Meanwhile, Grant had a fight with Newton on a personal matter, distantly related to all this, and got caught up in the middle. How's that, so far?"

"Brilliant. What about Hadrian?"

I was instantly deflated. "Hadrian, yes. He's insanely jealous; he had the opportunity—he's even practically confessed. But as far as we know, he's got bugger all to do with the church, and he's got practically nothing to do with Gaytour either. There's a container of hydrofluoric acid hidden under his studio, but when he was on the island he kept his acid in Newton's office, where anyone could have seen it."

"And he's nuts."

"And he's nuts. Some of the time."

I lay on my back on the floor.

"Getting a different perspective, caro?"

"It's like a huge jigsaw, and we're looking for one particular piece. I can't seem to locate it, but I know I've already seen it."

"I hate jigsaws."

"Hadrian. Hadrian...he needed to talk to someone, which means he knows something, and he's hiding somewhere. Where?"

"Why?" Paul added.

"Another good question."

"Was there any special sound in the background when he called? A tennis match? A Streisand medley? Anything like that?"

"No I don't think so. I could hardly hear him anyway. His voice was distant and fuzzy."

"Fuzzy...was he calling on a mobile? You know how my mobile sounds when the battery's low. It drops out a lot. It's a real pain."

"Yes. It was exactly like that! So he called on a mobile, which means what? He was on the move?"

"Or there was no land line available."

"No what?"

"Normal phone, caro. Was there anything else unusual about the call?"

"He rang at five A.M."

"Five is late," Paul mused. "Not like four, when people are still up."

"Did he have to wait until someone was asleep before he made the call?"

"I bet you he's holding up in the men's dorm at the YMCA! We should check it out right now!"

I gave Paul a sardonic look. "Is the men's dorm at the YMCA a place where nothing terrible can happen?"

"Hardly! Anything can happen! That's the beauty of it."

"Hadrian said he was hiding where no one would find him and nothing terrible could happen."

Paul pondered. "Some place where there isn't any trouble... behind the moon...beyond the rain..."

I plugged my ears. I knew what was coming.

"Heavens! Caro, listen to me, pull those pinkies out!"

I sat up. "I thought you were about to sing 'Over the Rainbow.'"

"No time for that. I just realised where Hadrian is! On the island!"

There was a pretty good chance Paul was right. The resort was secluded and inaccessible, with only a caretaker named Pratt in residence. I pictured Hadrian virtually alone out there, where the murder took place, hiding and brooding. If he was paranoid when he'd spoken to me, by now he might be totally deranged.

"Caro, we'll have to go back there."

My mind boggled. "How?" I asked.

"Fly, natch. We can afford it. We'll use the loot from Hiram's payoff."

"Oh." I had tentatively earmarked my share to upgrade my speakers and amplifier. Still, there'd be some left over. "Yes, all right. But how can we reach the island? The ferry won't be running anymore."

"Mmm, that's a toughie...let's take Darren! He can drive speedboats, and he's big and strong. Could be useful in case Hadrian gives us any flak."

"Darren? Oh, no. Anyway, he won't go."

"He'll do it for me. Now get on the blower and book that passage!"

I was extremely dubious about the whole scheme, particularly Darren's involvement, but I could see no other way.
Neither of us knew how to navigate, and besides, the island
was private property. Technically, we would be trespassing.

I rang the airline and was told by some underling there
were no seats available until Friday. I emphasised the urgency
of the situation, but they wouldn't budge. Then I remembered
Stewart. By some stroke of luck he was on duty.

"Stewart here," he snapped. "Can I help you?" He sounded
as officious as ever.

"Hello, it's Marc Petrucci. I'm trying to book three flights
to Mackay, and they say there's none till Friday—"

"I'll put you through to reservations. Just one moment."

"Wait! I thought you could help. This is Marc Petrucci!"

"Do I know you?"

"You remember! I'm on the cover of *Queer Scene*."

"Oh! You're not the man who's tattooed on every square
inch of his body? Darling! I didn't know we'd met!"

"What? No! I was on last week's cover."

"Oh." He gave an exasperated sniff. "Honey, I deal with
thousands of people every day. What is it you want?"

I explained.

He tch'd audibly. "Wednesday's the best I can do. Three
seats. They're not together. The flight's at 2:45 P.M. What's the
name again?"

"Pe-trucci. Could you upgrade us to first class?"

"Well! You'll never know if you don't ask."

"Does that mean yes?"

"No."

They say fame is fleeting, but my brisk conversation with
Stewart brought the truth of it home to me in vivid colour.

I rang June next and organised for us to stay with her. June
was delighted when I informed her the future was looking
faintly rosier for Grant.

All that remained was the question of Darren. Paul thought

we should confront him together, and late afternoon was the best time, when he would've been up for an hour or so and it was too early to walk the streets. We drove around to Paul's building—a 1930s block that had seen better days—and rapped on the flimsy security door of his flat. We waited in silence.

"There's no one home," Paul muttered.

"This is ridiculous! You've got keys, haven't you? It's your place!"

We let ourselves in. Paul is not the star tenant on the block by a long chalk, but the sight that greeted us was beyond any previous postparty carnage I'd ever witnessed. The lounge/-dining/kitchen room was utter bedlam. The couch had been tipped over. The indoor plant was gasping its last. Food was splattered and spilt from one wall to another, as if somebody had taken his meals while training for the fifty-meter sprint. CDs lay everywhere, and the few that had been replaced in their covers, I discovered, were in the wrong ones. That was the clincher!

"Paul, you've got to get rid of him. As soon as we get back!"

He looked shattered. "I'm afraid you're right, caro. He carried me away, but long legs can only go so far."

I started to clean up while Paul packed a bag in his bedroom. From the heart-rending screams, I deduced that Darren had been at his wardrobe.

I was halfway through soaking a second sinkful of crud-encrusted saucepans when the culprit himself strolled through the front door, munching a dripping hamburger.

"Ah, it's you," he said casually. "I thought it was a thief. What do you want?"

I summoned up my most authoritarian tone. "Sit down," I commanded. "I want a word with you."

"My shift hasn't started yet," he drawled. "If you're horny, come back at nine."

"Sit!" I shouted.

Paul stuck his head round the door. "Hi," he grinned.

"Paul, keep packing. I wish to speak to Darren alone."

Startled, he withdrew. I turned back to confront Darren's insolent gaze. "Paul and I are going to the island. We want you to come along to take us across and back again in a speedboat."

His mouth dropped open in surprise, but only for a moment. He flashed his usual superior smile. "No way," he answered. "I like it better here."

"We need you," I emphasised.

"What do you want to go back for? D'you leave something behind?" He sniggered. "Your little coloured maps?"

I took a step toward him and lowered my voice. "I believe you may change your mind," I said. "I've been thinking about your deal with Newton. The police don't approve of blackmail."

"Newton's not gonna complain."

"I'm more interested in the Lachie Turner business. Newton was wrong to pay you off, but you failed to appear, and that's a major offence. The authorities would be delighted to have a little chat about that! So would one or two contacts of mine at *Bimbeau* magazine." At the mention of this organisation, Darren began to look apprehensive. I pressed the point. "They're down eight-hundred fifty thousand because of you! They have some very powerful friends."

It was a desperate bid on my part. I crossed my fingers, hoping Darren hadn't seen the morning papers. Lachie's revelations of the previous night dominated page three of the dailies, and *Bimbeau* had already indicated they were buying the exclusive rights to his story.

Darren scowled. "I'm not gonna go back up there for nothing."

"I'll cover the expenses—flights and accommodation, hire of the boat."

"I want something out of it!"

I was amazed at his obstinacy. "We've very little cash," I said. "I only have enough for our expenses and Paul's got nothing."

"He's got this flat."

I peered at the newly created bomb site. "Yes?"

"Yeah! It suits me here, close to the groovy end of town and everything. Tell Paul to sign the lease over and we've got a deal."

"And what's he going to do then?"

"Who cares? Stay on with you, I guess."

I tossed it up. Clearly, Paul's flat would never be the same. He tends to move every year or so anyway, either through youthful restlessness or at the behest of shell-shocked landlords. Our current situation proved that we'd be able to maintain a civilised level of compatability *chez moi* until he found somewhere else.

"I'll do my best to talk him into it," I answered.

"Thought you might." Darren smiled lasciviously.

"Meanwhile, think about where to get hold of a boat. This is an undercover operation." How I relished the action-packed resonance of that phrase. If Andrew and Neil could see me now! "We leave in three days' time."

I had one more call to make.

"Our Lady of Sappho Healing Hospital. Sister Bonaventura speaking."

"Hello, my name's Marc Petrucci. I want to speak to whoever's looking after Claire Bornkamp."

"Oh, yes, the Dutch lass. Are you a relative?"

"A friend. This is quite urgent."

"I'm afraid Miss Bornkamp checked out two days ago."

This was surprising news. "I thought she was in intensive care."

"She was at first. She suffered a nasty fall downstairs, poor dear."

"Where is the poor thing now?"

She paused. "I understand she's being looked after at the home of friends."

"You don't have their number, do you?"

Her tone hardened. "I'm sorry, I can't give you that information. Goodbye."

She hung up sharply. Nevertheless, a germ of an idea had been planted in my mind.

CHAPTER 25

Our bus reached Murphy's Inlet at dusk. A strong wind was up; I was amazed how quickly the weather had turned in the short time I'd been away. Palm trees are suckers for a touch of turbulence, by virtue of their great, stiff leaves, and there were tufts of big palms around the old Seabreeze Guesthouse, whooshing and rattling in rehearsal for something major.

Due to the wind, our flight had been spectacularly bumpy. As a result, not a single thread of my clothing had escaped the stain of mushy carrot, chocolate cheesecake, red wine, or coffee. My first stop at Seabreeze would have to be the laundry.

As soon as we checked in, Darren strode off to town to hire the boat. We had decided to get across to the resort as soon as possible—not in the dark, of course, but ideally not in broad daylight either. Although I still didn't trust him, Darren seemed to be behaving himself and fitting in with our plans. As for Paul's part of the bargain, he had not yet agreed to move out permanently, possibly because he still knew nothing about it. I'd hoped to mention it, but the time never seemed suitable to bring up the subject of sacrificial eviction. I would have to deal with that later.

June was welcoming but she seemed preoccupied. Some old friend whom June hadn't seen for years was staying, and the woman was in poor health. She'd taken my favourite room, too. Still, I tried to be sympathetic.

"Don't you worry," I told June consolingly. "She'll rally; this is the perfect place to get over an illness. It's—er—nothing I might catch, is it?"

"Oh no," June replied. "I'm just a bit worried about her. She's not the happy little thing I remember." (It made her friend sound like a corgi.)

"Get some minestrone into her. That'll do the trick!"

"I made some this morning, love. Just for you and your friend. He's a sweet young fellow." She leaned close and hollered in my ear. "I don't like that other one, though. I've seen him about the place before. Shifty piece of work."

As if on cue, Paul joined us just as June was singing his praises. He'd changed into his "nautical adventure" outfit: white runners, pressed blue jeans, a promotional T-shirt advertising a popular brand of lubricant, and a lemon-yellow windbreaker.

Paul launched into a long story about his time spent as a chorus member in *Cats*. The story involved his tail getting caught in some moving scenery—a life-or-death situation, though he made light of it now. He'd screamed out for help while remaining "in character" as a randy old tomcat. The effect was bizarre, and several school parties had demanded their money back. Paul's tale had June chuckling away, but I'd heard it once too often and my mind wandered. Gazing around randomly, my eyes alit on a local paper lying in the recycling basket. What attracted my attention was a photograph of Pastor Matthew Paramor on the front page. His expression was self-satisfied and triumphant.

I rescued the paper. It turned out to be the Church of Divine Intervention's own broadsheet, "The Weekly Word," and the date was recent. The front-page editorial, written by the good pastor himself, referred to Crab Island. The more I read, the more engrossed and astounded I became.

NEW DEAL FOR CRAB ISLAND

Dearest Brethren of the Church of Divine Intervention,

As you know, I have been at the forefront of protest over the resort on Crab Island ever since we first discovered the sinful and ungodly use to which it was to be put. The thought that this natural paradise created by God should end up in unnatural hands sickened every one of us. On a more worldly level, I am also aware that many good Christian people of the Inlet who worked on the resort development are as yet unpaid for their hard (if misguided) labour.

Therefore, it is with full heart and greatest joy that I may reveal the following news, first here in our newsletter and later to the world. We have purchased the Crab Island resort!

For some weeks I have been in negotiation with the previous owners, Gaytour International. Following the unspeakable act of violence that took place on the island, these multinational associates of Satan have been looking for a way to withdraw from their original investment. I am not ashamed to admit I have taken advantage of their vulnerable position. I have secured ownership of the land and the resort itself for little more than the cost of the outstanding debt. In this I have been supported by our sister church in the USA, with whom we have recently been reunited, praise the Lord. However, we still require vigilance: I shall be conducting widespread fundraising activities in the near future!

How glorious that this beautiful place, which could have been home to obscenity and depravity, will now be dedicated to the Lord as a peaceful Christian retreat exclusively for our church members and their families at unbeatable discount rates. I have already had plans drawn up to convert one of the major buildings into a chapel and another into a fully functioning twenty-four–hour prayer centre.

Hallelujah and Praise the Lord. Our prayers have been answered as never before. Crab Island has been fully cleansed. I hope to see you all on Sunday, that we may give humble thanks for this gracious and most holy gift.

"Paul!" I said. "Sorry to interrupt, but cast your baby browns over this!"

As he read it, he ran through his repertoire of astonished

facial expressions and explosive sounds of disbelief.

"It's true, caro! *Blue Lagoon* for Bible-thumpers! Thongs and tea pots!"

Just then the phone rang. June toddled off to answer it.

"I can't believe Gaytour would do a deal with these people! It beggars belief. Hiram's so pro–gays and lesbians and so anti–everybody else!"

Paul rubbed his chin. "I can understand it. If you knew Hiram as well as I do—"

"You mean sexually for a very brief period?"

"Even so, I learned how he operates. Basically, life is war and there are battles on all fronts. That's his attitude. You win some, you lose some. If you don't thrash 'em here and now, you'll rape and pillage 'em later."

"And because of the debt and bad publicity, he lost this particular battle."

"Exactamundo! These are the terms of his surrender."

I frowned. "A very dishonourable one."

"Ah, but he's a businessman, too! They don't know shit about honour."

June wandered in. "There's a man on the phone for you, Marc," she said. "It's the one I don't like." She beamed at Paul.

I rushed to the phone. "Darren?"

"I'm at the dock, and I've got us a boat. Are you ready?"

I glanced out the window. It was almost dark. The wind howled with even more atmospheric intensity than before.

"I think we'd better wait till morning."

"We can't!" he answered. "You want to keep this quiet, don't you? Murphy's Inlet is a small town. If we go tomorrow, everyone'll know in five seconds flat."

"But it's dark."

"I only got the boat for the night. It's hush-hush, a favour. I said it'd be back in its moorings by dawn, no questions asked. Otherwise you can forget it."

"Damn. I suppose we'll have to."

"Why are you so keen to get over there, anyway?" he asked suspiciously.

"To find clues."

Darren's only answer was a snort.

It was indeed dark. The moon, if it was planning to rise, had so far been very tardy about it. When Paul and I reached the dock, we spied a glimmer of light at the end of a jetty: a flashlight, signalling. We ran to the spot to discover Darren below in an open boat, ready to cast off.

"Hurry up," he called as we got nearer.

The boat was slightly bigger than the last one we'd shared. It tipped as I stepped in, and I nearly fell overboard.

"Be careful, caro," whispered Paul urgently. Darren started the motor and we sped away into the gloom, like spies in a wartime newsreel.

The sea, stirred up by the wind, was very choppy. I instantly felt insecure in the digestion department. I closed my eyes and tried to picture calm desert scenes, but the pitching and tossing of the waves were not to be overlooked. While I kept a sickly silence, Paul gossiped.

"Paramor's cult have bought the island," he gabbled.

"Yeah, I know," said Darren.

"They always wanted it. Do you know he put some guy on the island to take dirty photos? We saw it on TV."

"Yeah."

"They didn't have to use them in the end. The murder was enough to turn people off."

Darren just grunted. Paul turned to a more salacious subject.

"What about Lachie Turner coming out?"

"Paul—" I began.

Darren cut across me. "What do you mean?"

Paul was delighted to be able to pass on such good news. "We were there. He did it at the *Bimbeau*'s Choice Awards. Told the whole world he was gay! I was so proud."

"Did he! Shit, ay? How did *Bimbeau* magazine take it?"

"They're buying the rights to his life story."

Darren scowled in my direction. "You knew all along," he snarled. "Fuck it! I could be making money out of this! And you wanted me to keep quiet!" He cleared his throat and spat in disgust. He was clearly peeved that someone else had got the better of him for once.

"Keep quiet about what?" asked Paul, but Darren wouldn't answer, and I was otherwise occupied with nausea.

An unusually large wave loomed in front of us, but instead of sensibly skirting it or throwing the engine into reverse, Darren drove us right up one side and down the other.

"Whoopee!" squealed Paul.

It was all too much for the delicate Petrucci sensibilities. I leaned carefully over the side and made room in my tummy for June's steaming minestrone, presuming I would ever get back in one piece to sample it. I stared into the deep water. Stars had come out and were shedding a tiny amount of light, though the sea was still an ominous black. Along the side of the boat, the vessel's name was painted: GOLGOTHA—a biblical reference. I sat up.

"Feeling better, caro?" asked Paul.

"Mmm," I said. "Darren, if it's not a personal question, where did you get this boat?"

"I told you. A guy owed me a favour."

"I see," I replied. "That's very interesting. And what favour exactly does Pastor Paramor owe you?"

Paul looked dumbfounded. Darren cut the engine.

"Not this old trick again?" I quipped with commendable savoir faire, realising too late that it might have been prudent to keep quiet till we were well and truly ashore.

"I should've done it right the first time," he said, producing a sharp fishing knife. He pointed it at us both, alternating from one to the other. The weapon gleamed threateningly.

"What are you doing?" shrieked Paul.

"This is where you get out," Darren barked.

"I knew you were involved with the cult, but I didn't figure out the extent of it," I said. "You were a plant in the resort, too. Along with the blob!"

Darren smiled. "The pastor suggested I pose for Sam's pictures, to make sure they were nice and juicy. I didn't mind! The idea was to drag Newton into them but that dumb boyfriend stopped me from getting close enough."

"And were you blackmailing Paramor as well?"

He laughed, delighted with his own achievement. "These guys at the top! They can't do nothin' right. He was shit scared somebody would trace the plane back to him."

"So he is responsible for Vasselina's death."

"Him and Jackson. Their first plan was to dump a load of leaflets—something catchy like 'Repent Now.' Ditching the propeller was Paramor's idea. Jackson didn't want to, but he gave in. I guess he reckoned it was for a good cause. I helped the old bastard load it onto the plane. Fuckin' heavy!"

"Where's Jackson now?"

"Dunno."

"So Paramor paid for your silence, same as Newton," exclaimed Paul.

"Lucky for Paramor, he didn't end up the same way," I muttered.

Darren crouched forward, brandishing the knife. "You know too much!"

"Dazzle!" Paul gasped. "You killed Newton?"

The pieces were falling into place. "You were the last to arrive at my seminar," I said, as a replay of that fatal afternoon flickered through my mind, "and you'd been running. Very cheeky to sit right up front! I presume you'd followed Grant and Newton and heard their argument."

"I was pretty pissed off with Newton, too," said Darren.

"He had stopped your payments."

"I needed that money, and I knew I had to show Newton

I meant business! So I nicked the boyfriend's acid from the office. When I got back up top, the other guy had gone and Newton was climbing out of the pool, cursing and shivering. 'This'll warm you up,' I told him and chucked it right over him! Served him right. Strong stuff, though, eh? I never thought it'd kill him. I only meant it as a warning."

Paul started to speak, but I interrupted.

"Then you ran down the staff stairs, the quick way, as the meeting was starting."

"Yeah, I got right out of there. Newton never even knew what hit him."

"You thought you'd got away with it."

"Yeah."

"But Hadrian saw you."

He looked impressed. "You been thinking about this, haven't you! Yeah, that little rat was hanging around near the pool. Little bugger was always sneaking round the place. I've taken care of him, anyway. He's friggin' terrified! The acid belonged to him. He knows if he puts one foot out of the house, I'll tell the cops I saw him throw it. That's if I don't get him first."

Paul piped up. "*What* house? You mean Hadrian's not on the island?"

"Where? Here? Why should he be? Nah, he's at home, hanging out with his drug-fucked friends in the next flat."

"Let me ask you one thing," I said. "What did you do with the container?"

"I left it up there."

"With your fingerprints all over it?"

"Yeah, well, I was a bit freaked. Anyhow, the thing never turned up. I looked everywhere the next day, when I was roping off the area for Hiram. Haven't a fuckin' clue where it went."

"The police have got it," Paul shouted. I stared at him. "They've identified your fingerprints of course."

"What?"

"They've heard the whole story."

Darren looked from Paul to me and back again. "Bullshit."

Paul smiled knowingly. "Dazzle, really! Do you think Marc and I would come out here like idiots without letting the law in on it? If you don't believe me, check out those fairy lights twinkling on the water! That's the police launch heading this way."

Darren stood and squinted in the direction of the coast. In the same second, Paul was on his feet. Exhibiting his graceful extension—the result of youthful ballet training—he kicked the knife out of Darren's hand and into the water. Unfortunately, the impact of the kick knocked Paul off balance, and he toppled over the side.

"Aagh! Caaaro!"

"Paul!" I cried. "Grab my arm!"

I lurched across and reached out to him. My sudden move caused the boat to pitch violently to the side. I heard a second splash. This time Darren had fallen overboard. They both cried out as they bobbed around in the huge, powerful seas. The fragile vessel was tossing and drifting; at any moment I could lose sight of them.

"Paul!"

A shaky hand gripped the side of the boat. I reached over and held it, pulling hard. The entire boat nearly flipped over. A face appeared: It was Darren.

"I'll kill you," he screamed.

Stunned, I unthinkingly let go and he sank, cursing and flailing, back into the ocean.

"Marc! Here!"

On the other side, Paul hung on for dear life. I carefully slid over and managed to get a hold of him under the arms. Drawing on all my strength, I lifted him up as best I could, and he clambered into the bottom of the boat. Coughing up seawater, he climbed over and hugged me tight. I put my arms around him.

"Thanks," he shivered breathlessly. "Where's Darren?"

"He's still out there somewhere. I had him, but he slipped."

"Quick, caro! The flashlight!"

Darren's flashlight was rolling around in the bottom of the boat. It was soaking wet, but amazingly it worked. I directed the beam out to sea, scanning the waves. Finally, it pinpointed Darren some meters away. He was swimming hard toward us but seemed to be making no progress. Paul, meanwhile, began fiddling with the engine.

With a shudder the motor spluttered into noisy life. Instantly, we sped away.

"We're leaving him behind!" I screamed. "Turn it around!"

"I'm trying! I've got to work it out!"

I kept the torch beam fixed on Darren, which was not easy as we lunged through the waves, making a wide arc back to him. His stroke seemed to be getting weak, but we were drawing closer. Suddenly, a swift wave picked up our boat and flung it in the air. The impact knocked the flashlight out of my hand. Desperately, I scrabbled around for it in the unaccustomed darkness. I found it, but now, of course, I couldn't get the thing to work.

"Hurry up, caro, I can't see him."

I whacked the flashlight hard against my leg. The bulb flickered on.

"Quick!"

I shone my beam out onto the waves once more. All it illuminated was swirling foam.

"Can you see him yet?" Paul called.

"No!"

We continued our circling as we scanned the water's surface. The flashlight flickered sporadically, then finally faded out. I bashed it again, this time to no avail.

"He's gone. Oh, shit!"

"I had a hold of him and I let him go!" I wailed.

Then I realised we were speeding in the direction of the

island once again. I could make out the jetty and a dim light in the nearby boathouse. There were no lights on in the resort itself.

"Where are you taking us now?" I demanded.

"I'm not taking us anywhere," Paul snapped wearily. "We just happen to be going this way."

"We don't need to go to the island. Hadrian's not there!"

"Caro, please. I'm exhausted. Let's just dock on the island and we'll go back in the morning when it's light."

"All right," I answered, crestfallen. "Good idea."

We concentrated all our energy on directing the boat toward the island. At the last moment, Paul cut the motor and we were carried roughly against the landing. We secured the line and dragged our bodies ashore. The jetty was hard, wooden, and smelly, but I loved it with all my heart. Another small craft was moored around the other side.

"Someone else is here," I remarked.

"Blobbo the caretaker."

"We'd better be quiet as mice. Or crabs!"

We crept along the pathway to the resort's main reception area. Halfway there we passed the old boathouse. A dim glow emanated from within, the only light source around. We snuck up to the grimy window. Paul, who is slightly taller than me, peered in.

"I can't see, the glass is so dirty," he whispered in shocked tones. "This place has really gone downhill!"

Sneaking over to the open door, we cautiously peeked around the frame. A burning oil lamp sat on the wooden bench inside, dimly illuminating rows of windsurfers and various other pieces of maritime holiday equipment. Beside the lamp stood a half-empty beer bottle. Around the walls were drums of fuel, ropes, and lines hanging every which way, their shapes transformed and distorted in the fluttering shadows. It appeared that the shed was uninhabited, but evidently not for long. We crept inside.

"Whoever's here is up to something," Paul whispered. "I can feel it in my bones."

"I agree! But who? And what?"

"Call me clueless. When did you figure out that Darren was the murderer?"

"I didn't, but last night I was tossing and turning, going over it all again in my head. There's so much to consider: too much for one murderer! And it occurred to me—maybe there's more than one story. You remember what Darren said in the boat? He didn't think the acid would kill Newton? And he was right. Newton drowned."

"Yes. Well?"

"What if one person threw the acid and somebody else took advantage of the situation to finish Newton off? Perhaps they pretended to come to his assistance, then held him underwater in the pool until he drowned? Once Newton was dead, this person dragged the body along the track and into the bushes out of sight. When Wade and I found Newton, he was dry again and, I'm sorry to say, by the time he was back in the water he'd been fried and dragged and beaten about so much it made the coroner's job a lot harder."

"So who was the person? The real, actual murderer?"

"It had to be someone who failed to attend the meeting. If we reject Grant, who does that leave?"

"Claire!"

"That's what I thought, but I'm sure that when I showed her Newton's body, she was taken completely by surprise. She's a levelheaded woman; she went into damage control straight away. But later on, she took a risk and changed her statement, lying to the court. My feeling is, she was covering for somebody."

"Who?"

I glanced quickly at the flickering shadow in the doorway. It had been there for some time.

"Somebody she was having an affair with," I continued.

"Let's work it out. You recall the meeting? Remember Hiram, shooting his pistol and ordering everybody to get off his land?"

"I'll never forget it. Pure Barbara Stanwyck."

I raised my voice.

"You aren't a very attentive journalist, Delia. Hiram introduced himself several times and yet, an hour later, you asked me who the man with the gun was."

Delia stepped into the room. She was covered in grime, and in her hands she clasped a large kerosene tin. Her face was a mask of hatred.

"So what?" she said, flinging the tin into a corner.

"It was you who asked Grant where to find Newton," I continued. "Not Claire at all! 'Drowning,' he said. I suppose that put the idea into your mind. Lucky for you, poor Newton was half dead already."

"So now you're the man who knows *everything*!" she scoffed.

I kept my cool. "Not at all. Why did Claire lie? Why did she present your story as her own?"

"'Cause I asked her to! I didn't intend to implicate myself. As far as anyone knew I was at your meeting, and I wasn't about to tell them otherwise."

"But you weren't there, were you? Not even at the end."

"I ran into Claire on my way back from the pool. She was looking for Newton. The last thing I could let her do was find him—"

"So you dragged her back to your room." I raised my eyebrows. "How was it for *you*? You haven't been a dyke for long, I seem to recall."

She shrugged. "I had no choice, did I."

"And at what point did Claire begin to suspect that you'd used her to frame Grant? Shortly before you pushed her down a flight of stairs?"

She laughed. "I'd like to see you try and prove any of this!"

As we spoke, the flickering light behind the boathouse grew stronger. Paul sniffed the air.

"Fire!" he shouted. "There's a fire!"

Delia bolted, with Paul close on her trail. I shuffled along in the rear. She ran in the direction of the jetty, but Paul sprinted round the other side past the boathouse to cut her off. She spun on her heel and hurtled back up toward the resort. I turned and followed, and Paul swiftly caught me up.

Ahead of us, Delia veered off the path and bounded up a flight of wooden stairs. Suddenly, she stopped in her tracks. She looked up, her eyes wide. The two flights of stairs above her were alight. The strong wind swept the flames into the closest trees and, as we watched, a large patch of scrub caught fire. Within seconds, all we could see of New Heaven was a cloud of smoke.

Delia scurried back down the steps to the lower landing. The heat was intense.

"Come on!" I called. "Get out!"

"This island is mine!" she screamed. "Not yours! Not Paramor's! Mine!"

"Do you want to die here?" I shouted.

"*We* don't, caro. Quick!" Paul cried and sprinted away, hauling me after him.

A blazing tree had fallen onto the boathouse, which was now burning fiercely. I thought of the drums of petrol it contained; any minute, the route back to the jetty would be impassable. We struggled forward, crying and wheezing, scarcely able to see our way through the smoke. The wind howled; the entire island was a holiday inferno.

At last we stumbled onto the jetty. Paul hopped lightly down into the boat and pulled me into it. Loosening the moorings, he kicked over the engine.

"What about Delia?" I cried.

"There's no time."

"We need her! Without her we'll never prove Grant is innocent!"

"We can't go back, caro! The whole place is ablaze!"

At that moment, I saw Delia limping along the path toward the landing.

"Wait, Paul, she's coming!"

I called out to her. She saw me and started to run faster. She was almost at the wharf when she came to a gradual halt, threw up her arms, and sank to the ground. As I stared in puzzled disbelief, I realised the whole landing was moving. It was alive with crabs! Hundreds of them, smoked out of their hiding places, were scuttling and scrabbling to safety. Delia was trapped in the very centre of their exodus. She rolled and thrashed on the ground, screaming as crabs of all sizes bustled over and under and around her, crazed by the heat, desperately making for the sea, and savagely attacking anything that got in their way.

Countless crabs, some burning as they fled, streamed off the sides of the jetty and plunged into the bright water like a living fireworks display. Delia had stopped moving. There was no way I could get to her. Paul turned the throttle and we sped off.

We headed out to sea and never looked back until we'd reached the mainland: a deserted beach, some four kilometers south of Murphy's Inlet. We dragged the boat up onto the sand then slumped, exhausted, and gazed out over the water. The horizon glowed a dull orange in the night sky: the last fading glimmer of New Heaven.

CHAPTER 26

My stomach was bursting, but I couldn't help myself. I had to order the banana crepe with prune ice cream and hot toffee sauce. Apparently, all of Sydney had been talking about it. I'd already polished off two very substantial courses, and the opera was to begin in an hour's time, but what the hell. Tonight's opera was an appropriate follow-up to this huge, rich repast: Verdi's late masterpiece, *Falstaff*. Tickets were hard to get, but Paul and I had them.

The restaurant Yikes! was the new sensation in Oxford Street brasseries, but that wasn't the sole reason Paul and I found ourselves seated at one of its coveted pinewood tables. This was also something of a farewell dinner. Lachie Turner was moving to the United States for an unspecified time. His new American agent, one who took a fatherly interest in young rising male stars, had arranged for a number of screen tests. That is not to say Lachie wasn't in demand in Australia: He was. Since he'd revealed the tortured secret life beneath his soap-opera looks, he had acquired depth and created renewed public interest. He had gained credibility as a genuinely versatile actor—especially when you considered all the straight love scenes he'd done in his television career.

Grant accompanied him. He had a film idea he was trying to flog, and with his new Los Angeles contacts, he hoped it wouldn't be too difficult to get a foot in the door. Unfortunately, *Surfside Motel* did not air in California, but, as Grant pointed out, one could always rely on the gay Mafia, if not to provide a job then at least to show you a good time.

Since Lachie had come out, the gay scene had taken him to their collective pecs with a passion. Mainstream fallout, as

Grant called it, had also been minimal—a tribute to his charm.
I recalled with delight watching Lachie being interviewed by
a very serious, leading current-affairs journalist.

"What does coming out as a gay man mean to you?" the
hack had asked with funereal gravity.

Lachie grinned and replied: "I'm just letting people know I
don't go through the usual channels." ("Soapie Star Switches
Channels" screeched the tabloids next morning.)

Not surprisingly, our meal was unavoidably public. Eleven
gentlemen had brazenly demanded Lachie's autograph during
the soup alone. Seven of them were waiters.

It was practically six months to the night that Newton's
dream had gone the way of all trash. The vexed question of
ownership had at last been settled, even though most of Crab
Island was scorched earth and there was nothing left of the
New Heaven Resort itself; the tropical-style thatched roofs
had seen to that. No sooner had the debris been raked over,
however, than Iris Murphy's last will and testament turned up—
the very will Newton had pronounced nonexistent. In it, Iris
left a gorgeous thirty-six–piece table setting to Delia Scott-
Merman and one tropical island paradise to the Roman
Catholic Church.

I'd seen very little of Grant since his recent release. The
charges against him had finally been dropped once Claire had
recovered and, together, we'd set the record straight.
Inevitably, the conversation at dinner swung around to the
subject of the murder.

"So," Grant inquired, "who finally filled you in? So to
speak."

"June!" I replied. "Who else? She'd known Delia as a child.
In fact, if June had gone to the island like she was supposed
to, instead of you, she might have seen Delia there and recognised her. Then none of this would have happened!"

"Don't blame Grant," mumbled Lachie through a mouthful of sticky date. "He went to defend my honour."

"I was defending my property!" Grant laughed, and Lachie punched him on the chest. "Ouch."

Paul took up the story. "Delia had visited the island when she was a kid; her parents were old retainers or whatever of the Murphy family. She'd had her holidays there every year."

"Didn't you hate how your parents took you to the same boring old place each year?" moaned Lachie.

"Young Delia got very attached to the island: the sun, the surf, and the crabs. Later, of course, most of the crabs got attached to *her*!"

"Paul!" I groaned.

"She spent her childhood sucking up to the old lady with her eye on a juicy little inheritance." Paul tossed his head. "I can't bear opportunists!"

I shrugged. "Unluckily, it didn't work out that way. Newton got hold of it. I can imagine how he reacted when Delia showed up, claiming she was the rightful owner! He would've roared with laughter right in her face."

"He would have sold her an one-hundred thousand–dollar share," smiled Lachie.

"Anyway, old Iris Murphy had the last laugh on them all, leaving the place to the Catholic Church."

Grant chuckled. "My word! If anybody knows how to hang onto real estate, they do. Hopefully, it's the last we'll see of Mr. Paramor's crowd."

"Oh, haven't you heard?" Paul bubbled over with gossip. "Paramor skipped town. Their big sister-church in the USA whisked him off to Guatemala or somewhere. Extradition proceedings are afoot!"

"Yes," I remarked, "the authorities are very interested in the pastor's airborne activities. Ever since they were tipped off."

Grant was effusive. "I have to hand it to you, Marc. You are all knowing! Perhaps you can clarify something."

"What's that?"

"Well, dear, if all of us were running up to the top pool and back at virtually the same time, why didn't we bump into each other?"

"Ah. Let me explain." I relished these Poirotesque details. "Firstly, you did! You bumped into Delia, because you both took the long route, up the hill. Darren used the stairs, which only the staff knew about."

"What about Hadrian?"

"He didn't go anywhere. He overheard your argument and decided it confirmed his own suspicions that Newton was cheating."

"So the little sook locked himself in his room," added Paul.

"It was only later, when he heard what had happened, that Hadrian recalled seeing Darren lurking around."

"What was the situation with Delia and Claire?" Lachie asked.

"I don't know the intimate details. But Delia latched onto her simply to get to the island. They met at some media event. Delia came on strong, Claire went goo-goo eyed, ditched her lover, and waited, but all she got out of it was a one-night stand. Claire's no fool; she woke up one morning and said to herself 'I've been had.'"

"I know the feeling," Paul quipped.

"Poor Claire," crooned Grant. "Let's not be hard on the gal. I'd still be inside if it weren't for her."

"How is she now?" asked Lachie.

"Well enough to work on Gaytour's new resort project," Paul answered. "Fire Island II, they're calling it. Hiram's outfit leased an atoll off Singapore. The story's in *Queer Scene*."

"Singapore!" Grant exploded. "They'll all be executed!"

"Singapore should be a breeze compared to Murphy's Inlet."

Grant raised his glass. "To Murphy's Inlet. Thank you, stuff you, and goodbye!"

"And to Crab Island!" said Paul. "Ditto."

Lachie showed us his famous ravishing smile. "And," he said, "to Marc and Paul. Thanks and *au revoir*!"

We downed our champagne and felt all glowing and warm inside. I might have known Paul, like a cheap Christmas tree ornament, would shatter the moment.

"What was it like in jail?" he gushed.

Lachie bit his lip and turned away.

"I don't want to talk about that," Grant said simply.

"What's your film script about?" I hastily inquired.

Grant looked amused. "Well, lovey, in a nutshell it's about you."

"Me?"

"You and Paul. Investigating a mysterious murder. Hmm?" His smile broadened. I was at a loss for words.

"I love it," Lachie enthused. "There are zillions of cop-buddy movies, but Grant thought it would be fun to revive the amateur detective. You know, clever but sort of, er, unprofessional. Never seen a gun, that kind of character."

"I've seen a gun," I protested.

"Brilliant!" cried Paul. "Do I get to play me?"

"I don't think the writer has much say in casting," Grant chuckled.

"I hope that's not true," said Lachie. "I've got *my* eye on the role of Paul."

"What about Marc?" Paul shrieked. "Who'll play Marc? Let me think. It'll need to be someone on the mature side of 20, but well-preserved and sexy as hell!"

"Do you have any actor in mind?" I was modestly curious.

Grant looked uncomfortable. "Not really," he lied.

"Whoopi Goldberg," confided Lachie at the same time.

Paul howled. "Perfect!"

"Isn't she a woman?" I asked Grant.

"Yes."

"Now, now, caro, don't get all huffy and peculiar." Paul patted me on the head. "Nobody in Hollywood would make a movie about a middle-aged queen who goes to the opera. You understand."

"Thanks, Paul, I feel much better. You may stop patting me. Speaking of opera, we shouldn't keep Sir John Falstaff waiting."

We bade our goodbyes and keep-in-touches. Lachie refused to let anybody else contribute one cent toward the bill. Grant gave me a huge hug.

"Visit us soon," he whispered lewdly in my ear. "Bring marmalade."

Paul needed to check out the men's room, so I hurried off alone to fetch the car. By some incredible fluke I had scored a park in Oxford Street itself, two blocks away from the restaurant. As I breezed up the well-worn avenue, basking in the warm evening air, I felt suitably lighthearted. Midweek Oxford Street regulars passed by, and I smiled benignly in their direction. One or two smiled in return. I reveled in my anonymity. No longer the man who knew too much, I was serenely content to be exactly what Paul described: a middle-aged queen on his way to the opera. Nothing more nor less.

I reached the old bomb and was letting myself in when a door across the street caught my eye. I recognised it straight away: the Bunker, that salacious cesspit where Wade and I had rekindled our passion. I'd never been near it since, but in a split second the scene flashed before me, right down to the ninja turtle tattoo. I felt a pang (not unrelated to indigestion). I'd liked Wade very much. He had such a sweet face and a frank and experimental attitude to life.

I pondered. Should I plan a return visit to those subterranean premises? Perhaps there were more Wades lolling about. Paul wouldn't object, though he might disapprove for reasons connected with hygiene.

While these thoughts skipped across my synapses, I noticed the entrance door to the Bunker glide open. Two leathermen stepped gingerly into the street. One was skinny and resembled a toilet brush; the other was bulky with an enormous grey moustache and beard. They both wore leather shorts and caps. The large one's blotchy, roly-poly sides oozed through the gaps of a tight leather corset. I swiftly changed my mind about a return visit. It wasn't really my scene.

I was ready to drive off when the bearded leatherman veered clumsily across the road and planted himself in front of my car, his hands resting on the hood. He stared at me like some loony Viking.

"Get out of the way!" I called, leaning out the window. "What do you want?"

"Always thought I'd see you one day," he shouted.

"I don't know you!" I replied. "Please go away. I'm late as it is."

He leant right over the car.

"You remember me, don't you? I'm Merv Jackson!"

I gaped. So it was! I locked my door and wound up the window as fast as I could. Then, in a panic, I flooded the car's engine. The late alderman pressed his nose to my window. I felt trapped in a blizzard of facial hair and animal hide.

"Open this window!" he bellowed. "I don't want to shout!"

"No!"

He thumped his fist on the roof. Very carefully, I unwound the window a teensy weensy fraction of a sliver. He put his face up to the opening.

"Hello," he said. "I wanted to thank you."

"Thank me? What for?"

He grimaced. "You may not be aware of this, but you were the first step on the road to salvation for Merv Jackson. I had a bloody nasty car crash after you ran off. When I was in hospital, I got to sorting out a few things. You could say I saw the light! And it was all thanks to you and a very patient nurse."

He flicked his thumb toward his skinny companion. The man waved limply.

"That's my mate Kelvin. Bloody good nurse. He knows a man's man when he sees one. Kelvin fixed me up and showed me where the real men hang out. He brought me here. It was, I dunno, like coming home again after years and years of being away. You know what I mean?"

I wound the window down a little more. "That's an extraordinary story, Merv. It's, um, almost touching. I'm sure you're making a big impression at the Bunker."

He gave me a dentally challenged smile (possibly another consequence of the accident). "Listen, Marc—it is Marc, isn't it? How'd you like to make it a threesome tonight?"

"Oh. Ah…"

"Join us for a beer then, hey?"

"Sorry, Merv, I can't this evening. Thanks all the same. I've made other arrangements."

He lurched off the car and tottered up onto the pavement. "Too bad. Next time for sure. Glad I caught up with you."

He staggered back over the road and wandered away, his hefty arm slung casually round the frail shoulders of Kelvin the male nurse.

I caught sight of myself in the rear-vision mirror: I actually looked like I'd seen a ghost! Prudently, I ran my fingers through my hair, flattening it as best I could. I yawned, rubbed my eyes, and blew my nose. I grinned rakishly at my face in the mirror. It grinned back. That was more like it!

I was about to meditate on life's infinite variety and the astounding unpredictability of mankind when I remembered Paul. He'd be wondering where the hell I'd got to. I glanced at my watch: it was fine, we could still make the first act. I drove off, humming quietly, in blissful anticipation of the evening ahead.

I'm awfully fond of late Verdi.